This Location of Unknown Possibilities

This Location of Unknown Possibilities

a novel

Brett Josef Grubisic

NON CANADA

Library and Archives Canada Cataloguing in Publication

Grubisic, Brett Josef, author
This location of unknown possibilities / Brett Josef Grubisic.

ISBN 978-1-926942-60-5 (pbk.)

I. Title.

PS8613.R82T45 2014   C813'.6   C2013-906591-1

Printed and bound in Canada on 100% recycled paper.

Now Or Never Publishing
#313, 1255 Seymour Street
Vancouver, British Columbia
Canada V6B 0H1

nonpublishing.com
Fighting Words.

We acknowledge the support of the Canada Council
for the Arts for our publishing program.

It is an error to divide people into the living and the dead: there are people who are dead-alive, and people who are alive-alive. The dead-alive also write, walk, speak, act. But they make no mistakes; only machines make no mistakes, and they produce only dead things. The alive-alive are constantly in error, in search, in questions, in torment.

—Yevgeny Zamyatin (trans. Mirra Ginsburg)
On Literature, Revolution, Entropy, and Other Matters (1923)

Studio City

Sow's Ear Silk

I.

Uncapped medium point felt pen in hand, the woman sat poised to read at the desk—ankles crossed, spine a staunch column. Before peeling back the script's cover page, she noted that so far as attention-grabbing goes, *The Prisoner of Djoun* gleamed with potential. Though shelling out for *The Spanish Prisoner* would never happen—the endless manly posturing and ulterior motives, all that Mamet talk, talk, talk—she slid *The Fugitive* into the player once a year at least. Titles rich with implication? Typically 24-carat.

She signed approval with a thick check mark and watched black ink bleed into the paper's filaments.

"Okay, let's find out about this prisoner." The low rumble of commuters along Ventura met her words.

The woman wore a favourite pinstripe blouse beneath a charcoal cotton-linen suit; tortoiseshell reading glasses rode low on her nose. The look meant *getting down to business.* Freshly delivered from the panoramic office suite of the Man Upstairs, a stack of three scripts brooded next to the water glasses on the credenza; she expected to chew through them before lunch.

Focussing, the woman ran an index finger along the page. Noix d'Amazonie, the new nail colour Byung-soon had applied yesterday, caught her eye. The woman followed trends selectively and had pounced on the forest-tone polishes of the season. A touch of glam earthiness would soften God-given edges, she reasoned. And as much her stomach might twinge at the term *lipstick lesbian*—what a godawful relic from the '90s, as ugly as those navy suits with the NFL silhouette she'd once scrimped for—experience had revealed over and again that approachability was key in the industry.

At first glance the script's opening paragraph—the scene establisher—seemed reliably professional; centred and laser-printed, its author had the presence of mind to buff his words with a recent version of Final Draft. That, she'd wager. While no guarantee of quality, neatness aggravated her infinitely less than the tatty, crudely stapled masterpieces complete with red ballpoint annotations in feverish physician's scrawl that showed up with surprising regularity and incited speculation about the sender's mental competence. Other than Unabomber types holed up in log cabins, who used a manual typewriter anymore?

Returning to the page the woman said, "Okay, here goes nothing."

SCENE 1

Split screen. Two authors at their desks, clothed circa 1900. On the left, a woman in a dark shawl writes at night, candles the only illumination. Her desk is neat, but the slope-roofed attic room appears cramped and shop-worn. On the right, a man dressed in brown tweed trousers, a matching vest, and a white shirt reads in a sunny room. The room and desk are messy, but modern art and bright flowers in a vase suggest a well-heeled bohemian atmosphere.

FADE TO:

INT. LONDON - ATTIC OFFICE, Feb. 1897 - NIGHT

The woman tagged "WTF?!?" on the script's right margin.

Oh my Christ, she thought, *another Liberal Arts major who's spent a couple of semesters in film school, now dreaming of hitting the big time with an art house crossover extravaganza, a highbrow drama that will have brand name critics fighting over the kudos needed to describe* a powerful, unapologetic work of art. American Beauty *meets* The Hours *meets* The English Patient, *starring Judi Dench, Cate Blanchett, Meryl Streep, Julianne Moore, Nicole Kidman, Jude Law, and*

Anthony bloody Hopkins. Abracadabra: armfuls of awards, doors of opportunity across the globe swinging wide open, reputations set in thick bronze. Cash for the asking, naturally.

Shoulders back and eyes closed, she took in a deep breath. A slow count to ten tapped on the desk's glass surface, the woman resumed.

FADE TO:

INT. LONDON - ATTIC OFFICE, Feb. 1897 - NIGHT

A homely woman sits at a desk and writes by candlelight. EMILY MORSE SYMONDS, age 37, appears tired, as though ground down by life's progressive hardships. Dour attire and the room's spare furnishings hint at Symonds' lack of wealth and an avowed commitment to the ideals of women's suffrage. Leaning close to a flame, Symonds recites words from a sheaf of paper titled "Lady Hester Stanhope."

EMILY MORSE SYMONDS

Seldom are true stories distinguished by a well-marked moral.

(pauses)

If we study human chronicles we often find the ungodly flourishing like rodents, and the righteous apparently forsaken and begging his meal. On occasional a human life illustrates moral lessons with the crudity of a Sunday-school story.

Symonds marks deletions and hastily scribbles in replacements. On a fresh sheet she writes:

There are few true stories that are distinguished by a well-marked moral. If we study human chronicles we generally find the ungodly flourishing like

(pauses)

a green bay-tree, and the righteous apparently forsaken and begging his bread. But it occasionally happens that a human life illustrates some moral lesson with the triteness and crudity of a Sunday-school book.

Clearing her throat, the woman circled standout phrases in the ensuing paragraphs—Pride goeth before the fall; All earthy glory is but vanity; Ambition that o'erleaps itself.

"This 'repent sinner' BS tests well in the Bible Belt," she said. "Flyover states can't get enough of that fire and brimstone spiel from the pulpit."

Seeking a break from the speechifying, she ran the marker down the page.

Satisfied, the writer stands, walks to the window, and watches the roofs of London basking in moonlight.

"Holy Toledo," the woman muttered. "Incredible! What's next, 'The writer searches the thesaurus for a synonym'? 'Symonds adjusts her corset for a minute'?" For a moment she considered shooting an email to the screenwriter—"Dear Mr. Dumbass." But, really, what could she hope to convey? They breathed different air, apparently.

She returned to the script. In the midst of character assassination, the garret-dwelling moralist's pen rejected the smallest breath of Christian mercy.

She was ambitious, and her ambition had been foiled; she loved irresponsible command, but the time had come when those over whom she ruled defied her; she was dictatorial and exacting, but she had lost the influence which alone makes people tolerate control. She entertained visionary projects of aggrandizement, and was met by the derision of the world.

"Okay, okay, we get it—you disapprove. This Lady Hester was hell in petticoats and paid the price. But. Why. So. Many. Words?" The woman granted that way back then people had nothing better to do at night than read. From Symonds' point of view, voices emitting from a radio speaker would represent the very height of futuristic.

> In a word, Lady Hester died as she had lived, alone and miserable in a strange land, bankrupt in affection and credit, because, in spite of her great gifts and innate benevolence, her overbearing temper had estranged friends and kinsfolk alike.

SYMONDS

'Estranged'?
Perhaps 'alienated' will suffice.

The woman spread ZZZZZZZ across the page. Sugarcoating belonged in a nursery.

Annoyed, brow furrowed, and fighting the temptation to hurl the script to the floor, the woman plunged a fat green straw into a morning-sized takeout cup. Straws in lattes currently served time as the latest in a short line of cigarette replacements, and this month being jittery and motor-mouthed had become second nature. A pound or two of fresh muffin top showed too. Better that than cancer, she'd remind herself whenever passing by any traitorous mirror.

"Okay, lady, you relax now, let's take a little breather." She shut her eyes again *with intent*, as the facilitator of the anxiety management class taught.

Regulating air intake and imagining breath flowing down to the toes while keeping the body alert were, she remembered, the next steps in the meditation exercise. Today, gentle downward air wafts stood no chance. Sarcastic exclamations rather than the placid rhythm of deep inhalation gushed from her brain; and annoyance caused teensy eyelid muscles to spasm.

The script's clueless high-mindedness astonished her, that dogged and hopeful—naïve? blind?—disregard of the market, not to mention the pretentious, in-your-face intellectualism. All of it spelled commercial suicide: death by a thousand syllables. Who would pay good money to stare at a drab wallflower from days of yore reading from one sheaf of paper and then scratching in corrections for five goddamned minutes? Librarians? Tweedy professors, maybe. Monks.

For everyone else on the planet five minutes on screen felt like eternity. Five minutes! Christ, Michael Bay makes two hundred cuts in that time and look at the vaults of ka-ching he earns. But here: no talking, no action to speak of, zero tension—writing doesn't count. And three steps to the window? They barely registered.

"This la-di-da Masterpiece Theatre crap might catch buzz at a multiplex in Oxford," she said, wondering, *Is there such a thing?* "But here in the real world? Not an iota."

The woman turned to the cover page and wrote a peeved X through the title. The name of the screenwriter meant nothing.

Stretching, she rested her palms atop the desk's sole personal touch, a chunky lucite frame. The sepia-tinted photograph suspended within had been the advice of Tamara, a Professional Strategies Life Coach highly recommended by a friend of the Ex, and comfortably matter-of-fact at the first assessment: "Simple, right, without a groundstone that office environment will bleed you dry. Balance your mental energies there. Success will follow."

Improbable with a Nantucket-evoking white Brooks Brothers seersucker dress and fortune cookie advice, Tamara insisted that the special item must bridge the present to the past. "Breathe and let go. Make space for the object's appearance in your mind's eye."

Like seance ectoplasm the photo had materialized.

In a cramped trailer-studio decades ago a rushed photographer had snapped her, Elizabeth-Anne then, in a flour-sack shift of rosette print calico; smiling gamely, she'd cradled a shallow iron pan of wet gravel. The novelty set up—her mother's inspiration—was meant as an homage to a legendary family matriarch, the plucky wife of a '49er believed to have staked a bountiful claim upriver while a ne'er-do-well husband guzzled whiskey and played cards in the tent settlement along the flats.

When the woman's parents finally swapped the Pasadena rancher for a retirement condo in Gardnerville Ranchos, they'd sent an envelope stuffed with photos inside a box of jumbled keepsakes. Never overcome with nostalgia when studying her twelve year-old face—having agreed to the corny idea only to keep the peace—she nevertheless admired her mother's inscription on the reverse side: "A prospector has to trudge through a lot of mud before striking gold. —Knott's Berry Farm, 1979."

Balanced mood reached, more or less, the woman sighed. *Trudge, trudge, I'm such a pushover,* she thought, recommitting to *The Prisoner of Djoun*—

As Symonds continues to scribble emendations, the screen returns to the split view momentarily. The focus shifts to the man on the right.

FADE IN:

EXT. TIDMARSH, VILLAGE IN S.E. ENGLAND, FEB. 1919 - DAY

CUT TO:

INT. THE MILL HOUSE - DRAWING ROOM - DAY

A man–tall, bearded, and thin–grabs a book from the haphazard pile on his desk. He stands at a window and reads the cover page–Little Memoirs of the Nineteenth Century by George Paston.**
He flips to the fourth essay and samples a passage.

"More books & silence?!?," the woman jotted in the margin. She sought out the companion asterisks at the bottom of the page: **Emily Morse Symonds published under the pen-name of George Paston. The woman imagined words materializing on the screen to explain this crucial point. "Very artful," she said. "Who cares?" Interest flagging, she rallied with reminders of a potential nugget trove and professional courtesy.

Pacing, the man reads a sentence aloud.

LYTTON STRACHEY
'In a word, Lady Hester died as she had lived, alone and miserable in a strange land–'
(Drops the book to the floor)
Emily Morse Symonds, who are you to pass judgement, you resentful old cow? Sanctimonious Puritan!

The man walks to a desk to compose a note.

Mr. Murry:
Thank you for the letter of inquiry. The biographical sketch of Lady Stanhope will be completed shortly as per our recent conversation. The Athenaeum shall have it within a fortnight.
Yours in gratitude,
L. Strachey."

"ZZZZZ," the woman wrote, picturing a smothering quicksand of words.

The man folds the letter and replaces it with another sheet, entitled "Lady Hester Stanhope."
He begins to write.

"She renounced the world."

He pauses at the period.
Leaving a few inches of blank space, he continues to write further down the page.

> "The end came in June, 1839. Her servants immediately possessed themselves of every moveable object in the house. But Lady Hester cared no longer: she was lying back in her bed–inexplicable, grand, preposterous, with her nose in the air."

STRACHEY

'Inexplicable, grand, preposterous.' Yes, that's it.

The scene dissolves.

I'll say, the woman thought. *It dissolves way before that.*

After poring over pages at random she skipped to the last scene. Eyes wandering from script to picture frame to credenza, the woman resolved only to push on to the next script. "As for you, lady prisoner in the desert, I'm going to let you stew for a bit."

2.

The woman pressed an intercom button. "Can you step in here for a minute, Søren?"

"Sure, I'm free right now," the assistant said.

The woman looked up as Søren—chestnut tanned, the Nordic white hair of ABBA's Agnetha, and dressed as if ready for a country club tennis match—opened the office door and brought in the steady hum of Studio City traffic.

"You're looking a tad frazzled, Liz." He paused at the door. "How many of those have you chugged today?"

"What are you, my mother? It's this script. I'm tearing out my hair."

"Yes, I can see stray platinum strands there, not to mention black roots." He enjoyed the daily dramatics of his boss and the boyish inability to let one hour pass without newly stained clothing or mussed hair. "Or is that grey?"

"Watch your tongue, spray tan," the woman said, smiling. "You're not here to talk hair-dos, much as I'm sure you'd love to. This, this divine script." She tapped the cover page with the Sharpie. "How did it get in here?"

"I don't know. The usual way?"

"Who the fuck let it though my door?"

"Technically, me. Mea culpa." He bowed in mock-penitence. "I dropped it off with the other three. But they arrived as a parcel, and that always means the same thing: direct passage to the holding tray on your credenza."

"Okay then, you're off the hook. Let me read a morsel to you. Just to whet your appetite."

"If you must." Søren placed a clipboard and cellphone on the glass desktop. "I'm counting calories, though."

"I must. Sit, please." She indicated a chair. "And close the damned door. Thank you."

The woman cleared her throat. "Alright then," she said, adopting a posh British accent, "are we ready?"

"Yes, Liz, any time. Tick tock."

"Alright, alright. In this scene the heroine is sick with plague and her kinda sorta boyfriend is tending to her." She read:

FADE IN:

EXT. THE DESERT, 1813 - NEAR DJOUN - NIGHT

In the near distance a straw-brick walled home, at which two figures stand in front of a double-door gate. As a horse approaches, the men hurry to open the gate.

CUT TO:

INT. DJOUN - CANDLELIT BEDCHAMBER - NIGHT

DR. MERYON

There, there, Lady Hester. Calm yourself.

LADY HESTER STANHOPE

Your suggestion is difficult to obey, my friend. I fear I may pass over soon.

(She coughs.)

MERYON

The illness courses through you. We can but wait.

STANHOPE

But wait?

MERYON

That is all one can do.

STANHOPE

Plague is a portent, a punishment.

MERYON

Nonsense. You are one amongst many. The lowly shepherd, the pasha's infant daughter—will you have me believe that each is a recipient of divine punishment for mortal sins?

"P U," Søren said. "When does fur-faced Moses show up with stone tablets?"

"Wait a sec, I'm nearly done." Neck tilted, she peered over low-slung glasses.

MERYON

Rest, my lady. This cool cloth will vanquish the fever's rage.

STANHOPE

You are too kind to a foolish old woman. I should sing your praises... although you are aware I am no Margaret Martyr!

MERYON
(smiles)
Your humour returns! It can be nothing if not auspicious.

STANHOPE
I cannot help but wonder, Doctor . . .

MERYON
Yes?

STANHOPE
If Fate has brought me to the desert.

MERYON
Rest, rest, dear one. Your philosophical musings will be the death of you yet. Here, you must take more of this thorn apple tea.

"I can see the cast's procession to the stage on Oscar night," Søren said.

"Ha! At first I only saw the script's procession to the shredder. It starts off even worse, but surprise, surprise it actually gets better." Lizzie patted the closed script. "Maybe not this guy's take, but the basic idea of this tough old broad fighting for a piece of the pie. There's potential."

"And so you want me to . . . ?"

"Oh, sorry. I just wanted a sounding board."

"Gee, that's me." Exasperation crept into his voice. "Nothing else to do, not a thing, ma'am."

"I'm going to run through it again. Get me Zora at V, but not now. I'd say in about ninety, I have an idea I'd like to fire by her."

Søren tapped a reminder note.

"You know, I think maybe we should send this out, get it in better shape, toughen it up. That script trainer in Silver Lake, what's his face." She doodled flowers over the X slashed across the title page. "It's flab, complete and utter flab, right now. But, and that's a big, big but—ha ha, don't even say it—there's something here. Core strength, let's say. I mapped out a couple of ideas, where the story could go et cetera, so don't forget to include them with the script. And tell whatshisname that VNetwork is the vendor I have in mind. He's a pro, he'll know what will and won't snag their interest. Just give me a hour."

"Sure, no problem. Anything else? Another latte?"

"What the hell, sure. I need to keep my mouth occupied. I'm pretty sure my heart can take it."

"Right. I'll be back in fifteen."

"Bueno."

She turned to the list of comments:

—Penniless aristocrat turns her back on England?

—Virgin? In love with doctor?

—Icon re: Elizabeth, Amelia Eirhart (sp??), Joan of Arc

—Loses mind? Visionary? Mystic?

—A woman that carves a place for herself in a man's world.

Liz added a final question:

—Where's the drama???

I

Point Grey to Burnaby

It's much more inspiring not to go to places than to go.
—Karl Lagerfeld explains Chanel pre-fall 2012
(December 6, 2011)

A Career in English!

I.

A transparent stream of mucous seeped from Marta's left nostril, slow as a glycerin tear. Clasping a tissue, she blew gently in hopes of avoiding the unnerving pop—Oh my, is this an aneurysm?—of distressed eardrums. *I cannot have caught a cold*, Marta thought. No, not a cold at all, she determined, merely aggravating invisible particles enveloped within nasal drool. Natural, normal, automatic immunoresponse triggered by diminutive organic motes suspended in odourless, life-sustaining air. The bad inseparable from the good. Serpents and fruit trees. Typical. Pseudoephedrine mood swings too, Marta noted crankily. Springtime. She'd experienced better days.

Tilting the desk chair back, Marta blotted the watery rims and pictured the lids as bee-stung, having swelled and grown blotchy. Bloodshot eyes too, quite possibly. Would students in the impending class look up from their phone screens and comment, believing she'd been crying? Surely they'd have no ready-made explanation for the spectacle of a weepy professor. What soap opera scenario might they spin? A lost grant, perhaps, or tenure unfairly denied. A sniping review. The visible handkerchief and a vague comment about the peril of pollen would suffice to nip murmured speculation in the bud. They'd readily accept that external source over the implausibility of crushing disappointment or, another long shot, heartache so fierce that it had spilled into the classroom.

Marta's desk clock and computer agreed: 12:45PM. Exactly five minutes before she must depart for the week's final class. She closed the skinny office window. It wasn't supposed to be opened, anyway. People had heightened sensitivities in these seasons of compromised immune systems. Everyone expressed keen awareness of bounding allergens and environmental flux; rogue microbes failed to recognize personal space, and protection had become imperative.

In lieu of the marvelous transparent domes and lab-engineered enhancements of science fiction, Grounds+Maintenance had just finished with a series of practical paper and email bulletins that explained how the building's renovated ventilation system rendered a breath of fresh air obsolete, *counter-productive*. Marta's eyes had settled on the falsely reassuring scientific language of the latest: *cutting edge technology* that *deployed* ozone and ultraviolet light for *optimized ionization* and *departicalization*. In short: hinged windows have become an outmoded indulgence, comrade, and the health of you and the university community relies on individual cooperation, thank you for the ongoing compliance.

As she cautiously dabbed the inflamed leaking rims a final time, Marta began to organize the papers on the desk, sliding notes—lined yellow sheets highlighted in purple (key concepts, pointed questions for students) and green (relevant trivia, humorous asides)—into the valise and pitching the scarcely read administrative announcements into the recycling bin.

Two white sheets remained.

Marta placed the letter into a folder labeled Homeward: Admin. She'd already secured a photocopy in the Correspondence: History file in the desk's bottom left drawer. The letter's duality, banal and momentous, was proving so difficult to resist. She'd snatched glances between classes that morning. If nothing else the offer promised diversion, a break—ludicrous and unprecedented but invigorating—from routine, she'd been telling herself. *Tempted by celebrity, so facile,* chimed in a background voice, less friendly.

12:48PM. She swiveled the chair away from the wall of books and studied the immense vista. The scene felt underdeveloped, a photographic study Ansel Adams might have discarded, since all the surfaces—turbulent inlet, coniferous mountainsides, densely cumulous sky—seemed mopped by inky watercolour.

Greywashed, a vision of springtime stripped of the usual green bursts and life-affirming connotations.

Black-pebbled concrete formed a thick frame around the inset window panes of the office. A home away from home, this stout fortress of a building. After the resurgence of seen-but-not-read Tolkien a few years ago, two arts students had said, "In the Dark Tower?" within the same week when arranging an office meeting—as though the roof sprouting paired horns or a wrathful amber eye would surprise no one.

Trends cycling as they did, though, the name's sticking was anybody's guess. The matte concrete slabs of the exterior had appeared on cineplex screens more recently as the barricaded compound of a fearsome African warlord in a mutant superhero movie sequel. Perhaps quizzical students now exclaimed, "I've seen that place somewhere before, I just know it" as they passed by. Or, equally plausible, no one commenting at all.

Marta conceded that the tower's facade—that of an unadorned modernist bunker—loomed imposingly. After that, she found the Tolkien analogy nonsensical. Early-, mid-, and late-career vanity and politicking flourished, naturally. But brooding evil, Machiavellian tactics? Hardly. Assigning a C+ to an essay barely indicated a sign of power, let alone chthonic malevolence. The *vin ordinaire* of any office environment, professional rivalries, intense resentments, and grievance accretions were likewise known, albeit stored out of sight. As for the elaborate class hierarchy—untanned latter-day devotees of Matthew Arnold still genuflecting toward Oxford nested at the tip of the pecking order; at the base, brown-skinned women with broken English providing custodial services: "If you find a moment today, er, Dhatri, will you please vacuum my office?"—Marta supposed that arrangement, like good and evil, reached far back, as old as tragedy.

The portentous architecture, then, meant nothing except unlucky coincidence. True, alongside the kind- and coldhearted, she did pass by hunched Gollums and tightly-wound Lizzie Borden types muttering in hallways from time to time; as with asylum lifers and feral animals, a simple rule applied: *steer clear, don't meet their eyes.*

Marta withdrew the letter and read the familiar words, for an instant miffed by the author's choice of a nostalgic typewriter font:

Dear Professor Spěk:
I have been instructed to contact you because our production team has the good fortune to be in your vicinity. You may have heard that The Prophet of Djoun, a biopic of Lady Hester Stanhope, is currently in pre-production.

Of course not, Marta thought once more, *why would I have? Oh, movie people and their egotism.*

Your expertise, as revealed through your book Imperial(ist) Empress: Mysticism, Écriture Féminine and the Levantine Writings of Lady Hester Stanhope, would be a tremendous benefit for our production. If you can spare some time, one of the project's executives, Mr. Jakob Nugent, would be happy to explain our offer and the technical details over lunch.
We thank you for your time and hope to hear from you soon.
Sincerely,
Lora Wilkes
Assistant to Jakob Nugent

Folding the letter, Marta shrugged: what's the harm of one meal? Alongside the usual low morale doldrums coinciding with the school year's sputtering out, distressed thoughts had been mushrooming about the shiny prestigious career she'd willed—through methodical labour, more or less—into existence, on track now and unwavering until the onset of decrepitude. That legacy brought to mind a luckless character from a Poe story, walled inside a dusty catacomb for eternity by pages instead of stones. Losing mental pliability year after year as bones grew porous and brittle: squinting at a hidebound future that hadn't yet unfolded drew Marta's breath short.

Marta pictured Poe pacing inside that leased white Bronx cottage on a swampy, sweltering August night, the air gassy and fetid; months earlier Lady Stanhope had passed away, obscure, half the world away. Stripped to a disheveled vest and shirt and grumbling drunkenly, Poe threw the tale whose plot he'd been sketching into the unlit hearth: "Preposterous, what fool would wall himself in? No, there must be a villain and a lure."

Guiltily peering into her unsettled state of mind, Marta saw first the luxuriant illegitimacy. From Chongqing to Zhenzhou, polluted industrial sprawls of dawn-to-dusk wage slavery were truly entitled to complaint. Ditto for a famished, war-pitted continent with medieval life expectancies. But not her, in an office with *optimized ionization* perched over a distant city of glass spires and postcard-worthiness. "A champagne problem," her mother's diagnosis, sounded accurate in its way.

Marta nonetheless leaned toward *crisis of faith* despite the exaggeration; mundane as dandruff, *occupational doubts* didn't quite capture it. *Misgivings? Discontentment*? A tad vague, undirected. Whatever the case, she'd trust intuition for the remedy.

Nudging Marta forward as well, the reasonable sound of her father's oft-voiced motto, "The proverbial knock of opportunity should never be ignored."

Save for the onslaught of final exam grading the semester verged on being history, and she really ought to get out into the real world—an elsewhere—more often. Life's a banquet; do or die; broaden horizons; not the fruit of experience, but experience itself, is the end; carpe diem's bravado stretched back to cuneiform. Presumably, she'd find equivalent philosophy carved into a Bronze Age tablet. Who could argue with such longevity?

Marta pinned the vintage brooch watch—a thrift store find decades ago—to her sweater; another reality, a thirty-faced composition class, demanded acknowledgement. She'd contact this assistant to Jakob Nugent later.

The computer gonged for incoming mail. Marta read the weekly announcement from Exconfessio.

Ex G.B (Seattle, WA)—
1. I always see full-grown adults at stoplights picking their noses and it makes me want to stab them in the face.
2. I lost my wallet once with 4,000 dollars in it and the guy gave it back and would not take a penny.
3. I love my wife and kids, but would help a dog over a stranger any day.
4. I worked for the government and abused the job, stole time and hated every second and every person I worked with until I quit.
5. I had a friend commit suicide the day after he said, "Keep an eye on me."
6. I saw a friend put his cock all over his wife's best friend's face while she was sleeping and then smack her lips with it and she never woke up.
7. I saw a guy fall off a 5-foot drop off into a mud pit and didn't help him; I only laughed hysterically from across the street.

Rereading, she savoured the cinematic fullness of each confession.

The week's offering was tamer than others but intriguing nonetheless. Another historical constant: people behaving badly (even when the story was patently untrue: what person keeps 4,000 dollars in a wallet?) had been enthralling onlookers for millennia. Gossip, rumour, whispered speculation, outrageous misdeeds. Such an excess of libidinousness—a perennial cup that runneth over—harbored in countless minds. Who could tell how it would manifest? Stabbed faces and hysterical laughter. Misanthropy over philanthropy at a ration of at least 10:1, if one believed Exconfessio. What malice! Marta's nominal professional interest dedicated scattered thoughts to pondering what people chose as worthy of confession. An essay about secular ethics would be publishable, surely.

Last semester a student had handed in a curious polemical essay condemning Exconfessio. The pious student's evident outrage—galled in particular at the site's "inappropriate" All

Confessions, No Reprisals™ mandate—initially drew in Marta. Actually signing up to receive the confessions (Seven Sins, Deadly Honest™ available in weekly and monthly allotments)? Whimsy, an afterthought. Reading the litany of offenses, she occasionally aligned herself with unseemly figures, the peeping tom or the supermarket housewife tsk-tsking at the vapid images of exposed cellulite and extramarital rendezvous in *Hello!*

People were capable of declarations of astounding perversity. The alarming fact reassured Marta. Besides, the audacity of the confessions rarely failed to impress.

12:50. Time to vacate the sixth floor. She applied lotion to hands now papery courtesy of Purell.

As for *Do You Know Yours Rights?*, Marta tacked the pamphlet onto the cork board, its message ready to revisit on Monday. The folded photocopy had been slid under the office door, one sentence highlighted in pink: "Managing perception of your brand is the essence of personality rights." For the moment the immediate puzzles—the identity of the anonymous messenger, that faceless interloper's agenda—dropped away. And personality rights might be useful to mull over. Trickle down from celebrity culture and Ratemyprofessors.com—Marta's middling score of 3.2 an affront, like coming across her own name on a bathroom stall. Everyone an unstable, easily snuffed-out star and in need of tweaks, damage control and, always, upkeep.

2.

Marta breathed thanks for a vacant seat. At this hour humid buses teemed with vigorous student bodies pouring from campus. The boisterous chatter—of parties or concerts to attend, planned trips to ski slopes or brilliant sand beaches, as though they weren't harried, overworked undergrads subsisting on instant ramen and shoestring budgets so much as carefree Gamma Phi Beta initiates and titanic football-hurling beer pong players filling scenes in an American frat house comedy—crowded the airwaves and made Marta feel depleted, lacking a vital genetic marker that would assure a place at the coveted centre, one of those smiling tall girls whose cascading, photographer-ready hair and beguiling doe eyes proved accomplishment enough, a surefire means to a ringed finger resting on the social pulse, not to mention a comfortable end.

She reached into her bag, faded black canvas and advertising a bookseller squeezed out of business and replaced by a clothing chain years ago. The CD player she withdrew looked so dated it could well have been a bulky 8–track player or a gramophone complete with wooden trumpet speaker. Marta understood that if detected her half-hearted activism—Just Say No to Built-In Obsolescence—would register as unfashionable, even retrograde, like picketing against lady parliamentarians. Or technology.

No matter. Marta suspected that pulling a mandolin or a lute from the tote would cause no huge stir. Students fully expected an eccentric penchant for the quaint and outmoded to accompany their professors' willful scorn for ephemeral styles and electronic indispensables. Bow ties, clock brooches, fountain pens, wing tip brogues, briar pipes, Peter Pan collars over well-aged woolens, hangers burdened with sturdy tweed: a professor's prerogative, one that went hand in hand with the lifelong membership at the Museum of Irrelevance, relishing fading words bound between obscure covers.

Marta caught expressions—wary, uncomfortable, at times perplexed—on the faces of coltish students dropping by the office with concerns over grades or assignments. Eyes eventually settling on the imposing shelves of books, they would summon a genuine frown, the diplomatically unasked question completely sincere: "A reclusive career tending to forgotten grave markers in an infinite text necropolis: why would anyone choose that?" Marta was also prepared to admit to an element of projection in the mind-reading attempt: a truly accurate breakdown of student reaction might be "Huh?" with soupçons of "Why?" and "Whatever."

If they pinpointed the crimson spine of *Imperial(ist) Empress* or the light-bleached powder blue of the slim Austen and colonialism volume—the second study branching organically from her first—they didn't succumb to any temptation to flattery.

Marta empathized to a degree. Any thought of Commerce, the nebulous career plan for the landslide majority of freshmen students, inspired only an involuntary moue.

"Miss Spëk?" Marta bristled. Miss Spëk had been summoned, a familiar dun spectre. Dr. Spëk had been designed as the estimable replacement.

Turning to look up, Marta smiled automatically. "Yes . . . ?"

The girl, pretty and soft-spoken, was a stranger wearing artful eyeliner. She crouched, now able to converse eye to eye.

"I'm in your Po-Co Lit class. Queenie, um, Queenie Liu."

"Right. Was there something . . . ?" Marta studied the black ensemble of layers, ruffles, and lace, recognizing the Kuro Lolita look, a subset of an exotic micro-trend on a campus otherwise clothed in surfer, snowboarder, and yoga brands.

"Oh, right. Sorry. Is it okay to talk now? Here?" She cupped her ears.

Marta slipped the earphones into the tote. "Sure, Mahler can wait. If you'd prefer it, we can set up an appointment."

"It's just that, well, the semester's been like really crazy. How do you feel about extensions?"

"How do I feel about them? In general?" When student imprecision did not grate on her sensibilities, it sparked pedantry.

"No. I mean, well, I mean, like, can I get, you know, an extension?"

"And you know the deal, Queenie: 'Extensions can be granted for legitimate medical reasons.' Every student has a crazy semester, so professors tend to shy away from anything without medical legitimacy." Marta fully intended to give the student what she desired, but waited to hear what ingenuity the student would air, or what species of tragic circumstance she'd cough up.

"Well, to be honest. My boyfriend's in this band, Dramaturd."

"Dramaturge?"

"No. It's a deathcore band."

Marta supposed the student expected a disturbed reaction or parental consternation. She said nothing.

"Anyway, I've been writing songs with him. *You know*." Widened eyes conveyed, "Boys will be boys."

Oh, the sweet bond of sisterhood, spurred on by love to make altruistic sacrifices for our men, Marta thought. But how unexpected that the student would try to bridge the generational gap and join arm in arm with that long procession of women who'd sacrificed so much to clasp a place of honour with the opposite sex.

"How about a week?"

"Agreed. One work week. Remind me about it on Monday, in class."

"Thanks so much, Miss—"

"Doctor. But please call me Marta."

"Okay, Marta." Strategic friendliness accomplished, the student returned to a friend. Marta exhaled, relieved too. Despite the front and centre lecture hall career, she didn't count people skills as a natural or well-developed talent; wherever the milk of human kindness might originate, her supply flowed a touch erratically.

Though transit experiences had taught her what to expect, Marta flipped awkwardly through folders of ungraded assignments; having them alphabetized before her stop would be handy. The student chatted across the crowded aisle.

"No way, I have an all or nothing relationship with chocolate," she said. Marta assumed that Queenie was replying to an offer.

"What if it's in baked goods? What about hot chocolate?" The friend's tone was incredulous.

"I'm hardcore against it."

"No way, that's like extremely will power-y. It's totally brutal."

Surrendering to cramped conditions, Marta slid the folders away and scanned articlettes in a throwaway newspaper—pausing only to savour "caustic and insolent," an evocative phrase serving to sum up and pillory a far-off artist.

For the final ten blocks Marta stared out at the familiar retail corridor of the route.

3.

The squat fact of Undre Arms was mood leavening every afternoon Marta approached the apartment building's proud coat of arms stenciled black, green, and gold on the glass of each entrance door. Years ago she'd substituted a set of hairy tradesman's arms lifting cinderblocks for the twin lions, oak leaves, and ersatz-medieval shields, and those imaginary armpits greeted her now.

Dating from 1969, the three-story shoebox came from an engineer's office with no taste for Age of Aquarius embellishment. Marta's forecast called for its numbered days. Homely touching on forlorn, the greying stucco and mildewed patches could be foolproof lures only to developers, whose search-and-destroy vision ranked low-rise apartment blocks as bygone low-density no-nos that should be converted into high-density, small footprint profit.

Compared to any of the recently erected city condos selling for obscene dollars per square foot, Undre Arms stood out as a spacious bargain; even with the scurrying, paper-devouring silverfish insurgents that bred in drains or beneath floorboards and never failed to startle, Marta fondly called the place, and its ample closets stuffed with books, home. She expected to linger there until making the epochal, adult leap to home ownership, a leap practically inevitable and yet so momentous—the daredevil's inaugural skydive or the suicide's posture on a building's top story edge—that with thoughts of the awesome expenditure she continuously pushed the date forward.

Marta's parents firmly believed in squirreling away for the unavoidable rainy day. Every time the real estate topic arose she'd wonder if that fateful hour had dawned. Delaying the decision again, she foresaw being pushed out: arriving on a Thursday and finding an unwelcome letter crammed under the door that announced the building's sale and imminent date with a wrecking crew: "Vacate the premises immediately." No doubt the owner's son, eyeing a future of conspicuous sports car consumption, would thrill at the stock phrase.

After settling—voicemail checked, mail read, take-home work filed, a dish of no-fat yogurt eaten—Marta dedicated a few minutes to the computer, checking campus email one final time before half-heartedly Googling name combinations, beginning with "Hester Stanhope biopic." She found little, and nothing of value.

Evidently no Amelia Earhart, Elizabeth I, or Virginia Woolf, Lady Stanhope warranted no big budget, no public relations underling paid to stimulate advance interest, and not even a compulsive blogger unleashing pre-production trivia. As for "Jakob Nugent Lora Wilkes" and the production company, the information was likewise scant.

Marta imagined local production companies laboured under such penny-pinched operating costs that they claimed notice only with a film festival debut. Less charitably, she supposed the Stanhope project might be a made-for-a-specialty-television-network movie and so destined for justified invisibility from the moment it was okayed. Or worse, she feared, the screenwriter might have disinterred *The Nun of Lebanon*—the biography's revelation about Stanhope's doomed love affair barely scandalous when published in 1951—and converted the woman's life into cloying syrup, all emotional anguish and tearful *au revoirs* with exotic backdrops.

Marta admired the long dead aristocrat's instinct for adventure, not to mention the willingness to thumb a nose at convention. Though "Film Consultant—Marta Spëk" might ultimately appear in the smallest of fonts as the credits rolled, Marta felt averse to collude with a production company that would sully Lady Stanhope, the forgotten accomplishments, or the old time derring-do. Stanhope had been an odd bird who grew increasingly eccentric each year, and her pipe-dream reign in the ruins of an abandoned monastery would be easy to misconstrue.

Granting the film's exploitative designs, Marta supposed her professionalism might fortify scenes, smooth rough edges, and cull vulgarity as well as anachronisms. Contributing praiseworthy lines—or an entire scene—stood out as another possibility. *Pop cultural immortality*, she thought, unclear about her actual perspective about that temporary apotheosis.

On this Short Day of Frost and Sun

I.

At moments of ordinary respite during the weeks preceding the interview lunch—in line for sushi at the Student Union Building, gathering wool along transit lines, and once in the midst of a notably arid departmental meeting—Marta placed herself on the bustling set of *The Prophet of Djoun*. That title wouldn't last, she gathered: overt religious politics limited market penetration. At first she'd pictured *Hester!*, but decided the tone would never suffice: it summoned an old Mel Brooks production, or one of those Technicolor biblical epics with the ballooning cast of extras. And, besides, irony-free exclamation marks had long passed out of fashion.

The scenes she formed wavered and collapsed like mirages, a habitual desire for accuracy warring with farfetched guesswork. She'd never visited a set before, but knew that since her notions about film production originated with features about movie-making they were both outdated and malformed, likely veering far from fact. The image of a barking bald German director wearing a monocle and jodhpurs, imperious and intent in an elevated embroidered canvas chair, a cliché of course, recurred frequently, an antique tableau situated nearly a century in the past. Perhaps physical sets—wood, paint, spray foam, props—had also been rendered quaint, supplanted by cavernous warehouses of green screens and unfathomable computer processes outsourced to crowded facilities in equatorial hubs.

What role might they request? Marta had no clue. Did the production company even anticipate a bodily presence? Assumedly, an on-set lackey could call or send email queries that long distance expertise would clarify: "Professor Spëk, the director wants 'Get a life, assclown.' What's the 1820s' version of that expression?" Then again, fate might orchestrate call centre tribulations: answering prompts while holed up at a desk in a rented office cubicle (or a tent—considering that Lady Stanhope had settled and eventually died in a remote dusty corner of Lebanon, the production required some semblance of sand). The absence of data troubled her.

Though city dwellers were aware their home had been crowned Hollywood North, with vast facilities constructed somewhere in outlying areas (Marta's Internet perusal added specifics: "Vancouver's the home to literally hundreds of film & video companies, talent agencies—people & animals—F/X & post-production facilities, shooting stages & water tank facilities"), the bulk of Marta's images sprang ready-made from American screwball comedies, hyperbolic and yet based on a thin tissue of truth. Colossally oversized egos, tragic deluded has-beens, difficult capital A artists, diva actors bursting into tantrum and shutting themselves up in luxury trailers stocked with idiosyncratic and required-by-contract necessities—an oxygen tank, Algerian bottled water, a Thai masseuse—clashing visions, sniveling, hangdog, or back-stabbing assistants, devastating insults and public humiliations, rabid oily agents with transparent get-ahead schemes and ready stashes of cocaine, ridiculous intrusions and edicts from distant and invisible but all-seeing—spies everywhere!—studio execs (young thoroughbred prostitutes across their middle-aged laps, lines of white powder running along the low-fat flesh covering exquisite arched spines): how close to actual did these shopworn figures stand?

And her, typecasting too, a fraction of another movie commonplace: heavy-framed utilitarian spectacles and tightly reined hair understood by audience and script alike as an unprepossessing bud disguising an inevitable flowery beauty; the dour, pencil-in-hand scholarly demeanor undermining a buoyant though compliant femininity. The situation could be undone by a fresh perspective and the right man, not to mention the off-camera discovery of a push-up bra and cinching belt, contact lenses, bright lipstick, and expert strokes of a curling iron.

During that monotonous departmental meeting Marta had snickered, thinking of Cyd Charisse's grey-suited Stalinist functionary ("*Nyet*, Comrade") in *Silk Stockings*, whose officious military façade melted into a cascade of pastel chiffon after the briefest exposure to French couture and gung-ho American joie de vivre. Little had Lenin suspected the fragility of ideology. Marta, reluctantly drawn to the sheen of the idea, wished for longer hair.

She resigned herself to waiting. If nothing else, a studio meeting would strike a bold line between fact and fancy.

2.

If the countless mysteries of the impending term of employment were mildly worrisome, a certifiable known served to buttress Marta's reluctance.

She hadn't dwelled on it in years, but Marta easily recalled a singular encounter with one man, later (and later still: the anecdote had circulated a few times) renamed SRLFI, the Stellar Representative of the Local Film Industry. The guy's preference, the Stevester, came nowhere close to eligible for use.

Regret entwined the memory, which also served readily as an ambiguous cautionary tale.

The situation seemed innocuous on paper, Marta had decided, potentially no better or worse than any other blind date—a contradictory phenomenon that demanded low expectations and a fine thread of optimism from all parties concerned. As she languished in the final semester of a second graduate degree, jittery and melancholic in turn, she'd been set up on a date by Judy, whose insistent refrains about growing really tired of Marta's lack of initiative had abruptly turned into a strategic initiative.

Judy zealously believed that the meager—"shut-in," "Norman Bates-ish," and "mole-like" her rotating choice of terms—routines of graduate students atrophied their social skills and thereby stunted their written work's heft: who could trust output by an intellectual with merely theoretical knowledge of life? Grad students befriending Judy were soon informed that "balance" encapsulated her worldview; innate evangelism also meant everyone in Judy's sphere of influence must convert. "Get out there," she'd said to Marta, "you're a virtual sciophobe." Marta, exacting with word use, gathered that Judy meant "afraid of your own shadow," but conceded a relative proximity.

A professed free spirit, Judy borrowed key lines from the American philosophical tradition of Auntie Mame; and she preached the Gospel of Carpe Diem too. Seizing opportunity—men, grants, choice seating in seminar rooms and the graduate student lounge—pulsed through her veins, natural, obligatory, the secret to the fully realized life. As for caveat emptor, Judy dismissed the phrase as Cowardly Lion's rationalization for quaking in the shadows, a living doormat.

Marta, despite years of feminism and post-this and post-that literary theory meant to gnaw away at the truisms of suspect, oppressive patriarchal convention, nonetheless viewed her friend as "having a touch of the tramp"—that term her mother's, once regularly deployed to help young and impressionable Marta to distinguish rotten apples from good eggs—because Judy occasionally, or frequently, depending on the semester's stressors, bedded men whose names she'd scarcely heard.

Judy's match up for Marta: an Assistant Director "producing," Judy spat, "detritus." Her honest used car dealer pitch admitted minor flaws while underscoring the sterling plusses. He currently slaved on *Transfiguro III*, the second sequel of a comic book franchise that degraded (as eye candy, food for thought, and sheer entertainment spectacle) and belched empty awfulness with each outing. But the features—showcasing the boundless ingenuity and wisecrack-accompanied feats of a superhero able to change shape as he pleases—made vaults of cash and kept local crews and their American bosses gainfully employed. A hot prospect, SRFLI's paper characteristics proclaimed *going places*.

When Judy said, "You could cut steak with the man's chiseled good looks," Marta, avoiding any questions about the logic or aptness of Judy's image and bowled over by her friend's force of nature personality, had shrugged in turn: "Sure."

"What's our commonality?" Marta had wanted to ask, and in retrospect lamented the question's failure to launch.

The last date in a skimpy, unremarkable series had been a thudding fiasco—with a preppy button-down Oxford cloth tenure stream History prof so dull and career-obsessed that the responses of ire and unveiled boredom, and, later, grey despair that came with imagining an entire life shared with such a blinkered specimen who evidently preferred crumbling folios to living flesh, had seemed predestined. With the new proposition Marta had thought *Why not?* with the irrational yet pigheaded assurance of a gambler already long into a meteoric losing streak. And, anyway, she reasoned, the single-occupancy shell that at the moment she felt so eager to discard could always and easily be revisited, like home.

Judy's goading expertise played a part too: "God, branch out a bit. Who the hell wants to date another graduate student? Too much braininess kills physicality. Ker-splat. You'd try to impress each other with your peerless insights about Lacan until 11PM and then shake hands like abstinent Christian teenagers on some pimply, tight-assed high school debating team." Marta refused to share the fact that she'd willingly, happily participated in debate competitions—with other teens in matching green polo shirts who, yes, kept the tetracycline industry bullish—throughout grades 11 and 12.

The date did in fact dislodge Marta from terra firma, which was, she'd admit, small to begin with. SRLFI chose an *It Space*, his idiot term, capitalized and italicized judging from the intonation, used to describe a fussy overdressed start up restaurant that begged for interior design magazine photographers and coolness credibility, not messy humans prone to spilling fashionable alcohol concoctions and filling bellies that bulged ever so subtly over expensive waistbands. Between courses, Marta watched, curious to see where he stowed the gum he chewed so tirelessly. He seemed the type to stick a wad under the table.

After eight oblong plates of Minutia—"Appetizers as a concept are just so 1970s-Galloping-Gourmet-scallops-wrapped-in-bacon-and-served-in-a-brown escargot-dish, right?" he'd sputtered, inciting a facial reaction less impassive and pleased than she wanted—they'd driven, Marta listening, SRLFI motormouthed, to *Transfiguro III*'s wrap party. "We'll check out the vibe," he explained before speeding into a tangled, angrily-toned story about the search to finalize the sequel's official name. Watching passive captives in other cars, Marta nonetheless caught "so-called marketing geniuses," "brain-dead focus groups," "La La Land," "child's play," "give me a break," and "total clusterfuck" before intuiting that "their heads shoved all the way up their asses" amounted to his summary statement and a request for her nodded or vocalized sympathies. "Unbelievable," she'd enthused.

Scrutinizing the narrow gastro-lounge restlessly—all shiny plastic beige surfaces, as though clamped together from *Space: 1999* set remnants—Marta counted people using their mobile devices. The average was 3.5 per dartboard-sized table.

SRLFI spoke at a canter, blithe self-love a fortress completely impervious to her purposeful arrows of silence. Marta fixed on him with a baleful, dismissive stare; she meant it to shout "O joy! A shallow movie guy who yearns to be a shallow fashion guy," and was shocked that—she supposed—the man misunderstood so completely, believing her to be conveying instead, "Please go on. I'm fascinated by each and every verb."

His conversational stride exhibited no sign of fatigue as he steered and prodded and nudged her through intimate groupings of crew, all the while oblivious to the affront of his trespasses into Marta's personal space.

Hardly a complete disaster—exoticism saved him from becoming a deadly bore, and the partygoers did not ever whine competitively about the job market, funding applications, tenure, students, busyness, conference papers, or research plans—neither could the date ever warrant being judged a moderate success.

Introduced to SRLFI's "peeps," Marta noticed how one after the next looked beyond her shoulder or else right through her with the keenly focused eyes of a dog bred to retrieve. The single guy who broke the pattern—tall, rail lean, black shirt unbuttoned two places below decorum—had turned the conversation to Alice Munro. Since he'd managed, moments earlier, to drop the names of a famous Manhattan fashion visionary and a Hollywood producer (likewise "truly visionary") with whom he claimed to be very close friends, Marta registered surprise at the sudden literary tangent. She perked up.

On the next beat he asked: "I heard she's a real bitch. Is that true?"

Marta eyes widened, aghast. Was he for real? She had wanted to slap him, douse the man's fatuous face with the table's bottle of Swiss water and exclaim "How crass can you be?" but had chosen a prim "Well, we don't really study authors in quite that way." Back on campus the vulgarity had made for an entertaining tale of heresy.

The gaze of anyone else seemed to lose predatory gleam—undisguised assessment complete, the eye tracked movement at distant tables—when Marta revealed a lowly, would-be lecturer status rather than "I'm a writer with a hot screenplay recently green lit and gearing up for cast." She thought, *I am not worthy of being prey*. Such relegation struck her as an insult of a strange kind.

A few of SRLFI's underlings persisted, wondering in coy tones if she had a little something in the works—as though they could not actually conceptualize a word person who wouldn't trade body and soul for a screenplay catching Hollywood's favour, or at least be readying an option-able book that had in fact been written with the movie version already in mind. Disheartening, the narrowness was not essentially different than the purblind careerism of her own tribe, whose members wore the Knowledge Producing Intellectual badge with undisguised pride.

Marta had actually choked slightly when after another long hour passed SRLFI leaned close to her ear and asked if she wanted to "do some blow" back at his condo downtown. Declining, naturally, she claimed loyalty to a long-planned early morning hike that demanded complete focus: "It's going to be epic." The lie hung in the air, a ludicrous excuse, and clumsy as well, so patently was she not outdoorsy or someone who'd describe huffing up a rocky hill as "epic."

Beneath the offer's sheer embarrassing banality—cocaine with a movie guy: where were the $100 notes, the loud sniffing, and Studio 54 clone when you needed them?—Marta felt bothered by a less welcome sensation: she'd never tried the drug and a priggish dread warned that something lamentable might happen. Instantly, an image had flashed from a moralizing television episode deep in the past in which a foolish high school A-lister experimenting with LSD had leapt from a rooftop fully believing that he could fly.

But worse was the idea that she'd look like a rank amateur, unclear about the real-life etiquette and technique of cocaine usage. What if the reality didn't match the vision: rectangular pocket mirror, rolled bill, hasty parallel lines of credit card chopped powder, eye-watering tingling in the nasal passage, hyperactivity, altered vision? She could live without the spectacle of someone laughing as she fumbled or coughed while snorting. Other than too-animated conversation, the story of what happened after inhalation refused to coalesce. Maybe he'd expect them to *get it on*: that would fit the disco- and Reagan-era pattern.

There'd been another murmured statement, too, directly after: "And then I'll eat your pussy." *Ah*, Marta had thought, *I am worthy of being prey after all.*

SRLFI's declaration had been accompanied by a trial wolfish leer that her eyes measured as being distinctly unsure, half-apologetic, and not cuspid-baring predatory in the least. The words might be those of a boy trying out an elder brother's surefire technique.

The silence that followed proved laughably absolute.

Thinking *My kingdom for a phrase!*, Marta didn't utter a syllable because she could not imagine a response with sufficient bite. What would Judy say? Playful witticism and blistering riposte eluded Marta equally. No one had ever offered cocaine. Cunnilingus matched to it floated well beyond the map of experiences, even fantasy ones; she'd spent more time pondering the existence of UFOs.

Marta had returned to the context later. In SRLFI's world, about which she could only speculate, how would a woman reply? "Sure, babe, bring it on"? "Uh huh, let me take off my heels"? "Drop dead, you worm"? "Are you fucking joking"?

In this case, though, shared awkwardness emerged as the single outcome.

Following instructions, SRLFI dropped Marta off a block before Undre Arms. Though making no effort to park the Audi, he said, "Nice place. We should do something sometime."

"Yes, I agree." Mutual insincere smiles had sealed the negative transaction.

Marta closed the car door without great force. Pretending to fish out keys as she trod toward the entrance to a building of strangers, she hoped the refusal to turn around and fondly wave would convey a simple message: "Get lost." The coupe sped off. The security of Undre Arms beckoned from two minutes away.

Mood beginning to curdle with the recollection, Marta reminded herself that the biopic consultancy didn't represent a career move; nor was it a blind date. The work contract would be for desirable professional expertise—not heart, not body, not soul, the deal not Faustian. If the studio meeting hinted at unsatisfactory conditions she'd easily refuse them, a diva in her own right.

Sardine Tin City

1.

Military thundering from the *Mishima* soundtrack pushed Jake out of sleep. He reached across the bed and nudged Gleek. "Hey chubster, what's happened to my feline alarm clock?" The tabby responded by coiling tighter. As the piece reached a tympanic crescendo, Jake rolled over to address the device: "Lower volume."

This early, the room's light-absorbing surfaces produced a restful muteness, an effect Jake thought might be akin to reclining within a Victorian crypt, or stretching out under a heavy canopy of autumnal trees: comfortable and sedating. Walnut-finish furnishings, mortar-toned drapes and bedding, and walls painted Sullen, Jake recalled, comprised the "complementary palette" the decorator had highlighted on her laptop's virtual model. Calling the stark black and white photograph of a spherical natural gas tank in Belgium an anchor piece for the living room, she'd replied with a sigh when Jake sputtered about the cost: "It'll appreciate in value, you know," peering theatrically over the balcony off the kitchen to survey the street below, "unlike that shiny German car of yours."

An enthralled audience of one, Jake had watched Marilyn, a bubbly and trucker-mouthed California blonde, sell a vision with a realtor's gusto, minus the false camaraderie: "Masculine, yes, but not Hemingway-running-bulls-in-Spain-macho, right, or Joe-Beer-Can-watching-the-fucking-Superbowl. Tasteful and refined. Solid."

Strutting around the condo, right hand chop-chop-chopping into left palm, she'd told Jake about taking pride in profiling a client's exact needs. "This developer's off-white completely misses the mark, obviously," she ran a hand of fingernails along the chalky wall, "unless you're cloning a Motel 6 next to the Arby's on Exit 234."

Jake had enjoyed the unexpected bluntness. After the rapid strings of description, he guessed what choice words she'd summon for the Joe Beer Can man-den pitch.

Down to the last detail the project had been Marilyn channeling Jake, and he was flattered by the implied compliments; he'd give kudos to anyone who intuited which buttons to press—knowing the right thing to say and not registering as kiss-ass, that art took skill to master. When she'd taken a misstep with a Tommy gun floor lamp—"ironic," she'd called it—Jake figured that even Mother Teresa had run into off days.

Tracing a line along his sleep-warm torso, Jake grabbed the morning's erection and pumped slowly at the base for a few seconds. *Now that is solid*, he thought. To greet each and every day with a substantial pole pointing outward, what a proclamation of intent. Carpe diem. He wondered if all men did so. Of course they must; it's the male prerogative: go forth, thrust, and multiply, Johnny Appleseed, the rush surrounding orgasm the never-diminishing reward. As hardwired as breathing, and the build up and jet-speed release felt better. He scrolled the blankets down and scrutinized the black hair and muscular undulations of chest and belly. Not quite rippled, but not at all bad for early forties, he nodded, I wouldn't say no.

Time to move, Jake thought. He'd store his juice till later.

Naked, Jake crouched and slid the laptop from the messenger bag. Veering toward the kitchen, he clicked on the television; blasts of noise kicked his senses awake. As for bladder urgings, he'd wait for the erection to subside.

In the kitchen he stared at the weather channel—drizzle till noon, mixed rain and sun from then on—before switching to *Murder, She Wrote*. As much as he liked the widow detective's observant, puzzle-solving mind and spotting the has-been guest stars, Mrs. Fletcher's happy amnesia intrigued him. Anywhere the woman moved she walked into a murder or two, about 300 stabbings, shootings, hangings, and poisonings over the 264 episodes of the series—Jake had ordered the DVD boxed set on a whim—and yet remained unflappably optimistic, her demeanour calm. Never taken aback or weighted down in the least by the littering of victims, she took the world's seething murderousness in stride as though it were no different than ho-hum traffic on the day's commute, when she ought to be in session for Post-Traumatic Stress Disorder and chasing her AM and PM coffee with Zoloft. Jake couldn't deny he'd be a paranoid wreck if every social setting festered with deadly secrets, ulterior motives, and a minimum of one stiff.

The mounting bombast of Philip Glass from the bedroom competed with Mrs. Fletcher's revelations. The player had been a gift, but along with puppies or teenagers it demanded instructions three or four times before the information sank in. In the hallway Jake bellowed: "Volume down." Hearing no change he strode closer to the mic: "Vol-ume DOWN." He'd assumed kinks in voice recognition software were buried in the past. Gleek didn't stir.

Throwing jeans on the bed, he decided to go commando. He grabbed a black T-shirt. Justifying the V-neck's $110 price tag, the clerk in Yaletown had stroked the fabric: "Your skin can tell the difference." He'd read the tag—Made in Malaysia—and told her to get real. He bought it anyway.

2.

As 8-grain cereal bubbled, Jake checked email, just the personal accounts. He'd save the occupational addresses for the office. Jake strived to keep mornings at home work-free; border patrol was essential with Hollywood, a demanding boss with Old World beliefs about fealty. And his ass already dragged about the location shoot in the middle of nowhere—a part of the job description that always felt punitive, not least because the move threw him from a comfortable orbit—and wanted to stamp that reality out of his consciousness until the last minute. It's a whore's life, Jake supposed, and not every john is a trustworthy high-roller paying big bucks for pillow-talk and snuggles, not by a long shot.

A respondent to Jake's online hook-up profile began with a false-step subject heading, "Cease the day!" The attached lure: a regulation towel-wrapped torso shot at a bathroom mirror. Jake leaned close to the screen inspecting the image. Not bad. A little pudgy and years out of date probably; the accompanying message scanned as moronic: "Hi: I thought u look Very Familiar to guy that work out from my gym . . . Do u by any change work out at Noth Vancouver . . . ? Go with the floor type guy here. Anyway I just want to say Hello . . . How is life threatening you?" Another dud in a world full of them, Jake lamented.

Before replying, Jake lifted the cereal off the burner and forwarded "Cease the day!"

He'd ordinarily pass one or two to Jeremy on any given week, those messages entrenched in his routine, like morning espresso. Receiving was another. Jake grinned opening "FW: check this out" emails from Jeremy since the message in the bottle—compelling or deranged: which kind to arrive was anyone's guess—often surpassed the snippets he sent. Jeremy prided himself on a curatorial sense of the exceptional, ugly though bizarre.

Incoming messages stoked Jake. The left-field and potent charge of the swapped mail reshaped the waking world, adding bracing fathoms of depth to the otherwise flat, death-in-life schedule of obligation and routine—"I really need to get that report finished before my 2 o'clock with Peter in Finance"—and rote sentence volleys about politics, movies, vacations, kids, weather, and real estate, solid performances but empty as toilet paper tubes. The incoming details exposed the customary assumptions about sex—clearly defined, biologically motivated physical exchanges involving insertion of Tab A into Slot B in bed once a week right after the news—as lacking, a popular belief posing as fact that actually came nowhere close.

This discovery echoed a sci-fi plot: with special glasses the hero can see past the deceit of surface appearances. Of course Jake didn't unearth the stealthy alien invasion of *They Live*. For now, extraterrestrials remained fiction; but realizing life contains more than the flock's clustered movements had the elegant simplicity of a truth.

Jake counted on stumbling into like eurekas even though no one's average with luck batted a thousand. He held firm that dropping out of the B. Comm program—the fast track to office tower hivedom—had been the wisest decision of his twenties. Concrete limits to shoehorning exist, Jake had seen. In a borrowed tie and so cleanly shaven his cheeks shone, Jake had shuddered with a cold sweat convulsion steps past Price Waterhouse's half-circle security desk on day one of a work-study placement. The glimpse of the office maze of muffling grey felt cubicles had swelled into a revelation: before him stood a hasty engagement that would never lead to marriage. The barely masked disappointment on the sensible faces of the parental units? A bargain compared to a future of ongoing regret.

Jake had viewed the ensuing fluke job offer from a buddy of a buddy to guard the crew lot for a Daryl Hannah TV movie shoot as icing on the cake. Naturally, years of climbing industry rungs revealed that despite expectations icing and a felt cubicle look dishearteningly similar. Calls, meetings—being the delegating boss in one room, toadying yes-man in the next—reports, long hours, desk slouch, chains of command, soul-snatching superiors: like death and taxes, corporate sand traps lay in wait, inescapable.

He'd quickly learned to make time to smell around for perks. Finding them? Instinct, a matter of catching the scent.

Last winter at a wrap party for a TV series cancelled halfway into its first season, Jake had spoken with a producer's date, an abrasive grad student in some WTF subject called Critical Studies in Sexuality. "You have no idea," she'd exclaimed, backing him into a corner with a full glass of merlot while spouting about German sex researchers she mistakenly thought as household names. "It's a psychological phantasmagoria." As Jake imagined a ball-gag in the prof's mouth—the Gatling gun laughter from her throat unfortunately close to strangled goose honks—she explained scenes, ancient and modern, and described bizarre fetishes that might keep shrinks in business for centuries.

He'd mouthed appreciation. Based on his own experiences and ingrained, occasionally compulsive wanderings through the

Internet, Jake couldn't help but agree. Jeremy's missives? Further assurance that reality and appearance rarely hung out at the same location.

3.

Jake read the first email from the kitchen laptop. Jeremy, in Hawaii now on a yoga retreat, had still managed to dig up material. After the subject line—"Dept. of Public Transit," an idea Jeremy claimed to have lifted from *The New Yorker*—he'd pasted a story, one regrettably void of attached photos. Jake would bet a month's pay that male affinity for the visual resided deep within, a vestige from prehistory's hunt-to-survive era.

Now he'd have to fill in the blanks—

> My girlfriend and I met a sissified husband at the bus stop begging for change. I'm a guy, but I think it's great for women to make men pay for their infidelity. This wife takes the prize for vengeance.
>
> He was wearing a pinstripe short-sleeved cuffed blouse over a spaghetti strap cami, earrings, ponytail with pink elastics, I am guessing panty hose, women's slacks and pink lip gloss and the most gorgeous set of acrylic French nails. The tips were at least an inch long. His nails are so much nicer than my gf's. He said he got caught cheating again on his wife of 11 years. I told him if he told me what was going on I would give him bus fare, but I lied.
>
> Anyways. This sissy's wife took him and got his ears pierced, waxed his entire body, got electrolysis on his face and eyebrows. Got a full set of acrylic nails. She took him clothes shopping and bought him this outfit and made him wear it from the store. She then dumped him miles from home penniless and told him to walk home. He/she showed me his blackberry with the emails from his wife. She actually called when I was talking to him. And he called a couple of friends to help bail him out. No takers

today. I actually heard him say that if the wife didn't have all the money, he would be long gone.

Fishy. Jake, elbows on the black marble counter, wondered about the writer's fawning attention to clothing and unmanly nail envy. Definitely suspicious and a bit girly. He pictured the sissified vow-breaker on the phone: "Uh, listen Joe, I'm in a bit of a jam. Marge caught me cheating—again, I know, I know, me bad—and so this time for punishment made me wax and cross dress and then she dumped me at a bus stop begging for coin. It's way humiliating. Would you mind picking me up?" What friend—what *brother*—would say, "No, sorry man, I really have to side with Marge this time. You gotta be taught a lesson. Becoming a transvestite beggar for the afternoon is a punishment that fits the crime. Good luck, buddy, catch you later."

True situation or fever dream, the pathetic scene made Jake relieved to be free of marital shackles.

Jeremy's second message came with generic paired photos, ass and erection to camera; Jeremy's subject-line summary looked apt—FW: Subject: Very Very Makulit.

> Well I look very snobbish at first but I do get along with people easily. I also am very talkative when I get warmed up. Hmm what else? I find it hard to describe myself, I think it would be better if you would just talk to me and get to know me . . . Since it is true that words are the biggest liars of all . . . I'm very very makulit! that was always my asset! I'm true to myself, and i like being the first version of myself, not a second version of someone else! I'm not looking for just a hookup so if your just looking for that move on. Love to swim, modern jazz music, watch porn (cmon guy, be real, hahaha!!!) if you wanna be my friend, mack me.

Jake loaded the dishwasher and tossed back the sweet, scalding demitasse of coffee in two gulps. He deleted Rambo's email and glanced at Jeremy's final selection, a mail-order groom looking for a ticket out of Russia. That one he'd seen before.

Amongst a galaxy of come-and-go contacts and IATSE comrades, Jake saw Jeremy as a fellow-traveler. Meeting a decade ago at Serpentine, a WASPy Toronto fetish night "for Discerning Adults," they'd circled restlessly—both of them novice experimenters in SM and deciding in tandem that the dabbling would be a one-off—and shared a brief and ultimately lame engagement with a kneeling blindfolded submissive named Raven whose clasped prayer position hands held a stubby braided whip. They soon settled on bottled beer and bar stools in stiff, freshly-purchased leather gear, and cast unimpressed glances at the black-clad proceedings—the men as gruff and humourless as *Mad Max* villains, and the women's overwrought fantasy costumes transforming them, in Jeremy's view, into background figures in censored outtakes from Heart and Stevie Nicks videos. Jake had been taken from the moment they'd watched each other listlessly prod Raven's lipsticked mouth with semi-hards; Jeremy's smirk and rolled eyes emerged as that forgettable evening's high mark.

Learning they were practically neighbours on the country's west coast, Jake welcomed the chance to hang out with another with a closely matched taste for adventuring. Jeremy zeroed in on an age demographic considerably younger than Jake's eye-on-his-own-generation preference, a convenient fact that suspended the ritual tussle over alpha and sidekick roles. They'd kept in touch, occasional nights on the town gradually becoming regular calls supplemented by forwarded boasting pictures or videos of successful conquests; and once familiarity allowed for it, admissions of limp performances, outright rejections, and embarrassing, thudding steps into human cow pats cropped up. The look-at-this and it-would-never-happen emails of today? Comic relief.

Jake deleted messages from other respondents—timid, unappealing, dodgy, or inexplicable—and typed, "Life is threatening me well, thx. U up for a role in the hey?" to the torso that couldn't spell. He had no intention of continuing with that. Readings completed, he turned for the bathroom; the stubble could stand a trim. For dieting Gleek he left a modest portion of food and fresh water.

Word from Lora: a "sardine tin city" work day. *Same old, same old*, he sighed. At this stage of pre-production back-to-back meetings barely sunk in.

Prep

I.

A punctual finish to the weekly kickboxing session under the joy-free and fat-banishing regime of tattoo-sleeved thug-warrior Franco—the man a shoo-in should a Russian gangster require a personal trainer—left Jake with half an hour to spare. Figuring he'd squeeze in a few sets of arm reps, he strode toward the free weights.

For a weekday morning the gym seemed crowded. Jake swapped nods with regulars and roving employees in bulging black nylon vestments, flashed a smile of encouragement to a husky newbie giving fitness another go—who wouldn't applaud *The Biggest Loser*'s hard-won transformations?—and didn't hesitate to foist his impatience on dawdlers, or work in with top-heavy XXL knuckle draggers who wanted nothing more than to monopolize equipment and suck back muscle-growth drinks like penned livestock, even though they'd piss out the unabsorbed protein hours later.

Polite deference had its place, but not at this grab bag of shark-grin realtors, pretzel-stiff nightclub security hued the tanning bed mahogany of *Predator*-era Schwarzenegger, gum-chewing junior execs, and stringently maintained spouses of white collar breadwinners: with everyone posturing in alpha mode, Push or Be Pushed hovered overhead as the one and only commandment. At peak times, the circuit machine line of heaving guys with corkscrewing neck ink re-cast the place as a middleclass mirror of San Quentin's exercise yard. In a lifeboat scenario, Jake would trust none of them.

Though committing to a block of ninety minutes every second day, Jake possessed no special interest in fitness and health.

Now that he'd attained the target specs he relaxed, focussing on maintenance; showing up was a perennial item on a chore list to strike a line through, and not an accomplishment to brag about. He steered clear of running groups, core strength evaluations, boot camps, half-marathon training programs, staff offers of body fat assessment, and any back-slapping locker room gab about protein drinks (soy versus whey), powdered supplements (ditto), and "absolutely kick-ass, dude" lat/delt/pec/ab routines.

Musculature was simply a goal, not the must-have lifestyle promoted by magazines he scanned, nor even a topic to discuss at length. He couldn't see it as anything except mindless repetition, although a necessary means to an end like a driver's license or a passport. If he could purchase a prefab physique with as little effort as he'd made for the condo's décor or the shirt currently hanging in his locker, he would. But he judged a shortcut like steroids as risky, a medically unsound gamble. And, besides, no guy dreams of shriveled balls. Otherwise, he'd write a cheque and be in like Flynn. Loyalty to routine, the next best option, stood next to an oil change as duty, good in the long run if tedious. Catching his reflection in a mirror, Jake confirmed dedication produced worthy results.

For work and leisure the semblance of being fit and healthy was crucial. Jake had noticed that since following a strict gym schedule people—men and women both, though in their own ways—checked him out. That truth applied even in shadowy places where his silhouette alone remained visible. Whatever the facts might be—his insides might be riddled with disease for all anyone knew—taut bulkiness conveyed the universal shorthand for health and capable well-being.

Jake recalled scanning a piece online about scientists who'd found that at some microcellular level humans intuit a cut physique as standing for reproductive durability; in sniffing out good genes, then, survival instincts fix on muscles. Health—or its body double anyway: wide shoulders, narrow hips, an erect posture, scant fat bulges—meant vitality, and that in turn gave the bearer presence and an advantage, not to mention a tasty dollop of social capital. And added visibility—of the right kind—meant legal tender. Any child could grasp that. He'd done the math.

Factory-built muscles obviously weren't a well-kept secret anywhere except the suburban obesity belt since on any given minute he could spot guys, younger ones typically, quickly lifting their shirts between sets to flex abs perishable as hothouse flowers, faces satisfied despite being set as masks of cool evaluation.

Jake didn't crave attention, not really, or at least not to the extent of the so-called talent he'd had the displeasure of working under in recent shows. Still, a fraction of limelight struck him as good for business, deserved too. Success should be the reward for putting in the hours, Harvey Weinstein and history told him so. Why not generate some buzz—"Looking good, Jake" or, better yet, "Who's that guy?" Sure, capturing the spotlight didn't equal commanding respect, but it stood nearby. The level of recognition struck him as proper, hard-earned. Jake felt certain that if he could enter the same party twice, one time in today's incarnation and in the other carrying his frame from a decade ago, his former self would wander the room freely and capture a sad fraction of the eye contact.

Being memorable, forgettable, or run-of-the-mill: as if there was anything to agonize over.

2.

In the white tile change room he toweled off, tuning out geezers in flaccid white Stanfield's who nattered about the hardships of telephone party lines back in 1962. Small talk commenced when Tim, another morning regular, sought Jake's gaze. The guy's name might be Tom, Dan, John, or Don—one of those meat-and-potato names Jake tended to forget. "Hey . . . ," Jake said when they chatted, never bothering with the follow-up.

Soon after they'd met, Tim had let Jake know he'd purchased a first time trial gym membership that very week, worked in a nearby supermarket as a short-term gig, and had plans to break into the movie business. Gamma-male, Jake had pigeonholed him, a born kiss-ass and pushover.

Tim lifted the black T-shirt's right sleeve immediately. "Hey, man, check it out." Jake read the shiny scrolling phrase, newly inscribed to judge from the puffy edges: "Pain is Just Weakness Leaving the Body."

"Nice." Soft and pale the surrounding flesh brought to mind raw breakfast links. Jake felt impatience mounting; the guy was all script and no action.

Jake wondered if Tim fantasized about getting discovered, as in the ancient Hollywood legend. By the weights or lockers, Tim would zero in on Jake and steer conversations to big budget productions currently in planning or being shot around the city and ask questions about rumoured upcoming TV series. He evidently followed fan chatter and inadvertently kept Jake in the loop. Tim hadn't passed a resume Jake's way or asked for an interview; he obviously wanted Jake to throw him a bone. As far as Jake was concerned, a bone of any sort was out of the question. Lumpen, Tim still wore baby pudge even though closer to thirty than twenty.

Despite the keener attitude Tim had never mentioned a target job in the industry. Accustomed to meeting people foaming at the mouth to charge into show business, Jake didn't offer to open any doors. Tim needed to grow a pair if he had plans for more than a locker room swap about industry goings on. Undiluted ambition and staking territory were part and parcel in Hollywood North. Wallflowers and apologetic dreamers wouldn't get far; Schwab's on Sunset had been a myth for seventy years, one with no local equivalent.

The men's year-old acquaintanceship of five-minute conversations fell into a set pattern, Jake responding to Tim by answering his queries. Left to Jake, their interaction would have plateaued at quick mutual greetings long ago. If Jake rubbed Tim the wrong way by asking no questions about his job or personal life—and refusing two early attempts at deal-sealing knuckle bumps—he didn't let on. Jake didn't give the situation much thought; he viewed Tim as easy game and used to playing the wingman regularly.

"So, what's new, man? Great day out there, eh?" Naked, Jake crouched to run a towel between his toes, hoping to fend off another growth of fungus. Tim sat on a wooden bench. Jake had never seen him strip, not even to underwear; dollars for donuts, the short and rotund newbie changed inside one of the private alcoves built to cramped toilet stall specifications. He had something to hide, probably.

"Yeah, not bad. Same old, same old with me." The agreeable words revealed nothing. Tim could connect the dots as he wished.

"So, you on hiatus now, buddy?" Tim pulled off the first of two T-shirts. Jake had noticed he chose off the rack macho—labels like Under Armor or shirts that advertised big-boy cojones via branding for muscle-building supplements. Today's, for Muscle FX, came emblazoned with a boasting motto about wolves. A pack mentality at best, Jake ceded.

"Just finished with that. Needed some away time from it all, you know?" Toes completely dry, Jake applied deodorant, gave his dick a tug, and slipped on clothing. He didn't understand modesty about change room nudity.

"For sure, man, I hear where you're coming from. So what's on now that hiatus has dried up?" Tim rustled through a gym bag as he spoke.

"We're in pre-production right now for a new feature, a MOW, locking down funds, locations, talent, crew, that kind of thing."

The men paused as the concrete floor reverberated, the thud of heavy weights dropped from a height a standard declaration of prowess repeated every five minutes.

"Storm before the hurricane kind of situation."

"Cool. Who's in it?"

"I gotta fill you in later. Time to head to studio. No rest for the wicked." Jake smiled and gestured with his palms up: *What can you do?*

"Good to talk, man. Have a good one."

"Take care." Jake grabbed keys from the locker and headed for the stairs that led to underground parking.

The Vague Land

I.

What clothing is appropriate for the interview? The question crept up on Marta before bed as she shuffled hangers and cobbled together an outfit for the next day's classes. A tried and true sweater and skirt combination, or something unexpected? She'd begun to favour a new purchase to clothe the hired-gun role—Marta Spěk, Film Consultant—but could not match the acquisition and sketchy persona to specific wardrobe pieces. Artful layers of black, an imposing suit, sporty casual wear? Impeccable credentials are what matter, Marta told herself, and nevertheless fretted each time she laid out a uniform for the workday. She concluded style was beside the point: only executives and actors weighed that; behind-the-scenes personnel fell off the radar so far as public curiosity mattered.

Still, the compulsion rooted itself: create a pitch-perfect first impression. Logic warred with impulse and lost, and between home and campus she window-shopped in earnest and grew watchful for fashionable pedestrians. As for what to avoid, she needed to look no further than faculty meetings populated with dust-hued woolens, practical fleece vests, and faded cotton trousers; based on available evidence, a life of the mind left little room for the frivolous evanescence of seasonal trends.

The resulting compromise paired a slightly marmish but well-cut tweed skirt with a costly and uncharacteristically bright patterned blouse—the sales associate's two cents: "Jewel tones are this season's Important Statement." The look achieved balance, Marta had thought on the date of purchase, a modest though confident notice-me declaration. Later, she squirmed over literal clownishness, a statement the store clerk would have never advised.

A few winters ago she'd overheard a student in a freshman composition class tell a friend, "Some personality and a little beauty would be nice" in response to a question she'd arrived too late to catch. The reasonableness of the comment had struck her, as had the friend's abrasive retort: "Yeah, but nice tits rule the runway, man." Placing the Film Consultant ensemble on the bed, Marta calculated—prayed—that her choice attained a reassuring degree of personality and beauty. As for modest breast size, nature's allotment served adequately.

The final step: details—no brooch, one cocktail ring, scent applied well before arrival. While glasses ought to be left at home, contact lenses inevitably led to watery eyes. She'd wear them and make the switch in a restroom at the studio. Apply a coat of nude lip gloss too. Yes, definitely.

2.

Paying my own way, Marta thought, *this cannot be an auspicious sign*. Even as internal bolstering, the emphatic *cannot* felt loud, empowering; Marta repeated the silent word resolutely. Jaw set and arms crossed, she conjured an appropriately stormy weather cinematic sequence of being seated immobile inside the train and watching the studio rep—young, panicked, job on the line—search for mysterious Dr. Spěk in vain, eventually having to return and report the vexing failure to appear, a wrench thrown into the works, if only momentarily. As vengeance fantasy it was mild-mannered and bargain basement cheap, Marta conceded as she embroidered the details, but pleasurable nonetheless.

A synthetic female voice declaring the approaching eastward station with an automaton's uninflected vowels interrupted Marta's rising pique: "The next station is Metrotown." She craned her neck again to study the cheerful route map above; only three stops remained.

An electronic gong activated, the doors whisked shut, and the cars accelerated in computer-directed increments.

Although the Skytrain looked nothing like the limousine buffed to an obsidian lustre she'd grown to anticipate, and a catered lunch at the warehouse production office dropped at the edge of suburban development did not match an exquisite meal at SpotPrawn @ The Four Seasons, the adventure of being airborne—gliding, nearly floating when factoring out tracks—embraced her, a simple and true satisfaction.

Marta respected the hygienic elevated trains for the utopianism they represented, smooth curved metal, glass, and plastic—untouched by grime, graffiti, litter, and, seemingly, corrosive time—that proclaimed sure faith in mind-boggling technology to remedy all past ills and usher in a future in which strife, poverty, and that pesky gap between pristine vision and pock-marked reality faded into relics, odd and distasteful curiosities from a bygone age, like slavery, night soil buckets, and rickets. Such hopefulness: it existed at a level of magnitude she could never reach. For that faith even obstinate biological limitations presented no hurdle; ingenious implants, prosthetics, supplements, and replacement organs promised limitlessness, an immortality of a sort. A veritable fountain of hale, unblemished youth.

Marta's gaze wandered to fellow passengers. That engineer's vision of a golden new age scattered, instantly undermined by the tangibly anemic flesh and myopic eyes of the skinny slouched teenager who'd boarded three stops before. One seat in front of the youth, an elderly balding man was rocked by a head spasm a bamboo cane and frailty belied. Deflated weariness prevailed on the many-hued faces. Sniffles, coughs, and sneezes of flus and colds—allergy-induced outbursts too, she'd hazard—rocketed audibly, staccato interruptions to the steady whirring hum of the forward-moving compartment. This constancy of imperfection—breathing in deeply she could detect faint traces of aerosolized nicotine and alcohol residue wafting from nearby pores, sour breath, and body odour of the armpit and mothball varieties—unmuzzled Marta's skepticism.

As Marta turned from the commuters she caught a spectral image in the glass, alerted immediately to practical outlet mall spectacles, national average height, and flat, non-cascading hair in the medium-brown of her mother's entire family. Traditionally, outbreaks of a neurotic fixation on the negative amounted to a consequence of nervous stress. Like a bad mood or a cloud today's manifestation would duly pass; on the return trip, interview complete and decision made, there'd be none of this saturnine, no joy in Mudville assessing of the disappointing world. Marta counted on it. She'd taken a lengthy personality test years ago and one of the findings she'd been happy to hold on to was an "even-keeled" rating; complex algorithms had proven her a steady ship on all currents, the image satisfying. As for the other, less trophy-worthy findings, they had been relegated to an indifferently visited self-improvement file located in a backwater brain cell cluster.

Beyond the glass, the enormity of the panorama was dizzying. All the evidence of ceaseless human industry staggered the senses. Each hill presented nature paved over with structures, and every house came completely loaded with stuff sliding toward obsolescence and an eventual RIP in teeming landfills. *So many families*, Marta thought, *an overwhelming archive of joy and pain.*

Marta retracted her attention, hugging the notes and books arranged in the valise close to her chest. She'd chosen a valise instead of the usual canvas book bag with hope that the mock-ostrich leather and vaguely European pedigree would broadcast an *au courant* world-class professionalism.

Marta had no idea what to expect, so she'd prepared for a job interview atmosphere that would be anything but convivial. While Jakob Nugent's assistant had sent options for meeting times and a choice of meals—via an impersonal email: another ambiguous sign to decode?—she hadn't bothered with information about what Mr. Nugent's agenda might be. Overcompensating, Marta had packed a copy of the Hester Stanhope study (with three laudatory reviews tucked inside) and two recent articles, though she supposed that reserving time to read the material hardly fit into the man's plans. Perhaps an assistant had already prepared a one-page précis. It seemed a solid conjecture.

Marta didn't wish for university-style interview conditions—which forever brought to mind ice-blooded pike in sheep's clothing—but believed that a combatant's readiness could only help cement her position; she'd even printed a creamy vellum CV copy for Mr. Nugent's records. The thirst for fortification was unaccountable: in no sense did she actually need the job. Cowed by the mere aura of Hollywood, then? She reminded herself who'd be the expert in the room.

Marta did foresee caffeinated impatience and a chronic attention deficit—"Okay, okay, so this *War and Peace*, what's the deal with it? Give me the gist in a couple of seconds, I don't need a goddamned dissertation. Wait a sec, I've got to take this call." The explosive mile-a-minute production executive with a chicken's attention span and the out-of-touch prosaic egghead: another pair of Hollywood script-types that she'd soon witness interacting in real-time. She had little doubt about crossed wired. For these people, perhaps, she would serve as a handy talking encyclopedia, fielding questions about early Victorian bubonic plague treatments, whether Dr. Meryon would have spoken such and such a sentence, or if Lady Stanhope's clothing ought to be cut this way. "Prof Spëk, pls examine these image files from the Art Dept for accuracy. Many thx, LW, Asst to Jakob Nugent": would this be the kind of email she'd receive?

A savant or a soothsayer without pretensions of divinity—that temporary occupation she could inhabit with ease: "Yes, according to medical experts, over 200 different species can serve as hosts. Plague carriers have included domestic cats and dogs, squirrels, chipmunks, marmots, deer mice, rabbits, hares, rock squirrels, camels, and sheep. The vector is usually the rat flea, *Xenopsylla cheopis*. Thirty different flea species have been identified as being able to carry the plague bacillus. Other carriers of plague include ticks and human lice. Yes, absolutely, fever, delirium and rosy lesions would be accurate for Lady Stanhope's 1813 plague bout. Not so much for the blue-black skin and hacking cough, which typically signals the terminal stages of infection, which *needless to say*—she might even throw in a clause or two of pedantry for the sake of cliché—Hester Stanhope did not reach. No, that phrase is *hopelessly* anachronistic. Yes, extant portraits of Hester suggest that a turban is fine. Natural silk or linen, nothing metallic—that would be anachronistic too. But, yes, turbans would have been all the rage for her in both 1800 and 1823. Fashion then was nowhere near as accelerated as today."

A marvel of knowledge, outgoing, useful as soap, typically full of good will but not entirely averse to the occasional sharp remark: that she could manage. Once conversing with actual people, she'd adjust the tone accordingly; overt sharpness would likely win no friends.

Yes, she might relish the role; there was only a minor difference between it and the one she donned for the classroom. The indispensable brainiac, foundational, a fixture. Or was it, she asked herself as she observed yet another mound of hill barnacle-encrusted with homes, remnants of the smart girl who wrote essays and took home the assignments for popular students in exchange for second-rate pay and recognition? A little of both, she concluded with resignation.

Marta realized she'd envisioned herself answering these questions from the quiet of her office computer. As the set was being built—or as banks of CGI technicians keyed in virtual sets?—and the script revised and scenes shot and re-shot and re-shot once again, she might be stuck in a trailer instead and poised for questions, a shade removed from the geriatric employee wearing a *May I Help?* badge in an airport. For the lags between queries, there'd be a few novels and maybe that laborious omnibus review article due in September.

Then again, an entire trailer suggested money to burn, an improbability since the studio didn't own a blockbuster about a sinking ship or a caped vigilante. But who could say? Although she'd dug up no useful evidence anywhere, posing questions was her prerogative. Jakob Nugent must possess everything she wanted clarified. Marta closed her eyes and returned to the scene. She might wander through the sets—to all eyes an embodiment of the absentminded professor—in search of a scone and a mug of tea. Or else: she could send a request for an afternoon snack and have it promptly delivered by an underling—who might be one of her former students for all she knew.

3.

The robot transit system voice announced Marta's stop: "Studio Way."

The doors parted and Marta stepped off. Searching the concrete platform for the escort the studio had dispatched—young, lowly, and instructed to please, she assumed—yielded no results. Not a soul approached as the platform emptied. She'd pictured the airport scenario: "Dr. Spëk" written on a cardboard sign held aloft by the anonymous functionary. One email from Lora Wilkes had mentioned that the studio sprawled five minutes by foot from the station, but at the time Marta hadn't interpreted the information as an invitation to march on over.

Marta decided to wait five minutes. *Raging for fame has its price*, she thought.

Beyond the grey platform the scene presented muted northern hemisphere urban rim—power lines, parked cars, low-profile businesses housed in dreary if spacious generic boxy structures, vehicle traffic, sooty concrete arterial roadways, and forlorn weeds, bushes, and trees flocked with grit. The sour tang of the air was distinctive: thousands of sticky cottonwood leaf buds peeling in slow, temperature-orchestrated synchronicity. Their pungency could be bottled, trademarked, and sold alongside maple syrup in tourist shops, Marta supposed: Fraser Delta Spring No. 5.

The short-term options, Marta thought, *are simple: walk to the studio or stand and wait for an inbound train and, later, a perplexed and likely curt email.* Calling a taxi would be silly.

She strode to the exit stairway. What kind of cut-rate studio is this, she wondered. Jakob Nugent will probably ask me to split the cost of our no-frills lunch. Or we'll each plug coins into a vending machine and retrieve plastic-sealed sandwiches. She felt stalled. While the effort of the walk might erode her composure, Marta suspected that not arriving at all would be a lapse she'd bemoan louder than the executive and his assistant, her daydream of crucial necessity revealed as being only that.

Grumbling as she trudged along the sodden makeshift path at the road's edge—strewn, she counted, with a narrow range of discardables: cigarette packages, torn condom wrappers, fast food takeout bags, soda cans and beer bottles, Styrofoam containers, trampled clothing, plastic bits snapped off from cars, and panties (panties always, why?)—Marta envisioned herself as the kind of crazed marginal individual who squatted beneath septic overpasses or within the dirty blackberry brambles that thrive on the perimeter ground between commercial buildings.

Hearing the volume of the fault-finding, she pressed her lips shut. Were these low utterances like a gateway drug—one unexceptional day you begin with a few choice expletives, and soon enough you're pushing a stolen overflowing shopping cart and warning passersby of precarious mental balance by muttering nonsense several decibels louder than what's acceptable in polite society? Marta switched focus to the approaching interview, sealing the portal to abjection.

At the foreground of the blocky mass of white stucco and vinyl-clad buildings a single guard waited on duty, soaking up afternoon sunshine. She'd leaned a stool against the plywood booth that housed gate controls, a computer, and communication equipment. Stray locks tumbled from beneath her police-style cap.

Lora had sent no pass code or specific instructions about a gated entrance. Her name, she supposed, must be on a list.

The guard did not move as Marta approached.

"Good afternoon," Marta said.

The guard nodded, but remained silent. She didn't remove the mirrored aviator sunglasses when she faced Marta. And though the creased woman appeared to be a child's throw from retirement age, Marta imagined she might be nicknamed "Sarge."

Marta patted the valise. "I have an appointment."

"Do you now?"

"Yes. With Jakob Nugent."

"Lucky for you."

"Excuse me?"

"Whoareyou?"

"Pardon me?"

"Your name, girly. What. Is. It?" The woman couldn't be bothered to mask impatience.

"Spĕk. Dr. Marta Spĕk."

She scanned a computer tablet. "Right, there you are. Be a doll, will you?" She handed Marta a clipboard and tapped at a line for Marta's signature. In exchange for the clipboard, the woman gave Marta a photocopied site map; with an incongruous bubblegum pink nail she etched the path to Building 7.

"Watch your step, honey. There's always some jackass PA running with scissors or some damn thing. They get younger every year, I swear to you. Little *cucarachas*." Insectile fingers scurried in the air. "There's a lot of material there, but it's not quite a dress. You know what I'm saying?"

"Thank you for the assistance." Marta thought the woman should work on her interpersonal skills; sitting through a course on hospitality similar to the one waiters must pass before serving the public could polish that gravel abrasiveness. The guard hadn't been rude, not quite, but close. Crusty. Salty. Odd. "Half a bubble off," her father's judgement. In any case the experience had been distressing. That schoolyard bully routine was the domain of overcompensating guards in banks and at border crossings, not grandmothers.

Marta's footfall echoed. Not one costumed extra wandered by; nobody carted fanciful props from one soundstage to the next. Likewise, the dangerous scurrying PAs she'd been warned about made no appearances. The locale appeared deserted, though the mild green of the day suggested a spontaneous group picnic rather than an angry work stoppage.

Paused at the entrance Marta told herself that the sign taped to the window of the entrance of Building 7—Desert Queen Productions sat over an image of the Great Sphinx onto which Elizabeth Taylor's face as extravagantly eyeshadow'd Cleopatra had been superimposed—was without significance. The graphic designer's little jest bore no relation to the ideas stored in the minds of Jakob Nugent, the director, the studio, or the screenwriter, which if nothing else would not be campy and would have commercial viability or artistic integrity as an ultimate target. *Hester Stanhope, Queen of the Desert*? That would be too ridiculous. The sign signified nothing, likely makeshift and the project of an underling with an excess of free time.

She climbed the stairs to the second floor. Cavernous and unimpressive, the space revealed only functionality and the kind of leased furniture otherwise found in used car dealership offices—dark woodgrain plastic surfaces, neutral metal cabinets sitting on tough indoor-outdoor carpeting, off-white electronic equipment. A residue of latex paint hung in the air.

Unable to locate a washroom where she could change into contact lenses, Marta walked to a woman at the nearest desk; the blonde immediately held up an index finger. Marta waited as she completed the call.

"Yes, what can I do for you?" She spoke rapidly, eyes attentive to far corners of the room. Marta, admiring the delicate coral shade of the woman's lipstick, expected the receptionist to rap the surface of her wristwatch at any instant.

"Hello, I have an appointment today with Jakob Nugent."

"Alrighty, my dear, that narrows things down to a small army." She wore a grey T-shirt with scrolling white lettering: "We Must Avoid Deluded Motives."

"Pardon me?" Marta's exchange with this woman was becoming as awkward as the tussle with the gatekeeper.

"Jake, er. Mr. Nugent has scads of appointments all day, all week in fact. What's the name?"

"Spëk. Dr. Marta Spëk." Why hadn't the guard made a call? That would be efficient compared to this lunatic repetition.

"Aha, hello, we were wondering what you'd look like. I'm Lora Wilkes." She cackled then, a sound like no other that suggested a perturbed parrot and a cartoon witch. Marta felt tempted to ask how closely she matched their predictions. Of course they'd want to guess. Fair is fair, she admitted, and after all she'd spent plenty of time charting the probable Hollywood excesses of her soon-to-be colleagues.

"A pleasure to meet you." Marta held out her hand, feeling stiff, under scrutiny, and overdressed. Lora—whose firm ample bust looked to be the product of elective surgery—had swiveled her chair toward another woman whose computer screen display caused an eruption of laughter. Marta intuited that this crew was familial and boisterous, if unprofessional;

while workmates, they'd still likely go out for dinner and drinks or catch a movie.

A composed and altogether more insular environment existed within the Dark Tower—a monastic one minus a hearty sense of community and surgical augmentation. Marta had informed few of her colleagues about summer plans and had heard nothing from anyone else except holing up with business as usual—grant applications, conference appearances, journal essays, reviews, and chapters for forthcoming books.

"Hold on a sec, love, I've got to get this. Newsflash: LA is king and he knows it." She tapped a hasty reply on a phone's glass surface. Lora glanced up and gestured toward the executive's partially open door. "The meeting of the minds is right that way! Have a seat right there, and we'll set it in motion. Hang on."

The Grandview Grind

1.

Jake deemed his driving suitably aggressive, ratcheting several notches above average. Harshly judging license holders with an incessant need to yammer while ignoring basic rules of road conduct—"They're called signal lights, you fucking moron"—he kept calls to a minimum. Restless and pent up today, he tapped the phone's glass surface at red lights and traffic snarls.

He planned to stop for fifteen minutes in a suburban park after shutting up shop for the day; and he'd already posted "Quick Service?", an ad listing relevant statistics and a time guesstimate. If that produced negligible results—and Jake could predict from past experiences that zilch was almost a given—he would search pay sites to better the chances for success. The number of his active online profiles fluctuated, sitting at an economical mid-range at the moment. Periods of duress or boredom rocketed the number from zero to three, though never—almost never, in truth—higher.

Like the law of diminishing returns, flux existed; and Jake took for granted that the course of his hankerings would normally run into peaks and valleys. As he charted the situation, he was human, humans belonged to nature, and winter/spring, ebb/flow and wax/wane represented cosmic principles, as fundamental as life and death. Simple. It all added up, most times at least.

In those rare episodes of self-doubt when comparing himself unfavourably to colleagues—contented with a home-cooked pot roast dinner and several hours of prime time talent contests on the heels of a celebrity infotainment segment with a 30-second clip about a hurrying figure in black sunglasses checking into a clinic for sex addiction treatment—Jake's normal-because-natural theory seemed filled with Swiss cheese holes. He faltered, seeing his too intimate commonality with back-in-rehab Americans, literally scabby off-Main prostitutes bartering orifices for tiny rocks of crack, and park denizens he'd catch sight of during a late night's ramble. The guilt by association discomforted him.

The doubts surfaced infrequently, and proved ultimately therapeutic. For their duration, Jake thought over his would-be degeneration logically, backing steadily away from the cliff's edge. Perspective had its uses. Side by side, he judged, no epic divide stood between 24/7 nights of TV with Honey Bear, the cubs, and a bowl or two of microwave popcorn and the codger at a department store toilet playing with a limp tool and waiting hours on end for action. They were the same species of pleasure-seeking, give or take, and each capable of sinking into the dull and imprisoning habit of going through the motions: the tubby, sedated, and glazed-eyed couch potato family laughing in perfect time to laugh-track cues and the inflamed, bat-eared satyr: flip sides of the same coin.

The main difference? One had acquired lower pariah standing than the other.

Anybody ever alive was born with the same potential; Jake never doubted it. Appetite for pleasure, a truth of existence, wound through strands of DNA. Who could argue with that? The billions—trillions, maybe, if you threw in porn—shelled out by generations of moviegoers gave jury-galvanizing testimony.

At a handful of off-the-wagon scenarios Jake had concluded that management presented the only true challenge. He possessed a ferocious sweet tooth that he kept in check because of the looming potential to become an insatiable urge, the fix a trial and error discovery. Allowing an overload holiday now and then throughout the year—a feeding frenzy of pastries or sex, and, years ago, the typical range of nightclub intoxicants—was surefire, he'd learned, a gratifying hedonistic release that while addressing the commands of brain chemistry didn't totally cave to its every demand. For the rest of the time, Jake found a routine walking of the proverbial dog kept systems in shape but well rested and less prone to ripping up the furniture.

If asked, he'd confidently assert that self-denial actually served as a salve on the fears of others—uptight puritans! And based on mirror time during visceral mornings-after, he'd also admit frequent indulgence came at too steep a price. The body had set limits. And he wanted no part in the ballooning beer-batter midriff and drooping man-breast phenomenon of peers. Or worse. As for waking with a pounding headache next to a stranger in a messy unfamiliar room: the bloom was long off that rose. One remedy of pungent medicinal shampoo and hurriedly buzz-cut pubes had led to a nervous dread of bed bugs and other skin crawlers. Better to skip the nosebleed or headache or artless exit-eyeing conversation and sleep in the laundered oasis of the bedroom for which he made regular mortgage payments.

Balance, everything in moderation, know your limits, those tried and true maxims floated up whenever Jake found himself up late at night—groin humming the urgent tune of its constant fervour—and prepared to drive somewhere for unknown exploits and, with luck, eventual gratifying spurts. *Pace yourself. Avoid remorse.*

2.

As Jake slowed at the Pet Superstore and Big Box Factory Outlet intersection he saw the flow of traffic streams merging. No surprise there, the story nearly identical Monday through Friday. He checked the phone. The first response to "Quick Service?" contained no photo and two words: "Ur stats?" Jake deleted it. He'd like to smack any guy who asked dumb-ass questions, especially when he posted the answer as clear as day. The second and third replies exhibited similar asinine traits. Waiting for the green light, he irritably powered-down the tempting screen. Pursuit exasperated him some days, he'd readily admit.

Approaching the studio grounds, Jake began to prioritize the day's meetings.

He expected a few department heads to report in; otherwise he'd be closely tethered to office phone lines. There would be plenty of time to check back online. Ads had a pastry's shelf life and responses would dry up shortly in any case. After that, producing results meant posting another—different words, same idea—or covert perusal of a site where he'd reactivated a profile. True, he could always drive to the park on the way home and throw the dice. All of it looked like work, though in separate guises.

Getting laid without effort did happen, though rarely, and men were considerably easier to locate than women for obvious reasons. Women never parked their cars near highway rest stops and waited, pants unzipped, in search of lusting monosyllabic strangers in ball caps; nor did they wander in solitude within the shade of forests and loiter near public toilets.

The persistent idea that they might circulated as fantasy fodder that men whispered to themselves and, in his dad's time anyway, printed in magazines. In the actual world scenes like that wouldn't be realized unless involving a hefty financial transaction, or else extensive pleading—"Please, honey, just this one time, please. You're a hitchhiker and I pick you up and rape you at the side of the road, c'mon it'll be fun." Jake felt that even though he understood female reluctance, the whole situation was regrettable—he'd like porn fantasies to come to life, at least some of them. *C'est la vie*, he thought.

When the wisdom of being fearful did cross his mind he snorted with relief to be a guy. He'd never expected violence despite hundreds of sexual contacts and shivered with nervous excitement in places his assistant or sister wouldn't dare visit after sunset: the bungee jump thrill of danger related to engaging in illicit activity, not bodily harm.

The adventuring rush was particularly acute to him with no name exchange—the drunken woman he chatted up at a lounge and eventually led to the toilet stall for a quick exchange—in order of frequency: tongue-deep kissing, handjob, blowjob, fuck, muff dive—or the wordless figure in the murky woods who'd drop to his knees or yank down grey sweats in proud exhibition of hard prick or ass. Striding full of secret knowledge, the return to the car or crowded room following the frantic rushed tussle—face flushed, greasy mouth wiped, hastily tucked clothing emanating faint earthy scents—elicited a singular pleasure. Jake never tired of it.

Quests for high-rev experience were nothing new to Jake, the germ as old as memory. Childhood forecasts for distant adult vocations included digging up the bones of dinosaurs, becoming an Egyptologist, a cat burglar, an assassin, and a spy. Those goals took him through elementary school. He considered the practical high school years when publicizing dental school plans as an aberration resulting from daily pressures—"Think in the long term, Jakey" (Dad) and "Try to be realistic, Jakob" (Mom). As for the vision of residing in Paris while slaving to make his name as a fashion designer? The briefest of phases.

3.

Home-shot thumbnails of Jake's towel-wrapped torso currently joined descriptive numbers and words on Mascskorpio and Muscgymdude, to-the-point generic names chosen for two commercial sex site profiles to point out relevant material—that his upper-echelon physique and disposition sought gratification with similar bodies that measured up. Why be coy or falsely democratic, Jake had thought when inventing these guises. Between the two profiles he expected to line up a few suitable options; he'd keep the programs running for an hour and comb through the mail then. Aware that the search might be fruitless, Jake's gut said go. Failing that, he could try another site. The choices online grew weedily; any one could be revived with a few screen taps.

Normally Jake preferred to reserve his juice for a bigger bonanza and rarely wanted the sort of expedient assisting to orgasm he'd find in a park—stand, gesture, unzip; be back on the road in short minutes. The compressed efficiency of hasty sex had its natural merit—like sneezing it demanded no time and blasted out the pipes, equally crude and effective—but Jake felt partial to sex as sport; in part, the spark resulted from being immersed in unknown conditions and improvising to control the outcome. It didn't pan out every time, of course, but the successes stacked up considerably, a refreshing splash over sporadic stings of failure. Today he was wound up; a quick park session made sense. Fully cognizant that five minutes of masturbation would unscramble the circuits, he resorted to that only in dire circumstances—even a quarter-adventure had greater appeal than the warmth of a solitary hand.

He rubbed his eyelids at the last of what seemed like hundreds of stoplights that morning. Dehydrated a tad, he suspected. Following work and dinner yesterday he'd stopped by The Recovery Room. Dark-paneled and lit with ultra low-watt bulbs amplified by a feature wall of beveled mirrors, the place was a magnet for a professional crowd that drank from the celebrated cocktails menu. Fashionably cool, it would have been called yuppie years ago. The men there checked expensive watches often and laughed with toothy, faintly predatory smiles, watchful of their pretty, carefully-tended women—whom they regarded as integral parts of their social profile.

At the bar Jake had met, shaken hands with, and sized up Antony, "no H, man." Cleanshaven with shaggy hair as black as Jake's, he was shy despite the outgoing appearance, a guy who lacked—and desired—the wolfish aggression of the other men. Jake responded positively to the man's soft give and pictured Antony's reluctant mouth accepting his tongue and, later, the slow and progressively deeper thrusting of his dick.

Antony, "in finance, but breaking into real estate," introduced Jake to Krysta—"That's with a K and a Y," Antony said with a grin, igniting Jake's hope—a freckled day trader with fair hair and a small frame blessed by an ample, gravity-defying rack.

The couple talked about work evangelically, as though they believed real estate and day trading were revelatory, soul-feeding subjects. Jake began to feel that he'd stumbled into the convention of an accounting cult. *What the fuck*, he thought. Young and active, they ought to have more to spout about than condo prices, interest rates, and the housing market's crazy rollercoastering.

"What do you two do for fun?" Jake decided that the conversation would benefit from shepherding. "Besides hanging out here with the beautiful people, that is."

"Krysta and I started snowboarding last year," Antony replied.

"Cool." Jake looked around. Maybe this venue was a shade too indirect for his drives tonight. Or, he'd shown up before alcohol had lowered inhibitions.

"And we're really getting into traveling." Krysta's perky addition confirmed the couple's von Trapp wholesomeness and that, disconcertingly, they couldn't follow his lead. "We went to Jamaica in February! It was great!"

Jake had pondered alternate options.

Bored with the glacial proceedings, he said, "Excuse me for a minute. Beer." He pointed downward, intending the physical detail to direct their eyes and to signal a reluctance to keep on with the office lunch room chit-chat. He emptied the green bottle in a gulp.

The walls of the bathroom were covered in hexagonal brass tiles and dark weatherbeaten-effect planks.

Antony came in as Jake soaped his hands. "Man, it's like yawning. Now I have to go too." He faced the wall above the urinal, scanning a page of game scores tacked behind glass.

Jake waited at the black stone sink. Testosterone and impatience edged him toward reckless disregard. "What do you two have on for later?"

"Later?" Antony seemed surprised. "It's a weeknight."

"Oh, I see. I was hoping to get some tonight." Jake smiled widely, inviting this new acquaintance to join a conspiracy.

Antony approached the sink. "Oh, I see. You mean us. No, man, you're way off base. Jeez."

"Oops." Jake figured the situation didn't need defusing, but kept his tone confident. "I misread you, the both of you actually, man, no sweat. Forget it. I just thought—" If something did happen, there was no chance it'd be tonight. Alone and with a few drinks in his bloodstream, though, Antony might cave.

" 'I just thought'? What made you think anything?" Within Antony's indignation, Jake caught an undertone of curiosity.

"A vibe, that's all. Hard to define. Don't sweat it. My mistake. Obviously I'm not a psychic." The words he'd initially planned—"We could take turns on Krysta, then maybe you'd let me tap that too"—remained stowed away. Limits existed:

Antony didn't look like a fighter, but you could never predict a guy's reaction when intuiting his ass and territory were threatened. "I'll see you around, man." With no handshake option, Jake nodded a goodbye.

Jake pulled open the door and made a beeline for the exit. He knew when to concede defeat. Approaching the rain-beaded car he'd mumbled, "Everything in moderation, Jakey."

4.

At the studio's main gate Pat tipped her cap and leaned into Jake's cabin. "Howdy, hoss. You're like clockwork."

"Hi Pat, it's the All Bran." They bantered easily. "Any problems at the corral?"

"As far as I can tell everything's running smooth as silk."

"That's what I like to hear."

"She's a beaut. New?" Pat slid a hand along the hood and returned to the side mirror. She'd been a teamster before taking the semi-retirement guard job and took an interest in all things automotive.

"The finest in German engineering, I'm told. The dealer's a buddy and let me have it for a week's trial run."

"Sweet." She whistled. "Maybe you'll let me take her out for a spin later? I'll give you my professional opinion."

"For sure, Pat. Come by the office on a break or after your shift or something to grab the keys. Just promise: not a scratch."

"You got it, boss, not even a bug smear."

"See you later then."

"Welcome to the compound." She waved Jake through.

5.

Lora greeted Jake with a hug and a short stack of messages on paper—blue for American callers, pink for locals. "Nothing's in crisis so far, Boss Man," she said. "Good morning to you."

"To you too, my dear."

Lora called their close working relationship plant-fungi mutualism. A biology major back in the day with a still breathing and high-minded, if typically highball-authored, ambition to hunt down pharmaceutical greenery hidden deep within the Amazon Basin, Lora willed selective blindness to stiff mortgage payments and a firm intolerance of all winged insects. She relied on Jake's talent for latching on to new shows; and Jake, who preferred the flower and bee picture for their symbiosis, never took the awesome organizational capabilities of his right-hand assistant for granted.

"Where's Chaz? I need him to make a run. No major fires to put out later?"

"It's pretty much business as usual, but remember that Dr. Spëk will be here for lunch at one."

"Doctor who?"

"You remember, 'Professor Gasbag' from 'that sunset industry.' " Lora's fondness for finger quotation had not abated in the years she'd worked at Jake's side. "Chaz will be back in five, I expect."

"Oh right. Jesus, that's today?" He foresaw the specimen: rigid and as void of humour as a budget department bigwig. Jake knew the type.

"That's why those clever gods in Cupertino invented the organizer calendar on your phone, Jakob, all pretty and highlighted in purple by yours truly."

"Jeez, Lora, I should kick my own ass. I'll be ready."

"Coffee?"

"Yeah, I'll get Chaz to pick it up. Same for you?"

"You know it!"

Inside his office, Jake typed the laptop's password. He scanned email, relieved to see a trickle instead of the usual Monday deluge. Pleasure before pain, he figured, and clicked on a new blast from Exconfessio.

Ex A.W. (Toronto, ON)—

1. I often smoke pot or have a couple of shots of whiskey (rarer) before I go to work in the morning. I'm a middle

manager in a corporate environment—suits, ties and everything—and I get off on being bombed at 8:30 a.m. while everybody is slaving around me.
2. I have recorded with my camera phone the hot secretary in my office who insists on wearing tight skirts walking down the hall. I can't beat off when she's in front of me, but I can when I'm at home later.
3. I've never cheated on any girlfriend . . . but I've never been offered the opportunity.
4. I once fucked a woman twice my age who I met over a chat line. I wasn't attracted to her in the least, and I almost couldn't go though with it, but I did. I came on her face.
5. I minored in Women's Studies in university.
6. Sometimes I eat my snot, but I'm cutting down on that activity lately.
7. Sometimes I smile at gay guys on the street, just for the attention.

"What a douche," Jake said, smiling at the global village of human piggishness the website exposed, and thankful again for his gut's aversion to suit-and-tie strangulation and office tower managerial drudgery. Exconfessio's honesty was as exhilarating as the sheer inventive profanity. As one of those villagers, he thought he should participate too and had even compiled two lists of seven. He'd send them eventually. Maybe: the thought of having them become part of the visible world, even anonymously, made him feel exposed.

Time to check in with L.A, he thought.

Contact

I.

Winking at Marta, Lora picked up the receiver. "Your one o'clock appointment, Dr. Spëk, has arrived, Mr. Nugent." She hung up and drew an arrow in the air toward Marta's destination. "Your meal will be along in a heartbeat," she said. "Question: You still like Thai, I hope?"

With thoughts settling on caged factory farm chickens and habitat destruction caused by Malaysian prawn suppliers, Marta answered with a smile. "Oh yes, thank you."

Furnished by a budget office equipment leasing firm, Jake's office—a painted metal desk with an imitation wood grain top, grey filing cabinets, spun-nylon chairs—matched Lora's exactly. The sparseness, so at odds with Marta's imaginings, served to assure her that above all filmmaking was a bottom-line business with deadlines, returns on investment, lists of hourly goals, and a high risk of failure.

"It's good to finally meet you, Professor Spëk." Jake stepped from behind the desk to offer a firm hand. "Please make yourself comfortable." *That smile opens doors for him*, Marta thought, cowed by the well-tended edifice of impervious masculinity. Well-proportioned and aware of the fact, she surmised, here's the strutting cock of the henhouse. At least he possessed the manners to not chew gum.

"Marta, please. 'Professor' makes me feel one hundred." Sitting, Marta fussed; the cuffs of the new blouse hung just a titch long. Jake's carnivore watchfulness unnerved her, recalling the momentary eye-squint—instantaneous assessment and dismissal—of SRLFI's industry cronies. Stiff-backed in the wheeled chair, she watched the man's flitting eyes and imagined a low-charisma figure reflected in them, strangely invisible despite festive colouration.

"Sounds good. Marta, I'm Jake. Jakob was my granddad's name, and it makes me feel about the same age." He sat and pushed into the chair's adjustable back. "I suppose you'd like a clearer picture of why we've invited you here."

Lora knocked, stacked Styrofoam-encased lunches in hand. "Lady and gentleman, luncheon is served."

Jake laid out the basics of the production with veteran efficiency. He dabbed a spring roll in shared plum sauce, bit off a third, and said, "If I'm going too fast, just say the word." Pencilling bullet points on a pad of yellow paper, he sketched the contractual particulars of the consultancy, and broke between each to lift pad thai noodles steaming in the container. "This stuff tastes like crap after it cools."

Marta, surprised to be charmed by the unusual intimacy of a meal with a virtual stranger, wrote in a notebook and asked questions, relieved that the anticipation of a hard-nosed exchange of terms had been completely unfounded. She'd sat through seminars with fiercer antagonism.

Jake's answer to Marta's unasked question, "Why me?" deflated her excitement considerably. "You know," he said "there's no one in the entire region—well, no one else alive anyway—that knows a thing about this Lady Hester Stanhope. She's no Marie Antoinette." Marta hadn't been vetted, then. No, her presence represented a convenience, a local one, far cheaper than flying in a biographer from England.

Having never haggled, Marta judged the terms of employment to be exceptionally generous; she didn't conceive of demanding greater compensation.

Jake felt likewise assured by their negotiation. Unaware that scholars often dedicated years to writing one volume and received a pittance in royalties, he warmed to the fact that Marta's expertise had been leased at an attractively low price; the deal-making would keep the bean counters off his back.

"We're looking forward to your input, Marta."

"Yes, I'm keen to help out."

Jake handed Marta a copy of the script—"Nothing's nailed down, so think of it as a work-in-progress, okay?"—and recommended flipping through it.

2.

Stepping across the yellow safety line and into the deserted city-bound car, Marta stood before the vista. Past concrete, asphalt, and mottled rooftops, she caught a glimpse of the dwindling streaks of snow on the city's backdrop peaks.

With the system's precautionary gong sounding, she slid into a seat.

The Prophet of Djoun and the accompanying notes in pencil demanded little effort. She'd filed the script—slapdash, she concluded, as though spit out by a computer with rudimentary AI—in the valise well before transferring to the last bus connection.

II
Penticton to Oroville

Help Yourself to Happiness™
—Golden Corral Corporation

Kerplunk

1.

Jake spotted the Location Manager within a gathering crowd of elderly couples who'd donned khaki shorts and sleeveless fleece zippered to the neck. With a gadget-stuffed utility vest the man was unmissable. Jake waved him over.

"How do, Jake. Welcome to Penticton, Palm Springs north. 'A Place to Stay Forever' is plastered everywhere. Sounds like purgatory to me." The man surveyed baggage claim's points of interest grandly with the slow-motion sweeping *Welcome Aboard!* gesture of a caricature cruise ship entertainment director. "Or maybe death row. Please observe the exquisite architectural details, fresh from knock-off Miami-Dade 1985 shopping mall hell. I've been stuck in some shit-hole Podunk airports in my time, but wow, man, this one takes the cake."

American-born, storied, and as maligned as tripe, Nikolas 'Baby Dick' Babadek attracted notoriety for a collection of all things *Star Trek* and the feather-ruffling habit of making stacked-deck comparisons between local destinations and ones further south. Shopping, buildings, restaurants, bars, art, sports, beaches, women, you name it: Canada ranked as third rate, a knockoff repository, all originals found in New York, L.A. or San Francisco. And those pronouncements were hard to miss: if honest, Nicos could not list personal space recognition as a top five attribute.

"Take a gander at Omaha next time you're in the Midwest, Nicos," Jake said. "Now there's a tragedy."

"Uh huh. Been there, done that. This is worse. Bush-league, definitely. Let's get outta here." Nicos's addiction to having the last word also made him no friends; raised in a Midwest household of armchair football tribalism, the man lived for pissing contests.

Though he excelled at scouting locations, Nicos was no one's first pick. Everyone mocked him with nicknames—Half-Black Napoleon and Baby Dick—whenever he moved out of earshot. Jake felt convinced the man loved the sound of his adenoidal voice; believing he kept his own self-satisfaction firmly in check, Jake rated visible narcissism in others as a glaring personality flaw.

With a hitchhiker's thumb, Nicos indicated the empty luggage carousel. "How was the flight?"

"Mercifully short and smooth. No highballs or Ativan necessary." Take off and turbulence jangled his nerves, and the *(Just in Case)*™ pamphlet peeking out from the seat pouch hadn't helped. "And way better than driving through hours of non-stop treescape."

The carousel lurched toward full speed. "Quick pit stop, hold on."

"Sure thing, boss dude."

Jake walked to the men's toilet. He loathed flying, but airports made him randy. He roamed through their terminal wings restlessly, on the prowl for searing eye contact, agreeable idle gab at whose foundation stood the pulse of quickening sexual deal-closing, and the occasional—exceptionally, sadly so in an era of lurking terrorist underwear explosives and career-killing entrapment by security personnel—head jerk that promised furtive unzipped flies in an out-of-the-way stall.

The uniqueness of the airport environment was, he'd say, sorely undervalued. Airports, enormous livestock pens basically, housed an oily concentrate of emancipated drive—beast of burden vacationers gearing up for a week's worth of unencumbered bar-hopping, solo business travelers leaving behind the sapping imprisonment of mortgage payments and minivans, and weary returnees keen to squeeze out one final drop of escapade before stepping back into the drudgery of 9–5 under fluorescent lighting, re-circulated air, and TGIF drinks at Shenanigan's. Temporary freedom, and even the illusion of it, bounced between neurons as a heady aphrodisiac.

The devil will find work for idle hands to do, Jake figured, and that wasn't a bad thing. He'd long considered the shoulder-perched whisperer a trustworthy acquaintance when it came to provocative offers. No diabolical scourge, the silver-tongued, black-eyed tempter made no promises that opened the door to an underworld of everlasting doom. Selling real estate, of a sort, matched his character: "Now consider the excellent amenities of this fine property, the seller is very motivated." Jake could inspect the details and close on the purchase, or say, "It's not for me, thanks. I'm going to keep looking." The choice? His alone: Yes, No, I'll mull it over, thank you. No gun barrel pressed against his temple.

With the exception of the whistling gnomic near-retiree mopping the floor, the facility revealed only emptiness. No bedevilment today. Jake stood at the urinal for a minute and cupped his warm sack as he pissed. After pushing the silver flush handle he washed diligently at a sink. He'd read that a full thirty seconds of soapy suds took care of germs. The last thing he'd want for this obligatory week in the trenches would be a cold. Now alone, he checked the mirror: tired, but not too shabby. Jake's gaze swept the room. This regional airport didn't merit a second glance. Adventuring can be such a coin toss, he sighed.

2.

Nicos stood, balanced cautiously, on the narrow edge of the battered metal luggage carousel. Jake had noticed that the man compensated for a jockey's height as a matter of course, though apparently drew the line at the elevator shoes rumour placed on his feet. He pitched a bottle of water to Jake.

Jake asked, "What's first on the agenda?"

"After luggage shows, I figure we can drop your stuff off at Kaleden and then I'll show you our sites."

"Kaleden? Never heard of it. What's there?"

"Not much, pretty much as you'd expect. I can't figure out why anyone actually calls it home. Anyways, Kaleden, aka Kaleden Junction. There's the concrete shell of an old hotel at the base of a bone-dry embankment. That's it, I think. Some orchards. It's not like I requested a grand tour from city council. The guide refers to it as a historic town, which means that in days of yore a train stopped there or something. I wouldn't call it a town, maybe a pit stop if you need to take a leak. The place you're staying at is cool, though. Adobe-style. At the top of a sandy mound on a back road. Nice swimming pool. Air conditioned. And it's just fifteen minutes or so from the production office."

"Okay, let's get to it."

"Ready to rock and roll?"

Jake sighed. Why couldn't people learn to edit before they spoke?

The men drove away from the flat, overgrown town and ascended a long-haul hill on the black ribbon of highway leading south. Jake nodded, pleased that the location matched the photo slideshow Nicos had emailed. "Dehydrated as a mummy," he'd written. The description seemed apt and a surprise considering the valley's pooling lake water: but from the shoulder of the asphalt all the way to the tops of the blunt-edged mountains, the austere terrain refused to entice with bright shocks of greenery. Instead, Jake discerned sun-blasted grass patches, low scrappy brown-leaf bush clusters, rusty scars of raw rock, and no shade anywhere. A bitch to work in, he could tell, but it would be a perfect stand-in for eastern Mediterranean desert.

"Are there snakes out there?" Jake imagined rattlers basking on flat rocks.

"Probably. Looks like it. I'll check into it if you want."

"I would. Snake bites, crap, those would be a headache."

"I'll say." Nicos tugged at a cigarette package in a pocket of the plaid cowboy shirt bunched on the seat.

"That's not going to happen while I'm in the vehicle," Jake said, deciding that *They'll stunt your growth* tipped the scale into plain cruelty dressed up as guy banter.

"Right, I forgot. Gotcha."

Jake stared out the window. In this blistering heat, a swimming pool might be the best part of the day. "Let's go directly to the office. I'd like to check in with Lora. I'll give her a call now, tell her to update them on my check-in time."

"No problem. We'll be there in twenty. That was Kaleden by the way."

"Huh?"

"That fruit stand we passed a couple of minutes back, that was Kaleden. Next stop, Bridal Falls. No, make that Okanagan Falls. I heard there's tourist traps there, a Foamhenge and something called Mystery Manor, but saw a grand total of nada."

Jake slid a finger across the surface of his phone.

In the Orchard

I.

Marta detached a brochure clipped to the shade of the room's bedside lamp. An Economy Facility for Family Fun, the Star-Lite Motel evidently counted every penny: "Guest credit cards will be charged $10 per missing towel, no exceptions." Looking around spare and clean #10—complete with a set of three water glasses protected by crinkled hygienic cellophane—brought to mind untroubled lakeside and mountain slope vacations tightly budgeted by their autocratic mother, Marta and Lester in one room with Dianne and George adjacent, inset doors normally connecting them. Possibly, decades ago, she'd politely knocked on this very door next to the bulky television, her thrifty parents requesting privacy in their room and—never the doting kind—respecting that of their children.

Marta now checked to confirm the lock's security. She inspected the closet and bathroom and found everything in order. Spotting no ashtray—times had changed—she slipped the car keys on a novelty holder shaped like a fishing lure for a world of giants. Though the rental coupe wasn't strictly necessary, Marta desired the mobility. *I can go out for a drive now*, she thought, *and enjoy a freedom unavailable in the city*.

The entire winding valley of prodigious manufactured fecundity was familiar enough, but from the emerald parcels she glimpsed during the steep descent from the crest there'd been substantial refurbishing. The single-family orchards and modest roadside stands with arrow-shaped signs announcing "Peaches, Cukes 4 Sale," so plentiful once, now slouched into history; magazine-ready viticulture and the affluent metropolitan tourist demographic it attracted—discerning eyes peeled for organic preserves, half

Ironman marathons, grape cultivar trends, and gourmet lunches on chic verandas overlooking luxuriant vineyards—had become the new economic order. A rectangular plot cut from the surrounding orchard of dwarf peach trees, the Star-Lite represented a 1950s vestige with a passenger pigeon future.

Capillary dirt roads still crisscrossed the arid valley, Marta had noticed, picturing a tour along them after hours, air rushing though open windows, dust plumes trailing.

The other burgs between the amoebic city sprawl and the Star-Lite's roadside solitude—scrappy agricultural pockets and malnourished communities built in close range to mined hillsides of tailings long abandoned and overgrown or close to exhaustion—did not appear to have been touched by the aspirant's grab-the-future-by-the-horns outlook so pronounced on the valley's wine grape plateaus.

Marta felt reassured as she journeyed by the hardscrabble outposts, recognizing gas stations, restaurants, motels, and log homes—entire main streets, in fact—possessing a trapped-in-amber quality that was cousin to the revived historic gold rush settlement deeper in the province's interior. Surviving off visitor dollars, that destination promised to bring one version of history alive by hiring hordes of students each summer and paying them to stroll the dusty streets in character, the select calico- and wool-clad population educational viewing for the whole family, G-rated of course: no rape, racism, smallpox, domestic violence, or situational homosexuality, and perhaps just one town drunk rendered as red-faced and obnoxious yet benignly comical, a pioneer Falstaff.

Although the gradual climb from sea level contained her within one time zone, Marta had been conscious of how barreling so easily beyond the embrace of routine registered as such a heartfelt charge. Passing from sopping dense forests of hemlock, salmonberry bush, and clinging boreal mists to arid, needle-strewn stands of skinny pine, she noticed roadside Great Mullein ("desert tapers," her mother's fanciful coinage, sprang to mind first), and, at last, caught sight of the gateway marker, a loaf-form mountain, velvety camel and puckered by dark undulating furrows. Marta's shoulders began to relax despite the tension caused by traffic: nearby called out the landscape of childhood vacations.

The silence from the production office about tomorrow's schedule gnawed at Marta's nerves. To her chagrin, the immediate future was not a mapped road but an opaque wall, and that made her peevish; as always, the lack of a specific plan proved irksome. Marta's core punctuality—6 o'clock does not mean 6:10—routinely stood at odds with a world of delayed services and detained, inexact people. *There's nothing to do now except stare at the phone*, she thought. *Of course.*

At the motel's front desk office, Mrs. Simms, the Star-Lite's affable and confiding owner/operator, had endeared herself to Marta with a sisterly offer of counsel—"You got any questions, Marta, anything at all"—she'd said with a sly conspiratorial tone, as though Marta might be seeking a back-alley abortion, or dry county moonshine—"you come right to me. My family's been operating this place for two generations, so believe you me, I've heard 'em all." Cross-legged on a stool, Mrs. Simms hadn't mentioned any calls. Fretful, Marta wondered if she'd missed an important email. One might have been sent after she left home.

The red light on the room's telephone wasn't flashing; she lifted the receiver to check for a dial tone.

To her knowledge no one—and by now she'd learned the office's unwavering chain of command: Jakob near the apex, Lora next, and one of the pawn-like PAs at the base—had sent information about a "session" or "pow wow" (Jakob's and Lora's preferred terms for meeting, respectively) following check-in, so Marta guessed she was at liberty to plan out the evening.

The prudent choice to wait could serve her best, she decided. Perhaps Lora's short term plans included a call to explain next day's schedule. Marta needed to sort out the per diem, too, excited by the novel concept of daily cash allotments handed out in discreet white envelopes, she imagined, like bribes in movies. She thought of dropping by to check with Mrs. Simms one last time, just in case. Advice about nearby restaurants could supply a reasonable pretext.

In the meantime, she'd try to relax inside the cinder block cube, vintage print spun nylon curtains drawn for solitude. The room was warm and smelled of the staleness of age as well as of lingering bathroom chemicals. She'd prop open the door after sunset.

Marta slid off canvas sneakers. Unpacking luggage could wait, ditto the drive and inaugural wander along Main Street to investigate three blocks of retail offerings. Poised on the edge of the bed—covered with a slithery polyester satin quilt that made her squeamish and would soon be folded away in the closet along with the untenable poly-cotton sheets—Marta grabbed the remote and found the channel guide.

She clicked on a station that specialized in drive-in classics and arrived in the midst of a favourite moment. Tracking the prostitute-fixated serial killer with the light of righteousness to guide them, Angel and Mae skirted around the murky brick alleys of Sunset Boulevard during a breezy California night that nevertheless caused no movement in the stiff curls of Mae's voluminous wig or Angel's beribboned hair.

The improbable scene—the 15–year old Angel/whore character being played as innocent by a 24–year old performer in thick layers of purportedly age-defying makeup that rendered her hardened and mannequin-like rather than sweetly, dewily adolescent—always prompted Marta to recall a sibilant-heavy review, one that for a time she'd delighted in quoting to fellow graduate students, whose faces reflected no empathy for her fascination with déclassé subject matter. The writer called the B-movie a "screwy, sickening, and semi-satisfying stew of shtick, sleazeball, and sentimentality."

Sleazy or not, *Angel* was also a fortunate discovery—and heartily satisfying too, Marta would argue—that became the subject of her debut conference paper, an analysis of notions of prostitution and feminine duplicity that compared the wily centuries-old archetype Moll Flanders to a contemporary descendent, the soon-to-be avenging Angel. *Plus ça change*, the essay had implied with a tentative finger of accusation.

2.

For an accidental find, *Angel* had proven invaluable. Touching on *Psycho* or *Marnie* here, *Dressed to Kill* there, Marta revisited and elaborated on the topic at subsequent conferences. Variation-on-a-theme papers were a venerable if unmentioned tradition at such gatherings: forever eyeing the publish-or-perish quota—the cliché updated as publish-and-perish by rung-eyeing fresh PhDs—the congregated scholars welcomed the efficiency. Utility aside, Marta enjoyed rooting through non-literary source material as much as the political dimensions of the subject; the male-penned account of feminine duplicity opened up as richly complex and imbued with an agreeable taint of controversy.

By the fourth time Marta stood at a lectern for the mandatory twenty minutes to uncover the intricacies of Angel's narrative—complete with audience-pleasing film stills placed atop a overhead projector—both the character and the speaker had ceased to be students. Over the course of *Avenging Angel*, *Angel III: The Final Chapter*, and *Angel 4: Undercover*, Angel could no longer be labeled a "high school honor student by day," having graduated and become a respected police photographer. Nor was she a mini-skirted "Hollywood hooker by night," though she agreed to pose as one—*for one last time*—in order to trap yet another prostitute-fixated murderer. Exempt from B-movie plot mechanics, Marta's better paying new role at the classroom's helm didn't demand so much as a change of blouse.

Hollywood's retread economy arrived as a welcome ideology to Marta since she exploited its reliance on low-budget reiterations. She viewed the timely latest installment as grist for the conference paper mill—her constant work generated with one primary aim: the mecca of tenure. Marta barely needed notes to explain Angel's tidal flux of feminine agency; a single sitting through the latest sequel had replaced the earnest and painstaking shot-by-shot explication of former days. As for the conference talk, she easily stitched together the required minutes worth of material during the flight. She felt proud if absurd when cluing into a fact: her rank as the leading scholar on *Angel*. Dr. Spëk, the globe's preeminent *Angel*ographer. Checking later, she'd confirmed the unique monopoly. Careers had been founded on lesser accomplishments.

Marta spoke about *Angel 4: Undercover* and listened to the panel's three other speakers—occasionally feigning the ritual expression of rapt interest evident throughout the audience. After responding to a request to clarify a point and throwing in a comment during the roundtable, she left the windowless room and walked at a brisk pace to the exterior doors of the brick campus building that housed the entire event. Bracing Idahoan air and a winding pathway soothed her nerves as she retreated from the unofficial goal of the conference—stiff and polite and nuanced after-session mingling that eventually stripped down to serial pissing contests. The crowing over publications and grant funding, 3.5 Richter scandals, and fathomless complaint always suffused Marta with dread and a rip-tide undercurrent of nausea.

Naturally no one needed to explain to Marta that any group—from kindergarten on—invented unique means of instituting hierarchies and channeling animosities. And she didn't need to be told that without tactical participation a career could atrophy. Landed in a group of any variety, though, she ordinarily and habitually conceived of reasonable exit strategies and then gravitated toward lone corners and peripheral tables of finger food and coffee urns. Or, if fortune was smiling, there'd be print of some kind to scan, publisher book displays at which she could devote long minutes. She likened the movement to a plant leaning toward sunlight; more than comprehendible, the perfectly organic and sustaining motion followed earthly laws.

For this one occasion, she forgave herself for not dividing the room into will nots, haves, has beens, and have nots, and then arranging contact with the haves, artfully dropping mention of CV-worthy accomplishments and exceptional busyness into measured conversations—chapters to write! funding applications! student thesis supervision! journal articles! far-flung conferences to attend! book reviews! classes to organize!—and illustrating how bold new grant-nourished research would ensure the ongoing skyrocketing of an esteemed reputation. Even a courtier's tongue required rest.

The conference was held in Boise, "The City of Trees"—so she'd read about the place, whose completely recognizable name had floated up unaccompanied by facts, images, or trivia. Say "Jupiter" and Marta conjured a solar system illustration, enormity, dozens of moons in whizzing orbits, pinky-orange swirls of volatile gas clouds, and the Great Red Spot; but Boise only summoned Idaho and with it the seemingly contradictory occurrence of vast flat potato fields and angular swathes of coniferous trees. Boise's cloak of anonymity fluttered attractively.

Early into the many-paneled conference proceedings—a hive humming with intellectual enterprise of varying merit—Marta had succumbed. She decided the ideal moment to "scratch an itch" (the phrase, along with "shit or get off the pot," jumped directly from her father's stock of tart phrases, marvelous and vulgar but never repeated aloud) stood before her. Aged two years, give or take, the condition was entrenched, she admitted, resembling one of those inconsequential yet apparently chronic maladies of television commercials, like dandruff, winter dryness, and the terrible shame apparently caused by dingy carpets and coffee-stained teeth. *Or feminine itch*, Marta had thought. It appeared to be a syndrome only the right medicine could heal.

3.

As she would for an oddly coloured mole, Marta had kept track of the rogue itch-sensation, and could identify the very second it had arisen, shark-like—cancerous?—and unbidden from a murky depth. On a Monday morning early in the autumn semester during a course about narratives of sexual danger in late-Victorian London, she'd been lecturing about *Strange Case of Doctor Jekyll and Mr. Hyde*. The mid-sentence epiphany—a cartoon incandescent light bulb illumination that caused her to stall, arms frozen in mid-gesture, and then react with a spontaneous, titter-spurring Cockney-accented proclamation: "Guvnor, I seems ta 'ave lost me train o' thought"—was unadulterated excitement. At the thought of a double life's prospects—pretense, danger, creative challenge—her pulse had quickened, the theatrical secrecy a kick too.

Long minutes later and in the refuge of her closed-door office, Marta could tell that the odd fleeting tingle in class hadn't entirely dispelled. Analyzed, the heightened sensation—racing blood flow and excited neurons, she presumed—looked analogous to creative fireworks, the febrile state identical to the promise of a budding writing project, when the sheer potential of the blank page appeared as an enigmatically wrapped and as yet unopened gift. Less diagnosable was the accompanying bodily symptom—vague: a shiver that transformed into a deep-seated and steady ember burn. A remotely sexual element lurked too. Then again, she'd smiled, it might as easily be gastric distress—a blot of mustard, a crumb of cheese. Or: unrelated, a simple coincidence. When she resumed thinking about Mr. Hyde and alter egos, the peculiar shiver failed to recur.

At home that day Marta had changed into a robe, reclined on her thinking chair—she'd been told "slipper chair" was the proper name; and her request for custom upholstery in mossy velvet had delayed delivery from Quebec for an unaccountable eight weeks—and closed her eyes. She tinkered with a working definition of alter ego as growth, a creative act, a vehicle of self-expression, and not a panicked disorder.

Sliding her hand along the furry plush, she thought, *It's similar to this chair, a reflection of the range of my taste and interests.* Contrary to puritanical Mr. Robert Louis Stevenson and others, an alter ego didn't have to be a dire symptom, one indicative of injured consciousness or pathological *dédoublement.* Well, not necessarily anyway. Yes, nobody could deny *Sybil* and the genre's shattered mirror motif—such incoherent fragmentation, so hopeless a case. Fear and propaganda. A perfectly seamless and unified selfhood is a consolatory fiction, she concluded, irked to be quoting from a source she couldn't grasp. Salient-shaped words competed for her attention: *inhabitation, augmentation, polymorphism, masquerade, guise.* With so many perspectives to consider, the possibilities tilted into the carnivalesque.

Worries about severe psychological abnormality tamped down, Marta had moved on to a less fraught topic: logistics.

Obviously, the location—a destination promising the least chance of the situation going awry—must also be the edenic place with the remotest likelihood of running into a colleague.

The standard moues of qualification aside, Marta respected guile and accomplished impromptu liars; though she could deceive when necessary, she required forethought and, if possible, cue cards. Without that preparation, she bungled lies, the stammering textbook examples limply ridiculous. Her sputtered improvised answer to "Marta, what on earth are you doing here dressed like that?" would sound glaringly awkward and false, peppered with inept prevarication that even a child could detect. Disastrous. From a secure distance the situation drew a smile; she'd rather eat glass than count the miserable real-time seconds of the concrete experience.

So: a different city, perhaps. Better yet, a neighbouring country. Curled on the chair, she'd pictured herself as vivacious and disembarking at an Alpine train stop, having shed off demure Marta Spëk en route. This new person, _______, would possess an icy Hitchcockian countenance, the exquisite angles of shoulder and cheek signaling *arrivisme* or perhaps *hauteur*. Marta had frowned. The woman—persistently French, a favoured affectation dating from junior high school—was untenable and risible, an elaborate surgical remake that owed as much to Kim Novak as to Cruella DeVil. A hopeless travesty. Even if she aimed for such an extravagant imposture, she'd never attain it.

When Marta had attempted a second version of the fantastical step off the train—a feasible charade, one based on her quantifiably modest capabilities—no new figure emerged. She only saw herself wearing the tan Burberry trench coat she'd splurged on last year. Evidently a merely superficial transformation would be a stretch. *Nonchalance* held greater promise than *hauteur*. *Where there's a will there's a way*, a voice chimed.

The perspective appeared off kilter, Marta came to realize. Assuming a role was not the same as a play or film she planned to watch or address in an essay. No, the role created a unique kind of theatre in which she'd inhabit actor and spectator simultaneously. Even so, to step into that character and actually *scratch the itch* could hardly unfold as simply as that inadequate figure of speech implied. For the proper payoff the sensation had to register deeply, and not feel like the ironic donning of a costume, or a jokey thrift store wig on Halloween. True, changes could be cosmetic to a degree, a purchasable ensemble, but there needed to be substantial dimension, fathoms. Sweating thespian as well as skeptical audience, every outcome she foresaw corroded an already tarnished, 14–carat resolve. Happily, the deflated state did give her insight into the practical challenges of split personalities and bigamy.

During solitary meals and quiet intervals sitting on transit, Marta had grown studious about the practical facets of the alter ego (the term itself sank into obsolescence, replaced by the lyrical, Bergmanesque persona). As for unconscious motivations or root causality, that persisted as a thread she'd resist pulling. "Trifling, I'll return to that later," a mewling retort to the intermittent voicing of conscience, kept the overall transformative impulse alive.

There were pressing factors to make allowances for, Marta came to see. Sensitive to narrative triteness she'd fretted in particular about the *ne plus ultra* of the venue. And to complicate matters, clarity about what she'd like to have unfold remained tightly wrapped. To appear in public as *someone else* presented a moderate challenge; but to commit to interactive, unpredictable socializing—and colluding in the outcome of whatever contact instigated—only summoned the spectre of woeful consequences from foolish actions with inexplicable motivations. Farcical messes. Or worse: bad dates, as *Angel*'s Mae would call them. Danger seemed a minor probability, but embarrassment loomed as certain as sunset.

Start small, she'd thought, a grimace shaping seconds after. Typical Spëk. No, comfortable or not, a *leap* it would be, "of faith" the preferable, courageous figure of accompaniment. "From an office building window on Black Tuesday" bubbled up contrarily within minutes.

The challenge of the live performance caused vexation too. Even in high school Marta had shied away from publicity although she'd pined—acutely, in fact, a pale teenage Pushmi-pullyu—for the notoriety it might bring, agonizing about a two-line role in *Our Town* before finally perceiving the stymieing thinness of her skin. Speaking in full view on the gymnasium stage before a cold-eyed jury of peers for three consecutive nights, she'd predicted, would induce torrents of perspiration, if not cardiac arrest. Shame-faced while dying: nothing could feel worse. For the nights of the play's run, she begged for extra shifts at the part-time job at the cedar-shingled public library and tried with patchy success to stay attentive to a pet project, developing a better technique for efficiently shelving books.

Pondering the surfeit of hazards this performance might attract while seated in the Dark Tower and nestled within Undre Arms, Marta conjured an adult roster of preparatory choices. A drop-in acting class for improvisation? Toastmasters? A few hours of introductory pole dancing—*ladies, shake away your inhibitions?* Marta briefly entertained the ideas. She'd pulled away from that nettlesome hitch—having clearly understood the term performance anxiety—and thought *save it for later.* She stopped picking at the implications of *later.*

Setting, an easier challenge, puzzled her even as she enjoyed sorting the pieces. Hotel lounge: likely mistaken there for a working girl and subject to harsh questions from a management type. She'd seen *Pretty Woman.* Or else viewed as a lonely lady and prey to a self-styled rescuer or, worse, a wolfish ladies' man. A nightclub: too *Looking for Mr. Goodbar*? Noisy as well. Where else promised hope? A bookstore or library? Overly familiar, claustrophobic, not conducive to living conversation. Pie and black tea in a café, now that might work. *Just right,* as with Goldilock's chosen bowl: Marta could map her limits well enough.

And she'd mulled over attire too. Since being virtually anyone was not impossible, she could also dress according to whim. Then again, no one could tell the difference if she chose ordinary clothes in a foreign place. She'd opted against outlandishness, settling on a new persona-synched blouse as suitable. Outlawed: wig, costume, accent, complicated back-story. Onerously far from a core of truth, such props represented an overreaching acting exercise. Things might go—*would go*—askance. And she'd be remiss to overlook the puckish need of the cosmos to throw an arbitrary complication into an ostensibly foolproof plan.

And last: the name. "I'm Marta" represented a complete failure of resolve, a shrinking away from the grand gesture. Sadie, she'd decided. Marta was acquainted with no Sadie, but the name had surfaced without effort. Old-fashioned and slightly exotic, but not freighted and antique (Evangeline) or silly (Chenille), Sadie would be both suggestive and inviting, hinting of ambiguous values, diaphanous cloth, and fragrant carnation. Better yet, she'd raise no alarms, no inquiries, and no smirks of incredulity.

Seeking to sabotage a worrywart nature, she'd resisted the urge to chew over hitches and chart probable consequences. Sadie she would be, one day.

For Sadie, Marta later purchased a tiny ampoule of Chanel No. 5. Sadie's bouquet was "classic, but totally posed for a revival," a clerk with a face modeled after an Art Deco doll had declared. "Perfect," Marta said, having given up on sliding "poised" into the conversation.

Ideal in its own way, Boise, home of fervent Broncos fans she'd read, beckoned, a natural locale for Sadie's inaugural test run.

4.

If the ensuing scene was not anti-climactic, neither could it truly be described as enthralling. Nor exciting; barely a molecule of intrigue existed for savouring. A bubble of relief buoyed Marta: at least the scene had steered clear of humiliation. As for dangerous, that concern melted away as soon as she'd entered the room. There'd been a belly murmur of excitement, at best; cold hands and nervousness—a distant cousin to the hoped-for ecstatic charge—seemed third-rate symptoms, letdowns. *Picaresque misadventure*, a dramatic unfolding for which she'd intermittently readied herself? Nowhere in the vicinity.

Whereas the pulp novel version of the excursion would result in terror (being hassled, at minimum, by a creep, and downhill from there), a torrid entanglement, intercourse, and morning-after remorse, or else Hollywood epiphanic (being hassled by a creep, experiencing being weak and helpless, taking a karate class, becoming self-reliant and empowered, *take back the night, grrl*), Boise's would-be narrative of danger turned out to be humdrum and uneventful, scarcely an episode, at moments on par with sitting in an airport waiting for the arrival of a delayed flight. No lady's man, no serial killer, no transvestite prostitute—*street-wise but tragic*—no honour roll student by day, no conversational pyrotechnics or improvised autobiography. An anecdote composed of virtually nothing, she saw.

Avoiding eye contact and collegial waves, Marta had left the conference and strode quickly across campus to the hotel room. After changing clothes and assessing the result—not for the first time—she stood at the forlorn smoker's refuge adjacent to the lobby and hailed a cab: "Downtown, please."

She'd pre-selected 3Squares, a Zagat-rated café built far from the conference site, calculating that its trendiness would attract a stranger who would nonetheless be a semi-familiar type. Factoring in this and that, Marta accepted early on that the conventional urban verboten zones of literature and film—from the decrepit back alleyway opium den doors Dorian Gray opens to the dive taverns bikers, dealers, and prostitutes frequent in *Angel*—embodied such foreign values that acclimating to the setting was impossible, never mind excelling in risqué conversations. She'd been moulded by years within an academic environment and did not expect to hold her own in a conversation with a quasi-alien—a sailor, a drug-addled bundle of tics, or a thug who rode a Harley Davidson. Really, what could they talk about?

At the café—disappointingly unpopulated for a Friday evening—Marta had nursed tea and tough-crust apple pie. Interacting with the near-monosyllables of the grandmother-aged server with tired eyes—"What'll it be?" and "That all?" from behind the diner's long counter—required no acting. Marta hadn't the slightest chance to answer "Sadie" to someone's warm, ordinary probing question. Nor had "Where you from, honey?" wafted her way.

No mishap snagged her, and for that she'd been thankful. But admittedly no extraordinary outcome transpired, either—the itch still nowhere close to scratched. Marta had felt accomplished because she'd been prepared for something and had actually left the conference and shown up—as Sadie—at this location of unknown possibilities. Drink and food only, yes, but she could not deny a readiness for another script. The exact nature—unrevealed and impenetrable—continued to tantalize, even as predictions of public humiliation and bodily harm crowded over the seductive image of this improvised persona.

Next time floated up, as alluring as ectoplasm.

5.

The phone rang. "Marta? Lora here," the voice said. "You all settled in?"

"Yes, I arrived not long ago at all."

"Good. Jake and I flew up earlier in the week, corralling crew, putting out fires, blah blah. Business as usual, in other words. I've still got a shitload of calls to get through tonight so grab a pen, okay?"

"I'm ready."

"We've set up a satellite—well, more like a broom closet in a trailer—for the production office on set, but the other one, the official HQ, is at a store front we had to rent for the month, right on the main drag. Between the Star-Lite—sorry about that, this backwater isn't exactly overflowing with four-star accommodations, you know, my place isn't the goddamned Ritz by a mile—anyway, between your room and the other sites, you'll have plenty of space to work from." Lora explained the route and gave Marta the address.

"We'll give you *le grand tour* in the morning. You need to be updated on things. And if you're unclear about anything, we can sort it out then."

"Terrific."

"It doesn't look like there's going to be much to do in this town except watch fruit ripen, but we'll be in and out before you know it. See you in the morning!"

"Good night, Lora."

Stretching out on the bed Marta returned to *Angel*. Driving could wait until she settled. Jake had mentioned that the script would go through a series of edits before she encountered it again, so re-reading the outmoded version seemed fruitless. Although Marta understood that her role did not pertain to the script per se, she thought mentioning at least a few of the key problems of conception couldn't hurt. She'd wait until the morning to pore over the latest printout. Grisly scenes before *Angel*'s bittersweet ending would be good company instead.

In the Midst of the Incomprehensible

I.

Rapid-fire knocks interrupted Marta's fraught minute of indecision.

She'd placed two outfits on the bed and stood back weighing options. Khaki walking shorts and a loose T-shirt would be comfortable, without a doubt. She kept out of the sun religiously and foresaw crew eyes sweeping down to her pallid legs, all the more outstanding and eccentric in this caramel-skinned Holidayland of bikinis, where the fact of a melanoma lesion was transmuted into a quaint myth like a unicorn or leprechaun—*Of course I've heard of it, but I've never seen one in reality*. Denim provided cover, true, but stiff twice-laundered fabric? A hothouse. Marta never wore denim, firm in the belief that its currency and approachable casualness did not jive well with a professional demeanor. To her the match looked like a nun in a halter-top: transvestic and unconvincing, a misguided leopard failing at changing its spots. Nevertheless, she bought a discounted pair at Banana Republic along with a gauzy unbleached peasant blouse a week before leaving the city, *when in Rome* chiming insistently. Even the aged studio guard wore jeans, Marta recalled.

Tightly fastening the robe, she crossed to the door and released the chain. A harsh white field of sunlit gravel reminded her to buy sunglasses, the only pair she owned stuck at home in a drawer; sepia lenses would return the glaring, faintly hostile landscape to the palatable bucolic hue of postcards.

"Hi, I'm Chaz," the stranger said. "Lora's assistant. We didn't shake hands back in the city, but I noticed when you came to the studio. It was cute, you looked pretty bowled over." Swarthy with freckles the man presented a solid figure, a few Big

Macs short of husky. The abundant thicket of black curly hair was damp and pasted to his temples. An oblong face, not recently shaved, glistened, the profuse sweat like a film of petroleum jelly; a razor gash still healed at the point on a bull neck where the beard petered out.

Marta imagined he'd be huffing and spent halfway up a short flight of stairs. *At this rate, he's going to be on diabetes medication well before forty*, she thought. The man's shirt and trousers—yards of black denim—would be no help.

"Hi, it's a pleasure to meet you. I'm Marta." She held out her hand. "I gather you're here to deliver a message?" Holding the door ajar, the heat rushed in. Marta shielded her eyes, thinking of dust bowl migrations and frenzied locusts in ominous cloud formation. The man's hand felt warm and moist but not unpleasant.

"Well, no. My car died, or something. I'm not very mechanical. Anyway, I'm wondering if you could give me a ride to the production office. I called Lora already and she told me you're due there at nine bells." Chaz mopped his forehead with a handkerchief.

"Oh, I see." Marta evaluated the uncreased span between Chaz's brow and hair line as a shade disproportionate.

"If it's a hassle, I can hitch. I don't think this town has taxis. I dunno. The heat's kind of much already, though. I can already feel the sweat streaming into my butt crack. I'll probably get a rash." He checked the time. "Sorry, that's probably more information than you'd want from a stranger at the door at 8:35 in the morning. At least I'm not holding *Watchtower* magazines and warning you about next month's apocalypse. Beware sinner," he waved with mock-prophet enthusiasm, "preparest thy soul."

The burly man's performer reservoir took Marta aback. Chaz seemed to be a natural, though lampshade-comic rather than *Hamlet*-soliloquy. When she summoned the actor's mask in a classroom, she knew the cost of the short-term loan.

Chaz shifted his weight from one foot to the next. "Man oh man, I can feel the ground through my flip flops. It's like Mauna Loa. And I thought my room was hot."

Animated and chatty—a huge percolating dose of caffeine—Chaz disconcerted Marta. Marta viewed morning as solitary and low-key. Were she to meditate, the inspiring stillness following sunrise would be optimal. Her school year routine included a brisk walk around the neighbourhood, followed by yogurt-topped oatmeal. She reserved weekend mornings for a newspaper and a few magazines. During the workweek she prepared a pot of Earl Grey and hastily read a chapter from a canonical writer, a self-imposed assignment. Smitten years ago with the idea of cultural literacy, she'd compiled a lengthy list of key texts with which she managed—some consciously, others not—to have no lasting contact. Aristotle through Zola, the thousands of pages would take years to complete. On occasion a bright student made reference to specific lines of *Paradise Lost* or "The Miller's Tale," and Marta regretted relying on the therapist's classic turnaround—"What do *you* think?"—and the extended bluff: "Would you say there's sufficient evidence from the text to support that interpretation?" That strategy never failed. The alphabetical list served to remedy that professional eyesore as well.

Marta waited silently until the man stopped performing. "It's not a problem, the ride I mean," she said.

"That's great, sergeant." Chaz smiled and saluted. "Hey, do you have A/C? In there, I mean?"

"Just a fan. When I arrived in the early evening the drapes were closed, so it wasn't too bad. Perhaps units around back are equipped with it."

"It'd probably cost extra, and there's no way the production's gonna swing for that. For me, anyway. For you, maybe." Marta wondered if he wanted an invitation inside.

They paused. Birds chirped and tourist vehicles, weighted down and sluggish, passed by on the 97. In the lot a tumbleweed—skeletal, improbable—bounced by; Marta tracked the soundless ball's wind-borne ramble.

Chaz clapped twice. "Okay, anyway, I've got to change my footwear. Lora will kill me if she sees me in these—'Safety first,' that's her motto. I'll let you get ready and be back in five. Um, there's a coffee maker in my room. Can I get you a cup?"

Marta had already brewed tea. "Sure, that would be grand. I'll be ready when you return."

She opted against shorts, but folded them inside the tote.

2.

Car doors locked and safety belts secured, Marta switched off the murmuring radio announcer. Though she'd referred to the map several times, she placed it in the bag atop shorts, the script, and a copy of *Imperial(ist) Empress*. While the route from the Star-Lite ran directly, summer raised the possibility of road work and a detour. Marta studied the morning's vista before signaling left. The highway was a corridor, a narrow band between dense, sprinkler-soaked orchards. On elevated plateaus in the valley: lush vineyards unfurling like bolts of luxurious dense cloth. Still higher, indigenousness—lifeless Martian rock, scrubby sage, meagre grass patches, indistinct growths of bush, long stretches of inhospitableness, an unmerciful landscape that could make anyone fall on their knees in gratitude for petroleum products, air conditioning, and shopping mall food courts.

Chaz turned on the radio and stabbed the scan button for stations.

Marta had read facts and figures about road etiquette and expected to drive without the distractions of noise. Without looking at Chaz, she reached for the dial and rotated the volume dial slowly until the speakers fell silent.

"It's just as well. That station is such complete bullshit. 'The greatest hits of all time.' Yeah, right, I happen to know that 'Silver Threads Among the Gold' was huge in the 1870s, and they've never played it, not once. And what about 'Greensleeves'? That was a monster hit, it rocked out for decades in the 1600s."

Marta smiled, amused even though she believed he'd practiced those lines before.

"Ten and two position on the wheel, eh? You're really intent," Chaz said. He'd adjusted the seat and sprawled. "Not a speed demon, I see."

"I rarely drive." Marta had deduced that the passenger would be a fidget by the time he'd opened the glove compartment.

"We're actually going slightly below the limit."

"Oh, really?" Marta said, thinking, *Typical, probably expects me to offer him the wheel.* "Actually"—two heartbeats—"it is significantly faster than walking. Isn't it?"

"Okay, gotcha. No one appreciates a back seat driver. I'll shut up."

Marta guaged the growing volume of traffic ahead.

"This car is pretty new, eh? Mine's a heap."

"It's a rental. I think agencies always have recent models." Marta could not bear to talk about cars. It was a dead-end topic—filler for family visits, elevator rides—and as inane as Christmas plans or the weather. "Have you been working in the film industry for long?"

"Nope. I'm an office PA."

Marta frowned at the inadequacy of the answer.

"Oh, it's just that . . ." Chaz stopped. "Well, just between you and me, if you meet someone on set and he's been a PA for longer than a year, it means he hasn't been working full-time or else he's a completely incompetent tool. Pardon my French. I'm competent."

"And therefore you're new. I understand now." Vested road crews and heavily loaded vacationing families reduced traffic velocity.

"Want this now?" Chaz held up a stainless steel coffee mug.

Marta shook her head and focused on the vehicle flow.

"Okay. Well, being a PA is a probationary period, a rite of passage," he said. "After the time's up, you expect, and you're expected, to rise in the ranks. Picking up cigarette butts and guarding parking lots and equipment is shit-work, anybody can see that, especially during the six or so months when the clouds are pissing and you're stuck outside. Or in my case: going on coffee runs for the muckety-mucks and getting chewed out when the soy latte doesn't have three shots or whatever."

"Oh, I didn't know. You've made a career change, then? I've always admired people who just make the leap one day, walking away and never looking back. My profession has a painted-into-the-corner quality to it." The words sounded unconvincing to her ears. "I don't know what else I could do. Under- and overqualified simultaneously."

"You're doing this."

"True." She saw no need to correct the assumption.

"My story isn't quite like that. It's crappier. It's like a movie, *The Incredible Bulk*." Chaz spread out his hands with a magician's flourish. "Picture this: I was a bloated-with-mac-and-cheese grad student in Biochem and after my cap and gown moment—that outfit was for my parents, I didn't give two shits about it—I got hired by a lab working on a hush hush Next Big Thing project. It was the beginning of a promising career and then my world went topsy-turvy." He bit a knuckle in mirthful imitation of silent film anguish.

"Oh my."

"I know, sounds dramatic eh? It wasn't that bad. I was working on DIDIs for Vedmedica Animal Science, a high-tech place just outside of Seattle," he said. "You know, Discrete Interval Dormancy Inducers."

Marta, watchful of the dirty elephantine RV—and its execrable bumper sticker: "How's My Driving? Dial 1-800-EAT-SHIT"—wobbling drunkenly in the lane ahead, tapped a beat, a signal for Chaz to continue.

"It's a would-be new class of veterinary drugs, a potential profit bonanza, as mammoth as SSRIs. Since you're blank-faced about it, that's because R and D got snagged by 'isolated anomalies' "—the accent of the quotation vaguely Nordic—"DIDIs haven't made it to the market, in other words. Yet. Research is a toss of the dice. Pharmaceutical companies are the first to say so, especially at quarterly earnings meetings. But every so often there's a Viagra or Prozac and everyone's pockets Scrooge McDuck with cash."

Marta believed that doctors over-prescribed anti-depressants and conned people into accepting chemical imbalances as the cause of unhappiness—when evidence pointed to miserable marriages, unfulfilling jobs, past traumas, and overall lack of purpose as the culprits. She thought it abundantly self-evident that Valium had not been prescribed to legions of suburban housewives because they all suffered from malfunctioning brains in need of molecular fine-tuning.

"Anyway," Chaz said. "The plan was to design DIDIs to cause short-term hibernation. So when Jane and Joe Audi go away for a weekend at Whistler or Vegas, they slip Ginger and Sheba a pill that'll knock them out for forty-eight hours, give or take. Suspended animation, kind of, but just lasting seventy-two hours, max. The pets wake up groggy and in need of food and water, but that's the only shortcoming. Sure, the drug has professional applications, but mostly it's designed for the recreational-slash-consumer market. And that's a colossal market, just massive. Money in the bank. Do you know how many billions people already spend on their pets?"

Marta figured the question was rhetorical.

"Well, I'll tell you one thing, it's way more than they spend on feeding starving people in third world countries. Anyway, in trials, just a few mind you, some test subjects remained asleep. Comatose, in fact. Indefinitely. Okay, and a couple of them died too. Whatever. Anomalies. Thousands of people die every year from taking aspirin, so I don't know what the big deal is. Man, could that car go any slower? Christ!"

Marta expected Chaz to reach over and blare the horn, lean out the window with a cocked shotgun.

"So, the project was shelved after animal rights do-gooders got wind of it and made it the story du jour for the media. 'Inhumane and cruel,' that kind of thing." He adjusted the door mirror. "It's ridiculous considering how many animals we kill for hamburger patties and chicken nuggets every frigging second. I'm surprised you haven't heard about it."

"I guess hiring a petsitter is too much bother for people?"

"That's not the point, Miss Marples. Sorry. You've heard of capitalism, right? From a corporation's point of view, a sitter is wrongheaded. No profit in that is there, young Skywalker?" He spoke with his hand, as though a puppet covered it. "But if each and every pet owner uses a drug a few times a year for the duration of the animal's life ... well, it's not advanced calculus. There's, like, seventy million cats and dogs in the US alone. I woulda been rich. But whatever. The whole situation burned me out. Politics and finger pointing! Scapegoating and covering asses, you wouldn't believe it.

And now here I am, answering phones and schlepping coffee, poised for my meteoric rise to the top."

The RV and its boxy trailer of off-road motorcycles pulled over to let the impatient line of vehicles pass. "About time, eh?" Chaz said.

"It wasn't bothering me. We're almost there. It's Marple, by the way."

"Oh really?"

"I think so, yes."

He surveyed the roadside. "Gee, not much to say about this place. I'll bet it wasn't much even during its glory days."

"I spent a few summers here when I was a child. The city hasn't really grown."

"It's probably shrinking as we speak. If I was growing up here, I'd already be planning my escape."

"Urban living isn't for everyone." Even though Marta agreed, the man's boundless opinions irked her. She pointed. "That fruit stand has been there since the 1950s. Wonderful tomatoes and peaches." She'd passed by it countless times but had never stopped. Even as a retirement destination this town held no allure for her.

"I'm not much for fresh fruit and vegetables," Chaz patted his belly. "But give me a chocolate glazed any day."

Marta slowed the car and kept watch for a parking space. "There. That's the address Lora sent me."

Lora had described the production office as "old retail," and the description looked accurate. Marta pulled in front of a glass-fronted shop that in former times had housed a clothing shop, the crackled gold lettering of *Joan's of Oliver, Fine Fashions* still catching the eye.

"There's a space," Chaz said. "Rock star parking!"

"Another advantage to small town life."

"Yeah, right. I hope this place has a Starbucks. Otherwise everyone's going to be acting all premenstrual. Pardon my French."

Marta wondered how often pubescent Chaz had heard "Think before you speak" from parental adults. Apparently the man's stock of lessons learned couldn't fill a room. She remembered Lady Stanhope's complaint about Dr. Meryon, "doing mischief everytime he opens his mouth."

"Shall we?" Trepidation slowed her pace on the baking sidewalk. She counted classes, research, and conferences as ingrained routine, no more noteworthy than a blanket; years had passed since a facet developed in her occupation. *I'm literally walking toward a new role*, she thought, reminding herself to smile and inhale deeply.

"Crap," Chaz said, struggling with the door. "We're going to need a carpenter to align that asap."

The production office showed no evidence of the frantic circus atmosphere Marta expected. Feet up in a long unoccupied room and a telephone on her lap, Lora waved from a desk, indicating with a peace sign that the call had begun to wind down.

As Chaz investigated the perimeter, Marta sat on an oval-backed chair upholstered in peony-print chintz, its curved legs painted gold. From Joan's pinnacle, she guessed. Dior's atelier rescaled; now stripped of glamour and perfumed with must. Cross-legged, she tucked her feet beneath, gratified that the stomach elephants—butterflies scarcely the case—of only a minute ago had receded so quickly.

Lora finished and typed a quick message. "Good morning to you both. Welcome to our makeshift command post, complete with soupy air and free-floating mould spores. We've got quite the day planned. Chaz, glad you could make it. We need you to snag and taxi a few people within the hour. You can use a production car, for now. I hope to hell you've taken your heap into a shop." Lora strode toward them. In flip-flops and military-style fatigues but adeptly bronzed, Marta noticed, instantly feeling overdressed. Chaz had led her to expect steel-toed boots. "What's that on your lips? They're kinda stained or something. Communal toilet is down the hall straight that way, across from Jake's office."

"Oh crap. Cherry popsicle, does it look gross?" Chaz scrubbed his mouth. "And, yes ma'am, I called this morning and the guy's going to pick it up before noon. I left my keys with the front desk lady."

"We have a clump of VIP arrivals. I'll call them in a sec. They're leaving Vancouver in thirty minutes, so you can fetch them in Penticton before noon. Marta, Jake's holed up in that back office. We'll meet him in ten."

"Thanks again for the ride, Marta," Chaz said, ambling toward the hidden office. "I'll try to check in with you after the first wave."

"See you then." Seated on the queenly chair Marta nodded and studied the room, relieved at seeing a previous tenant had removed every drop ceiling tile save for the three suspended directly above; only the spare black grid frame remained intact. Low ceilings depressed any soul, their very presence symbolizing one's stepping nearer to dead-end serfdom, data entry division.

3.

"Okay, Marta. Let's get to it." Lora, wearing noisy flip flops, led them to the building's dimly lit rear. "We've got a situation, kind of a good news/bad news scenario. Well, sort of. You'll see. Coffee?"

"I'm fine, thank you. Chaz made me a cup for the drive."

"He's such a peach—a sweaty one, though, you have to admit."

"A situation?"

Brows raised, Lora corralled Marta forward.

The back office was empty except for remnants, a stout oak desk and two folding chairs. Jake, typing at an aluminum laptop as they entered, did not look up. Marta imagined Joan in the room decades earlier, noisily firing off letters on an indestructible Royal and smoking furiously as she gossiped with the floor manager about the lives of the clientele, homespun farm wives with callused hands to whom she peddled—on affordable layaway, naturally—modern visions of city sophistication and ease.

Lora cleared her throat until Jake's fingers stopped. "We're good to go, boss. You remember Marta, yes?"

Behind the desk, Jake continued reading the screen. *He's slouched and will be monotone,* Marta thought, *like back-of-classroom students*. Jake focussed on the computer intently, as though to communicate *I've got better places to be*.

Lora knocked on the desktop. "Yoo hoo, Jake?"

Jake telegraphed Marta his confident automatic smile. "Sure thing, we're good." Leaning back and clasping the back of his neck, he flexed grapefruit biceps. "You're settled okay, Professor? Everything in order?"

The clipped delivery encouraged a military reply. Marta thought to say "Yes, sir," but felt uncomfortable joking with a man she'd scarcely met. "Everything's fine, thank you. It's Marta, please."

"Alright then, we'll start with the good news," Lora said, pacing the room like a zoo animal, one newly captive and wide-eyed rather than sleepily domesticated. "The next while can be a surprise holiday for you, all expenses paid. Surprise!"

"Accommodation and per diem plus the weekly salary," Jake said.

"Okay, what's the bad news, then?"

"*The Prophet of Djoun* has done a one-eighty." Jake drew the sudden change with an index finger half-circle. "Major change of plans, it's deep-sixed now."

"Keyword: it's been re-purposed," Lora added. "There's a new buyer and a new concept. The script's been revamped." Lora settled at the desk's corner.

"The nature of the beast." Distracted, Jake's eyes flitted to the screen.

"Oh." Ignorant of production company deal-making, Marta awaited further explanation.

"Basically, it's a matter of economics," Jake said. "But money was already allocated for your consultancy, so it's still yours. The contract had been signed, et cetera. Legally you're entitled and we're obligated." He snapped shut the laptop.

"I don't understand." Marta disliked this new status as a technicality and a legal obligation. "I'm entitled to what?"

"We'll give you the *Reader's Digest* version," Lora said. "Network A backed out of their commitment, so *The Prophet of Djoun* went bye-bye." Marta watched Lora wave and wondered why she believed that pantomiming the situation would help clarify the ambiguity. " 'We're over-committed' they claimed, and needed to lower overhead. 'These uncertain times' and 'Return on investment,' and so on. The usual business doublespeak, but the gist is they backed out at the eleventh hour and put the kibosh on the whole deal. If I had a dime for every lying wanker in the movie industry . . . Christ, men and their cold feet."

"Keep your eye on the track, Lora," Jake said.

Marta's confusion hadn't abated. "So, the movie isn't going to be made?" Since they sat inside Joan's on location in Oliver, Marta assumed that scenario was remote: what imbecile would demand a disrupted schedule and hours of driving from the coast only to have her turn around, fat cheque in hand?

"Not exactly. *That* movie isn't going to be made. *Prophet* is out, *Battle* is in," Jake said.

"*Battle* . . . ?" Marta sensed resentment flowering. How long would it have taken to email an update? And couriering another script wouldn't have broken the bank. *They forgot about me, obviously*, she thought.

"Network B got sold on a different vision, you see," Lora said. "Scripts are wet clay, basically. They're easy to shape. A bowl becomes a vase in no time and it might become a bowl again by the end of the week. Or a cup. Poof, like magic! And we deliver what the buyer demands. They announce, 'No cup now, we need a plate' and we know what to do. Demand and supply." Despite Lora's words and remedial pottery class motions, Marta wanted to hear elucidation without weird digressions or geared-to-children analogies complete with Theatre 101 hand gestures.

"Enter *The Battle for Djoun*. That's just the working title. Lady Hester Stanhope is gone, but now there's Lady Harriet Swinburne, a strong independent woman that's similar. Likewise, the other characters have been changed a bit and renamed. Again, it's a legal thing."

As Jake drew out the production company's bottom line, Marta learned the otherwise insouciant man paid close heed to the letter of the law.

"The Stanhope woman has living relatives in England, or somewhere, so there's concern about character assassination and defamation, or buying permission, or some damned thing, if you can you believe it." Lora had resettled at the desk perch. "Question, Marta: she's been dead for, like, ever, right?"

"Yes, since the summer of 1839."

"So, there's another character, one based on Lady Stanhope?" Marta thought vaguely about libel laws and the term "Inspired by True Events" so often appearing in film promotions.

"You got it. Lady Swinburne has the same back story," Jake said. "She's strong and outspoken, left England rather than face hypocrisy, and so on. She doesn't put up with other people's crap, basically."

"Basically," Marta said.

"She's a sexy middle-aged alpha-female, an Amazon, tough as nails, Lara Croft meets a young Queen Elizabeth I with a touch of Amelia Earhart. Set up a commune in a hostile foreign territory, renowned for miles, and all that," Lora said.

"But Network B angled for a script that's more action-oriented than the original biopic," Jake said.

"Action-oriented," Marta said, annoyed by her own parroting.

"That right, honey. It's re-genrification," Lora added. "Happens all the time, the law of commerce, as old as Adam Smith."

"All the time, you'd be amazed," Jake confirmed.

"Action? Like *Transformers?*" Marta asked. "Or *Saving Private Ryan*?"

"Yeah, exactly." Lora nodded. "Or maybe *Aliens*."

"The epic battle between good and evil, it's classic, old as the hills," Jake hinted at the revised thematic content. "But no robots."

"Robots?" Marta said. "Really? I don't see how . . ."

"The new script"—Lora drew the shape—"will explain everything. Trust us."

"Anyhow, we're not quite so concerned with historical accuracy now. The viewers aren't going to quibble about things like that. The network's demographic is teenaged boys, basically," Jake said. "And men that act like them. As far as they're concerned anything before Playstation is a long boring stretch of prehistory."

Who act like them, Marta silently corrected.

"Precisely. These guys are stunted, nerdy dweebs that play with gadgets while they watch TV and drink six-packs of Coke and still get hot watching *Xena* reruns. Ancient Rome, Medieval England, World War I, it's all the same. Their primitive brains register gore, action sequences, and flashes of T and A, not whether Lady So and So would say or do such and such in 1829 or whenever. Did I mention gore? Exploding bags of blood, decapitation, that kind of thing. I should know, I live with two of them, teenaged version." Lora paused. "They're rude little monkeys. . . ."

"The track, Lora, the track."

Watching, Marta discerned how their variation on good cop/bad cop had developed organically.

"Right. The long and the short of it is that viewers are the bread and butter of the network, and those viewers want action sequences and D-cup video game vixens and don't give a fig about much else. Hester Stanhope's speech-making would lull them into comas. They'd switch channels in a heartbeat, so the plan is that Lady Swinburne's kick-ass battle royales will flick some caveman switch in their thick heads."

"Exactly." Jake flexed, ready to move on. "And we're here to deliver the product they expect."

Marta read the yellow LIVESTRONG wrist band and the tattoo beneath the dense clipped forearm hair: there, for onlookers, a high-rise stack of letters spelled "Fortune Favors the Bold." *Comportment*, she thought at random, a fusty principle. And faintly absurd too, like *white man's burden*.

"We'll give you the latest script now, Marta. Take the day off. Look at it and think about what you want to do. Like I mentioned, we've got a shitload of work to get done today, so we have to cut this meeting short." Lora held up the cellphone to indicate the day's hectic schedule, blocks of different colours along a time line.

"Alright." Marta wanted extra minutes for interrogation, but Lora had made it plain that the moment didn't look propitious.

"If the vacation idea doesn't cut it, you can check out and head home," Jake said. "It's a good deal either way. Free money."

"We'd prefer that you're nearby, just in case," Lora said.

"Just in case?"

"Well, you know."

Marta had no idea.

"You look a bit dazed, hon." Lora's expression suggested parental tenderness. "This business is crazy."

"I'll stop by later." Marta turned for the door.

Grunt Work

I.

Jake picked up the phone and dialed Nicos once he and Lora brought their schedules into synch. He watched his assistant's bustling stride toward the frontmost desk.

After the morning's first outburst—"C'mon, Jake. This is going to be an ordeal, and you know it"—she'd been puffed up and radiating annoyance. Wise with experience, Jake and Chaz hung back as Lora spent her energy on visiting crew, whose questions she met with a cyclonic fury. Earlier, Jake had pointed out the necessity of striking the morning's appointments: no, he wouldn't put off the tour any longer, and no, ma'am he wasn't being superstitious. The location inspection—the physical walk-through of both camera-ready sites—demanded full attention. Now, not later. He'd scrolled through plenty of site photos and renderings, but like porn the images served as a passable substitute only when he couldn't grasp the real material.

Though stomping around on site and kicking the proverbial wheels reassured Jake with the sheer physicality, the precaution was also smart. A slim volume of gut-souring episodes in his career had hammered home the fact that each level in the hierarchy of delegated activities called movie-making represented a fuck-up in the works. The unambiguous instruction—"Find a cliff-side crash site and build a partially buried spacecraft there"—might seem a no-brainer, but between the executive mouth from high above and a crew ear a few notches below, everyday air currents sheltered anarchic long-chain molecules of Murphy's Law, whose very essence guaranteed sound wave distortions. The cliff might not measure up, the crash scene look too this, not enough that, or the alien craft put together somehow wrong—mangling proportion, colour, shape, or style took no special skill. Jake's concern: when and where—not if—the fatal failure of communication would occur.

There'd been no production—nowhere over a century of history—in which an idiotic decision hadn't hobbled easy progress. Jake would wager a month's salary on that. Inevitably, things going sideways proved as fundamental to moviemaking as water cooler small talk in office towers. Virtually every veteran accepted that as the nature of the beast and grew cautious—the philosophical crux: *Watch your ass*—in order to stave off the sort of disastrous miscalculation that stole time and money from the demanding string-pullers who green-lighted work and signed pay cheques.

Jake had witnessed the results of even one wrong step and understood the consequence. Having your professional competence questioned was the first sure razor cut of career suicide. Six months or so later you'd be telling anyone in earshot how you'd "had it with the game" while handing out freshly printed business cards—Certified Real Estate Agent—and throwing catchphrases like "seller's market," "no better time than now," and "investment in your future" with a televangelist's wheedling intimacy and undercurrent of desperate threat.

"Hey Nicos," Jake said. "Yeah, I'm settled. The place? Fine, no complaints. Good views and quiet. Comfy bed. Where are you? Where's that? Okay, how close?" He held the receiver away to muffle Nicos' barked instructions. "For sure, fifteen minutes is fine. Finish your breakfast and then haul ass. Don't bother with parking, I'll come out when I see you there. Yeah, yeah, I know, just honk if you don't see me."

"Where's the crash site, by the way? Close to the Swinburne compound?" Jake leaned forward to study a map left on the desk by Lora. "Right, what's that? Hold on a sec, I'm looking. Never mind, the address means nothing to me. Christ, it's like varicose veins. There's a million half-assed roads around this town, God knows why. That location might as well be Timbuktu."

The urge to crumple the map into a tight insignificant ball flashed angrily, but Jake let it pass. He'd always despised last-picked-for-the-team scenarios and avoided involvement in practically anything—golf, tennis, karaoke, poker—that he could not master: he saw no point in showing up if he didn't have a hefty chance of dominance. *Love of the game*, what bullshit.

Map reading, a subset of sense of direction, was another item he could add to a steer-clear-of-it pile. It embarrassed him to realize that in a dire situation—being lost in the wild during winter with no food or matches, vultures circling, and a supreme urgency to find the trail home—he'd be a lousy person to get paired with. Trudging forward with gung-ho bravado, he'd bellow out his top dog status and mislead fatally, shepherding survivors in a straight line due south toward warm safety when a lazy spiral culminating in hypothermia and carrion birds feasting emerged as the geometric truth.

And salt in the wound Nicos, Mr. Know It All, always stood by with a knowing look. The guy possessed senses on par with one of those mystifying urban legend dogs that shows up at a distraught family's front door an entire year after being forgotten at a camp site one thousand miles distant. Jake could see no advantage to disclosing that information. He'd let Nicos pilot the way because that was part of a LM's job description, an obligation reflecting nothing except a lesser rank on the totem.

"Anyway, Swinburne's compound for a walk-through, then the crash site. See you in fifteen." Jake felt eager to stop Nicos from speaking; he'd hear plenty from the motormouth inside the cab of the pickup.

"Right, I'm sure it is." From the restaurant Nicos griped about a rubbery breakfast omelette, the result no doubt of inferior Canadian chickens, eggs, or kitchen talent. "Let's keep it at fifteen anyway. A few loose ends here."

Jake re-read an old delivery from Exconfessio he'd been scanning during the call.

Ex A.W. (Vancouver, BC)—

1. I pissed on my ex-boyfriend's new female roommate's bed before I moved out.

2. I put dog shit under some asshole's car door handle (he he he).

3. I threw dog shit at my neighbour's house.
4. I rubbed my ex's mom's hand mirror all over my snatch and asshole before returning it.
5. I hate women who either marry into money or inherit money and have a nanny to take care of their kids five days a week so they can go to the gym (cunts).
6. I hate men that comment on how great of shape these bitches are in.
7. I'm a bitch and an asshole driver.

Jake figured that the final admission counted as two, technically. He deleted the staggeringly vindictive message—he believed in an absolute line between titillating misbehaviour and non-stop ugliness—and emptied the computer's trash. Today's confessor sounded dire; the poisonous admitted bitch looked like a juggernaut of trouble from the *Fatal Attraction* school and gave nothing to savour, only depressing, mouth-puckering bitterness.

Jake saved the lively confessions and revisited them in the same way as he imagined other people turned to a newspaper's Daily Smile quotation with its tacky retro humour—"What is practical nursing? Falling in love with a rich patient!"—and kept each of the miniature episodes archived and ordered (and, when restless, reordered too: Righteous Citizen's "I would be happy to handicap any able bodied person who imagines they have a right to park in the handicapped parking spot" recently losing priority status to Slacker Drone's "When I worked in an unsupervised position at my current job, I would do things like take off to the casino for hours and smoke a joint on the way"). Intoxicating snippets from the lives of strangers, they never lost their caustic zing. Stitched together, the scenes would make for an awesome, unsettling movie.

The envy-consumed turd handler, though, merely stood out as an unpleasant reminder of how awful and twisted people could grow. The woman—or a guy text-transvestite: Exconfessio made no claims to verify the legitimacy of the confessor, and Jake had read many supposed admissions that triggered suspicion about the writer's true motivation and real identity since guilt or braggadocio seemed beside the point—reminded him of the coffee mug of Mick, his second boss in the industry: "Yeah, I'm an Asshole. Just Try Me." Though forthright, the mug's honesty didn't compensate for hours spent under the unbearable man's hairy thumb. At least, Jake hoped, he'd never meet this scheming malevolent creature face to face. He felt leery of anyone who acted like an asshole and patted himself on the back for possessing brutal directness. Such wastes of space made his sac contract tight. Cruelty dressed up as courage: another performance the world could get by without.

Jeremy had sent just one bit of trivia. A slow week, Jake guessed.

The subject line: "FW: 'Roid rage?"

> "Muscled Pumped and Raging - 38
>
> I'm a ripped, very well muscled guy looking for other muscular guys only! If you're fat, fuck off! If you're soft and flabby, fuck off! If you're thin and don't work out, fuck off! I'm only interested in other guys with the mojo to dedicate themselves to work out and invest in what they have. If you have the cojones to not be offended by this ad, then I'd like to hear from you."

Jake thought he might have seen this hulking tool at the gym, fatuous and infantile in his unending self-absorption. He imagined the swaggering testosterone worshipper trapped in an elevator with the hateful could-be hag from Exconfessio. It'd be a caged death match for sure, bloody, despicable, and no-holds-barred—Japanese fighting fish in a puny tank but substantially less graceful.

"Hey, Jake, your chariot awaits," Lora yelled from the kitchen. "Jake?" His phone gonged seconds later: "Hey, did you hear me?"

"I'm on it, panic button. What's up with you, anyway? Did you forget to take your meds this morning?"

"You know I take them religiously. 'A centred worker is a productive worker.' "

"Man oh man, I wished you'd never taken that seminar. Motivational speakers are just cult leaders minus the polyester suits. It's best to avoid contact with them. Besides, the whole deal was probably underwritten by PharmaGen BioLabs as a cheap human trial experiment. You sound like you're about ready for the grape Kool Aid. Hello?" Jake spoke to a dead line.

"We've been over this, Jake." Lora stood glowering at the doorframe. "We all have our crutches, Mister One Night Stand."

Jake related anecdotes from time to time during morning lulls at the office. He selected bits cautiously and even toned them down, an educated guess being that if Lora—for whom going braless would be a tour-though-the-wild-side act of sexual bravado, and who grew pursed and distant whenever he used the word monagony and visibly unsettled the one time he had in the spirit of earnest but jokey disclosure categorized himself as trysexual—discovered that she had been exposed to the iceberg's mere tip, she'd be appalled (low probability), astonished (high probability), or merciless as Ming with jibbing (100% certainty).

Lora embraced the rare poetry of birds that mate for life. Her visionary's third eye wide open, she'd call for the looming conclusion of Jake's galavanting; the stars predicted the sea-change as plain as day. And he'd be wise to prepare for the moment true adulthood began. "Your horoscopes have been making that claim for years, woman," Jake always replied, "time to find a better system. Tea leaves maybe. Tarot cards."

"Okay, okay, touché, Madame." He stood. "I should get out there or Nicos won't shut up about it. I'll call from the second site and we'll get a game plan in order for the afternoon."

He disconnected the laptop and pulled open a drawer. The tussle with Lora reminded him about his own daily regimen. He grabbed two chubby capsules from the messenger bag and washed them down. He'd been assured by the natural pharmacist that the arginine, tongkat ali, and catuaba bark combo added up to a "surefire male enhancement." On a whim, he'd also bought a year's supply of Enzyte after catching ads on TV promising suburban guys that they'd be walking hard-ons, the envy of all the other Joes on Pine Crescent and secret wish for the unfulfilled Janes.

While the vision of a pill-popping middle age drew his breath short, the strong throb of a lower centre of gravity possessed supreme appeal. And naturally, years of searing inbox spam promises—"So hard you can break an egg"; "Become the sex magnet of your 'hood"—had branded unguarded bits of primal cortex. As with in-your-face D-cup cleavage, Jake found a too visible big package to be crass but unnerving provocation: people typically stared and turned away nervously, primly judging the display to be crude while helplessly responding to the voluptuous contour over and again, animal instincts triggering a gush of saliva and compelling them to bend over and take a sniff, or else cop a feel.

Jake had used up half the pill supply. Each day he swallowed the doses half-heartedly: he hadn't noticed the constant hum of enhanced vigour or suffered terrible side effects; he figured there must be something to them. Still, placebos yielded positive results. Everyone understood that.

Knees, heart, hair, career, looks, sex appeal, good fortune: sturdy's a white lie, a feeble house of cards that can collapse into flat debris at any moment. Years ago Jake had shared philosophy over beers with Randall, the accountant Warner Brothers had sent to supervise the weekly budgets of a superhero series, the studio's globally syndicated moneymaker. Jake's senior by a half a decade, the man spoke as a war-weary veteran: "You know what, man, one day you wake up and you notice your skin. It's different, looser, like the elastic waist of old underwear. Sagging steadily and then, I guess, just gone. Bibs and diapers at Sunset Manor creeping nearer every day." When Jake attempted to counter the accountant's fatalism, Randall had brushed the logic aside as smoke and mirrors, the fruit of relative youth: "Come talk to me when you reach my age." *You can keep your resignation*, Jake had thought, viewing such passivity as a fatal character flaw.

He tugged at the legs of his jeans and passed by Lora. Spillage: going full commando with low-hangers could be painful. "Oh, where's good coffee?" he asked.

"Working, Jake, working."

Outside, Nicos sounded the horn at the impatient regular intervals of a New York City cabbie sent over from Central Casting. "You'd better run," Lora said. "Christ, any minute now a representative of Oliver's finest might show up here waving a badge. Say hi to Nicos for me. And Jake?"

"Yes?"

"I'm glad you're enjoying my Christmas present, really, and I know you like to smell pretty, but we could all live happier here with you applying one less splash of Terre in the morning."

"Okay, ma'am." Although firm, Lora's mothering was well intended.

"Talk to you soon."

2.

A Red Bull canister fell and clattered on the asphalt as Jake swung open the door. He tossed it into the pick-up's empty bed. "Hey, Pig Pen," he said, observing the litter—balled napkins and food wrappers lining the dash, empty energy drinks crowding the floor, and Styrofoam take-out strewn alongside water bottles on the bench seat. Nicos maintained the lustrous exterior of his vehicles with the anal-retentive standards of a military boot camp CO, but expressed a profound shift in philosophy for interiors. The weird split always struck Jake, who thought a midpoint between extremes seemed realistic, closer to cosmic balance; anyone comparing his desk and bedroom would notice matching tidiness levels.

"Hey, boss, you know me. I like to nest." Nicos swept discards to the floor and patted the seat. "Okay princess, here's a safe place for your hairy Royal Doulton ass."

Jake, bested by the subordinate's rapid-fire brain, slid into position without a reply. Nicos revved the engine.

"We ready to rock now?"

"Go." Jake sniffed, relieved that the interior's air-conditioner blew away any stench from Nicos' putrefying snacks. As for the heavy smoker's residue, he'd just man up about that and hold his tongue. He unlocked the phone and tapped out a message to Lora: "Tell me again, why'd we hire this guy!?!"

A life-of-the-party personality, Nicos' compulsion to talk ballooned exponentially when he'd passed long hours alone. Jake calculated that the Location Manager must have been solitary overnight in a motel and likely granted minimal contact during breakfast despite firm efforts at the quick fix of chatting up the waitress or diners at nearby tables. Sharing the cab now would not be too different from circulating in a room of desperate speed-daters eager to spill as many words as possible in their three-minute allotment of "Let me tell you all about me, *please*." Stalling for time was possible, Jake could see, but texting work missives could grab only a few moments of privacy.

Nicos's mouth switched on as he shifted out of Park. "The compound's not even ten kliks away, right," he said, louder than necessary, "but the crash site is a fair bit of a haul. It's out of the way for sure, but I figure the pay off is worth it. You'll see. It blew me away, that's for sure. A-f-ing-mazing, considering what we had to work with, anyway. It's not exactly the Himalayas out there—it's a fricking desert, well kind of a desert, technically the Osoyoos Arid Biotic Zone, whatever that means, but everyone says Okanagan Desert—so finding a sheer mountain face was no small feat. I mean, c'mon, Christ, talk about unreasonable expectations. Dunes woulda been a cinch. Even CGI woulda been easier, way easier." Nicos turned to face Jake, drawing attention to the sloping Bob Hope nose—another incongruous item for slow-day office speculation. "But I lucked in anyway, chatted up these hippie wannabe dudes on longboards and they told me about this retired gravel pit that I would never a found by looking at any map. Sometimes I'm pretty impressed with myself. Yeah, it's a gift, that's all I can say."

From past truck ride episodes, Jake was fully aware that Nicos could—and would—say much more. "Hold on a sec. I need to get this sent." Jake tapped the glass, scanning old online profile messages and photos, and waited for Lora's reply. Being on location and away from city amenities always made his testosterone levels spike, he'd swear. Hormonal torment: maybe the herbal pill magic had begun kicking in, after all.

"So, you were saying there's nothing closer, eh?" Jake said, no longer able to ignore Nicos' swiveling head and quests for eye contact.

"You saw the pictures, right?" Nicos turned to Jake again, expression obscured by shuttered mountaineering sunglasses. "There's some hills with a few scattered rocks, yeah, but nothing epic as per orders." Nicos flipped through a binder, steering with one hand. "Here it is. See, right, the list of requirements actually put in 'grandeur' a couple of times, so that's what I looked for. Grandeur, Christ! And found, kinda sorta, you'll see." He detached the copy of the email and thrust the sheet at Jake. "Anyway, the other option was way the hell over there in the sticks"—he thumbed southward—"and that would of pissed off everybody. All the talent pussy footing around and complaining would of been a sight, I gotta say. But the cost . . . killer. K-i-l-l-e-r. Not to mention the fact that we'd have to hire helicopters or a fleet of Humvees to access it. In no time we'd be hitting James Cameron territory with budget overruns. Hell to pay and all that, your head on a silver platter, the whole nine yards."

"Right," Jake sent a follow-up message: "The tide is rising." He'd let Nicos spew it all out. Like a baby, Nicos would tire eventually and maybe hit some kind of equilibrium after a painful few minutes of squalling. That strategy also worked when Hurricane Lora approached.

Lora's text opened with a smile emoticon: "With great power comes great responsibility. Reward him with a gold star and Good Luck!!! Rearranging YOUR schedule now so can't talk. ttyl biatch!!" Jake smiled. Schadenfreude: he would have typed the same.

Jake stared out the window while Nicos spoke, unconcerned about the failure to contribute. Nicos didn't expect an exchange of sentence for sentence reciprocity; a second body created the necessary illusion of conversation.

As the truck passed a barely there trailer park on a low sandy rise, Jake followed the abrupt change to greenery, a hand-planted oasis promising reassurance in an otherwise unwelcoming—though harshly striking—environment. In place of imposing barren rock outcrops and the invariable parched grass plains between them grew countless trees—vibrant, groomed, and healthy, a domesticated wilderness planted in fertile, easy-access grids. The layout appeared ingenious in its efficiency, but unlike the cold brutality of an auto plant, the orchards and their fluttering summer grace invited attention. Jake foresaw entranced drivers slowing and pulling over, eventually giving in to the desire to stroll around the luminous unthreatening forest, blithely setting aside the important lessons about the malevolence that awaits in stands of trees learned by Hansel and Gretel or those doomed kids in *The Blair Witch Project*. And that duo from the bible too.

Jake made a mental note to wander through a few rows before the shoot wrapped, ideally during the weak light at sunrise or sunset. A roadside sign—"U-pik fruit"—offered a handy solution to the trespassing problem.

"We're just about there," Nicos said. "Behold," sweeping across the view with an open palm, "the Djoun compound. Well, in a minute. Hold on."

Without signaling, Nicos swung off the highway and on to a narrow dirt road, swerving at a jackass speed that prompted a RV's angry horn blare and, for Jake, a short cinematic vignette of the lifted wheels that precede a tumbling crash, bloody wrecked bodies, a cloud of settling dust, spilling gas, and appalling final silence.

Jake leaned gamely with the truck's turn velocity—he'd heard Nicos' boasts about Dakar Rally-worthy off-roading expertise, but trusted his skill anyway. Curious about the pilot's shows of manly aggression over the past hour he figured he deserved an explanation. "You're testy today, man. Need to get laid or something?"

Nicos smiled widely. "Nah, it's the great outdoors. Brings out the animal in me, so I guess I'm testes. Get it?"

The homemade road mowed a line between two parcels of farmland.

A uniform green span of fruit trees fluttered visibly from Nicos' window, and on Jake's side the orchard spelled decimation, a flat expanse of plowed dry dirt clods and leafless wood carcasses. Errant partial rows of upturned stumps implied a work-in-progress; in the middle of the former orchard plot whole spiny trees had been dragged into one high pile that, Jake guessed, would soon be torched or fed into a chipper. The trees looked too puny for lumber.

"Disease?" Jake asked, thinking of the photograph of anthrax-infected livestock buried in shallow desert graves that Marilyn had suggested as a décor option for the fireplace wall. He'd felt better about the eerie industrial site photographed by the German couple, sterile metallic gloominess ultimately proving easier to come home to than decaying cattle with milky dead eyes.

"You'd think so, but no. I asked a guy here about that. When the time comes, they rip up the whole thing and plant new ones. It improves profit in the long run. I think orchard plots are like thoroughbreds. I mean they're super productive while they last, right, but they run out of juice quicker than a mongrel—or whatever they call non-thoroughbreds—so you put them out to pasture."

Nicos slowed to a rolling stop to examine the wasteland, then pushed the pedal for a demonstration of pebble-spitting acceleration. The Red Bull clattered and bounced in the back. "Or they chop them down and burn them, as the case may be. It'll make for a wicked bonfire, like at Burning Man. And sometimes it's a market demand thing, they're not sentimental these guys: they get paid more for apples than for pears or something, so it's out with one and in with the other. That's why there's so many grapes everywhere now: city yuppies pay through the nose for Chardonnay, not apple juice. They're businessmen these farmers, so I guess optimal fruit production is key."

"It's a long-term investment, I guess. You'd think trees would take years to grow to that size."

"Yeah, but we're not up to speed on agribusiness, you know, so maybe there are new hybrids or something that grow really quickly like bamboo or those trees they've developed for toilet paper. Synthetic growth hormones maybe, chickens and cows are pumped full of 'em, so why not plants. Gene-splicing too. Mondo-sized trees in just six short months! *Sleeper* here we come." Jake guessed that Nicos' veins flowed with the blood of a conspiracy theorist.

"I suppose so." Jake hadn't heard about toilet paper trees, and he didn't ask. It would please Nicos to offer up another information session that began with "I read somewhere . . ."

As the truck reached the back end of the orchard the road widened into a yard of ankle high grass. Obscured by trees, the farmhouse to the left hinted at a spiritual closeness to the stucco mid-century rancher of the suburbs and confounded Jake's expectation of a gabled Walton family homestead in aged white. The old-time barn at the edge of the stump field butted a round-shouldered mound of mountainside; with a sagging profile, mullioned windows, and planking weathered a powdery grey, it stood ready for second unit crew exterior shots.

"That's great," Jake said.

"Got it video-documented already and filed away. It's too country and western for us, right?"

"Right. Unless we get another script change."

"Okay, here we are. Behold the Hebe family farm."

Nicos slowed to wave at a lanky ball cap teen—Hebe Jr.?—inside the glassy cab of a yellow tractor. After a gentle right, he drove toward the barn and made a sudden left, where a dusty clot of weeds huddled. Jake hadn't noticed the gap between one hill and the next; the sun's glare on the identically hued humps of tall dry grass produced an optical illusion similar, he guessed, to snow blindness.

"How'd you find this place? More insider info from skateboarder hippies?"

"Nope, just old-fashioned footwork. Some luck too. I was driving toward town and noticed the stumps. I figured the farmer might be cash-strapped and open to an offer to lease the field. We could set up shop there and it'd be cheap for us, so what the hell. It wouldn't hurt to ask. Turns out there's more to the property than meets the eye."

Nicos waved to the young woman who approached as the truck turned. The PA pointed Nicos toward a makeshift parking area—a shallow U of orange fluorescent tape—with expert traffic-cop gestures. Jake didn't recognize her; the vested newbie must have been okay'd by Lora.

"Who's she?"

"Loree, I think. Rory. Lottie, maybe. Something like that. She's got more tattoos that you and me put together, that's all I know. Showed up yesterday. Considering that she's been parked on her ass guarding an empty lot, she's doing alright."

"Nice."

"I heard that she's not into dick," Nicos said. "A carpet muncher, get it?"

"Yeah, I figured that out when you said she's not into dick."

The building crew was nowhere in sight. Jake scrutinized the rampart wall of the compound. From the distance it appeared fully prepped. The caramel colour of the plaster contrasted nicely with the faded beige field on either side. Jake nodded: so far, so good.

"Not bad, eh?"

"Yeah, looks that way. From here, anyway. Where's the house?"

"The gate's on hinges. Open sesame and the rest will be revealed."

Adjusting to the radiance and desert wind, Jake walked to the far left of the wall. Though he'd worked on countless sets, the simple act of stepping behind the façade never failed to amuse. An illusionist's clever trick, it stayed magical even after the secret had become public domain.

He stepped up to the house façade and tested the rounded plank entrance. The doors gave the impression of heaviness, and the plywood's paint job—big wood knots, rough edges, thickly drawn lines of grain—read as being hand-hewn from whatever trees that grew in Lebanon back in the day.

The set designer, a pale over-caffeinated novice keen to make the right mark that would elevate her into A-list feature film Olympia, had agonized—right down to wringing hands—about the lack of material about Lady Stanhope's home base: "But there's a dearth of extant documentation" and the like in person, as well as by phone and email.

"Don't sweat it, Brainiac," Jake had replied with minor variations—"Professor," "Calculon," "Einstein," "Spock."

After the offhand comments designed to calm her, he'd grown bullying and blunt: "Relax, okay, it's not like we're making a documentary for the Lebanese Museum of Natural History or whatever. There's no curator, okay, there's no committee of experts with asses to kiss, just TV viewers wanting a good story. TV viewers. Got it?" And as the script changed: "It's the idea of a generic desert compound in the 1820s. No one—and by that I mean no one: viewers or studio—will care that you filled in the blanks with an educated guess. The reference is to other movies, not some old painting or *The History of Middle Eastern Architecture*. The viewers will care more about the surface of the UFO's hull and the alien's face than the goddamned gate of Lady Swinburne's compound. So how about you go watch *The Mummy* or *The Jewel of the Nile*. Okay?"

Submitting, the woman had asked no further questions. If he caught sight of her again soon, he'd commend the effort.

3.

Inspection complete, Jake walked back to the truck. Nicos waited inside, music blaring inside the sealed cab. When Jake thumbed toward the highway, Nicos revved the engine while sliding down his window. "Next?"

"Bingo."

"It'll be about twenty minutes, boss, thirty max."

Nicos signaled left at the highway. Weaving impatiently around lumbering RVs, he flipped between radio stations and remained as quiet as predicted while Jake tapped an update to Lora and tormented himself with virtual contact with the city.

In short minutes they climbed north from the serpentine highway of the valley flats to a sparsely inhabited area of rolling grassy fields whose rear borders disappeared into dark conifer islands.

When Nicos announced only a few turns remained until they arrived, Jake looked around and frowned. There'd been no word of a prairie crash site from construction, and the process photographs he'd viewed focussed on close-ups of spacecraft details. Rounding yet another corner, the roadside fields irregularly parceled by barbed wire fencing were interrupted by an austere institution lifted directly from a script—the sort of sci-fi thriller that centres on covert extraterrestrial visitors, black-suited governmental operatives with opaque aviator sunglasses and black Suburbans, and a terrible conspiracy that corrupts all the way to the innermost circle of power.

"Pretty cool, eh," Nicos said, glancing at the dazzling white radio transmission dishes that grew like cybernetic mushrooms from alfalfa fields. "Too bad we can't use them."

"Never say never." Jake charted plot turns capitalizing on the primo location. Jumps through space-time weren't an unheard of concept for the network, after all.

"You think it's available?"

"I don't even know if it's operational. I can ask, so just say the word."

As they turned off White Lake Road, Nicos said, "You, know, I never found any White Lake. I looked too. Weird, maybe it dried up."

So far as Jake could tell the cracked mud access road only led them toward an eternity of low grassy slopes. With nothing to call mountainous he huffed with concern that his Location Manager's instinct had failed. Jake hoped the crash site would be majestic but harsh, as though the craft had plummeted to the base of Everest; judging by the placid landscape outside the window, any UFO here would appear benevolent, as though it had touched down gently, prepared to disgorge philanthropic visitors possessing kind bulbous eyes, soothing curves, and valuable, softly-glowing technology their delicate amphibian hands gladly shared.

The road forked and Nicos swerved left onto a narrower stretch, bumpy and overgrown. "It's not exactly ideal conditions, right, I'll grant you that," Nicos said. "I figure we can set up base camp here and taxi crew and talent to set. It's a hassle, but that's less than nothing compared to the other option over yonder."

After stopping to open an improvised gate of barbed wire and scrap lumber, Nicos sped up, spewing rocks and creating a momentary fog of tinder-dry earth. With a final right, the truck descended; the path terminated at the bottom of a deep bowl.

"Ta da! You'd never guess, eh? It's the former property of a bankrupted gravel company, now administered by the town. They abandoned the pit a while back, but the local kids still come here to party and make out on weekends. I drove out here last Friday night. It was pre-gaming tailgate parties and steamy windows, like stepping back into my youth."

"Right on!" Jake said, smiling. He'd received his first blow job—though nowhere near the best; even with whispered course correction, "Um, can you watch it with the fangs?" Janica Detwenko had been slow on the uptake and accidentally taught a fumbling early lesson about the commingling of pain and pleasure—at a gravel pit during junior high school. "Stop here, okay?"

Nicos skidded to a halt and popped the door locks; the men stepped out, stretched, and wandered toward their destination.

The largest portion of the bowl broadcast its uselessness—rusted equipment, low sandy piles overgrown with determined clumps of weeds, and tall piles of loose rock that looked like nothing except gravel pit. Jake imagined that in a pinch the location could serve as a make-out spot in a teen comedy or a gangster's forlorn execution site.

The remaining quadrant, a pint-sized and unexpected striated granite face—vertiginous, infertile, pitted, lunar—could be better only if it stood taller. Partially buried in front of the cliff, the crashed spacecraft possessed reassuring solidity: even before being framed by a camera the wreck would momentarily convince a passerby of its authenticity. The alien technology read as adversarial too: the sharp angles, jutting armored components, and crude oil-effect surface conveyed stealthy malevolence with ease.

Nicos pointed to the extreme right of the cliff face. "No idea what the deal is with the tunnel, it's not like there was a mine," he said, "but maybe they found the gravel part first and when they expanded they found the harder granite or whatever, and got a bit of gold rush fever and made some preliminary digs to see what was there, I dunno."

"Why isn't anyone here, a PA at least?"

"No need right now. Right?"

"Yeah, I guess so." Jake knew an oversight of that type could bite him on the ass. "We need someone here as of today, though. It's safe? The cave, I mean."

"I dunno. I stuck my head in it, but that means squat. It'll be good for second unit, I bet."

"Maybe, yeah. Give me a minute, okay?"

"Bullets in the cylinder?"

"What?"

"You know, you have to take a crap, like now."

"Christ, man. No."

Jake walked to the tunnel's entrance and stared inside; without a flashlight the depth was impossible to gauge. The shaft would be of little use except as an exterior shot, that he knew; it looked cramped and, besides, there'd be hell to pay for wasting an interior already built on set in the city. A few strides into the damp shadows Jake paused at a lichen-splattered wall—as good a place to piss as any. As he lowered his pants to mid-thigh Jake felt cool air flow between his legs. He wanted to spray the rock wall with a full surge, but Nicos loitered just outside.

"You thirsty or something?" Jake asked. He'd oblige even though it wasn't really one of his kinks.

"Oh, sorry, man," Nicos said at a near-whisper decibel.

"I gotta return some of my organic coffee to Mother Earth. I'll be out in a sec."

"Marking territory, gotcha. I'll be waiting in the truck." The hibiscus flowers of Nicos' Hawaiian shirt retreated into the glare.

Within seconds of returning to overhead sunlight, Jake felt sweat rivulets funneling down and settling in his ass cleft. He strode toward the spacecraft and stopped, holding up outstretched hands to mimic a camera's lens frame. Viewed with one eye shut, the alien's crash site registered well, closer to cineplex quality than cable network product. Peering out of the pit and into the perimeter of the sun's aura, Jake decided the location measured up. He lifted the hand-camera again and strode toward the Ford; with each step he watched Nicos fill the frame.

Comfortable in the air-conditioned oasis, Nicos didn't open the window as Jake approached; he shifted into gear when Jake planted his feet at the grille.

"Very funny," Jake muttered, wiping his forehead with a sleeve.

Nicos continued to creep forward when Jake reached for the passenger door.

"You are how old? Suck my dick, man."

Nicos pretended to adjust radio controls.

"C'mon, man, don't jerk me around." At the bottom of the pit, his voice echoed.

Nicos refused to brake. He popped the door lock seconds later.

"Bet you're thirsty now."

"As a matter of fact I am." Jake regarded his colleague fondly: fair is fair. "Asshole." He could hear Lora's routine chide: "Keep them in your pants, boys." He reached into the bed for the Red Bull and threw it into construction's scrap pile.

"You stoked?" Nicos revved the engine.

"Yeah, I think I am. Everything's smooth so far."

"Maybe it'll be the exception to the rule."

"Maybe."

Apprehension

I.

Marta opened the script before turning the ignition key. Even with Lora's suggestive story-as-wet-clay analogy, Marta couldn't re-cast Lady Stanhope—or, as it turned out, the stand-in required by the legal department—as tomb-raiding action hero material, "kick-ass" or otherwise. True, the flesh and blood Victorian aristocrat had placed herself in the midst of scheming political factions and petty civil war skirmishes in the Levant region; perhaps the script dwelled on her as a female Machiavelli adept at half-truths, well-timed flattery, and ally choice. If that emphasis warped the truth considerably, the courtly intrigue would nevertheless give the plot necessary punch.

With the exception of drawn-out family quarrels haltingly enacted through letters transported by camels, horses, and ships, Marta concluded, there were simply no other places to insert searing conflict or daredevil plot elements into the caravan-paced episodes of Stanhope's life.

She read a sheet stapled to the cover page—

THE BATTLE FOR DJOUN - OVERVIEW

Djoun, Lebanon, 1825.

A middle-aged aristocratic English woman lives in exile with servants and her doctor, Basil Potter, a weak man who has loved his patient for years but has never spoken the words. Lady Harriet Swinburne turned her back on England and its hypocrisies years ago, and has used a formidable intellect and powerful charisma to carve a place

> for herself in an unforgiving desert land ruled by stern men who view women as expendable possessions.
> The local populace, peasants and wealthy alike, fear and respect her.

Marta wondered whether this information would scroll on the screen following the opening credits. She'd ask. So far the changes were cosmetic.

> Lady Swinburne is called the Empress of the Desert, and many believe she is a prophet close to the ear of God. She has a reputation as a healer, a philosopher, and an oracle; each and every day men and women in need of guidance or medicine show up at the gate of the Djoun compound seeking a minute of her attention, a touch from her hand, or sage words. Legend speaks of a savior, a woman dressed in a man's clothing who will arrive from a distant land. The credulous believe that she alone can free the land of wickedness and lead the people into paradise.

"The same back story, so I see," Marta murmured, wondering about the aptness of Jake's description. Perhaps he'd meant "an English lady living in the desert." This fabrication, she judged with pursed lips, had more in common with the hokum of *The Ten Commandments* than Hester Stanhope's life. Marta knew the mother-love looked silly, but she felt protective of Lady Stanhope. There'd been a name change, at least.

Marta patted her forehead and continued tracking the story's trajectory.

> One night a bright comet streaks across the starry sky, followed by a thundering crash. In the following days villagers tersely whisper about massacred sheep flocks, dead birds littering the ground, and entire farmer families vanishing overnight. Strange portents—flashes of light, humming sounds—fill the night skies. People begin to fall ill

with a new kind of plague, one that Lady Swinburne and her doctor cannot heal.

Puzzled and desperate for answers, she eventually leads a small group on horse to the mountainous area where the comet appeared to land. Near a cave they find a great metal machine half-buried in the sand. The group has seen nothing like it before.

Aghast but mesmerized, Marta skipped forward several paragraphs.

The outlying grounds have been reduced to smoking rubble and the villagers have gathered with Lady Swinburne and Dr. Potter for the last stand. The creature appears at night only, and the rag-tag group had hoped to make an offensive assault on the metal machine during the light of day. Having failed, they can only wait for the creature's certain arrival.

Marta would never have predicted the inclusion of an alien. Re-purposed, indeed. She read the final lines.

As the creature bends to feed on Dr. Potter, Lady Swinburne, despite being frightened and wounded, summons the strength to avenge the death of her beloved and loyal companion. She attacks with a farmer's scythe and slices the creature at its throat. The creature shrieks and struggles, but Swinburne's assault pays off—however, she is too late to save her faithful friend.

Following the somber victory celebration the scene returns to a cavern near the crashed spacecraft. A few feet inside, the dry stone becomes wet with webs of organic material; suspending in them are small translucent orbs. In the final moment, an alien fetus squirms inside its egg.

Serviceable enough B-movie plotting, Marta thought. While she'd encountered better ideas, she had also, in the name of conference papers, sat through worse. *A B-minus movie.* And the news wasn't only bad: her dread over an inane script featuring a grotesque named Lady Hester Stanhope, so palpable moments ago, could be laid to rest.

Marta heard laughter and looked up. The trio striding by held skateboards at their hips. The tall shaggy-haired leader closest to the car stopped to slip the board between his thighs; facing towards a hardware store, he drew the curves of a woman with index fingers that sliced through the air. Marta couldn't hear the words of the exuberant tale, but watched the cartoon thrusting motions. She filled in the blanks: "36-24-36."

"Dude, no way," the skinny friend to the performer's left replied.

The youngest followed suit: "No way!"

As the storyteller leaned on the hood and continued with the va-va-voom-era *Playboy* fishing tale, Marta wondered how far he'd strayed from the truth and for how many millennia men had etched that universal contour; archeologists had likely discovered identical figures at Lascaux. *Women never draw the equivalent ideal,* she thought, and reached for her notebook. The movement alerted the storyteller's friend, who turned and pointed; grinning, the three mimed smiling universal peace offerings—Ma'am, we've removed our hands from the vehicle, we're backing off, no harm intended, peace—before tearing down the street.

2.

Marta adjusted the seams of the close-fitting denim. *Hermetically sealed and perspiring in my car, this is ridiculous,* she thought. Surely she could locate a place for breakfast along the main street. After releasing the safety belt and re-checking the emergency brake, she stuffed *The Battle for Djoun* into the canvas tote and swung open the door. A toasting blast of air outside easily bested the car's greenhouse interior.

Marta followed the direction of the storyteller and his rapt sidekick audience. Homeless men with homemade cardboard sign pronouncements—"A dollar short of taking over the world"—were nowhere to be seen, she noticed, and wondered if the city council, eyeing the dollars of happy tourists, had drafted a zero-tolerance policy.

The sign outside the O-K Café teetered awkwardly; the chrome music stand holding a tray-sized whiteboard promoted the daily special: *2 eggs any style, ham/bac/saus, tst, hash $3.99.* Marta could see no other options. Dry toast and tea would be fine anywhere, she suspected.

The O-K epitomized a style of restaurant that had passed out of fashion in big city centres long ago. The spaciousness alone would make the monthly rent prohibitive. A row of blue vinyl booth seating occupied the left wall, tables stood pell-mell in the middle, and on the right ran the O-K's social hub, a stretch of grey laminate counter where any customer on a stool faced a mirror, sundae glasses, milkshake and coffee makers, a metal rack holding single-serving cereal boxes, and a friendly middle-aged woman wearing an apron over a snug waitress uniform the pastel green of bygone hospital corridors.

The restaurant's oscillating fans and quiet invited her in. Marta guessed that the town's breakfast rush crested shortly after sunrise. A second music stand directed foot traffic: "Please Seat Yourself at a Clean Table." Marta crossed to a booth and slid in. The seat offered a full view of the restaurant and street.

The waitress broke from a conversation and strode to the kitchen's ordering window. To the woman's bellowed question—"Loon, will you pick up that single?"—Marta heard no answer.

Marta watched as Loon approached.

"Good morning, ma'am," the waitress said. "Did you see the special?"

"Yes, I did. An order of dry whole wheat toast and black tea, please. Thank you."

"Orange pekoe and wheat toast, that all?"

"A glass of water too, please. No ice, if that's not a problem."

"Happy to oblige, less work for me. White or brown?"

"Brown," Marta frowned at the woman's distractedness. "Thank you."

"It'll be back in two shakes." Marta heard the waitress call out the order: "Henry, stack of brown."

When Loon returned with a small metal teapot, Marta asked, "Do you have soy milk? The unsweetened kind would even be better." She was averse to being pigeonholed as a fussy special-needs urbanite, but the diligence of her diet represented a trickling source of pride. A wrong turn into bad habits began with one seemingly inconsequential choice.

"Creamers there on the table is all we've got."

"Thanks anyway."

Marta pulled the script and a pen from the bag. She reread the treatment and dragged a finger along the script's edge. The nail caught a page and she flipped the script open near midpoint.

"Here you go. Three shakes at most." The waitress slapped down a bill.

The toast was slathered with buttery goo. "Excuse me." Marta picked up the plate and raised it high. "I'm afraid this toast isn't dry."

"Well, I'll be." Accepting the toast, she placed the coffee pot on Marta's table. "I figure my messed up orders will reach the ceiling by the time my shift ends. Today's one of those days. I'd forget my head if it wasn't screwed on."

"I know it. We all have them."

Marta returned to the script.

DISSOLVE TO:

EXT. DJOUN - GATES - DAY

Riding their horses slowly toward the Djoun compound, Lady Swinburne and Doctor Potter formulate a plan.

LADY SWINBURNE

It is unholy, an evil from the depths of the Inferno.

DR. POTTER

(laughs)

My dear Lady, such feverish imaginings!
Too many years in the desert with these credulous superstitious pagans, I suspect.
As a man of science, I implore you to clear your mind and proceed rationally. Now is not the time to take leave of your good senses!

Swinburne halts the horse suddenly.

SWINBURNE

What do all your laws of science lead you to conclude? Pray tell, Potter, pray tell!

POTTER

This is wondrous strange, I grant that.
Without further investigation, however, I must stoop to base conjecture.

SWINBURNE

Be that as it may, Sir!

POTTER

You force me into a premature conclusion, Madam. But if you insist . . .
In place of your minions of Beelzebub, I suggest vestiges of a lost tribe. Local legend speaks of an ancient race of powerful warriors cast into exile for unspeakable sins.
It may well be there is fact at the basis for this fanciful mythology.

SWINBURNE

(laughs)

There are more things in heaven and earth, Doctor, than are dreamt of in your philosophy . . . Dear, in all honesty, your science sounds no better than my superstition."

POTTER

We are at sixes and sevens, my old friend.

SWINBURNE

No matter.
It is incumbent on us to lead these poor farmers and secure their continued safety.
They may not possess simon-pure souls, Doctor, but it is the obligation (in French) of our kind to care for them.
Without our leadership, they shall surely perish. Let us retire to my chambers to formulate a winning strategy.

Get thee to the Batmobile, Robin, Marta thought. *Shakespeare must be a godsend to hacks.*

At the gates they wait for an attendant. Swinburne is impatient.

SWINBURNE

I wonder where Abdul might be.

Marta flipped to the last page.

The waitress returned. "Bone dry," she said. "You one of them movie people in town?"

"Yes, that's me. Today's my first day up here on location."

"Lornette Spang—she's one of the waitresses here—was talking," the woman turned to check the order pick-up window, "she heard you people might be hiring on some extras."

"Certainly. In fact, there are several scenes that require extras." Marta patted the script knowingly.

"Do you need any experience? To be a movie extra, I mean." As she moved to pour coffee, Marta rattled the teapot's lid. "I did a commercial for OK New and Used up Penticton way last year. I played 'young mother buying a minivan.'" Marta watched Loon's paired quoting fingers, aloft like rabbit ears. "I'm Luna. Luna Kwakowsky. Maybe I'm too old?"

"Please to meet you. I'm Mar," Marta swallowed back "Sadie" as equal parts impulsive and foolhardy. "You'd be perfect, I'm sure." Luna looked well under thirty.

"Ha, that's nice of you. Mar, eh? That short for Margaret," the woman asked. "Martha?"

"Marta, actually, but Mar works best." Marta disliked abbreviated names. "Why don't you write down your number? On the back of the script is fine. I can pass it along to the Production Coordinator."

"Will do, thanks. And don't you worry about the bill, it's on the house." She grabbed the coffee pot but remained at the table. "We heard that Michelle Pfeiffer is staying up there at that fancy hotel at the Burrowing Owl winery."

Think smaller, Marta thought. "No comment. I really ought to go over the new script."

"Keep me in mind."

Marta nodded in reply and flipped to the final pages.

INT. SWINBURNE'S COMPOUND - NIGHT - MOMENTS LATER

Potter advances toward the alien hesitantly, palms open to show his peaceful intentions.

DR. POTTER

In the name of civility, stranger, I urge you to diplomacy.

The Alien hisses and crowds Potter into a corner. Lady Swinburne enters with stealth and watches events unfold. She holds a grain scythe.

POTTER

We are... We are men of Science. We must communicate!

As Potter stretches out a hand in welcome, the alien swells up and covers Potter to consume him in a frenzy. Lady Swinburne uses this opportunity for her assault.

LADY SWINBURNE

(rushing in)

To hell in swift dispatch, demon!

'*Get away from him, you bitch,' or its early nineteenth century equivalent*, Marta thought. *Obviously*.

The alien spews liquid from gaping wounds and shrieks in pain. Lady Swinburne commits to a final attack and the alien falls away from Doctor Potter, whose wounds are too severe to heal. Lady Swinburne rushes to him and places her face close. She is in tears.

POTTER

(whispering)

The eyes of science have been blind, Lady. Demons do indeed live.

SWINBURNE

(grabs his hand)

Reserve your breath, good man.

POTTER

I have loved you always, Harriet. Always.

SWINBURNE

Fear not, we shall commune again on the other side.

POTTER

Au revoir.

SWINBURNE

Au revoir.

Lady Swinburne turns to the doors of her chamber. They open and the few remaining villagers rush in. They stare horrified at the alien and then begin to chant Lady Swinburne's name in celebration.

Marta agreed that there would be little need for historical accuracy. In cut-rate movies like this desert dwellers in off-white robes would suffice; attention to actual details of national fashion was pointless, a costly indulgence. And the audience, as Jake and Lora had underscored, cared about cleavage, scary aliens, and gory action sequences, not fidelity to cultural history.

Marta waved to the waitress as she exited the booth. The woman strode to the till and handed Marta a scrap of paper. "They can leave a message if I'm not home."

3.

Marta gripped the wheel, poised to shift into gear but unsure about the next destination. With her lettered expertise rendered as useful as an expired coupon, she'd been stripped of qualifications. What menial tasks Lora had in mind, Marta couldn't guess; this time tomorrow, Lora might ask her to go on coffee runs or taxi studio dignitaries alongside Chaz. Perhaps. Errand-runner was such a distant cousin to the nerve-centre job she'd projected that it scarcely registered. Speculating if she'd swallow the insulting demotion, Marta saw herself on the Skytrain platform on the day of the studio interview, a living definition of a sinking feeling. Still, the ready silent answer now—"Definitely not, if only for the sake of saving face"—comforted her.

Idling moments later, mitigating factors weakened her resolve. While cramming clothes into a suitcase, hurriedly checking out, speeding toward the coast while spewing a cloud of *eat my dust*, and being well paid thanks to someone else's oversight—the easy choice—made perfect sense, Marta felt invested in the chance invitation and the radical change of pace. And backing out because of fizzled plans smacked of unadventurousness, a species of cowardice.

The prospect of staying at the Star-Lite for even two days sounded dreary nonetheless; she hadn't packed many books and always wrote in close proximity to a library, a real one. The all-expenses-paid summer holiday the production's legal counsel told Jake to offer also had a limited appeal—vineyards and orchards would quickly fade as interests, and reclining under an umbrella at a lake while buttered with sunblock looked no better than biding time in a darkened motel room. *Maybe it's time to revisit* Angel, she thought. While no respected critic named *Angel* an underrated masterpiece, it definitely overshadowed *Angel 4*; she could in similar fashion strive to guarantee that *The Battle for Djoun* became all it could be—not gold, but containing use-value nonetheless, like copper or zinc. Quality was quality, and serviceable B-grade ranked higher than *Mansquito*. The office weighed in too; frantic and quarrelsome, yes, but the overall Gemütlichkeit atmosphere refreshed with a tonic's effervescence.

Options existed, then. Marta backed up; touring around for a few hours would allow for productive brooding.

4.

For the unscheduled free day Marta challenged herself with an assignment: to wander without items on a to-do list. She deemed fretting and organizing irrelevant; she'd been tasked with arriving at a decision and well over half a day remained before Lora required the answer. Disappointed at the turn of events and apathetic about Lora's proposed choice, Marta guessed that being penned up with plans and schemes in room #10 would only squander time and breed resentment. As the solution gestated, she'd answer the beckoning of the valley's lazy bends and their powdery byways.

The habit of writing a few points in a notebook to outline the day's agenda was, as always, compelling; Marta resisted, tentative in her belief in the advantages of a break in orthodoxy. Still, she couldn't drive blind; she mimicked arbitrariness instead. About to signal a left turn for the sloping ersatz-Spanish main street of Osoyoos—a questionable master plan begun by one town council and abandoned by another—she accelerated directly onward, stopping at a roadside stand for cherries before approaching the low-volume border crossing. Her memory of Oroville, the region's flat farming hub on the American side of the border, wavered slightly. While overlaid with images of other small towns, the recollection of her grandmother struggling to change gears—"Cheese and crackers," she'd mutter at distressing grinding sounds—in the black interior of the shuddering red Chevy Nova while en route to the shopping bargains there possessed a photograph's detail.

The place hadn't grown much, though its economy still flourished with agribusiness; pallets and faded red plywood bins, fruit processing plants, farm machinery, sprinklers, and ditches bursting with weeds stood out as the only interruptions to the acres blanketed with trees laden with ripening fruit. Further south in higher altitudes the climate dried out further and business switched to resource extraction of another kind. Besides the region's searing winds, Marta recalled cattle pens and windowless slaughterhouses, stilt-legged truckers with plaid shirts and etched silver belt buckles proclaiming loyalty to truck brands, and an annual stampede with a parade of covered wagons, beauty queens, carnival rides, deep-fried batter, and widespread animal cruelty. She would drive no more than ten minutes southward today.

After another impromptu turn, Marta stopped for water—and toilet tissue, to replace the Star-Lite's supply, criminally flimsy yet seemingly manufactured from recycled bark—at the deserted supermarket where her grandmother had shopped for discounts decades before. Pulling over again minutes later, she spent a few silent and appalled minutes exploring a forlorn collectibles shop that specialized in settler cast-offs and grime-filmed ashtrays shaped like cowboy hats. Eyes watering, Marta tugged down a leg of her jeans, surprised that the snug fabric didn't amplify the impact of the heat. Further stops and starts to gawk at Americana struck her as ambitious as well as needless, especially since such a bounty of government-funded Points of Interest towered nearer to the Star-Lite.

Marta threw the final cherry pit out the window before approaching the return border crossing. There, a stiff-postured guard waved her through with a half complement of questions. *It must be my honest eyes and unthreatening face*, she thought.

She met the remaining destinations of the day with tinges of unwilled nostalgia. Before nosing the car up to the Anarchist Mountain lookout to ponder the immense blasted panorama with a congregation of RV travelers, Marta crossed the solid yellow line at an ice cream shop housed inside an imitation Dutch windmill. Standing a few paces from the menu fastened above the order window—the same hand-painted sign, although updated with taped-on cardboard adjustments to flavour offerings and of course prices—she concluded that besides the area's inevitable tourist- and retiree-targeting real estate build up, the only significant change appeared to be personal: a radically diminished tolerance for dairy products.

Following take-out lunch from a Thai restaurant in Penticton—eaten while seated at a willow-shaded picnic table facing Skaha Lake—Marta drove along gravel roads running toward railway tracks and farm houses and climbed higher on the banks for sips of wine flights at plateau vineyards with clever names. As much as she enjoyed the meandering, by day's end Marta felt satisfied that she'd seen enough. An additional week? None other than a sentence in a prison masquerading as a recreational paradise. *Just ask Robinson Crusoe*, Marta thought. Solitary confinement on the Island of Despair cannot be disguised by lush plant life and seductive beach sand. Whole days in the valley, heated stretches of hours—not a chance: Marta's limit for leisure was hardly a secret; and as mellifluous as the words looked on the page, *dolce far niente* didn't enchant her in the least.

Yes, she'd explain the situation to Mrs. Simms, pack, and speed away into the night. Chaz might pass by and report the vacated room to Lora. A few days later she'd send a terse, unrepentant email with instructions for payment, the relationship terminated.

5.

Marta pulled in front of #10 moments after the early evening sun—pretty but strange: fulvous, the yellow-brown of topaz—had dropped behind the mountains. The sky had turned darker than comfort for driving, but an exasperating search for the public library—simple pragmatism: the motel offered no computer access—delayed arrival. Eventually spotting the set of green awnings the gas station clerk described, she soon unearthed nothing about one of the script's co-authors. The second, however, kept busy: his name appeared promiscuously as a contributor to an extensive list of straight-to-discount-bin feature films as well as TV movies and apparently lacklustre episodes of short-lived series, the names of most Marta didn't recognize.

Marta noticed that the writer possessed talent of a diminished kind, adept—if that word fit—at churning out sequels and enfeebled formulas: science fiction, action, romantic comedy, holiday-themed dramas and issue-of-the-week specials. Dismayed, she read that he shared co-responsibility for *Ms. M.P.*, a ridiculous updating of *Mildred Pierce* she'd watched with condemning eyes late at night a few summers before. As visual and intelligible content it had struck her as depleted and sad, like a black and white photocopy of a Rothko canvas. Obviously, a predatory alien traipsing around in Lebanon circa 1825 wouldn't faze the screenwriter whatsoever; the man could cobble a script together during the office commute.

Marta removed the plastic DO NOT DISTURB sign she'd hung outside. The room was warm and as stale as before but undisturbed. She preferred to make the bed herself and avoid exposing the presence of sheets packed at Undre Arms.

After shucking off the canvas sneakers and jeans Marta stretched out on the bed and stared at venous ceiling plaster. Since no note had been jammed under the door and the phone's red nub of a message indicator light threw no light, Marta sighed: she'd have to swallow the reluctance to call Lora. And though that simple conversation hinged on a response—yes or no—Marta realized that the day in the valley had not resulted in one fateful answer; her mind vacillated instead. Marta looked once again at the door step: no envelope. Lora hadn't mentioned per diem at the production office, and Marta guessed she might have to pick up the cash-laden envelope in person. The nocturnal drive to town might steel her nerves; and by the time she reached for the glass doorknob at Joan's, a solid answer would have coalesced.

Marta recognized Chaz from the thudding knock. Retrieving the jeans, she said, "Hold on a moment, please."

"*Zdravstvuj*," he exclaimed as Marta swung open the door, "I brink you givt from Rossiya-Matushka." A donut sat atop the napkin resting on his outstretched palm. "They're scrumptious. Sour cream and chocolate. From a bakery run by a Russian Doukhobor family. Who knew? They have pyrahi and borscht too." He pinched his cheek. "Boy, I am going to pay."

"It's been years since I indulged." From the door frame Marta took in the scene. The cloak-like ambiance of a cloudless night, incandescent bulbs of Christmas-tree wattage, and fluttering moths now softened the glare and heat of their morning exchange. Traffic—an occasional flash of headlights trailed by a glowing slow-motion ray of red—was similarly transformed, subdued by insect chirps and the delicate rustling of breeze through leaves.

Chaz turned around to follow her gaze. "Yeah, it's nice, eh. No wonder strippers like soft lighting."

"You have a poet's eye, apparently." Marta felt the peculiar bloom of the moment vanish.

"So, is that a 'No'?" He coin-tossed the donut into the air; it landed perfectly in place.

"Actually, it's a 'Yes, thank you.' " Marta wrapped the corners of the napkin around the donut and clutched the packaged gift. Refusing would be impolite; she'd seal the donut's fate later. "Thanks again."

"Sure, no problem." Chaz extracted a beer can from a back pocket and lifted the tab. "So, I hear you were pissed about the script change."

"I'm surprised you heard."

"Any production is a small town, basically, so gossip's a fact of life, and our office is the information switchboard. Even the lowest of the low gets word eventually." He stepped back and sat—arms crossed, beer bottle wedged between thighs—on the hood of the rental.

"Would you like me to disengage the alarm?" Marta noticed that she'd crossed her arms as well, hip against the doorframe.

"Yeah, sure, or you could haul out a chair. I've been on my feet all day." She opted for the former. She expected he'd return to his room momentarily.

"Okay, where were we?"

"Change of plans."

"Right. The re-genrification."

"You people are fond of that word," she said. "I've never heard it."

" 'You people'?" Chaz's widespread arms encompassed miscellaneous crew at the Star-Lite. "We people make them up, of course. Every group has its jargon, right? You oughta know. I sat through enough seminars lorded over by self-involved gasbags, and their vocab made my ears bleed."

Marta smiled: outmanoeuvred. Naturally, she was no stranger to a slow rotation of fashionable terms imported from Europe that would be nonsensical only steps from campus: *Verneinung*, alterity, liminality, *méconnaissance*, aporia, space of abjection, opacity of the subject, regulatory discourses, Ideological State Apparatus. As with spices, she used them sparingly; she too had attended flatulent seminars.

"Anyway, TV's a different pile of bull." The hood proving unyielding, Chaz moved to lean at the driver's door. "It's cheaper and crappier, more bottom line too, basically Entertainment Product. And it's parasitic, right, like those knockoff designer purses you can get at the Chinatown night market: the script borrows—that means steals—ideas from better and box office big-performer feature films or recycles plots and characters from other successful TV programs of the moment and puts them in the mash-up blender. Sells it for cheap too. It's like when porno flicks capitalize on the names of multiplex movies. *Foreskin Gump* and *Hung Wankenstein*; *Shaving Ryan's Privates*, get it? They leech on to the trendiness of whatever they're borrowing from because they want to—" He drank from the can. "Ah, better. It's like when you mention that you're friends with someone famous. The connection makes you a celebrity by proxy, well kinda. Same deal with TV, sort of, but with cable the budget's way smaller. Cash in on somebody's else's success.

"So *Battle for Djoun*'s no different. Ready to shoot, but not even close to original. It's Cheez Whiz—factory fresh, yes, but with no socially redeeming value. Um, kinda like a forgery too . . . *Predator*, *Aliens*, *Star Wars*, even bits of *The English Patient*, *Pride and Prejudice* and that movie where Sally Field rescues her daughter in Afghanistan. I forgot *Outlander*. The script picks off lots of meat from that carcass. It's a 'dwarfs standing on the shoulders of giants' kinda deal."

"I suppose." Marta detected rationalization. "By the way, it's Iran, in the Sally Field movie. *Not Without My Daughter*. Possibly *Norma Rae* too?

"Sure, why not. Some anal Film Studies grad student could probably find the source of every single line."

"You're awfully cynical."

"Nope, not at all. I'm not writing or directing or really doing anything creative. I consider myself part of the production, like a secretary or a factory worker. If it was—or is that were?—1974 and we were—um, was?—talking about my job at the Ford plant assembling Pinto hatchbacks—a crap car if there ever was/were one—you wouldn't say, 'Oh, you're so cynical, knowing that your daily grind contributes to another ugly death trap being on the road.' No, you'd say, 'Wow, that gig's union,' or, 'Think you can get me on at the plant?' You're paid to deliver the goods on time and maybe under budget, and that's what you do. I don't think you have much of an idea what it's like to work in the real world."

"Thank you for the psychological profile." While hardly novel, the assessment stung. "You can call me old-fashioned if you want, but I'm invested in the longevity of a work. Why bother with so much effort only to arrive at *product* that winds up in a virtual landfill, like plastic junk from a dollar store? It's counter-intuitive." If Chaz knew about her own dabbling in junk he'd see the disingenuousness of the claim. Marta couldn't pin down her earnest stance on the matter; her responses bleated out abstractedly, in the spirit of debate.

"Okay, gotcha. If I had a job assembling crap plastic whistles that would end up in a dollar store, I could still say I was making something meaningful—someone buys it and plays with it and has fun and, oh, by the way, I've fed my family. That's not nothing. It doesn't all have to be *The Cremaster Cycle*, right?"

A man from #9 poked his head out, the glaring expression a perfect substitute for words.

Chaz stepped close to Marta. "Christ, chill man. It's not even close to eleven."

"We've just managed to get the twins to sleep," the man whispered. "The wife and I are grateful for the break."

"Okay, we gotcha, man. I hear ya. My sister has kids and says they're quarter-pint vampires that suck out her life force." The man closed the door gently. In low register Chaz said, "Christ, it's not like the Pope held a gun to their heads and screamed 'Procreate!'"

"I'll take this awkward moment as my cue to depart. Thanks again for the donut. I'd better meet with Lora before she disappears for the day. She's still there, right? We need to hash out if I'll be helping out tomorrow."

"Yeah, I'd say so." He checked his watch. "Oh, right. My car won't be ready by the morning, so I'll have to impose on you one more time."

"Okay, we'll see. You're in my debt now. Goodnight."

Experience Itself

I.

Sunken into a wilted lotus position at the centre of the bed, Marta massaged the tender underside of her bare foot. The muted television splashed irregular shapes on the walls of the otherwise unlit motel room, and as she slowly rotated a thumb along the puffed arch Marta felt her eyes drawn away from the broadcast—a cartoon breakfast cereal square dancing and singing, elfin smile set wide and spidery stick arms flailing for a convincing performance of glee—toward the stillness beyond the frame of the open door. The murky space past the asphalt lot might be siren-calling to a reawakening nocturnal instinct, but Marta's unlimber muscles, tendons, and ligaments wailed louder yet. Simply untying laces had been a chore; after removing the left shoe and sock she'd postponed the bother of the next foot until an indefinite later and chortled at the idea of sleeping through until morning half-shod and fully clothed, like the fiery-bearded vagrant she passed by on workday mornings en route to the campus-bound bus.

Never in her career years had she been so tired; she could imagine individual cells deep within her body howling, their microscopic brows furrowed and nostrils flaring in fierce outrage at the animated cereal square's infinite joie de vivre, calculation and bloodlust erupting from their tiny pounding hearts. *Factory workers in poor countries have every right to malign their bosses*, Marta thought, bonded in sisterhood with the truly oppressed for fleeting seconds.

Alongside religious zealots and tabloid devotees across the continent, Marta had long assumed Hollywood's legendary appetite for cocaine to be symptomatic of a bottomless moral vacuity. And yet after the grueling, eye-opening, and Industrial Revolution-like schedule of Day One—a trial by fire, not one minute under fourteen hours—another strictly utilitarian purpose had been revealed. If I continue on here, Marta concluded with resignation, sugar and caffeine, cocaine's legal surrogates, are going to become my new best friends. Neither sat in short supply at the production office; stockpiled chocolate bars were there for the taking.

Bleary-eyed and hunched over a cooling foot, she replayed scenes from the inaugural shift, peevish and silently castigating her imagination for being so blithely disconnected from servile, workaday actuality. While a reasonable ignorance of specific details of filmmaking had been made clear from the start, the surprise and dismay resulted from fathoming the inaccuracy's totality.

In the room's solitude she realized that if the day had not exactly pummeled her with a series of public humiliations and admonitions—the proverbial spanking in the parking lot surrounded by unsympathetic onlookers clucking their approval—the overall experience had been humbling nonetheless. Relief, such as it was, arrived in the form of awareness that the day's cautionary tales—conveniently sized and ready-made for Sunday school lessons: pride goeth before the fall, look before you leap, and so on—had played out in the wholly private arena of her consciousness. Through Lora or Jake's eyes Marta would have appeared no different than any other novice, charging ahead half-cocked and making wrong assumptions left and right. And for them the gaffes and apparent naiveté might have been endearing one minute and irritating the next, but never worse; her raw hubris and patent exceptionalism had been disguised by a professional skin of polite reserve.

Marta saw the distasteful truth, though. The queenly disposition galled her especially. She'd grossly inflated her worth and envisioned a lofty arrival, the rich aura of professional entitlement granting the power to select whatever she deemed suitable—like venerable Dame Such and Such dipping bejeweled manicured fingers into a box of exquisite chocolate truffles. The pearl before swine snobbery looked grotesque, laughable: no to this and indubitably no to that, but perhaps—just maybe—she might dabble here, infuse one cog in the movie-making machine with a patina of unadulterated quality by virtue of a singular gift—penetrating intellect, courtesy of top notch genetics and impeccable ivory tower grooming.

Eyes squeezed shut, Marta saw herself in a sideshow: ladies and gentlemen, feast your eyes on the philosophunculist extraordinaire!

2.

The day came nowhere close to meeting her expectations. Nor had the discussion with Lora the night before. That exchange had turned out to be less a negotiation than a tipping domino trail of firm negations uttered between cackles—"No way, Jose," "Good luck with that one," "Ha, out of the question."

Marta had knocked on the front door of Joan's of Oliver happy with her resolve—at last—to lend a hand to the production, but the ensuing conversation only clarified the resounding difference between objective reality and Marta's fantastic version of it as well as the total unionized rigidity of the enterprise from root to flower.

In no time she'd learned that she lacked seniority of any kind and that scholarly credentials counted for naught; and without any professional affiliation—paid membership in one of several unions, that is: another prerequisite Lora and Jake might have mentioned at the studio—she possessed no real access to the key positions into which she'd generously slotted herself; neither here nor there, she floated, a non-entity. Marta had suggested working with words, naturally, "doing rewrites," or adding lines and even scenes in the interest of an alchemical elevating of the leaden script.

"Thanks, but no thanks," Lora had replied brightly.

When, grasping for straws, she mentioned Script Supervisor, Lora—all business now, the mask of affable informative hostess secured away—had pounced on the idea: "No go with that, sweetie. You see, she's already in place, hired on ages ago. And, besides, do you even know what a Script Supervisor does?" Marta didn't, perfectly aware that the only responses she could give, "Not exactly" and "Supervises the script," would sound preposterous, so she held her tongue and waited for Lora, whose face appeared avid with ready answers.

The phone rang exactly then, the timing from a drawing room farce. Quick to answer, Lora swiveled the chair and slid open a filing cabinet drawer. She handed Marta a thin volume of stapled paper.

After reading the cover—*On Da Set: A Guide 4 Da Green*, which featured a hand-drawn daisy character wearing hip-hop pendants and opaque sunglasses; the hipster-flower crashed bull-like through an old-fashioned film set—Marta turned to the table of contents, not alphabetical but a listing of positions ranked by importance. Chaz's gloomy account of his cur status had basis in fact, she saw: PA stood at the very bottom of the sheet. She flipped to the guide's mid-point:

"Script Supervisor: The script supervisor (aka, continuity script supervisor), is responsible for many key tasks before, during, and after a film's production. A script supervisor's main duty: to document all details surrounding movie scenes—as they are filmed. That means keeping track of everything from (1) the types of lenses cameras operator uses to (2) the exact positions of the performers. A script supervisor also marks lines through the script to keep the director up to date about how many of the scenes have been completed, or *covered* in film speak."

I'm way off the mark, Marta had thought. Accustomed to being regarded as knowledgeable as well as to feeling competently informed, Marta felt a blood rush of embarrassment at Lora's explanation of the job by proxy.

Only later did a fallback occur to her—the flash of insight arriving via the all-purpose adage about life, lemons, and lemonade: she'd branch out and learn a new, possibly valuable skill set. Failing that, a consultancy position, something not mentioned in *On Da Set*, held promise if only because the uniqueness appeared to excuse it from being subject to territorial union legalities. Script consultant, creative consultant: were those possibilities?

One might be, she guessed, although any screenwriter would resent an interloping amateur with a snob's tilted nose and delusions of literary grandeur.

Once finished with the call, Lora preempted Marta's case-pleading with a palatable suggestion. "Look," she began, features arranged to appear tentative and pensive even though any child could see Mom's mind was set, "before you vote on anything, why don't you show up tomorrow morning and see how we operate. You can hang at HQ, take the temperature of the place, inhale the funky air of the three-ring circus up close. We'll get Chaz to ferry you around, take you out to set, et cetera," she said. Lora's chirpy afterthought, "It'll be fun, like visiting Disneyland," contained the false inflection of a camp counselor's prediction for an unpopular and skeptical child that "things might just work out, you'll see."

Suffused with worry, Marta nonetheless agreed. In the jutting angle of Lora's jaw she'd perceived a dare, an unasked for challenge. A hard kernel of schoolgirl inside her understood that backing down meant shame and cowardice; without thinking, she met the taunt. *Okay, pile on the degradation*, she thought, unclear about the nature of her victory.

"Sure." Her ego smarted from being relegated to the sidelines and deemed burdensome babysitting material for harried Chaz. "I'll see you bright and early tomorrow."

She recognized a Hobson's choice: she could scarcely stamp her precious diva feet, storm off set, and cause the production to fold into chaos: as a non-essential, she could hole up at the Star-Lite in the morning and wait there in vain until sunset for a pleading call, or a concerned knock on the door with an urgent messenger—couriering four words: "We need you, please"—standing outside. A one-shift experience, then. If unpalatable, she'd be packed and ready to slip away without explanation.

3.

The promised visit to Disneyland turned out to be eventful—a complex obstacle course of errands and tasks, in fact—but altogether uninteresting. Throughout, nostalgia for the classroom had appeared, unbidden like a sneeze. Marta had held that feeling at bay, convinced she suffered from nothing other than culture shock.

The production office's steep learning curve related to connecting names and jobs and positions on the rigid hierarchy to phone voices and a parade of faces stopping by, and Marta began to reconsider an earlier upbeat commitment to climbing it: dedication to the summit of Everest could be construed as heroic; ascending a mountain of rubble could not.

Before noon, she'd been introduced—"____, this is Marta," as though her name alone, like Charo's, would suffice to explain character, value, relevance, and purpose—to various brusque department heads and their careerist assistants, as well as to a throng of carpenters, teamsters, couriers, delivery men, electricians, PAs, and a motley assortment of shaggy-haired, instantly forgotten others who dropped in and called with questions, concerns, requests, complaints, or emergencies—all urgent and in need of immediate response.

And she'd sat quietly in the SUV with studio reps and mysterious higher ups as Chaz, adopting a subdued facts and figures delivery persona, drove and conversed between airport, sets, and office. Between the pick ups and drop offs, she'd assisted on runs for office supplies (fans, markers, paper, power cords, and a white board, as well as coffee, snacks, bottled water and diet soda, fruit, and mounds of chocolate) and answered the insistent phone several times, confident that she could at least intone the secretarial phrase, "Please hold, ____ will be available in a moment," with panache. Even that last, technically a no-brainer, had proven onerous; her lack of familiarity with every member of the crew seemed only to inflame the commandeering personalities emitting from plastic receivers.

The secretarial function had been thrust at her throughout the day, as though she looked the part. When one man, an imperious and pushy extras wrangler with a cell phone perpetually clamped to a portly face, had instructed Marta—"Hey there, honey, would you . . ."—to fix him a coffee, Chaz, a godsend, had intervened and pointed toward the kitchen set up: "Help yourself, man" within earshot and "Douche pile" thirty seconds later. Soon after, he'd explained to Marta "who's gotta kiss whose ass."

Marta learned too that a short-term non-unionized consultancy offered a single perk: practical exemption from the Byzantine system of obligations and favours. *I've already encountered enough of that for a lifetime*, she'd thought with relief, frowning at the image of pallid, under-exercised buttocks beneath Tenure Committee woolens.

4.

Marta's eyes regained focus when a mobile blur interrupted the darkness. Chaz stood at the doorframe.

"Knock, knock," he stage-whispered. "Wow, you're pretty zoned out, eh?"

"That would be an understatement." Marta swung her legs to the edge of the bed in one gymnastic movement. "You frightened me. I guess leaving the door ajar is an open invitation."

"Don't give it a thought, I'm a pussycat."

"That's reassuring, though I'd guess that any psychopath worth his salt doesn't announce gruesome intentions up front." Aiming for lighthearted banter, fatigue had landed her nearer to paranoid accusation. Overworking always brought out an inner scold.

Without further word, Chaz walked into the room. "For you." He handed Marta a white envelope.

The quiet solemnity bore into Marta, who anticipated a letter of termination: "Attention Professor Spëk: We regret to inform you . . ." The man's face still shone with moisture, she noted, and now smudges here and there of dehydrated red sauce, likely from the over-salted pizza the office had ordered hours earlier, lent him a boyish appeal.

Chaz waited, leaving Marta no chance for a private viewing. She tore open the envelope and withdrew an illustrated birthday card. The caption exclaimed "Redneck Push-Up Bra" in large copper foil letters; in the foreground of the accompanying photograph a buxom woman stood arms akimbo and wore a homemade brassiere of short ripped strips of pewter duct tape. Befitting the cliché, the woman—who in real life would be called trailer trash—scowled, lustily gap-toothed and plastered with makeup that coarsened her in such a way that a career in subsistence prostitution seemed probable. Naturally, her brown hair was bulbous with beer can rollers. She stood in front of the aluminum screen door of a battered mobile home; a lit cigarette protruded from the corner of plum lips. The only item missing: a rolling pin clutched as a weapon.

"I thought of you when I saw it."

A surreal puzzlement washed over Marta. Here she breathed, perched on the side of a soft mattress in a no-frills motel room late at night after fourteen hours of work at a strange demi-job in a remote location where an odd man had just handed over a bizarre card months from the date on her birth certificate while making a ridiculous and insulting association that she utterly failed to comprehend.

Stalling, Marta pretended to read the card's interior punch line, *Why?* resounding silently. What possible connection could Chaz have made between this card and her? She tallied its qualities—the stacked levels of crude humour, the woman's pendulous breasts and cartoon Appalachian aesthetic, the overall cheapness—and found no commonality.

"Should I ask?"

"Huh?

"Well, to be honest, this is baffling." Watching him, she struggled with the degree of tact required and whether to return the offering. "It's not my birthday and that leads me to conclude that you see similarities between me and this, this vulgar stereotype, and . . ."

Chaz pursed his lips but made no move toward an explanation.

"Let me put it this way," Marta continued, eyes on his. "If I gave you a card that, for instance, featured an unattractive computer nerd wearing one of those novelty caps that holds two cans of beer, and then said I was reminded of you, wouldn't you find it just a touch insulting? I mean, what purpose could there be to giving someone a 'thinking of you' gift card that could only ever be interpreted as an insult? Or am I missing something?"

"Oh, wow. I guess I'm a 'Don't look a gift horse in the mouth' kinda guy."

"Well, there's that. I'd say I belong to the 'Beware of Greeks bearing gifts' camp."

"Huh, I thought that saying only applied to life during wartime." Uncomfortable, he adjusted his cap. "So I get it, Herr Doktor Freud. Your job is all about interpreting layers of symbols and that, so you read into things when there's no reason to."

"I see. So, the association between Appalachian Annie-Lou here"—like an auctioneer's assistant, she held the card up for a full view—"and me is random and therefore means nothing? You might have just as easily picked a 'Happy Birthday, Father' card or a 'Get Well Soon' with a photograph of a Hawaiian sunset or a fuzzy kitten and thought of me?" Though Marta felt no actual ire, a biting tone intruded virally into her sentences. "Remind me to decline an invitation to exchange Christmas presents. Or next time, if there is a next time, that is, you may want to choose something with flowers on it. It's a safe bet; women understand bouquets. Or perhaps there's something I've misunderstood and you can enlighten me? Dadaist humour is a bit much for me to navigate at this hour."

Chaz started to speak, but stopped, pressing an index finger to his lips. He pried the card and envelope from Marta's fingers and ripped them into chunky confetti while taking histrionic strides backwards and exiting the room. Curious, Marta watched as his clenched hand reappeared and knocked on the frame.

Marta grinned as she realized Chaz's ploy. "Hello?"

"Hey, professor. I was on my way to my room when I noticed your open door. How's it going?" Chaz wore a theatrically false and endearing smile. "Since we didn't have a spare minute to stomp around on set today, I thought we might do that now. What do you think?"

"Pardon me?" Marta relaxed, admiring the man's effort. "Now? As in, leave my room and stumble around in the dark after completing a fourteen-hour shift?"

"Bingo and bingo. Desert air, cool wind in your hair, a mini road trip, like that old Eagles song: who could say no to that?"

"You can't be serious."

"C'mon, it'll be fun. I can make you a coffee or something if you need a little pick-me-up."

"Burning the candles at both ends isn't really my, well, *modus vivendi*." Marta studied the shifting expressions on Chaz's thrill seeker's face.

"I'm not sure what that means, but, anyway, we'll be back within an hour. I promise it'll be relaxing. You'll sleep better."

The man's enthusiasm seethed potently. "Why not?" Marta imagined that an alert mind could kick-start spent limbs. "You have some tomato paste on your chin, by the way."

"I'll be back in ten." He rubbing his chin with a shirtsleeve. "I need to change out of these clothes."

"See you then. Shall I?" Marta's gaze drifted toward the paper litter.

"Allow me."

5.

When Chaz returned just five minutes later, Marta noticed that he'd traded the day's black jeans for a less faded pair; the black T-shirt featuring yellow lettering, "Bacon is My Fragrance," led her to conclude he favoured duplicate purchases.

"I'll drive, okay?"

"That's a problem, sorry. The rental agreement's for one driver."

"Driving is part of my job, so I'm excellent. Bend the rules a bit? Less tiring for you too."

"This once, alright." A head-on crash in the dead of night seemed remote.

The breeze that passed through the car grew moister but only slightly cooler and, Marta recognized, Thanksgiving savoury with grass stalks and sagebrush the further they drove from the irrigated orchard flats. Marta peered outside. Except where the twin headlight beams on the highway shone, little detail flourished, only road shoulders and the silhouette of trees—and, later, untended scrubland, choppy lake water, and fenced rolling fields—scarcely discernible from the night sky.

"I read somewhere that for every kilometer one exceeds the speed limit, the probability of an accident rises two-fold," she said, having read nothing of the kind.

"Really?" Chaz accelerated slightly, features lit and exaggerated by the glowing red console display. "Interesting, I read something by Aldous Huxley once: 'Who lives longer? The guy who takes heroin for two years and dies, or a man who lives on roast beef, something, something, till ninety-five? One passes his twenty-four months in eternity. And all the years of the steak guy are lived only in time.' Relax, ma'am, I've never even had a fender bender."

Marta returned to the barely revealed landscape. Though she could pinpoint her fatigue—muscles heavy, eyes dry, thoughts cluttered—the night cover energized her.

Intently focused on the road's frequent curves, Chaz didn't ask questions or unreel anecdotes. At the crest of a long hill, he slowed, leaning close to the windshield. "We're nearly there. I think so anyway."

Ordinarily comfortable with silence, Marta now sensed the need for conversation and struggled with a suitable topic. She glanced at the radio, but Chaz had switched it off pulling away from the Star-Lite. Only shop talk, which she hoped to avoid, presented itself.

"So, what are your plans in the industry?" The words sounded flat, perfunctory.

"Let's not talk about work, okay?" he said. "It's depressing, and besides I'm kind of into this drive. My pupils are dilated; I think darkness triggers adrenaline production or something. I'm alert like a jaguar or a blind person, you know what I mean?"

"Yes, we could stop and hunt prey."

"Or howl at the moon." He glanced out the side window. "Well, if there was one. Sometime, though, I'll tell you all about my first job in the business, my foot-in-the-door story. At Cine/wurst Adult Studios. We had to pronounce it German-style,

Cinevurst. 'U dollar sign A' was part of the name too, which no one knew how to pronounce. Sounds sleazy, eh?"

"Yes, and definitely more intriguing than mine." Involving a fatal mid-semester coronary and a suddenly open tenure-stream position, her success story made listeners uncomfortable, as though she'd cheated and personally served the man Mormon Tea to induce cardiac arrest and get ahead. Aside from that, she lacked riveting anecdotes. Graduate school tribulations invited only yawns outside of the ivory tower, Marta knew firsthand. And she felt unprepared for a public launch of her other rite of passage stories. Sadie's adventures in pop culture would remain in cold storage for the time being.

Chaz slowed at a stop sign. "Weird to have this out here in the absolute middle of nowhere." Other than the immediate road and shoulders of dry tall grasses, they might be in deep space. "A reassuring outpost of law and order, I guess."

Marta, regretting the weak depth of field, peered outside for the furtive eyes of roving coyotes. Lulled by gentle bumps and turns and contented with the conversational hiatus, she leaned into the door and let drowsy eyes cease their work.

6.

Shortly after returning from Sadie's abortive trial-run at the Boise conference, Marta had been struck by a continued restlessness as well as the inadequacy of the explanatory metaphor she'd come to use—Idaho hadn't been a pressure valve, nor she a machine with a noxious buildup of steam. As for "an itch to scratch," that she kept. Allowing time for the model description to coalesce, Marta settled on the tried-and-true in the meantime: figuratively, she was all dressed up with nowhere to go.

And while conceding that an appearance as Sadie could be accomplished with ease in an off-the-grid city destination, or, even better, in the vast suburb spillover, the chance that she'd run into a colleague—or student: of the thousands she'd taught, surely restaurants had hired a handful or two—further cemented an already entrenched reluctance. The solution would be longer term, she concluded, paying closer attention to posters in departmental hallways and email announcements for conferences at universities in Trieste and Honolulu. She'd hold Sadie in suspension; and for now, of course, the unavoidable demands of teaching, grading, and publications took precedence.

The Benefit of Risk, about which she wrote a hostile review that lambasted the author's methodology ("paltry slapped atop abysmal," the exact wording), would have been remembered as a demoralizing waste of paper if it hadn't sparked the *Holiday Archetype Personality* manuscript—and provided Sadie with temporary new lodgings.

The author's thesis—a loud, dizzying barrage of MBA business-speak about venture capitalism coupled to a simple-minded, fascistic notion of evolutionary triumph—read as laughable drivel, but in its message of risk-taking she'd felt a timely nudge. "Starting Today, Nice Guys Don't Finish Last™," one of the author's registered motivational speaker refrains, managed to give Marta pause.

Over three months worth of weekends, Marta signed out volumes of well-used *O Magazine*—refusing altogether the purchase of a lone issue—and a complement of miscellaneous self-help and popular psychology bestsellers from the public library. She pored over the lot (amongst their number *Nice Gals Finish Last?*, written by someone with an alleged Ph.D. from a university she'd never heard of, and numerous variation-on-that-theme women's magazine articles about breaking through the glass ceiling), pilfered the flimsy ideas, and redirected them; and she mimicked their tone, vocabulary, and penchant for pithy coinages for use in the extra-curricular project. Marta dabbled at the venture exclusively at home. While not a secret she'd take to the grave, neither did it represent the sort of prize endeavour worth mentioning to colleagues.

Marta realized with surprise that the actual construction—breaking the book into segments, wholesale invention of plausible ideas for a pitiful audience—had not surpassed her abilities. Honing the jocular sales pitch tone became a true hurdle. The visionary's persona required art; being neighbourly, trustworthy, folksy, and yet authoritative in print was no mean accomplishment. Marta persisted, eventually producing an acceptable facsimile. If she sent the manuscript out, months would pass before a reply; at that point and with a letter of unqualified offer, she'd have time to iron the patter smooth.

She judged the end product to be literary fool's gold. A travesty or else a vapid parody of the genre, it also looked no different from cynical *product.* From the title onward, the thin manuscript existed as a con for the gullible, one whose very purpose transformed Marta from being a last-place-finish nice gal to a predator of the weak and foolish; both roles lacked in appeal. Pangs of apprehension pulsed across her abdomen.

In the ruminative period between completing the manuscript and sending it off, she left the sheets in plain sight. Alone on the vintage yellow Arborite kitchen table, the papers and their implication could not be avoided. That constant visual cue forced a thoroughly deliberated choice: to act or not to act, that was the age-old question she returned to. Over those three weeks—a gestation period, she came to think of it—Marta toyed with diagnosis. She viewed *The Holiday Archetype Personality* as a shameful mutant, a monstrous birth of a disturbed intellect, a consequence of being overworked, living proof of a bookish woman's variant of a nearing-middle-age crisis, a symptom of an unhealthy immersion in a competitive professional environment, and an empty lark. At last, she chastised herself—*give it a rest.*

Tiring of one's own quirks and neurotic tendencies was as easy as getting fed up with those of someone else, Marta believed, convinced of the drawbacks of the over-examined life. Wedged between narcissism and abject self-loathing, she extracted some comfort with the trick of using self-knowing to undermine her internal drive to fret and over-analyze. As far back as kindergarten her mother had chided her for "making a mountain out of a molehill." Perhaps Marta didn't possess self-awareness at all; she'd only internalized Dianne's point of view. Sensing imminent, paralyzing uncertainty, Marta focussed on action.

From those public library books she also selected a remote publisher whose tawdry range of bus reading and disposable bold-typeface titles—*Must Love God!: Confessions of a Teenage Jesus Freak*; *The Coming Panic (& How to Profit from It)*; *Marriage Secrets of the Alpha Delta Pi Sorority*; *Just Pray No: Finding True Love and Stopping Relationship Addiction Syndrome*; *The Oneida Community Diet*—aligned perfectly with the market niche of the project. And if Apate+Global Publications of St. Petersburg, Florida eventually sent a kindly-worded rejection, she would file it away in the home desk's Correspondence: History folder and recycle the manuscript. The entire effort would then be remembered as an ignoble experiment; and she'd forever consider *The Benefit of Risk* so complete a failure that even an idea it had inadvertently spawned amounted to four minutes of chewing for the paper shredder.

Marta included sufficient return postage. Rejected or not she wanted the manuscript secure in her possession, disposal of the body always a crucial point.

The book's concept unfolded easily, simplicity necessarily the foundation. Intricate systems or any ideas that made demands, she'd discovered, were not part of the best selling self-help author's stock of attributes. The lost, curious, or dejected didn't care for and would not read Judith Butler syntax. Simple yet pithy—the trusty voice of common sense—became key, preferably with the promise of thundering Shakespearian or biblical profundity—*love thy brother as thy self*; *to thine own self be true*—but stripped of the antique, off-putting language, of course.

"If every person has a favourite holiday and a seemingly natural affinity for it, that's because holidays evolved in response to archetypal human traits," she wrote in the enthusiastic letter to the publisher, deciding against an exclamation point in the draft's final edit.

The two-pager explained the basic schema—Halloween as Dionysian, Rabelaisian, festive, anarchic; Easter as introspective, melancholic, Thanatos-oriented, and so on. Before sounding too unappealingly academic and high-minded, or as flaky as a kaftan'd Santa Fe Jungian mystic draped in turquoise healing stones, the letter transitioned from the speculative overview toward what the Director of Sales would expect: practical, tangible, mass market, and salable applications. *HAP*'s qualities, she hoped, would jump of the page as fresh, relatable, and roundly marketable.

Honing the pitch, Marta zeroed in and highlighted the zodiacal parallels: how each individual matched a basic type and possessed, moreover, an *adjunct disposition*, à la Aquarius rising, that could be calculated with ease. Readers could find self-improvement too. For these seekers, new awareness could lead to informed, perhaps life-altering decisions about career and romance. For good measure she added an Enneagram-ish healthy lifestyle component (yes, the functional Halloween archetype can be attained, and the commonplace dysfunctional kind might, with steady effort naturally, be rehabilitated) and provided an example of the romance tie-in: a Halloween person with Christmas rising ought to stand way clear of an Easter type, dysfunctional or otherwise.

"HAPpiness in Your Grasp!" the bankrupt, virtually meaningless tag-line mentioned in the letter, eventually appeared on the book's back cover. Typing it, she'd imagined the phrase appearing on a trademarked cosmetics ad, as empty and alluring as a bubble.

On a par with the zodiac or tarot cards, the concept seemed sensible enough, especially if mental interrogation demanded mere circumstantial proof. Marta had heard people describe themselves as being a Christmas person or as loving Halloween. Some, she figured, would be reassured about the cosmic and fateful explanation for that fondness: "Oh goodness, no way, we're both Easters!"

While polishing the hopeful soft sell, Marta ran into a snag: what name to sign?

Clearly, the wrong choice would be Marta Spěk, Ph.D. Besides the obvious reasons—the manuscript's appalling bad faith, the titanic lack of merit—Marta understood that any faculty trolling the mass market in unabashed pursuit of commercial success would be regarded as ethically compromised and sullied, equivalent to a monk on a talk show circuit or hawking knives on a shopping channel. Not that she would be publicly shamed—she was no Hester Prynne and, in fairness, only a handful of her colleagues could be labeled dour Puritans. Even so, Marta freely believed she'd detect the sulphurous tang of smug unspoken judgment—*At what price tawdry fame, whore?*

Until Sadie's reappearance, Marva Longknife and Hortensia Propp—names courtesy of a random literary name generator website—rivaled one another high on the shortlist. Stepping off the campus-bound bus one morning, she discarded them. Sadie glimmered perfectly, of course. Marta had come to view Sadie as a fond middle name, a part of her complete identity, if never used. When the time arrived to append a family name to Sadie, Lightbody materialized, like a stubborn memory disinterred by a hypnotist. The name's unthreatening and airily visionary undertone sounded right for *HAP*, and when Marta thought of the faint but sinister echo with Lucifer, she judged it a weird coincidence, one nobody would spot.

Sadie Lightbody made her first public appearance as a signature. For an authentic touch, Marta used a left hand to sign Sadie's name. Sadie would remain unlettered, Marta decided, street wise and intuitive rather than book smart, a distant cousin of *Angel*'s Mae.

With the adoption of a new pen name, Marta thought that a laissez-faire, just-do-it attitude would serve best. The exotic and reckless choice had a singular appeal: it was so atypical. She resisted the mores of civility—good will, integrity, sincerity, honesty—in favour of the wild, nature-sanctioned amorality of *The Benefit of Risk*: capitalize on the thoughtless organicism of the market, survival and dominance of the fittest, and so on. That bracing shift in perspective gave her permission to drop the manuscript in the department's Mail Out basket.

Apate+Global's letter of acceptance stressed the publisher's commitment to Sadie's enterprising vision. Later emails also recycled words—monetize, incentivizing—and the phrase "capitalize on holiday buying season opportunities" with machine regularity. A+G rushed the manuscript to print, though not before first trimming the "fat," material the editor had drawn Xs through: arrows to cutting felt pen remarks on the margins identified problems: "obscure" and "$2 words" and "egghead." Marta insisted on not making the changes; seeing the relative truth in the adage about leopard spots, she replied to say that market-readiness ought to be left in the hands of A+G's in-house editorial team.

Before signing the contract Marta explained the need for anonymity. Pseudonyms were a dime a dozen in this industry of lifestyle experts, the Spirituality and Self-Improvement Editor told her over the phone. The press accepted Sadie Lightbody, and both sides agreed that Ms. Lightbody's chronic aversion to public appearances added mystique. The seclusion would be good for business—millennia worth of seers had taught the public to expect a masked sibylline cave dweller, or at least an introvert with a great reluctance to bathe in limelight.

A+G updated her with emails about the book's "cleaning up" over the buying season. By late spring the product run flatlined. Not uncharacteristic, *Holiday Archetype Personality* circulated fleetingly, a flash in the pan—her mother's phrase, dredged up unexpectedly. Marta felt tugs of sadness and relief with the subsiding of Sadie's presence on the popular culture landscape. However many barriers between the limelight and herself she'd insisted on manufacturing, Marta couldn't deny enjoying degrees of its luxurious warmth.

Even at moments of ethical entanglement—reading but never daring to compose replies to aching letters from Carol S. in Atlanta or Shirley V. (hailing from Milk River, a town in Alberta so small that Marta had opened an atlas to confirm its existence)—she pinpointed tingles of pleasure upon receipt of letter bundles and forwarded emails that arrived with requests from A+G to reconsider a publicity tour. Amidst deep sighs and muttered complaints about the effort, *the lady doth protest too much, methinks* never slid far from her tongue's tip.

Marta didn't succumb to the temptation of taking Sadie Lightbody on the road. Savouring the idea of the adventure was satisfactory enough.

A+G sent word about the "mother of all PR events" for a contingent of their authors, the Sacramento Psychic & Well-Being Lifestyles Fair. Like all other colossal opportunities, Marta turned it down as recklessness incarnate: one oversight, a single random moment would tear down her house of cards. The Fair's coinciding with the semester break wormed into her brain; she flew to San Francisco, splurged on a sporty coupe (asking, in Sadie's stead, for royal blue, but settling for black), and wandered around, an anonymous face in a teeming crowd of believers.

If the Floridian publicist had exaggerated the splendour of the gathering, she'd been accurate about the enormity. Wandering through aisles of beeswax-scented booths Marta emoted erratically, astounded by the complex interplay of hope and despair. Crystals, herbs, oils, cards, texts, dolls, rune-inscribed stones, Psychic Answers 100% Guaranteed, zodiac forecasts, each a curative proffered before a staggering—and apparently endless—litany of woe: heartache, addiction, cancer, depression, curses, bad luck, and worse karma. Stretched out table after table, Marta saw, lay evidence of the human condition. *Sadie Lightbody will not be joining the fray*, Marta had thought. No contrarian voice piped up to debate.

7.

"You know, I was thinking it over and I dunno." Chaz reached over to nudge Marta's shoulder. "Hello, you there? Marta?"

"Reverie." Marta refocussed, unsure whether she'd fallen asleep. "Sorry. But I have mentioned that I am not really accustomed to fourteen hour shifts, yes? You were saying?"

"Never mind, it was no big deal."

The rushing air sent pocket currents of pine and coolness through the cabin. They had traveled in silence on an empty road for long minutes when Chaz said, "Crap." He pumped the brake pedal and made a sudden turn right. "Man, almost missed it. Again." The lights shone on a gate. Behind it, a two-track roadway sliced into dry grass fields. "Just a sec." He pushed open the door. "Things look so different in the dark."

Insects flew into the beams cast by the headlights. Marta watched a dust cloud settle as Chaz untethered the gate and returned to the cab.

"Hold on, it's bumpy from here on in. Do you want to drive down the hill or hike it?

"Let's hike." Marta would have chosen the other option if Chaz had slowed to a reasonable pace.

"Deal." He braked and shifted into Park.

Marta searched outside for lights. "There's no one here." The headlights illuminated the road's compressed dirt tracks and another periphery of dry grass. "I guess that's not really necessary."

"There should be. 'Budgetary considerations,' maybe." He swung open the door and stepped outside. "Safer here too. It'd be a different story if we'd pulled up in the city."

"Will that drain the battery," Marta asked. She listened for crickets and heard only the cooling engine's pinging.

"It'll be fine. Otherwise we'll be stumbling around in pitch black. And that's an accident waiting to happen."

"Coyotes could be prowling."

"Another reason to keep the lights on. Let's get a move on."

Surefooted, Chaz strode ahead and followed the fading path of light generated by the rental. The beams vanished as they descended; Chaz brought out a metal flashlight. After a Boy Scout salute, he said, "Be prepared."

Still walking at a dedicated pace Chaz stretched a hand back; Marta accepted the assistance and clutched his thick wrist.

"Oh," Marta said, tread unsteady on the soft loose ground, "I couldn't see this from the road." She noticed the partial echo of their footfall as well as of her own voice. In the weak light the pit lost definition; Marta imagined them as nocturnal explorers surveying the strange barren vastness of the Barrington Crater. *The blackness of eternal night encompassed me*, she thought, remembering, though never admiring, Poe's peculiar brand of gothic melodrama.

Watchful of eroding gravel edges, Marta soon breathed regularly, suffused with relief when the road flattened out; cracking an ankle at the bottom of a dark pit was no one's idea of fun. She relaxed her grasp on Chaz, who slowly circled like a lighthouse beacon and cast rays toward the pit's far reaches. The revelations wavered spectrally: at medium distance rocky piles and conveyor-belted machinery that decades back had carried industrial goods from A to B. Senses alert though hardly superhuman, Marta found the scene—derelict equipment, blurry weeds, argentine flashes of darting animal eyes (rabbit, owl, groundhog?), awesome shroud of sky, and resounding silence—eerie, even otherworldly, and not frightening.

Situated at the base of a cliff, the partial spacecraft commanded attention. Marta raised her brows, impressed by the effect created by the flashlight's beam on the low-luster surface, the tent-fabric skin like a stretched latex glove swabbed with creosote; the jutting mechanisms registered as foreboding and potent, just as evil should be.

Chaz tossed the flashlight underhand toward Marta. "Crap, sorry about that. Take a look, I'll wait here."

Marta retrieved the flashlight from the basin's floor of gravel crumbs and wiped it clean on the denim. She aimed the light toward the craft and traced a path toward her feet: the way was free of impediments. Camera-ready and crew-proof, she supposed.

She looked back at Chaz, whose hand now cupped his mouth. The man's smoking didn't surprise her. Donuts, candies, cigarettes, coffee: a sybarite as far as a future gastroenterologist would be concerned, she surmised, only half-serious. Or a case of maladaptive oral fixation. An object always hovered near Chaz's fun-loving mouth. Like the zodiac Freud had his uses, Marta had found, especially when applied to others. Herself, she'd been labeled as anal retentive at least a few times, though she preferred a pathology-free descriptor like well-organized.

Pitched at seventy-five degrees and circled by the debris of heaped earth, the wreck looked convincingly disabled. Marta stood close to the surface and inspected the details.

"There's a miniature or two for close-ups in studio," Chaz yelled. "This one would look like *Plan 9* crap under the microscope."

Marta walked to the ship's edge and shone the light upwards. Behind: ground strewn with lumber, cables, and PVC piping; the complex wooden skeleton provided no hint of the aerodynamic sleekness of the opposite side.

"You okay back there?" Chaz called out. "It's pretty lonely over here."

Marta returned to front of stage. "Don't move, there's a coyote on the hill just over your shoulder."

"Very funny." He squatted to stub out the cigarette as she stepped closer. Marta caught a cloying scent, not uncommon on campus and city streets.

"Will you be okay to drive?" Marijuana caused only drooping lids and dumb hunger when she'd tried a brownie years before. Marta tossed the flashlight to test his reflexes.

He caught it without effort. "Of course, I'm a pro."

Famous last words, she thought, even as she opted to trust his self-evaluation, a hedged leap of faith. Marta stopped and craned her neck. From the bottom of the pit—crickets, crunching gravel, and breathing the only sounds—low meandering clouds obscured starlight. "Cool, eh. With that black halo it reminds me of what macular degeneration must feel like." Chaz flicked off the flashlight.

"You're quite the romantic." The scraped gravel floor and complete blackness reminded Marta of a rehearsal in an empty threatre. "I can picture you with Wordsworth in that long belt of flowers. He'd be waxing lyrically about dancing with daffodils, and you'd say they looked like fried eggs or tiny suns going supernova." When Chaz didn't reply, she sought his expression in the shadows. Nothing. Attempts at banter warped in her mouth and burst out as scoffing, like Lady Sneerwell's malice except not safely distant on stage.

Recent sentences loitering menacingly in the air, Marta wondered about apologetic phrases. "Sorry about that" had the merit of elegant simplicity, though it ran toward patness. And if "My tongue acts on its own when I'm nervous, sorry" sounded less mechanical, she had to wonder about its truth.

The beam reappeared and illuminated the gravel. "Okay, I guess we should get a move on," Chaz said, "busy day tomorrow." He directed the light to the road's incline and gestured for Marta to lead.

Enveloped by blanketing night and the fragrance of summer grasses, Marta resisted the urge to speak.

Chaz walked a few steps behind, guiding the way.

As they approached the crest he caught up and rested an open hand on her shoulder, swerving to pull her close. The bolt of alarm passing through Marta dispersed as quickly, her realization coinciding with Chaz's stumbling over a stone and pressing his lips inches shy of their target.

"Ah." Nearly dumbstruck and confused about the details of the situation they'd fallen into, she tamped down thoughts of crafty Greeks embracing the hope of a winning military strategy.

"Christ, was that smooth or what?" Like a storyteller preparing to scare a campfire audience, Chaz placed the flashlight beneath his chin. He touched Marta's jaw. "At least I didn't draw blood."

"Or chip a tooth." Marta smiled and watched Chaz swing the beam toward the car. "Thanks." The simple word covered sincerity and an apology for earlier abrasiveness. "The guided UFO tour under the cover of night couldn't have been better."

"Great, ma'am, it's the little things that make this job so special," He tipped an imaginary hat. "Gratuities help too."

In the distance the lantern glow of twin headlights grew steadily into a scalding halogen glare.

"The cavalry's arrived," Chaz said. "Still kinda weird that no one was posted here."

"*Mystery of the Missing Guard* solved."

"I read all the Hardy Boys."

"Me too." Nancy Drew as well, but that news would hardly come as a surprise.

"I'd better go wave the white flag, let the PA know we're the good guys. Wait here, okay?"

"By all means." *Cowboy paternalism*, she thought, *how cute.*

After Hours

I.

Sequestered and untouchable in the shadowy back office—no ringing phones, no hasty meetings, no professional rulings to make, and no Lora, who should by now be settled into REM sleep—Jake scrolled through online postings. *Hope springs eternal*, he thought, free hand tucked between thighs. *Especially when fueled by festering hormones*. He reconsidered. *Volcanic hormones* had a better ring to it.

His tongue snaked as Jake read, sliding into pliant hollows before returning to the precise location high on the mucous wall of his left cheek where yet another pearly canker sore had hunkered down. Aphthous ulcers, his grizzled doctor called them, and after he'd explained that Jake did not suffer from Sutton's Disease as Jake's dedicated internet searches had lead him to conclude—yes, cankers were a familiar growth in the fertile greenhouse of his mouth but, no, they weren't chronic, not technically—he'd also said with a tone of undisguised exasperation that virtually anything, from citrus juice and spicy foods to stress and abrasions, caused the painful little incidents, and that if they ran in the family, well, you're prone to them and they'll be a tiny thorn in your side for life, boo hoo.

Muttering intolerant words about the trifling infirmities of each post-war generation, the doctor advised rinsing with salt water and taking B12 if absolutely necessary. *Don't be such a baby* hung in the man's office air like spores.

Jake's tongue roved on, but the agent of obscure retribution returned to the white ulcerous jelly to jab the pain-trigger surface. Proneness to anything evoked picking-up-soap *Oz* scenarios and hapless flipped crabs circled by gulls, and Jake wanted nothing to do with that; he'd take predator over prey any day. He decided to head to the kitchen for salt after checking out the next few postings. Annihilate the squatter.

He switched between sites, each one facilitating social networking—ha, what a term, so chaste—of a kind, and clicked on tantalizing city postings as well as graspable local ones, surprised at the global village similarity. The city contained a steadier volume, of course, but the sheer variety of tastes and extremities of kinks seemed reliably common.

Locals ads weren't plentiful tonight, and of those few the bulk raised alarms—either bizarre ("Selling used bras . . . dont ask a million questions. They my exs bras left over, misc sizes, have 30 or 40 bras. Take them all $40.00") or illiterate ("I have grate stemina, I'm good looker, and decease free"), or both. And, as always, the holier-than-thou finger pointer patrolled the border:

> A Word to the Wise - w4m - (Everywhere)
> I see so many men on here saying they get no responses from women - only gay men. I have two words to say on that: Dick Pics. Now I'd like to say that I am a 100% completely heterosexual woman, but I am completely turned off by pictures of your penis in:
> a) various states of hardness
> b) various states of softness
> c) posed next to a water bottle to display length
> d) posed next to a beer can to display girth
> e) posed with your hairy balls and/or hairy ass
> All I have to say about dick pics is gross, gross gross gross and gross.
> If you are truly interested in getting a response from a woman as opposed to a gay man, then display a tasteful body pic. The rest can be seen at a later date. Have discussed this with many of my female friends and we are all in agreement on this. So, if you want a chick then don't post your dick.

Jake thought of responding to Miss Unsolicited Advice with a photo of his erection planted next to a bottle of shaving cream—or a Heineken bottle: his photo collection was sizable—and one letter: "f."

As with Exconfessio, anonymity here encouraged free expression of belief. The site appeared democratic, wonderfully so in theory, but as with any town hall free-for-all or a gathering of drunks lack of inhibition repeatedly forced everyone to face the concrete fact of heaping opinions they disagreed with or didn't care to hear in the first place. He'd say the site's blunt racism set civil rights back by a century.

Jake didn't reply. An internet flamewar would just waste time. *There's bigger fish to fry*, he thought.

Jake checked sites routinely, a moderately bad habit he told himself, and not an addiction—even if you granted the possibility of such a thing. Sure, the ads entertained—as sideshow oddities, porn, and Jerry Springer trash-talk all rolled together, and consequently as a reprieve, akin to a coffee break or recess—but spectacle alone would not sustain interest for long.

If asked, Jake would define himself as a doer, not a voyeur. He'd sought out low-wattage venues on several continents where viewing heaving entangled bodies was as customary as white lies; and while he'd stand nearby until dilated pupils picked out the details, soon enough he'd wander off in search of quieter corners. Groups got on his nerves: too many signals to interpret, unpredictable complications, and one bad apple spoiled the barrel. Sex—one tab in one slot, his usual choice—raced ahead as the real draw, not laborious community-building, UN negotiations, or Cirque acrobatics. What else? Just looking? Why only watch when you can act? Action always trumped spectatorship, the one infinitely superior to the other.

He returned to a local prospect, which struck him as worthwhile enough despite glaring shortcomings. From the headline alone—"I'm drunk and right now I'm so in love with you - w4m - 32 (Close to Vaseux Lake)"—he could tell Sherlock Holmes didn't need to point out the trouble brooding. And the ad's content hammered down any clinging uncertainty:

> I just got home from a disappointing [arty and I am WASTED. looking to be impaled. just took some Gravol and waiting for it to kick it. bang me and leave kinda deal. Tall, drak, hansome, get ahole of me asap.

The woman, accepting the ad's truth, was plainly a three-car pileup of a wreck. Unsuccessful at love, and so accepting the bare minimum from a stranger instead. Not to mention wasted and on Gravol—he checked Wikipedia about side effects: dizziness, unusual bleeding or bruising, drowsiness, constipation. She'd be fever-hot, oozing musk and boozy sweat.

Okay, it can't hurt to check in, Jake thought, recognizing recklessness, and sent a standard line of statistics followed by a tentative statement of interest: "Hi, gdlkg, 6feet, 185, hairy chest, hefty endowment (see attached pic), discrete and after late-night impaling fun."

He conjured the image of slick, sweat-streaming, and feral Christina Aguilera in that boxing ring video and levitated her to a lakeside rural Canadian trailer park where, still drunk and feisty, she'd crash-landed on a narrow cot, short plaid kilt flipped up and showing a taut tanned bare ass and dimpled cleft, a locale of unresisting promise; above the waistband peeked a tattooed inspirational saying, a winding thread of reading material for quick-draw guests.

Jake factored out the gruesome possibility of Gravol and multiple respondents: a dizzy and bruised Xtina doppelgänger suffering from cramps and constipation defined anti-aphrodisiac, as did idiotic small talk in a room full of ill-at-ease guys jockeying for the lead fuck.

The fantasy continued to resist his designs. Jake pushed away another figure—mobile home Xtina's sad emaciated city cousin, a rickety crack whore wearing a platinum wig that he'd once caught alley-servicing a lard-assed salesman in a boxy suit (hefty briefcase of sample wares tucked under his arm) at 6:30 in the morning near the set of a failed 16-episode superhero series—that kept shoving her way into the scenario. The logical mind's reminders about likelihood rarely bothered with subtlety.

Stalled about committing, Jake walked toward the kitchen; the blue, green, and red glow of stand-by lights on faxes, printers, phones, computers, Lora's air purifier, the kettle, and coffee maker provided sci-fi illumination. He dumped a handful of salt in a glass and added hot water; swishing the briny medication he clamped his throat, trying to avoid swallowing a drop. A body refuses the intake of that concentration of salt and he'd be happy to make it through the day without heaving up a meal.

His mouth tasting of ocean, Jake returned to the desk. The lovelorn drunk had replied with a classic snapshot—halter top lifted at a house party—and, "k, but make it quik." She listed the address and wrote, "u cant miss it."

2.

Jake knew that five minutes of masturbation would snuff out the night's compulsion. That practically always settled him. Even so, he couldn't denying the supreme charge of watching himself sink to the hilt inside another warm body, and this chick's assets—in photos at least—hadn't sagged yet. And jack-ass go-for-it-ness—showing up at a red-flag location and seeing how it all played out—seldom failed to arouse. The unknowables, the strategizing, and the potent whiff of danger intermingling with the scent of victory: Jake imagined the primitive hunter brain whirring into wakefulness at the onset of each and every trek. Abiding by the law of hormones, he guessed. He'd be fighting Mother Nature by refusing the opportunity.

He found the lake by the address of Gravol Xtina on a map. Convenient: it stood on the left side of the highway about half way between the production office and his swank bed and breakfast on the hill. "Couldn't hurt to check it out," Jake mumbled. While the laptop confirmed the address' legitimacy, squinting at the screen couldn't unearth a mobile home from amongst the satellite map's blur of pixels.

He tilted back on the chair and reached under his waistband. After a full day his junk was still passable, not yet tacky and ripe. He lifted his arm; the pits smelled okay too. He'd prefer to be freshly showered even though the Vaseux Lake skank could probably use a rinse as well. And if the deed proceeded as planned, inspecting his piece for a soapy fresh scent would be the least of her concerns: a randy goat, she'd be ready to go. That approach worked for him; small talk, dinner, flowers, compliments, and all of the usual suspects could be scrapped. It'd be hassle-free, instead, just like porn: get there, get on, get in, get off, go. He dabbed Terre on his neck. Just in case.

Stuffing keys and phone into the messenger bag, Jake flicked off the desk light. 10:30: plenty of time to finish the job, grab a swim, and find enough sleep to play an A game in the morning.

3.

At this late hour driving felt impossibly rural, a mute vista from the past, expansive and as empty as the panoramas of *Badlands*; even the parking spaces on Main Street stood free, skittering tumbleweed and a silent hitched horse the only missing elements. Further on, no tourist traffic clogged the northbound highway. On the nameless flatland that emerged after the still plots of orchard, Jake swerved the Ford from one road shoulder to the other, enjoying the adolescent moment before the tragic action sequence—a sudden oncoming fast-moving semi, no time to swerve, head on crash—nudged him back to the proper side of the yellow line.

The right hand high on his thigh teased his dick with warm proximity. He welcomed the sense of blood flowing and the start of an erection; he itched for release. Cock-proud, Jake was no stranger to semi-public j.o., putting on a show under a treed canopy in a park or near the shady trails where the beach butted into the forest. His policy: look but don't touch unless a hot prospect changed his mind.

The GPS chime—Jake had asked Lora to switch out the robotic voice—indicated a left turn onto a gravel road that he would have otherwise missed. He drove slowly, the angel on his shoulder whispering "Bad plan, Jakey boy" as it called up cautionary vignettes with a preacher's ease.

Halfway along the soft curve, Jake pulled over and snapped off the headlights. The problem stared him in the face: Xtina didn't live alone; no solitary trailer parked there, enticingly anchored on a dry empty lot. Nor did the trailer belong to a bustling community where one vehicle arriving would catch no notice. Six single-wide trailers crowded together in the middle of an acreage of dried grass; one, three, and five sat unlit and sleepy. Pulling in front of the address couldn't be inconspicuous; he'd draw prying eyes. Snuffing the lights and walking the distance? Maybe, but that had *CSI* episode written all over it. Or else, his visit would be nothing unusual; the neighbours would sigh or huff, "Christ, not again," and roll their eyes, already too worn down by slutty Christina's procession of gentlemen booty callers to pick up the phone or kick up a fuss.

Outmanoeuvred, Jake thumped the steering wheel with his fist. Gunning the engine seemed apropos, but American bad ass wasn't his thing. Door 1, 2, or 3? Door 4 rated as viable too: turn around and write off fifteen wasted minutes. His brain continued to fire off loser eventualities: an insomniac roommate, a kid asleep in a crib, a boyfriend foaming with jealousy, a protective dog, a visiting mother. Letting loose a frustrated snort, Jake said, "Looks like there's no tasty treats for you tonight, buddy." He unbuttoned his jeans and awkwardly coaxed them to mid-thigh. Lifting the T-shirt over his head, he tipped back the seat. Pent up and stretched out half-naked and semi-visible from the roadside, Jake could tell he'd shoot in no time. Closing his eyes, he returned to prone Xtina's lifted skirt. She groaned, her sleep restless and bladder distended from beer. In the trailer's solitary stillness Jake dragged his thumb from soft voluptuous oyster folds to a puckered hole whose coaxed elasticity welcomed penetration from a bigger implement.

As predicted, he spewed after minimal strokes; opting for a bare-chested drive to Kaleden, he wiped off the results of the fantasy with his T-shirt.

Only one light shone in any of the trailers when Jake shifted into reverse.

Remote Kinship

1.

Despite a heavy dreamless sleep Marta arrived at Joan's feeling bedraggled. Phones trilling, she scurried to the kitchen and mixed a sweet milky coffee, stirring the concoction with a melting Kit Kat finger.

Marta bowed to Lora's recommendation for the shift and continued to role play as Chaz's sidekick. Outfoxed, feet dragging, and yet fence-sitting about returning to the city empty-handed, she oozed testiness despite feeling badly about the crash site blunder and vowing to mend fences. Early on Chaz quipped, "You're my bitch today" and Marta's mute disapproval had closed that avenue of banter and all other communication for several minutes. Firm lines must be drawn with this recalcitrant man-child, she reasoned, and if he wanted a helping of bitch she'd serve super-sized portions.

Even with the unpromising start, the hours that followed were invigorating, if chaotic, like working at a fire station; at any moment a stretch of low-call-volume tedium could be interrupted by an emergency, an incoming request filled with complicated instructions, the fundamental point of which always sounded identical: *Get it done now*. During those frequent gofer trips—from the production office to main unit behind the Hebe farm, to second unit at the crash site, or to bigger towns north and south of Joan's for supplies—Chaz charged ahead, a lively indispensable guide. At one lull as they waited for word from the director to emerge from video hut seclusion, Marta learned that the barking hands-on autocrat of her imagination overflowed with inaccuracies. Punctuating an explanation with snickers of disbelief, Chaz called her notion "a wee bit dusty, lassie."

As she watched the crew—who looked at ease with the rapid cycling between extremes: attentive with purpose, then slack, smoking, and lighthearted—and the glacial shooting of a single scene, Marta registered constant surprise, amazed that the actors could in fact inhabit a role with so much interference abounding. Desert sun, intrusive equipment, and a medieval village of crew confounded the mind, as did staccato cessations stemming from errors of lighting and sound quality, camera position, crew and performer gaffs, technical malfunctions, and directorial changes of heart. She'd never imagined a breeze could matter so much.

Compared to stage actors, the imported talent here would find focussing difficult and maintaining the integrity of the role an apparent impossibility. These conditions helped explain why, Marta concluded, so many movies featured stars whose daily selves seemed inseparable from their character.

At the Hebe set distractions sprouted with the resolve of weeds. The lines spoken, a pause of several minutes, a variation of those lines uttered again, the camera repositioned slightly, light or sound rechecked, a short conference between walkie-talkies, equipment adjusted, the line's inflection modified, another line (flubbed this time), a second conference, laughter, walkie-talkie squawk, and then joking, lots of it, as though the crew milled about a faltering party that desperately required levity to revive: Marta thought *halting progress* placed an elegant facade on a blunt, onerous fact.

Stationed far from the camera, Marta continued to watch after Chaz whispered a need for seclusion to take a call. Relieved the spoken lines remained more or less faithful to the page, Marta's face also tightened with surprise and chagrin tracking the actor—pale, brown hair, English, unknown to her—whose handle on the character deviated so ludicrously wide of the mark.

Over the scripts she'd read, earnest, pedantic, and faithful Dr. Meryon—historically real, though not a charismatic, movie-ready figure in the least—had become earnest, pedantic, and faithful Dr. Potter, Lady Stanhope's foolish right-hand man of science; brought to life now on the flattened dry grass near Djoun's entrance gate, the man's dogged traits evaporated. A simpering, flamboyant airhead supplanted rational if lovestruck Potter.

Marta knelt to the tote to confirm the misreading.

CUT TO:

INT. DJOUN - ENTRANCE GATE - DAY.

DR. POTTER

Sargon, dear boy, prepare two horses. Your Mistress, Lady Swinburne, and I wish to imbibe the flaming sunset from the ridge.

SARGON

Yes, sayedy.

POTTER

Make certain to brush the horses so that their coats have the luster of gold in the light.

The actor's initial improvisation threw in an abundance of fey gestures alongside the audible lisp—hand on hip, effeminate finger strokes to pat flanks of hair into place, and an off-script line, "Be a good boy," followed by pursed lips and eyebrows arched in the shape of coolly sexual evaluation as the youth ambled away. In case anyone missed the obvious, the actor placed elongated stress on the "f" in "flaming," the hiss of air leaking from a tire.

Static noise burst from the Assistant Director's walkie-talkie, the director on the other end, Marta presumed—"Dial it back already. He's not Liberace, for Christ's sake"—resulted in fresh crew joking and, for the actor, a fresh manly register as well as the loss of ad lib lines, implied pederast interest, and fussiness about hairstyle. The hand on hip persevered, though now rigid with martial intent.

Before the scene wrapped Chaz whispered that he was gunning to leave. Northbound on the highway, he joked and guffawed, contented to field Marta's question about the kitschy take on lovelorn Dr. Potter; he explained that *they*—the umbrella word referring to the production company, client network, and back-room deal-makers—had called for a comic relief character to balance out the sombre action. "Just ask Aristotle," he said with a smirk, outlining how the rules of ancient literary convention required a smart ass or wimpy trembler to break the monotony of a pack of virtuous but humorless heroes.

"I mean, think about it." Chaz took a swig from a water bottle. "Let's see, off the top of my head, the Cowardly Lion, Dr. Zachary Smith on *Lost in Space*, Count Baltar on *Battlestar Galactica*, I mean the original series from the seventies, the porky little sidekick of Frodo in *Lord of the Rings*, even that sleazy Company Man from *Aliens*, all cut from the same cloth. They're there, spineless jokes, to put the heroism in relief, right; and good or bad, they usually show their gonads right at the end. And then the movie ends, and the hero doesn't have to worry about the audience digging the wingman more than tall, dark, and handsome, who is, you gotta admit, a bit of a wet rag to hang out with when there's no baddie to dispatch."

"But when the alien eventually kills this ridiculous version of Dr. Meryon, there'll be no pay off, no emotional investment," Marta replied.

"Oh, there's the big switch, right, when the character reforms; I haven't read the script, but you watch: he'll drop the fussy faggishness—pardon my French—but what else are you going to call it?"

"Dandyism? Aestheticism?" Marta squeezed the passenger door grip. Driving with one hand resting atop the wheel, Chaz's attention wandered restlessly.

"Yeah, okay, whatever, Professor PC. Anyway. The Jesus-y self-sacrifice and redemption, that happens, but it doesn't erase the fact that he's been a total wanker up until then. He dies, for sure, but he's redeemed himself—usually, kinda, sorta—with a scene of twenty-four carat heroism. The selfless act: one ticket to paradise. Not like anybody who's watching it on a rainy Saturday afternoon gives it a second thought.

"Like the Cowardly Lion, right, he'll grow a pair." Chaz swallowed in gulps. "Okay, that's not exactly what happens with the lion, but it's the gist. But then—in this case, an action movie has its own variation of the rules—he still has to die because he was such a weak asswipe before. He was a sinner, see, so has to pay the price, praise the lord. But with that last-minute transformation he realizes the error of his ways, so acts bravely. He goes to Valhalla, right; if he'd minced around 'til the end we'd known he'd burn instead."

"Or shiver, as the case may be. Don't you think that's reading into things a bit, professor?"

"Oh, you've cut me to the core. Mind if I open the windows all the way?"

"Sure." Marta held up a thumb of approval. "Isn't the writer outraged," she asked, feeling empathy for the person whose storytelling might be the only facet keeping audiences awake. "I mean the liberties being taken with the original script are, well, exorbitant."

" 'The liberties'? Man, what century were you born in?"

"You know what I mean."

"I can't fathom whether 'is sensibilities was outraged by them lib'tees, Miss Austen," Chaz tested out a spotty cockney. "It's not like he's here to protest. In fact, the guy's probably already written a sequel and two other scripts since signing off on this one. The guy wants a pool or a new Beemer, not a grave next to Shakespeare or whatever. Anyone writing for TV, especially cable, knows the drill. Plus, if they're not hacks already, then they have, um, lowered expectations. If they really want to make capital A art, they obviously won't sell their precious baby to some crap heap production company responsible for *Alien Implants 3* and *Splendido, Inspired by the Harlequin Novel*. I mean c'mon, get real. Gross." He pointed to the roadside, where a pair of crows squabbled while hopping on a coyote carcass. "Vancouver's famous for pot, right, but the city's non-black market money-makers are dragons, robots, aliens, and superheroes, bargain basement cheap right through to big budget. You have no idea. It's Porno Valley, only for sci-fi: spewed out formula year after year. Same for

Toronto, only there they take on occult, cops, spies, um, oh yeah, chick flicks too. They compete, split mutants and Xmas movies down the middle; it's like those gang bang movie chicks, Annabel Chong versus Jasmin St. Claire. And then, same as pot, it's sold anywhere. If there's a cable channel anyway."

"That's quite the monologue." Marta wanted to refocus the conversation. She'd missed half the references and couldn't guess where Chaz's tangents led. She posed another question. "So, obviously a serious writer would choose a different venue?"

"Bingo. They'd find a way to get their masterpiece read by a mover and shaker, and that, as you might guess, is no small feat. Everybody and his dog is writing a script and thinks it's going make it on the Black List and get the go ahead. Lottery tickets are a better bet.

"Plus the pay's good, right, so they're happy to sell out. Fifteen grand, minimum. Not bad for a few weeks of typing, I mean toil. I met this guy who wrote a short story. Just one, right? Worked on it for, like, ever, sent it out, got rejections months later or no replies at all, worked on it some more and sent that version out, eventually got paid. Three hundred bucks. If you broke that down into dollars per hour, you'd be looking at something like one-tenth of minimum wage, if that. Chump change, make more working at some Third World Nike plant. Christ!" Chaz blared the horn. "F-ing RVs."

"It's not all about the pay cheque." Marta knew the fraction would become smaller if applied to her first book: its sole royalty payment might have bought a dinner for two at Le Crocodile if she'd opted for a house wine and skimped on the tip.

She guessed Chaz's parental reply: "You can't pay bills with artistic integrity." He swerved to check for oncoming traffic. "Anyway, I'm thinking you're mixing up Art and Commerce."

Chaz's phone rang. "Right, okay, how soon?" He pulled over, craning to check for oncoming traffic. "Crap, I gotta switch lanes and drop you off at the office."

"The no cell phones while driving law is for other people, I take it?" Acclimating to Chaz's driving style, Marta relaxed in the easygoing camaraderie—the banter sharp and stimulating but not mean—of the cab. Relieved, she sensed no aftermath to the gravel pit encounter. An onlooker would never guess what had transpired.

"Yeah, that's right. Rules, bending them, you know the drill." He handed her the bottle. "Have some, you look thirsty."

2.

While scrambling between telephones and labouring clerically alongside Lora at Joan's, Marta grew resigned about the repurposing of the stay in the valley. Real movie-making possibilities presented lottery odds and there'd be no getting around that fact, Marta concluded as each hour passed. Production was a wound clock, she'd seen that; and with all the intersecting gears already screwed into place and set in motion, a role for her could only ever be minor. When her part in the metaphor refused to manifest, Marta dropped its pursuit. The obviousness of the predicament didn't deserve a poet's special treatment anyway.

After Lora's firm late night "No can do, sweetie" declarations and the unpersuasive wish upon a star note she'd concluded with, there'd been no mention of significant—or new—challenges for Marta. Consulting about this or that remained the hope, but once the secretarial assignments began, "Let's see what happens" had metamorphosed into "Would you mind getting the phone?" Buried within the undertone: "Let's never mention consulting again." Reluctant to push and now fully cognizant of her non-unionized liminal ghostliness, Marta couldn't summon the daring to campaign for under the table writing duties or propose other escape routes from dead-end Dickensian clerkdom. "No use in flogging a dead mule," her father would say. For the interim she'd delight in the unabashed weirdness of the office—silly and uproarious when it wasn't busy and tense—and lend a novice hand, become an assistant's assistant and function as a semi-useful instrument, an intern without any big dreams of climbing the totem, or a constant need to impress difficult bosses. *Experience itself*, she recalled, had represented a philosophical call to arms once upon a time.

Between one call and the next Marta realized another plus: she'd write off the entire as moderately interesting, a novel anecdote for the Speck family Labour Day barbecue that would be hobbled somewhat by the fact she could hardly claim to be rubbing shoulders with tabloid-worthy, tantrum-prone celebrities. Still, she could bank on the story being better received than another account of conference proceedings—"dishwater dull," her mother's verdict—or book chapter progression ("In English, please?"); even low-budget B-movie-making possessed greater mystique than academia ever could.

And for once she might forestall her older brother's annual jibe—"Rrrriing, it's the Venetian, sis. They're looking for a Joan Rivers replacement. Are you free?" For as long as he'd been saying it, Marta had suspected that beneath the jokey utterance lay half-baked sublimation, a tough shred of inert anger about her panicked grad school decision that never dissolved. He'd cure those supposed bleeding ulcers of his if he'd let go of issues like that. Lester wanted to be known as Les Speck, and tolerance for the attendant jokes and Zero as a nickname was his prerogative; an umlauted "e," one discarded consonant, and legal paperwork had given Marta sublime peace of mind for a time.

Driving around with tourist bonhomie remained a solid alternative, true. Instead, Marta thought that arriving at Joan's after an unhurried people-watching breakfast at the O-K would be satisfying—well, satisfying enough. She'd miss the genteel winery tours and raucous jet skiing promoted by the local tourist board, but liked the idea of that routine. Owning the unrestricted leisure of a contented ghost, she could show up and disappear to suit her whims. If she awoke one day with a craving for a family vineyard and flights of tart small-batch wines, those choices would be recreational too: which estate, when to go, what to wear? The production wouldn't miss her—a dogsbody VUP, the quintessence of non-vital personnel—at all when she slipped away.

Unplanned and all-expenses-paid, the stay in the valley could be called a workation, she concluded, one whose day began with chirping birds and startling blasts from the noise generators farmers invested in to prevent those sugar-loving marauders from swallowing their entire livelihood. Marta had risen early for years; her body's internal alarm ran automatically, turning it off required medication. And if her mind relented and sleeping in occurred, the blazing perimeter appearing around the drapes each morning penetrated as inescapably as the mechanical bird-scattering commotion; even a night mask couldn't stop a response to the sun's infernal nudging. The Star-Lite indeed.

Wrench

I.

"Problem, boss man. A biggie. Shitstorm's arrived, more like it," Lora telegraphed from behind the desk as Jake fussed with Joan's obstinate front door.

That the tumult of words—and skier-facing-an-avalanche pantomime: spread hand high in the air, a doomed self-preservation effort—preceded his assistant's customary seize the day greeting of "Good morning, boss man, want me to send out for coffee?" informed Jake that the set schedule had already plummeted into the mud, even before he'd clicked on the laptop or punched in a single call. And since there'd been no head's up en route, he gathered that whatever bad luck had dumped in his lap the pile fumed angrily.

"Now we have to pull a rabbit out of our asses."

"Well, that's news from left field," he said, crouched to fist pound a hinge.

Along with everyone else at the office, Jake had long been resigned to the inevitable: something always fucked up and without fail fires needed extinguishing. Ho hum, that was the nature of the job. Cold sweat resulted from the severity—how many hours to fix it? How many dollars would it siphon from the budget?

"Okay, what's up? Who did what? Who didn't do what?"

"Seems our Dol'rez slash Lizzie needs replacing—pronto," Lora replied, still at the desk and evidently on hold. "Good morning to you, by the way, strong coffee's on."

"Bring me up to speed." Jake strode to close the distance. Coffee could wait a minute; Lora's bellowed news broadcast had shattered the morning's blue sky calm.

"Okay, from what I've heard it went down like this: crew guys were setting up and sound was running into a technical glitch that was taking up tons of time, business as usual in other words, and that's when they heard 'Omygodomygodomygod' and a shriek. Turns out that Dol'rez had shown up at the crack of dawn and was 'getting a feel for the scene'—Little Miss Method—and when the crew started making noise, the airhead got huffy and told them she 'needed space,' so wandered off toward one of the fields in the back of the Hebe place. . . ." She raised an index finger. "Okay, okay, sayonara to you too, buddy," Lora said, slamming down the receiver with hammer force. She grabbed her bucket hat, jetted the chair back, and began a hasty offensive toward the front of the building, spitting out "Hold on a sec" as she strode by Jake. A moment later she paced the sidewalk.

In the kitchen Jake sniffed the coffee. Watery or strongly acidic, Lora's brews pleased their maker alone.

"Anyway, sorry, taxi drivers aren't FedEx, not by a bloody long shot." Lora rushed in and used a dish cloth to dry agitated hands. "It's so goddamned hot already, who the hell can take it, Christ!"

"The chair, Lora." Jake recognized incipient meltdown. "Let's ease up on momma's little helper for a couple hours. Alright, Betty Ford?" Even though experience had taught Lora the wretched results, she chain-drank coffee the instant Category 4 stress manifested.

"Okay, okay, I hear you." Lora sat, hands on lap.

"Can you continue now, my little hummingbird, or are your nerves shot," Jake asked, arms crossed and back at the kitchen counter. "Need some agua? A nibble of Klonopin?"

"I'm just fine, thank you." Lora tore off the hat and pitched it toward her desk. "Oh, where was I? Right, okay, Dol'rez screaming, I'm there," she said, resenting Jake's kindly but firm nurse routine. "Apparently—this comes from Baby Dick, who by the way is in fine form today—she'd seen an old irrigation thing, you know, a flume, like a small aqueduct, I guess farmers had built one high on the hill decades ago and then left it there to rot after they got the modern system. She went to check it out. I have no clue why, maybe she thought laying hands on a relic would help her get into character. Who can say? Then—get this—just a few feet away she slips on something soft and totally freaks out, thinking it was a rattlesnake. The woman—and I'll quote her resume: 'an ex former model based out from Europe'—was born in Manchester and now lives in Burbank, so I doubt she'd recognize a rattlesnake if she did step on one."

"A snake attack?" Jake snorted: when asking Nicos about snakes he hadn't been serious. The budding smile died as he pictured the actress's tainted blood racing as she tore through the grass, venom creeping stealthily toward an unsuspecting heart: between media attention and insurance payouts, this accident could be fatal in more ways than one.

"Nope. Who knows, it was a cow pie probably. You ready? When she spazzes out, she takes off screaming down the hill and veers off into a little rocky area and trips." Lora's grin spread. The hassle of it all aside, the situation didn't exactly inspire shock and dismay. What snake-fearing fool wanders off alone when she's in rattler country? "Mind you, she also told me that she'd been a 'hare's breath' from being the spokesmodel for Chanel, so you gotta wonder."

"Okay, so, sprained an ankle?" Jake guessed. No big deal, they could work around that. "Broke it?" Less fortunate, crutches would be a hurdle.

"Nope, way worse. She fell, face-planted actually, into cactus. Rocketing at full speed. Brittle prickly-pear cactus, they're called—that's more info from Nicos. They grow wild in patches here. Long stiff needles pin-cushioned her entire face. Keyword: she's a hot f-ing mess."

"Fucking Christ!" Jake tapped his fingers on the desk. "Just her face, though, that's good."

"Um, no. They jabbed right through her robe and into her scrawny carcass. She's allergic, not to mention skinny as the rails I hear she's fond of snorting on weekends. Apparently, Dol'rez looks like a piglet ambushed by a rabid porcupine, then drowned. That's Baby Dick's call on it. First Aid's arranged for the ambulance trip already. She's totally out of the picture. Totally."

"You have got to be joking. Crap!" Jake turned for his office. "Man, looks like I need to make some calls. Where the fuck is Chaz? Where is everyone? I need some real coffee, then set. Maintain the fort till I wrap my call, okay? Is Nicos in the vicinity?"

2.

Jake lowered the receiver, feeling the gratifying flush of reward. *Good ol' dopamine*, he thought. Brain parts had been humming in unison—problem to spatialize and resolve; motivating fear of humiliation, failure, and punishment; duress of the ticking clock—and in congratulation a few extra squirts of a feel-good chemical currently flooded neural corridors. He hoped the feeling wasn't a champagne toast at midnight, *SS Poseidon*-style.

"Okay Lora, we've MacGyvered something," he bellowed, closing the laptop. "We're going to meet about the details. Can you hold down the fort?" The question required no answer.

A Baited Hook

I.

The day's earliest plan: to grab a quick breakfast with Chaz. He'd told Marta she could ride shotgun afterward while he drove all over hell's half acre. Chaz had hinted that the intermittent quotation from Tarantino and vintage double-bills, the director's stock-in-trade, was meant as jest. Marta didn't believe that for a minute. Winked references saved him from the appearance of sincere *Easy Rider* worship, she knew—guilty herself of a similar attitude when it came to the conservative yearnings for *Kinder und Küche* wrapped within the DNA of the chick lit she dipped into now and then before sleep—but Marta found that mapping Chaz's interior life as a hoard of fantasies built atop macho scenes of B-movie anti-heroism made sense. She'd bet that *Mad Max* iterations represented a key part of the man's Halloween costume history, donned with claims of ironic intent, naturally. Right now a cache of the remainders might well be hanging in his condo's storage cage.

Chaz knocked a few minutes early and waited outside as Marta rushed to finish dressing, all-weather jeans now an emblem of cemented honorary crew membership.

"Change of plan for me," he murmured, voice close to the security chain. Lacking an alternative, they'd planned to eat at the O-K. "Problem at HQ."

"Oh, really. What's happened?" Marta spoke loudly toward the closed door.

"One of the actors freaked out or something. Lora didn't go into gruesome detail. 'Get in here asap' was her message for me, basically."

"Who melted down?" Marta brushed her hair and peered into the bathroom mirror.

"That Irish chick with black hair," he said, now at the window. "You know, the one playing the maid."

"Dol'rez Chase, she's English."

"That's the one, yeah." He breathed asthmatically into the door frame, "Leia, my daughter, the Force commands you to move with great haste."

Marta unfastened the chain and swung the door open. "Thirty seconds, alright? I need to apply sun block. Then I'll drop you off, how's that? I'll make my way to the O-K. I can get you breakfast to go if you'd like."

"Sure thing. That rocks." Warm air rushed into the room. "Chuck me the keys, alright. I'll wait in the car and get the AC blasting."

2.

Marta parked near Joan's and waved after Chaz said, "Catch you later." She watched his nimble gait—rapid, a hustling stride about to accelerate into a trot—before securing the car. A few paces along, she halted. She'd stowed the tote in the back seat; the script in it would be handy over breakfast.

"Top of the morning, Dr. Mar," Luna said as Marta chose a booth. "Hot enough for you?"

"It's not bad so far."

"Just you wait, the day's young. Where's your friend?"

"He was with me until three minutes ago. There's trouble on set."

"Oh wow, what happened?"

"Apparently there was an accident of some kind. I really can't say more."

"Okay, my lips are sealed." Luna mimed a zippered mouth. "The usual?"

"Yes, please."

Marta removed *The Battle of Djoun* and flipped through pages marked with coloured tabs. Back when she'd actively planned to attach scenes and words as beneficial as fish oil, Marta had pored over and annotated the mutated script while wearing, she supposed, a catalogue of expressions that ran between ire, amusement, and confusion. Defeat would have shown there too. She'd paid closest attention to the transformations of Lady Stanhope of course; as for the re-purposing of the bit players, those she noticed as well.

Unlike the rest of the crew Marta had hands-on awareness that with the exception of her indispensable Mrs. Elizabeth Williams, the former flesh and bone servants of Lady Hester Stanhope had been condemned for eternity in trans-continental dispatch exchanges filed in humidity-regulated storage deep within the Victoria and Alberta Museum's Special Collections Department. She'd visited those insulated storerooms during one of two research trips to London, where thrift had turned out to have as much importance as the contents of the acrimonious and sporadically paranoid letters.

Lady Stanhope's procession of servants had been characterized wholesale in damning ink as shiftless and rude gossips, or as petty thieves who connived and resisted authority—another bundle of proof that victors write history. The letters accused the alleged laggards of not knowing their place; line by line they became synonymous with problem children whose constant misbehaviour practically begged for the harsh reprimands and occasional bouts of corporal punishment meted out by their imperious governess. Scrubbed of distinctions they languished in near invisibility, skulking background figures, interchangeable, vaguely malevolent, and as irritating as bottle flies.

The Battle of Djoun kept the unwashed mass as extras that swept, gardened, and cooked, existing primarily as mobile edge-of-frame scenery before the predatory alien's grand entrance. They were dispatched horror film-style soon after, unsuspecting and one by one—and silently too: speaking roles cost a mint. The alien enjoyed their deaths like low-calorie hors d'oeuvres, biding its time before ascending the social food chain, intent on savouring the tastiest morsel—finely marbled aristocratic flesh tartare—last.

The script dispensed with steadfast Mrs. Williams altogether while amalgamating the servants' surplus of reputed bad qualities and stuffing all of them into Lizzie, a vain first-rate conniver granted no family name. Charcoal eyes squinty with schemes, face drawn habitually to reflective surfaces, and feckless grasping hands forever slipping pricey baubles into impoverished hand sewn pockets, she owed her existence, Marta concluded, to Iago and that free-floating population of maligned figures, from Cinderella's step-sisters to Leona 'only the little people pay taxes' Helmsley, whose resolute jowls relayed a steady conviction of being owed a princely sum, far greater than the pittance their owner felt life had supplied.

And like those reality-TV contestants who proclaim "Winning is my destiny" to any nearby microphone and without a modest blush of hesitance—as an indisputable fact, as though the very cosmos would overturn timeless, absolute laws to assure the outcome and confirm a clock-like order to existence that served the particular needs of Addie-Mae Chesterfield from the outskirts of Mobile, Alabama—Lizzie's faith bubbled mightily, an effervescent tonic that caused her mind to brim with sure thoughts that the ill-gotten reign of Lady Swinburne, a cruel and undeserving mistress, would never endure. Any day, and by the swift act of a just God, servant would become master. Order restored by divine intervention.

In a show of ladylike kindness, Lizzie would then reserve a place for the fallen and humiliated mistress. After all, with so many other fertile lasses vacating their posts in shame, a reliable maid, one in no danger of becoming pregnant and receding into the shadows during the blackest hours of the night, took priority status.

Though the maid role wasn't pivotal, the underhanded motives did provide a necessary subplot—larding to help stretch out *The Battle for Djoun* to the contractual 88 minutes. In scenes set days before the alien's crash landing, Lizzie conveyed a fondness for machination primarily through facial expressions and inflections of voice since the speaking parts appeared sparsely: "Yes, Ma'am," "Right away, Madam," and "Milady, the Doctor requests your company."

Marta imagined that Lizzy would look the part; a combination of subtle qualities—facial shape, makeup, hair, manner of dress, body posture—could transmit her uppity villainous qualities at a glance. Later scenes, soliloquies really, took place in the kitchen and in Lady Swinburne's bedchamber, and swept away any lingering doubt.

Lizzie's penultimate appearance also contained the longest speech. In it, the solitary maid withdrew one of Lady Swinburne's formal gowns from a steamer trunk and clasped it closely while directing a gaze to the polished sterling silver back of a hairbrush, held up with a free hand. Marta had tentative faith that an actor of the right calibre could squeeze pathos from the thudding words:

INT. LADY SWINBURNE'S BEDCHAMBER - DAY.

LIZZIE

My dear Sultan, you are too kind indeed.
(curtsying at the brush)
Verily, I cannot accept so extravagant a gift. That you hold me in such high esteem is surely enough! You insist?
Such a wealth of gems could only attract the covetous eyes of my impudent servants.
True, I am indeed perhaps too kind to them, too kind altogether. And yet to cut off the hand of a thief, as is the custom in the land over which you reign, that extremity, if I dare say so, is contrary to the lawful civility of my fair island home.

She pauses, as though listening to the Sultan speak. A beat.

Oh, if it pleases you I shall place the necklace of rubies upon my neck.
My, they're so lustrous.
A complement to my own fair beauty you say? You flatter me so, Sir!

(giggles)
'Tis so, kind gentleman, I must inform you.

After sunset, Lizzie's ungoverned ambition propelled her to strike a diabolical bargain. Once Lady Swinburne had retired to the bedchamber, Lizzie harnessed a horse and rode toward the crash site. The consequence: predictably dismal. The maid's blithe negligence of folklore—no one signs a contract with a demon and wins—foretold a severed head planted in the sand minutes later. Though in a roundabout way, Marta conceded, Lizzie did receive poetic justice in the form of a bloody ruby necklace. *Very Angela Carter*, Marta thought, touched by the screenwriter's unexpected flourish.

Marta could see that Lizzie's revelation scene would appeal to any young actress on a quest for clips of CV-worthy material. Even with the dimwit echo of Lady Macbeth the hairbrush scene contained meat to chew through. Well, gristle anyway.

Lizzie's rationale for forming an alliance with the alien stayed opaque to Marta. The servant lived to better a lowly social status and drape her body with the aristocratic finery that she saw as a birthright. But the alliance with the alien could not result in a marriage of any kind; even for loopy logic of *The Battle of Djoun* a cross-species liaison was no possibility. Perhaps Lizzie lacked the backbone to murder Lady Swinburne and consequently needed to enlist the alien. The reptilian predator certainly had no qualms. If so, what could Lizzie hope to offer in exchange? Nobody debated the alien's self-sufficiency. No matter, Marta had decided. Plumbing character psychology hardly defined the story's central principle. A functionary, a necessary sacrifice to a bloodthirsty plot, Lizzie read as a villain, and the eventual headless corpse toppled in the sand provided reason enough for the scenes devoted to her. Gory punishment—the reassuring Romans 6:23 message T-shirt worn by the pro-wrestling fan who'd swear on his mother's grave that bad things happen to bad people—reared up as the pay off. Revealing the drives of an embittered illiterate maid with delusions of silver-spoon refinement? Not a chance. The screenwriters must have skipped classes on kitchen sink realism to chase Tyrants in *Resident Evil* instead.

3.

"Well, speak of the devil," Lora said, breaking off a conspiratorial huddle with Chaz. "Question: Are you ready, lady? We think we've come up with a special job, just for you." Although Lora smiled gamely, Marta heard undertones of mischief in the bubbly voice, notes of a dark promise. The task, Marta suspected, would be belittling and unrewarding, in line with the miller's daughter's literally do-or-die assignment in *Rumpelstilzchen*.

Marta believed her mother had thrilled at intoning "Once there was a miller who was poor" with a strange, richly portentous relish, the eventual emphasis in the telling underscoring the miller's empty boast rather than the troll's comeuppance. As Marta grew older Dianne served the tale alongside a real-life snippet from high school that involved pushing an uncooked bratwurst down a hallway with her nose, a sorority initiation rite that doubled as a queer public humiliation in a Prairie town of Teutonic immigrants. Eventually she dropped the fairy tale; the sausage parable, however, had staying power.

Both stories, to the speaker at least, existed only to teach the same lesson: the trusting person is wise to grow a hard shell; wariness prevents injury. Thanks to Dianne, Marta's childhood imaginings had been populated with normal-looking people with secret elaborate schemes and fairy tales with sinister parallels to daily occurrences—beware millers and false promises, beware popular girls carrying deli meats.

"Chaz tells me you're up to speed on the Dol'rez incident."

"Not exactly. I heard there was some problem with her."

Lora had already unraveled the detailed version of the incident several times. She reduced it to essence for Marta: "There was an accident on set and now we really need to replace that actress."

"Nothing serious, I hope," Marta asked.

"She'll recover eventually. Anyway. That's not our biggest headache. We can re-order the shooting pages for awhile, but our goal now—and I mean pronto—is a new Lizzie."

"What can I do?"

"I need to pow wow with Jake first, but it'd handy for you to manage the process, not casting the actress of course but organizing the information flow. Liaising, in other words." A paper shuffling frenzy competed with Lora's words. "While you're waiting, check out Cast It Systems online, that's how we'll start the process. Use the computer thingy on Jake's desk."

Right, be careful what you wish for, Marta thought. "Alright, sounds good." She recognized clerical drudgery beneath the gilt of responsibility: administrative secretary rather than data entry temp, a half-step promotion.

"Let's hit the road, Chaz." Lora already waited at the front door, hat and celebrity-scale black sunglasses protection from external hazards—UV bombardment, perhaps, or unhinged fans. "I'm driving."

"Oh, don't bother with the calls, Marta. Anything that's important will get forwarded to my cell." Lora raised palms of helplessness as the phones broke into chorus. "We'll be back when we're back, sooner than later I hope."

Marta wandered to the kitchen for a granola bar. Chewing, she sat at Jake's desk and tapped halfheartedly on the screen. The actor casting website required navigational expertise, not to mention a membership and password: a dead end. Besides, Marta had learned enough to sense that slacking off wouldn't be foolish. In the stretch of minutes between Lora's departure and return, the entire situation might change, and with "Okay, we're going in a different direction" the promise of greater responsibility could easily be rescinded. It wouldn't surprise her that after Lora's meeting with Jake and a rapid series of amphetamine phone calls between offices in various cities, they'd discarded the maid role altogether, Lizzie killed off without explanation. Or that an extra—a previously mute guard, cook, or shepherd—had been awarded with career-stimulating bonus scenes. Or: extended episodes of alien stalking and bloodshed added as substitutes.

Anything was passable, Marta supposed, so long as it supplied minutes of useful screen time. Her prediction called for the line of least resistance—lowest cost, smallest effort—prevailing.

Wandering from desk to desk Marta enjoyed the sunless quiescence of Joan's. She settled behind Jake's desk and listened to the refrigerator's whir, incoming pages of the fax machine, and the orchestral ringing of telephones. After a quarter hour restlessness assailed her. Still, there was no point to beginning any project because, Marta suspected, Lora and company hovered in the vicinity. She'd outlawed the only option—checking in—telling herself that an absolute break from campus and city routines had to be advantageous; ear plugs for the siren call of work would be a nudge in an untried direction, so postulated the theory. And though the zeitgeist declared that constantly being in touch via email and a mobile phone emblematized success, the eroding of the line between career and the rest of life rankled her. If anything, the division should be shored up.

Years ago on a whim Marta had called Judy—who'd opted, on the heels of a short-lived and ill-advised flirtation with auburn dye, a pixie cut, and a rebranding as Lilith, for "respectable yet icy" Judith. She'd also kissed the pursuit of a doctorate goodbye, widely proclaiming that any fool could see the results of even the most rudimentary cost-benefit analysis: serious time wastage during one's prime. When Judith answered, Marta asked about the background noise. "Waves," Judith said, explaining that her toes pointed to turquoise water on a beach in Hawaii; she'd thought it best to stay in contact "in case a listing should move." That state of mind Marta wanted to permanently extinguish.

The compromise—to check in with her research assistant, who'd agreed to take care of the balcony of thirsty plants in need of repotting at Undre Arms—became null and void when Chaz pushed the door open and held it for Lora and Jake. The trio thundered in, an excitable herd with immediate goals and directions. Vacating Jake's chair, Marta sped toward Lora; technically, Jake held boss status, but his brusque indifference made Lora the easier choice.

"That was quick. I barely had time to accomplish a thing."

"We passed by each other on the highway, so we met roadside and turned around," Lora said, watching Chaz loiter near the front door. "Alright, Chaz, you know the drill. Or do you need a map?"

"No, ma'am." Chaz started toward a desk.

"Marta, we're all on the same page now, so we'll bring you up to speed," Lora said.

Jake passed by, phone in hand. "Just give me five. We'll meet in my office."

"Question: Did you check out Cast It?" Lora said.

"So far as possible. Full access requires membership." Marta followed Lora's trail from desk to kitchen to fax machine.

"Oh, damn it, I forgot, right, I'll get that to you in a jiff."

The meeting in Jake's office washed over Marta as déjà vu: agitated Lora—in fatigues and a bright T-shirt advertising a chainsaw manufacturer—perched fretfully on the desk's right corner while rock-ribbed Jake, self-assured with the baritone, set jaw, and black T-shirt, sat tipped back behind the desk, eyes darting to computer screens.

"The big cheeses," Lora began, "thought of a few solutions for the cactus incident. I'll spare you the details—and there was a fricking tornado of proposals—but the gods have spoken: Lizzie will stay in the script."

"So now all we need is a new Lizzie," Jake added. "Yesterday, preferably."

"That's where you'll come in because Jake and I need to focus on rearranging the shooting schedule. Thanks to Little Miss Method the whole thing's totally cockeyed now."

Envisioning a snaking procession of actor profiles, Marta said, "How can I help?"

"I've outlined it all there." Lora handed Marta a yellow pad of paper filled with words and a pencil etching of one-way arrows. Marta studied the messy oval flow chart. "Who gets called first, what everybody will want and expect, and so forth. It looks bewildering probably, but it's a cinch."

"Alright."

"First thing first is the casting exec in the city," Lora said, finger on the thickest arrow. "She's already alerted and will have rounded up way too many wannabe Lizzies. Actors are about the same as us rubes buying lottery tickets: very few winners but a dreamy boatload of hopefuls."

"Anyway, the idea is to hire a look-alike," Jake said, "so that some of the scenes shot with Lizzie in the background won't need to be re-shot. Eventually we'll come up with a short list, a really short one in this case, and we'll pass it over to the network, and the director and production execs here and there. Got it?"

"Yes, I do," Marta stood. "Lora, it would be great if you could show me how to access Cast It."

"No problem, c'mon," Lora said, on her way out. "Then we'll line you up with Blanche at MetroPolis Casting. Oh, she's a bully and will talk your ear off, so beware. She's from some Baltic, no, make that Balkan, one of the two, republic where pushy brow-beating is a way of life. Anyway, it'll be Canadian casting, guaranteed. Tax breaks, sweetie, always depend on CanCon rules, a required amount of local hiring. You can report to Jake, or to me if he's not around."

Lora explained the process, the arduous part of which rose inescapably: conferring with so many different people with such distinct and likely competing agendas. The production company, casting directors, and network decision-makers would each have directions and opinions and needs, and all would require updates and progress reports—and accomplished, if possible, in hours. "Lizzie the Second spitting out lines before Friday," Jake had promised.

Reassuring Marta about the inevitability of minor disasters, Lora added that obvious solutions rarely worked out: the back-up plan dating from initial casting was currently in rehearsal at "some dinner theatre in the f-ing burbs and totally unavailable."

"Let's get this going." Jake's bark sounded chilly with impatience.

4.

Marta spoke on the phone throughout the day, leaving messages, talking to assistants, and answering questions from executives; exasperation clouded the atmosphere. The sun had set by the time she finished, left ear throbbing, nose bridge pinched on dozens of instances; if asked how much she'd achieved, or how near a Lizzie replacement stood to signing a contract, Marta couldn't judge, the day's biggest discovery being that movie people, despite the appearance of direct speech, clear motivations, set goals, and, above all, yes/no decisiveness—using, in other words, the black and white language of the business world—prevaricated habitually; vagueness and doublespeak poured from their mouths.

In Department of English offices Marta recognized the approximate truth behind bureaucratic non-statements, but here she hadn't fully grasped the rules. Promissory declarations—"Okay, let's pursue that," "For sure, we'll liaise about it and get back to you pronto," "Absolutely, she looks like a keeper"—often dispersed into nothingness, causing Marta's stomach to flip at each of Lora's frequent requests for progress reports. Marta felt battered and strong-armed, treated as a minor functionary with a forgettable name at one moment and as a nettlesome impediment the next, like a gate with a rusted hinge.

Zone

I.

Slumped and feeling atrophied behind the desk, Jake wondered about what women feel. Fingers tapping nonsense Morse on the smooth oak, he zoned out; the laptop's screen clock ticked the fact that the day's third marathon conference call with Vancouver dawdled behind schedule—half of every shoot was spent on the phone, he'd swear, sure as well that he'd gasp no surprise when his MRI scan eventually revealed a grapefruit-sized brain tumour.

The question floating to mind sidestepped the matter of what women want—not *Cosmo*'s bread and butter: how to be happy, romantically fulfilled, paid attention to, and validated to the core while achieving multiple orgasm and large-carat birthrights. No, he wanted to comprehend exactly the physical sensation of being pent up, horny. Since he couldn't walk a mile in lady shoes, Jake thought to pose the question to Lora; right after a shocked face—and a quip: "You could always ask, Jake. You know, just before sneaking out before morning"—she'd tell him straight up.

He'd bet the sensation shared traits with hunger or thirst, real if challenging to describe, and needing to be slaked or else. Or not. Maybe being peckish was closer: not so much, "If I don't have it now I will die," but instead akin to, "A piece of chocolate would be tasty right now," and then five minutes later she might still be thinking about it, or, equally possible, would have moved on to another topic. Similar to his, yes, but also categorically different.

He'd have to be cautious with Lora; she would jump down his throat about chauvinism if the phrasing sounded off kilter. "Jake, that's totally inappropriate": it wouldn't be the first warning. Though "asswipe" and "prick" remained in heavy, office-wide rotation, she'd deep-sixed the circulation of "gash" and "snatch" with repeated mumblings of "out of control" and "union grievance officer."

His libido refused pleads of compromise, Jake knew. A sex drive was a hurricane force, the iron grip of winter over an Arctic town; and while he ordinarily thrived off the forward thrust—when a studio rep at a wrap party a year ago said some French painter had crowed how he painted with his prick, Jake had nodded with approval and recognition—the burdensome, bullying side irked him, much like a spoilt child whose super-enthusiast parents have brainwashed him to believe the world revolves around his every need.

Jake's sac had been weighty and full of urging for days in fact, and this morning his shaft was showing signs of unasked for off-and-on engorgement, depending on mobility. As it rubbed against fabric when he walked, Jake thoughts had wandered doggedly from set crisis management to available orifices, and further wood resulted. That only led to a new volley of compulsive thoughts—textbook vicious circle. And morning, he knew, would bleed into evening. His dick might be primitive and the polar opposite of Mensa material, but it had a wolf's grasp on targets. And mole-like too, its instincts led him to places where that satisfaction would be within closest reach.

Jake had taken care of the immediate problem early this morning in the rinky-dink toilet room in the back of Joan's, quickly, a low groan accompanying a nominally satiating spurt of release. A wank's merit, a relieving of pressure and nothing more, merited no poetry. The act wasn't a letdown so much as muted, a partial sighting of a blurred metallic orb in the night sky when you really craved being beamed up right inside the heart of the mothership.

After the thudding non-event outside of trailer park Xtina's—the address now a twice-a-day at least reminder of what could have been—he'd been gruff with need; bossy aggression lurked just below the surface of all his moods as a result.

And while any morning jerk off staved off the groin's urgent immediacy—when, mutated into a rutting animal, he'd be drawn to pushing into unyielding surfaces (the routine age-old: Jake's first sexual memory the result of standing pressed in front of the vibrating washing machine) and begin to size up anyone within eyeshot, or have sudden, unwanted clarity about dogs humping legs and pillows—that solution had the same appeal of driving at the exact speed limit. And who committed to that?

Jake surveyed options. Lora was too much of a sibling to register, and something unappealingly stringy persisted about the professor, a brown minnow in a vast colourful sea. And that tightly-reined librarian fantasy had never held Jake in its sway. He pictured the tattooed lesbian PA at main unit, the grizzled married-with-kids gaffer on set who'd blown him with surprising expertise in a studio bathroom a couple of shows ago, and Nicos—rumours whispered that he swung both ways, and he'd seemed pretty keen to get up close and personal that day at the crash site cave. There'd be weird repercussions, though, awkwardness the least of them; and, anyway, that taboo law of the jungle about not crapping where you fed made sense, as did going fully corporate and outsourcing.

Jake watched Lora's gesticulating conference with the professor; when he stripped them, the image landed elsewhere—not as saloon odalisques with long curving backs and inviting liquid eyes, but as trembling POWs, arms crossed, resentful and afraid, and anything but aroused.

He peered past them to the street. The restaurant down the street offered the best bet: a waitress—less entanglement, more laissez faire.

2.

Make hay while the sun shines, he thought, checking for incoming email.

A website Jake relied on when traveling listed the hotbeds of regional activity; nearby locations such as parks or rest stops ranked south of iffy—one star and year-old comments: "Dont waste ur time" and "I'll be there Oct 5, 1–5PM."

Craigslist, the other frontrunner, let Jake know that what few opportunities existed in the valley could be found in the area's largest city, an hour at least even if gunning it. The sparse local titles posted extremes—from "Personal Pain Slut" to "LTR or Bust: Ring Me"—and spelled nothing but trouble, and, besides, he craved a normal player—sexually awake, not a tub of fat, geriatric, or an emotional freak show—likewise on the prowl for a hassle-free one-off. Simplicity itself. If nothing else, he'd have to place his own bait; and if that flamed out chance-taking also loomed: an outdoor location and deadly small talk with a horny geezer while watchful for tasty arrivals who might never arrive.

Despite himself, Jake hoped for better than barrel scrapings. The country, in old jokes and movies at least, seethed with beef-fed hay bailers who'd grab hot urgent sex from wherever they found it—women, men, livestock, a hole carved into a melon—as well as farmers' daughters and sultry diner waitresses, full-hipped women chomping at the bit who'd missed the olden-days lecture about female propriety and whose primal nature trumped nurture. So why, when he'd give eyeteeth for a randy farmhand who'd readily fuck in a chicken coop, were ads for panty-clad married men, pervy senior citizens spending their sunset years at rest stops, and deranged trailer trash, all he ran into?

"Jake," Lora yelled from out front. "Vancouver's ready now on line two, sounding ready to rumble."

Wisdom and Blood

I.

Frayed, bleary-eyed, and talked-out when main unit's window shot wrapped, Marta could only focus on saying terse farewells and racing to the Star-Lite—cinder block and sterile, yes, but a monastic and winningly anodyne sanctuary nevertheless. Leaving Joan's meant the solace of a freedom she couldn't wait to breathe in. She'd hoard the per diem funds and skip another meal; becoming so swept up in work—call after incessant call—meant begging off for a half-hour break, a decadent, out of the question luxury. All day she'd grazed on cereal bars, chocolate, and pinches of trail mix instead. Her taut and leaden midriff complained, as though she'd swallowed a wheelbarrow of hay.

Beside the simple, remedying pleasure of solitude, Marta needed to be away from the tentative hugs and hushed reassuring there-theres—or worse, embarrassed wordless loss of composure—arising once an outburst became public spectacle. Her jaw clenched in certainty that any moment or the smallest of catalysts—dropped keys, a paper cut, another photocopier jam—would trigger frustrated tears. They'd erupt with geyser force; there'd be no stopping the sobbing torrent, and in that instant she'd be revealed as infantile and green, merely a novice incapable of coping, a tearful woman in a man's bellicose arena.

Growing rhinoceros hide might happen eventually, but defenselessness ruled today. Marta harboured a big squalling baby beneath a competent surface; she was determined to let no one catch the least glimpse.

Shutting the door of Room #10, though, guaranteed a saved face: should the gale of weeping arise, the scene's setting in utter privacy would preserve the outermost facade of her pride.

2.

All day Joan's had been closed in and discomforting, and escaping—walking into the sunset cinematically steadfast, no looking back—seemed the only sensible response.

Marta repeatedly imagined a shoulder-to-shoulder group in a stalled elevator compartment. Over the tiniest gap of minutes, a brutal new, albeit short-lived, social order would coalesce, leadership and second-in-command jockeyed for, oppositional party formed, weak followers assigned negligible duties or told to shut up. Upon the eventual release, the regime would disband, each individual fleeing the doors frantically with a single goal in mind: a quiet place, an Eden of solitude that no other body, voice, or personality could invade.

Throughout the shift's unending transmission of calls—complete with a random assortment of soothing musical genres when some kind soul placed her on hold—Marta had felt vulnerable and bullied when she believed she ought to be calloused, agenda-setting. Apparently she needed to "play hardball," "be in the big leagues," and "step up to the plate," the routine catch-phrases spouted by industry people during those conversations, but lacked the crucial gut instinct and "game face" that would result in the mandated, foe-demolishing "A game." Buffeted by sport and the idiot kill-or-be-killed jargon it generated, she returned to fantasies of the classroom ease.

That peculiar mettle wasn't foreign so much as unnecessary in her professional life, the official one anyway. In classes she lectured and facilitated thoughtful dialogue; at times when the subject was politically sensitive, the conversations normally remained even-tempered. There, the AC circulated calming motes of an implicit agreement: hotheaded impoliteness—anger, accusation, exasperation, abruptness—had no place within the Quaker-like community's serenely intellectual boundaries. A fiery attitude belonged to a lesser society, one that would sell its eye teeth for contestant status on *Big Brother* and the ilk, where bellowed outbursts, tearful makeups, and threats of physical altercations transformed into the gold of ratings success.

Speaking with self-important strangers in Vancouver and Los Angeles during the day, Marta sensed the pricks of their impatience; their tones shot out assertions difficult to miss: *Get to the point, I haven't got all day*; *Why are you wasting my precious time?*; *I'm valuable, who are you?*

The jarring rhythms of the conversations—cutting her off in mid-sentence, marooning her in on-hold limbo, demanding that she repeat sentences, misnaming her Margo and, inexplicably, Minta—hurt Marta's feelings and left her floundering: clout and the upper hand obviously claimed trophy status, but Marta wished for an even playing field, as Blanche from Vancouver would say before hauling in "Okay, let's get down to brass tacks" for the tenth time. The woman—if that's what she turned out to be: Marta imagined a clammy underworld deity with sunken, seen-it-all eyes set in a boneless androgynous face–wouldn't recognize finesse if it bit her.

In sporadic moments of calm logic during the shift, Marta believed communal laws governed the conversational tenor, making it no different than any other group idiom. With that, she decided not to take the aggression personally: speech sounded abrasive because that was how these people communicated with each other. A behavioural script, her soft science major students would call it. The same rule applied to car salesmen and realtors, she supposed, all a matter of perspective. An outsider eavesdropping at an academic conference would group the whole lot as pompous windbags of pedantry, while in truth only a small percentage deserved the title. The pushy rudeness she perceived at the other end of the receiver was probably similar: a couple of the calls had been with ill-mannered individuals, while the rest reflected no more than the lingua franca of movie industry segments.

Still, when actually conversing with the casting director (by turns overbearing and aggressive, as Lora had warned; a woman who peppered sentences liberally with "up our game") or her nasal assistant (short-tempered; expert at cutting retorts; capable of a scornful tone that Marta saw peeling paint) in Vancouver or anyone in the production hierarchy above Jake (*impatient* at the head of a lengthy list of undesirable traits), Marta found that remembering the soothing, explain-it-all mantra of plurality and cultural difference moved out of reach, an impossibility. Acceptance—this is not rude, not bad manners, not wrong, no, just a specialized form of communication—imploded. Rising from the wreckage: condemnation.

She began to think of those unreasonable, far off voices as sadistic, halfwitted, and stunningly coarse; longing to spit tacks and blurt out obscene strings of invective, she bit her tongue instead.

Marta pictured herself as a starchy diplomat's assistant uninformed about and therefore unprepared for the social habits of the brutal, cannibalistic tribe assigned to her. She craved a map of enemy terrain, or else a guidebook, *Industry Rules of Conduct*. But that access, she learned, came bundled with a proverbial caveat: easier said than done. *Go with the flow*—the disposition she aimed for—proved equally unapproachable.

By the end of a day of parading mercurial moods, she'd given up on adjusting to their ways or adopting them. Rather than engaging with the speaker at the opposite receiver as a person whose heart pulsed with warm blood and valuable insights, she grew as sullen as a teenager, monosyllabic voice progressively stripped of goodwill, lastly a series of utilitarian functions: "Yes," "No," "I understand," "Will do," "Okay." Every "Thank you" strictly pro forma. The responses mimicked Jake, she recognized, unsure whether such impersonal efficiency indicated a sign of victory or defeat.

Go!

1.

Jake ran through a mental checklist: bean counters and bureaucrats from higher up (appeased), new pages of the shoot (set to go), replacement Lizzie (coming into focus), Pinky (yes, the housekeeper confirmed she hadn't caved; ears blocked to pitiful mewls, she'd fed Gleek spartan diet portions).

The niggling rest could wait until the morning. The sun had set. Eagerness to put the business side of the laptop to sleep burbled throughout his limbs.

2.

Handling calls, emails, quick conferences with Lora, and trips to set, Jake had still managed to carve out a potential time and place for the evening's extracurricular session.

Even with the slim pickings—a shade short of a famine overall, and (once burned, twice shy) not an eligible woman to be plucked—he'd exchanged promising details with a pair of guys: a local who claimed to live on a family peach farm and a wine tourist in a hotel fifteen minutes to the south. Johnny Peachpit, likely skittish and a probable no-show, or the tense "on the DL" hotel guy with scant details and a shortage of photos to trade: with his gut instinct retracted and mute, Jake opted to let the fates choose. He grabbed a penny for the scattering of coins on the desk and tossed it. Tails. He typed, "Good to go. Address?" and waited for Peachpit's reply.

The promptness blew away the hovering pessimism; Jake's heart picked up the pace. Getting dicked around by slow replies was a fatal telltale, he could claim from experience; it meant the player on the other end had opted to yank his chain. Or toy with him: and cat/mouse feels worthwhile only when you're the cat.

Jake jotted down the information: "South, on the way to Deadman Lake, turn right at sign, The Singhs, fruit stand, parked tractor."

To the alleged tourist holed up with blue balls at the deluxe resort, Jake typed a message, "Not happening, bud. Gd luck." Karma inspired the courtesy; no one likes to be left hanging.

Sex outdoors—a camping site, a parked car, a park, even an alleyway—always packed a charge; and an orchard stretched before him as virgin territory. Jake felt pumped with excitement.

Beautiful Objects

I.

Marta collapsed on the bed fully dressed and thankful in the reprieve of darkness. She alternated between staring myopically at the ceiling and turning over, face pressed into the lavender-scented Egyptian cotton quilt that she'd packed at home—a once upon a time luxury item which, like English soap and an ampule of high-tech moisturizer concocted in French laboratories, had become a daily indispensable.

With the single image of a shut door and secured brass chain whispering alluringly, the road to the Star-Lite had passed by unnoticed.

Marta exhaled deeply, relieved at staying dry-eyed, albeit perspiring, inside the tomb silence of the room; not even a foreshadowing of tears crossed her face—no telltale film of excess eye moisture, slight trembling of the lips, or uncontrollable tugging of a frown. Without the stimulus overload and the fraught negotiation called conversation, her former self returned. Even-keeled.

After ten minutes she relaxed: no outburst would arise.

Marta imagined her nervous darting eyes—those of a deer sipping at a stream where predators lurk—steadying, announcing the end of mental disarray. She sat up and clicked on one bulb of the bedside lamp. The hunger she'd staved off with salty banana chips and mixed nuts returned, but late-night restaurants of any stripe seemed improbable nearby. Though Marta believed that late meals were unhealthy—when a yo-yoing maven of daytime TV had publicized her diet guru's rule banning carbohydrates after 7PM, Marta accepted the wisdom of the latter-year Sermon on the Mount without a second thought—the day's exceptional difficulty granted leeway.

She foresaw a drive on deserted streets, a quest for the glow of a diner, *Nighthawks* circa 2010 promising warmth, security, and comforting light, but serving shade-grown and fair trade organic coffee rather than watery swill soaked with DDT and harvested by exploited peasants. Turning over one page in the wafer of a phonebook made her realize that gorging on junk food from a gas station would be as close to that nocturnal idyll as she'd get. *That can't be worse that pacing in a solitary hothouse*, she thought.

Three thuds on the door followed light taps running across the window.

"Yes," Marta switched the bedside lamp to full intensity and crossing to the security chain. The only surprise possible would be somebody other than Chaz.

"What are you up to?" Chaz had already changed clothing, and Marta read his new T-shirt: "Chuck's Pub. What Wood You Like?" The beer-slinging barmaid in a short skirt and halter top was a woodchuck. D-cup, naturally.

"Well," she started, mouth volcanic with complaint. "When I arrived here I wanted nothing except escape from the office. I don't know how you people do it." The impulse to continue with invective stagnated on her tongue. "Anyway, for the past couple of minutes I've been thinking about chasing down something edible. I looked through the phone book, but practically everything is in Penticton and Osoyoos. Do you have any good ideas?"

"There's chips in my room, but that's it, sorry. Anyway, I thought we might go swimming."

"Really? I mean, are you serious?"

"But of course, madame. Earlier today you mentioned going to the canal, and it kinda stuck in my head."

On the highway, Marta resisted and had finally given in to Chaz's request for examples of the bad behaviour of her youth. She'd felt reluctant. His presumption: colourful yarns to spin, revealing glimpses at the rocky contours of a stowed-away wild side.

Marta's face had warmed with embarrassment about a history with a startling lack of delinquent bite—nothing except for mild-mannered disobedience: resisting adult rules in minuscule ways, such as an afternoon of swimming in the reputedly dangerous currents of the canal behind her grandmother's farm. No poignant story of running away from home was hers to tell; and no shoplifting, cheating on tests, risking alcohol poisoning and waking up in a ditch, or obtaining a body piercing on the sly. She'd never been fined for a late library book return. The revelation, then: she'd been judicious and faithful, easily comprehending the wisdom of laws and parental authority, and had little drive for hormonal, Id-orchestrated acting out. That chapter made Marta feel as rebellious as an orthopedic shoe.

After hearing the pitiful bad girl list Chaz, mumbling about a checkered past and pleading the Fifth, agreed to reciprocate, full of defensive qualifications to render the severity harmless.

"It was a long time ago," he'd emphasized, "so keep that in mind, and not all at once. I barely recognize that guy now. My parents were getting divorced and, really, it's not nearly as bad as it looks." Had he been caught, the misdemeanors would have landed him in juvenile detention or worse: spray paint vandalism, shoplifting, defacing library books, underage drinking, "petty dealing of party drugs," "B and E," including a church, and arbitrary acts of targeted violence which, he confessed, might be classified as hate crimes today. "You know, typical redneck town shit, jocks roughing up the class queer and pushing around the two Asian kids."

For Marta, also raised in a community of similar size, the rap sheet highlighted appalling efforts. And, aside from fantasies, she'd never struck a soul.

"You gotta believe me, that person is a total stranger. I'm one hundred percent pussycat now." Chaz continued to disavow that self and whatever truths it revealed. The final words of his defense: "C'mon, last winter I was a Sister of Honour at a lesbian wedding. A Wiccan Joining Ritual, I mean."

Inside the cab, they had painted themselves into an awkward, silent corner; Marta's surprise had been interpreted as total condemnation.

Though hungry and frazzled, Marta grasped that the chance to let Chaz off the hook had wafted into the room. With the exception of the bully barbarism, she'd sensed a twinge of her own envy, in any case, not judgment alone: a sensible, well-mannered childhood does not convert into intriguing memoir. "Okay." She sought alternatives. "Well, how about swimming on the weekend?"

"How about 'Make hay while the sun shines'?" He slumped, back against the doorframe. "You don't have to swim, just show me how to get there. How's that? We've pushed shooting forward by a couple of hours tomorrow, so you'll have time for beauty sleep if that's your worry. Besides, it's that or *Exxtreme*—with two Xs—*Labradoodles: Caught on Tape!* on TV."

"Well, you're practically wagging your tail down there. That's hard to resist."

"Excellent, I'll grab the chips." Chaz sprang to his feet and saluted a goodbye.

"Ten minutes, okay?" Marta thought of the peasant blouse with the beaded drawstring neck. The gauzy medium weight would be ideal for canal-cooled drafts.

"No problem."

2.

They walked in silence by the bug-splashed noses of cars toward Marta's rental, parked next to the Star-Lite's front desk office. Hours past sunset, all the surfaces—asphalt, concrete, stucco, room doors painted red—radiated with dying campfire heat, but chilled breezes rushing down from valley peaks and through orchards whispered promises of a comfortable sleep.

To reach the canal from her grandmother's alfalfa fields, Marta had needed to fight through fifteen minutes of reverted farmland, a parcel of gnarled roots, antelope-bush, tall grasses, and woolly rabbit-brush that snagged clothing. She remembered that service roads ran parallel to the channel, and drove toward Joan's certain that the point of entry would appear, clear as a beacon. Since Chaz hadn't asked, she guessed he trusted her internal compass.

Unaccustomed to driving at night Marta sighed in gratitude for the deserted highway—and Chaz's restraint: little animation, no fidgeting with the radio, no comments about the speed limit. The orchards stood mutely, revealing sentry indivisibility when the headlights flashed across their leaves.

Marta followed the tug of memory and turned right when approaching the town's prominent intersection. Her concern mounted—odds favoured the access road's accessibility for municipality officials only and gates for anyone else. Spotting a small bridge ahead, she signaled right again.

"Whoa, slow down, sister!" Chaz said.

"You held your tongue the entire way, that was impressive. I do have to slow down for a second, only to get my bearings, but I promise to speed up again."

As breezes rushed through the cabin, they passed by windowless fruit storehouses, forlorn lots, and scrappy back yard orchards. Chaz pointed out a municipal sign, the destination now plain. A yellow metal gate blocked passage.

"Well, that's that." Marta listened to the idling engine. Beams caught metallic flecks in the paint and made the heavy bar glow with unambiguous purpose.

"Just give me a sec, okay?" Chaz reached for the door handle. "And eat some chips before I scarf down the whole f-ing bag. Deep-fried potatoes, that's the last thing needed by this Buddha belly."

Marta watched him walking to the gate. Chaz bent before turning to the car with a smile. "It's not locked." He strode to her window. "Green means go."

"And that," she sighed, "is how criminal acts begin." A statement of formality only: Marta could see that canal swimming was a foregone conclusion.

He's already turned for the gate. "An unlocked gate and not a Do Not Enter sign in sight. I think we'd have a legit case."

"I have to agree."

Chaz unhitched the gate and re-secured it once Marta passed through, tiptoeing back to the car with cartoon villain sneakiness.

Pebbles spat noisily and Marta noticed the car drifting slightly as the tires followed the road's gravel curves. She clenched the steering wheel; the surfing motion awakened her nerves. "You know, it's interesting, this canal system was dug before the Depression, when the government decided to develop this town," she said. "It planned to create a settlement for World War One veterans. Before that the whole area got by as a minor gold rush hub and a major cattle ranching area. Beef for the Empire."

"Cool, Professor History. Maybe I'll read about it when the book comes out." He reached outside with scooped hands; the air pushed his lax arms along the window frame. "How much further?"

"Bridges were built at even spans all along the way. As far as I can remember, they're more or less identical. I can pull over any time, so just say when."

The curve straightened and she drove with relaxed shoulders for five quiet minutes.

"Okay, next one," Chaz exclaimed.

"I'll keep the headlights switched on." Marta slowed as a bridge came into sight.

3.

Willowy vegetation clotted the canal's banks; if clandestine swimmers had cut pathways, none parted from the road.

"Wow, it's not the Gold Coast is it? Looks like I'll have to blaze my own trail," Chaz said, beginning to slide down his jeans. "No, er, cracks about a full moon, alright?"

"My lips are sealed." Work had blessed Chaz with a farmer's tan. His face and forearms blended into the night while the rest did set itself up for lunar jokes.

"You're sure you don't want to come in?" Chaz stood wearing striped boxer shorts.

"Between log boom death traps at home and the deadly currents of the canal, my family was phobic about death by submersion." Expecting a piercing and tattoos, Marta was surprised to discover nothing except an ursine endowment of unclipped chest hair in a thick T. "You'd think we'd had a maritime family tragedy that everyone desperately wanted to never repeat. But, really, the water is too cold for me."

"Okay, here goes nothing." Chaz shucked the boxers and quickly turning for the water. He hopped over sharp rocks and a yarn tangle of branches, muttering about pain until disappearing. "Mother of Christ, it's . . . okay. Actually it's not that bad!"

A translucent miasma of haze drifted in from distant orchards, and Marta concluded the swampy setting would look better from a distance. She hiked to the centre of the white wooden bridge and peered over the edge to watch the foamy rush of water beneath; bats swooped and fluttered across the wide night sky.

Chaz yelled and gesticulated, but Marta couldn't decipher a word. She waved, growing uneasy. If he swam too close to the bridge and its narrow corridors of swift current, she'd gesture madly to alert him. The set up seemed classic as a would-be tragic accident: "Yes, officer, it was late at night. Yes, he was swimming alone. Yes, he may have had a beer or two. No, I couldn't hear what he was saying, and by the time I rushed down to the water he was too far from the shore; I couldn't really see him, so rescuing him was out of the question." She wondered if being a passive witness counted as criminal negligence.

Watching Chaz from the bridge, Marta envisioned herself standing atop the plank railing, cinematically lit, balanced precariously, wearing a bone-white bra and, matching her bruisable, faintly indolic flesh, panties reminiscent of sodden newsprint. The image could be an indelible outtake from *Blue Velvet*, and she—vulnerable, overwrought, mottled with grotesquerie—a woman about to make a despairing or euphoric leap after a sublime moment of trailer court anagnorisis, perhaps, or to undulate crazily while lip-synching to a dubious torch song from the 1950s.

Marta had read enough to recognize that a leap into the dark void came freighted with implications, soulful and profound. If in a novel, the catharsis of the leap and the immersion into the water would be a complex, essay-worthy set of associations that might reference baptism rituals or the Freudian unconscious; she'd analyze the passage in a classroom expertly. The difference was, jumping off the ledge and sinking into the roaring current tonight wouldn't announce any breakthrough. Inky water here simply meant dangerous, not symbolic; and if surviving the plunge turned out to be the lucky outcome, the arrival on shore would presage the mood of a wet cat only. The literary moment—doused with a convenient new outlook, now weightless and ready to grab life by the horns after the special audience with Platonic truth—would prove wishful thinking. She'd be cold and uncomfortable, and flustered later while driving on empty roads in damp undergarments clamped to puckered skin. She hadn't even brought a towel.

Chaz floated otter-like below. He let himself drift for a moment with the current and then kicked frantically to return to territory he'd already claimed.

Marta waved again and walked toward the car. Staring into the murky thicket hollow where Chaz had disappeared, she began to discern a crude pathway. Branches jabbed and the granite bank tricked her feet, but the current's silvery reflections guided her forward. No sandy shore met her: rock one step, canal the next. Alert for the insidious hum of ravening mosquitoes Marta crouched on a flat boulder, pondering whether to dip a toe into the frigid water.

"How's the water out there," Marta yelled over the current.

"Invigorating!" Chaz turned over and began swimming toward the bank. "Actually, it's cold as a witch's tit. That was my Dad's favourite."

"Colourful. Mine still says, 'Cold as a well-digger's ass.' "

"And 'Don't know shit from Shinola,' " Chaz said. "Never knew what that meant."

"My mother preferred 'chewed dates.' " Marta ran fingertips along the surface of the water. "My father's comparison was—well, is—always 'ass' and 'a hole in the ground.' "

"Wow, 'Good grief, Charles' for my mom. The foulest thing out of her mouth is 'Cripes!' And that's when she's really 'browned off' about something. It's time-warpy, but kinda cute."

"My mother grew up in a Prairie household of hockey player brothers."

"It's weird that our generation doesn't have better sayings." He paddled near the shore. "Saying 'dude' all the time doesn't count." The current mellowed at the water's edge and Chaz corrected the drifting with an occasional kick.

"Cold as a stock-trader's eyes?"

"That's not bad," Chaz said. "I was thinking of something to do with terrorists, but it seemed too obvious and Republican. Phew, that's enough for me. With all the shrinkage, I'm starting to feel peewee league!"

"Your clothes are where you left them on the car hood." She could feel the water-cooled air passing though the cotton's light weave. "Do you want me to grab them?"

"Nah, they'll be warm. I'll make a run for it."

Marta guessed they were both conscious of the scene's picturesque oddity, Chaz the au naturel elephant in the room. Knee-jerk propriety occurred to her as she stood: fig-leaf hands over the groin for the man; and for the woman averted eyes, or, perhaps, nurse-like efficiency, as though a nude body—a mere object to be shaved, wiped, or prodded—existed as part of a routine, as unnoticed a line in the job description as beeping heart rate monitors.

Comic relief slipped out instead. "This way, Sir," she said, gesturing with the bland helpfulness of a flight attendant.

"Thank you, Miss." Chaz slipped out of the canal and into the trail with a motion whose fluidity was broken by yelps and grumbling caused by pokes of angular gravel and sharp webs of branches.

Though she'd never stood at this exact location and hadn't ever conceived of sneaking out to the canal deep into the night, Marta inhaled deeply and, facing the water, surrendered to a contentment cousin to nostalgia. Cascading swirls of moist and warm air, enveloping murmur of current, mobile chiaroscuro along the surface: the bubble of time exceptional and perfect, otherworldly yet as rooted as ivy.

With the headlights illuminating the return climb, Marta avoided the snags along the path.

"Hey, I should have mentioned it earlier, but I looked online. There's a twenty-four-hour truck stop-style restaurant ten minutes south of the motel," Chaz said as Marta emerged from the darkness. "It's either that or the dregs of the BBQ chips."

"I'm officially starving, so chips won't cut it."
"Pedal to the metal?"
"Okay, for you. Just once."
"Let's go," he said. "I'm buying."
"As you wish, Charles."
"Ha ha, let's not go there. Just my mom calls me that."
"I understand you completely."

Colossus

I.

Jake's chest nudged the steering wheel as he scrutinized the poker-faced landscape: one sliver-thin dirt road looked no different from the next, and the solid blocks of orchard between them helped him in no way. He felt elderly slowing to catch sight of the dwarf road signs. At least no other drivers zoomed by and registered—*honk, hooonnnkkk*—the crawling speed, stops and starts, and brake light frequency. Jake, almost positive he was pointed in the right direction, fretted about the sketchy details; he thought enviously of scouts and trackers in movies—never having met one in real life—who could glance at a patch of dirt and verify who'd been there, what went down, and how long ago. Close to the real McCoy, Nicos would have sniffed out the location in a heartbeat.

Reaching the summit of the low rise, Jake spotted the landmark he'd been told to watch for—a small plywood fruit stand whose roof-top sign trumpeted fertility: a basket-weave cornucopia spilling over with plump ripe produce. Supposedly, the rendezvous location stood just inside the next roadway.

A minute too early, Jake spat gum out the window and popped in two fresh cinnamon pieces, hoping that the courtesy would be reciprocated. He'd walked away from breath-of-the-damned types before; and he'd head for the nearest exit if up close and personal with any body's rank orifices and funky pits. He rifled through the messenger bag for lube. Spending next to no time on trivial chat and negotiations would be key tonight.

Tractor-wide, the target road stretched out, as nondescript as the rest. Jake braked to a crawl. Since parking on the puny road shoulder was out of the question, process of elimination led him to the orchard itself. If anything went wrong, he'd tell Old MacDonald or Officer Joe that he'd pulled over to take a leak: tired, a long day on the road, etc, etc, no harm, no foul.

Positioned at the edge of the neat tree line, Jake flicked off the headlights and waited. Short minutes later he swung open the door—a furtive stranger inside a dark car could be intimidating, after all, shorthand for danger. Leaning against the grille with crossed arms, he saw shadowy forms and detected no sound except rustling leaves and the guttural croaking of distant toads. A cattle-hauling semi sped by, illuminating the arbour, for that instant a diorama at a natural history museum: "The Age of Agribusiness," complete with an old-fashioned thresher and piped-in livestock pong. During the headlight flash Jake darted his eyes from one tree trunk to the next. Not a soul. And when darkness returned he was blind for a half minute and anticipated the snap of a twig or a voice—"Hey, man"—from the near distance. Still nothing save for the sound of his breathing. The butt of a joke, he predicted, the sensation unwelcome.

2.

It's time to take the bull by the horns, Jake thought. "Hey, anyone there?" he asked, voice low but friendly, as when approaching a dog. Jokily: "I can't see past my nose."

The breeze cutting through the trees answered enigmatically.

He sighed a gambler's lament, pissed about wasted time and squashed expectations. Ecstasy's possible, Jake had been shown time and again, as is being stood up, running into a repulsive case of false advertising, or coming face to face with a thudding lack of chemistry despite everything lining up on paper.

Buttressed and warmed by the vehicle, the idiocy of trying but failing to attain a cool, devil-may-care pose struck him.

Jake's eureka called for the lowering of jeans; he'd work his tool to optimal hardness and jack with teasing showy gusto. A proud Colossus of Rhodes stance might entice the shy watcher; that manly siren's call never failed to work in porn. Outside of porn, the spectacle played out differently: a comic set-up with a punch line about Pee-wee Herman and being caught, or worse, a crushing indictment—the mark of a sex offender, a solitary loser, a characterless nobody with an overgrown fantasy life who can't disguise the fact that the very existence of the bad habit is third-rate, less a proud enlightened choice than a pathetic last resort.

With the tumult of thoughts he kept the jeans buttoned.

Why did the act need to mean anything, Jake wondered. Nobody thought scratching an itch harboured deep implications, or stood for loneliness, laughable social skills, or butt ugliness. *Philosophy in the dark*, he thought, *what's up with that?*

He squinted into the murk of the rustling tree rows, expectations dwindling and spiky anger rising.

Exhaling sharply—annoyed, dissatisfied, insulted—Jake returned to the vehicle and backed up, momentarily pondering the hotel visitor he'd brushed off earlier. "Cursed hellhole," he said, "no wonder people go to real cities." He turned right at the highway. Despite the black cloud mood he drove off slowly. Someone might be there, hidden and watching—a coward or a sadist—and he refused to give the game-playing asswipe the satisfaction of catching any sign of his short-lived but intense regret.

Commoner Elements

I.

Perspiration rivulets tickled Marta as she signaled at the 24-hour Husky pillar, the towering red plastic portrait of the gas station's trustworthy namesake atop a secondary invitation: an electric blue circle at whose centre stood utensils—fork, knife, spoon—in giant silhouette. Shivering, Chaz had admitted the canal water to be far nearer to antarctic than arctic, and requested heat blasts along with sealed windows for the drive. The scent of vegetable broth filled the cabin as he thawed.

"Cool, Peterbilts, look at all that chrome," Chaz said during Marta's tour of the parking lot. Cooling and leonine, a few semis were sprawled near the highway; Marta, braking to survey the options, swerved toward a third-rate spot facing the toilets. A stop for truckers, she reasoned, so the might-is-right rule must apply.

"That'd be the life, eh? 'I don't pay no union dues,'" Chaz sang.

"I think that song is about being a tramp." Marta pondered the likely cleanliness of the women's washroom.

"Same idea: no fuzzy cubicle, no telephone noose, no nothing to tie you down." Chaz twisted around to survey the trailers. "'Believe in the holy contour of life,' right?"

"Men seem keen on that Kerouac mystique. When I think of him, I picture debt, a string of bad marriages, and death by alcohol before reaching fifty, an esophagus filled with blood. Not very romantic." Marta checked the parking brake. "As for the truck-driving life, sorry but I just don't get that, either. Sitting in a loud vibrating metal box all day, working for a quota-spouting boss, popping NoDoz. That sounds no better than an office, only with hemorrhoids and high cholesterol from a diet of fried food."

"Okay, Professor Killjoy. You're right, but every job is just a job when it comes down to it." He swung open his door. "You gotta admit, there's something about a shiny big rig on the open road."

"There used to be a drive-in right over there, the Silver Sage," Marta pointed, in no spirit to admit anything. The night air, summery but overlaid with acrid notes of gasoline fumes, was refreshing after the sultry automobile interior.

"I'll join you inside. I want to take a closer look at those babies."

Marta wandered toward the coffee shop under the metallic orange glare of mercury vapour lighting, each lamp's output, she guessed, as blinding as the sun. The canopy was deserted; weary families did not fill tanks at this hour. The Peterbilt drivers likewise stood out of sight, apparently in sleeper cabins or eating inside.

When Chaz bounded in Marta returned the sample menu to the cashier's stand. "Look who's here," Chaz said, pointing. "Hey, Jake! Let's go in."

"The sign says 'Please wait to be seated.'"

"That's different. We'll be with Jake, so it's like we're meeting somebody at our table." Chaz had already begun crossing the room.

While Marta felt no desire to sit across from Jake, a way out failed to materialize. Choosing a separate table would appear impolite. Reluctantly, she trailed behind Chaz.

"Small world, eh?" Chaz slipped into the booth. "What brings you here?"

"I went out for a drink with the AD and some crew. They're staying at the Watermark, down on the lake." Jake twisted a thumb toward Osoyoos.

"Ah, so that's where the A-listers are."

Marta looked around as the men talked shop. Solitary nighthawks comprised the Husky's population; a few thin men—plaid shirts, faded denim, cowboy hats—looked pallid and worn, yet held animated exchanged with the waitress and the line-cook as they sat at the long wood grain counter. Up close the restaurant's lighting, a beacon to drooping-eyed drivers on the highway, beamed harsh and unforgiving. The floor, seating, and tabletops were moulded from plastics, Marta observed; an industrial product, the pre-fab room expressed durability and efficiency. Barring fire, the formica would be wiped by generations of waitresses. If replaced, scavengers in the distant future would yank the eternal woodgrain from landfills and speculate in awe about the wondrous era before the Great Disaster.

Chaz pitched a career-growing strategy to Jake. "It's branding, right. You are your own brand, it's your skill-set as a product that's marketable."

"You mean like your porn name?"

"Huh," Chaz said.

"You know, that old joke—you take your first pet's name and a street you grew up on, and that's your nom de porn."

"Cinders Dupree," Chaz said.

"Rex Magnolia," Jake nodded with approval.

"Spotty Ponderosa." Marta pictured insects that devastated vast forest swaths.

"No, this is serious. I went to a seminar about this in the city. You choose two words that best describe you, professionally I mean. The idea is to distinguish yourself from the nameless horde, and to specialize as a way to define your niche."

"Are you sure it wasn't a cult, like that thing Lora joined?" Jake said. "Sounds idiotic."

Marta agreed. "What use does it have after you've defined your two characteristics? Do you print cards that say 'Chaz Murphy X and Y' and network with them at parties?"

"Hey, baby, what's your sign? I'm a Taurus with Scorpio rising," Jake said. "Man, that's just like movie Indian names. 'Pleased to meet you, I'm Big Sweating Bear.'"

In classrooms no one would throw the I-word into a conversation without carefully announced precaution and distancing finger-quotes; Marta kept quiet with the hope of discouraging Jake's insensitivity.

The waitress, buxom but haggard, slammed two sweating glasses of water on the table. "Ready to order?"

"The pie, is it locally made?" Marta asked, no stranger to buyer's remorse. "I wonder if there's lard in the dough."

"Um, let me check with Julia Child in the back," the waitress huffed, on hold for further tourist demands. Her tone edged toward exasperation: *the hoops I jump through for a lousy tip.*

"Thank you."

"The truck came from Spokane," the waitress answered when she returned. Marta caught the woman exchanging a glance with Jake. *Is this chick for real?*

"Oh, okay," Marta said, peevish. She had passed by at least half a dozen roadside fruit stands minutes before, but the pies on display here arrived boxed and frozen in a long haul trailer. And though the cherries might have been picked and processed by seasonal workers in one of the nearby orchards, the relentless logic of capitalism demanded pie production elsewhere. *Small wonder there's global warming*, she thought. "I'll try a slice of cherry, thank you."

"Whip?"

"No, thank you. Plain is fine." Marta added "whip" to the inventory of laboratory discoveries in her midst.

"Can you ask Wolfgang Puck back there if the gravy's organic and locally-sourced?" Chaz directed a full grin at Marta. "And can you tell me the cow's name?"

"Get a room or something, you guys, Christ."

"Maybe I'll have a Royale with cheese," Chaz said.

"Hamburger with cheese," the waitress said. "Fries or slaw?"

"Fries with gravy. On the side, okay?"

"Right." She turned to bark at the kitchen, "Yeah, alright, alright, in a minute, okay?" Facing Jake with raised eyebrows she asked, "You done?"

"Yes, ma'am."

The waitress frowned at the half-eaten meal and walked away.

"Looks like someone's taken a shine to you," Chaz said to Marta.

"You know, Chaz, the dangerous part of trying to be a hipster," Jake paused to drink, "is that the trying portion is way more obvious than the hipster portion and you end up looking like a total wanking loser, some lame wannabe in an entourage that thinks cool will miraculously rub off if he makes the right purchase. It's like those douche bags wearing Ed Hardy shit from head to toe and saying 'dude' and 'peace out, bro' every five seconds. I mean, c'mon, it's fucking pathetic. Every wannabe's been quoting that one scene since 1994. Christ, even the waitress knew it. Maybe you can bring back 'chillaxin' while you're at it, *dude*."

Marta shifted on the bench to measure Chaz's reaction. Masculine posturing in seminars wasn't new to her and, as a result, she counted temperate refereeing as a skill. She felt blood surging nonetheless and imagined a hot pink flame of anger streaking across her cheeks.

"Ouch, man, that's harsh. Next time, be sure to tell me what you really think." Signing defeat, Chaz extended his hands, palms up. "You're my boss, including after hours, so I guess I'll just bend over and take it. Hope you enjoy the ride."

"I guess anyone could be seen as making a sad grab for hipster status," Marta said, moved to defend the underdog. "For instance, a tattoo in Helvetica on one's forearm. How unique is that?"

Jake replied after several beats. "Touché, Professor." He couldn't even drag in the excuse that it stood for a folly of youth. "Look, I'm wound up and irritable, it brings out the dick in me." He stared out the window. "You're not a douche bag, man. Okay? I gotta get back to Kaleden. Eat up, the food's on me." Jake slid out from the booth and strode toward the cash register.

"He kinda walks like Chuck Heston, don't you think? 'You Maniacs! You blew it up! Ah, damn you! God damn you all to hell!' "

"Pardon?"

"*Planet of the Apes*. That's not entourage-y is it?"

"I really couldn't say."

Inward Impediments

I.

Though Marta had acclimated easily to the impatient nudge of a personal solar eclipse—opaque rectangles of stiff, densely woven drapery a soothing contrast to the invasive corona of brilliance foretelling summer's ongoing assault—she winced at the intensity of the morning's fiery display. *It must be late*, she thought. Pressing fingertips to temples firmly she massaged with slow rotations. She ached dully, as though suffering from the aftermath of excess alcohol or amidst deep-set sinus congestion. Fatigue made her eyes seem dehydrated, faintly sore.

Operating at full capacity required a completed cycle of sleep, and Marta knew each hour chopped away caused a punishing escalation of symptoms—wandering focus, irritability, and muted wit, the disincentives substantial. As a result she'd rarely been one to tempt fate and stay up late, not even when at university doing so meant Brownie badges of accomplishment and belonging, first partying all night and protesting boastfully of massive, splintering hangovers—"Holy crap, I can't even see straight!"—in an undergraduate lecture hall and, years later, typing in 4AM finishing touches on the most recent would-be publishable masterpiece, this one about fascism and nostalgia in T.S. Eliot's late-career essays for "Contradictions in Modernism," Professor So and So's exacting graduate seminar.

The delicate condition, as she thought of it, belonged to that class of retrograde feminine maladies—constitutional but unwelcome—experienced by the enervated angel of the household in a Victorian three-volume novel. In fact, she might be distant cousin to the delicate wasp-waisted specimen prescribed beef broth and ample bed rest after inexplicably collapsing—the poor dear—into a dead faint during an unusually hasty promenade through the rose garden.

Clutching the quilt, Marta sat up. Chaz snored lightly.

The habit didn't surprise Marta. Neither did the unconscious annexing of mattress territory, the ease with commandeering three quarters of the top sheet, or the restless cephalopod traversing of her body throughout the morning's earliest hours—inquisitive forearm resting below her breasts, thick trunk of a leg across her imprisoned calves. She peered into the bathroom. Check: even without glasses, she could discern the raised toilet seat.

In the hour of drifting toward wakefulness, Marta's mood oscillated between stars and gutter: queasy, vaguely out of sorts, and distressed—besides lacking sleep, she was entangled and sweltering in the flannel smock of a nightgown—while bubbling with a novel excitement-dread. The latter, she gauged, did not reflect the uncontaminated innocence of a well-fed suburban child on Christmas morning so much as the sour-sweet disaffected adolescent's mixture of enchantment and cynicism: "Yay, presents! . . . Eww, bad presents! . . . Ugh, God, how long do I have to sit listening to these worn out family stories?"

Rolling the quilt downward—cautiously: she'd hold off on shaking Chaz into consciousness—Marta found that her shoulders had grown stiff in unaccustomed and possibly unwelcome ways. Marta guessed that in reaction to Chaz's roving she'd slid far from the mattress' centre, half-sleeping while facing the drapes. The other options, entangled limbs or staked and defended turf, had seemed unfeasible and uncharitable, respectively, and since #10 wasn't large enough for a sofa bed the self-imposed edge-of-bed banishment represented the lesser of evils.

And Chaz scarcely wrestled with the fine points of bed-sharing diplomacy; he seemed the type who could nod off during a blitzkrieg. Stray light, a dripping tap, or sudden thoughts of the classroom: Marta had long ago accepted inevitable tossing and turning as another constitutional given.

Sleeping alone was a pleasure to which she'd happily grown accustomed. Although anyone could not help but be aware of snickering, judgmental words surely invented to categorize and dismiss—spinster, crone, old maid—Marta normally remained untroubled about what Dianne in a poetic if blunt maternal turn had christened her "friendless bed," George and Dianne having slept bundled together like kittens since their Niagara Falls honeymoon.

Contrary to the holier-than-thou forces of tradition—and mournful verse that spoke of lonely trees and cracked cups—Marta didn't believe in the destiny of an unpalatable fate, a punishing Sisyphean future of turning over crisp sheets on a fallow mattress each and every night until she grew withered and grey, eyes rheumy and remorseful.

And even if she stumbled into romance and eventual cohabitation, she'd certainly reserve a bed, or better yet an entire bedroom, for single occupancy. Animals might instinctually nod off in packed furry clusters, but Marta questioned sleeping in such close proximity, received wisdom far better in principle than actuality. Brushing aside the twitching motility, Chaz's other deep sleep companions—muttering, snorting, snoring—validated this sage perspective.

Marta straightened the nightgown after a moment's deliberation. Struggling to unfasten the row of pearl buttons, she pulled the yoke collar and peered beneath, expecting to discover a mark—an abrasion, light bruising, creases—but found instead narrow expanses of undamaged flesh separated by yesterday's underwear.

The clothing looked wrong—too plentiful, for one, with an Austen heroine decorousness, and also ridiculously virginal-yet-matronly—but the fitting morning-after ensemble did not coalesce no matter how long she pondered it. Naked merely felt exposed, and without access to the full sheet she could not hope to accomplish a come-hither Marilyn look; and utility-grade bra and panties alone returned her directly to the *Blue Velvet* universe. A sex kittenish oversized T-shirt à la Bridget Bardot seemed too far of a reach; and for that she'd need accompanying hair extensions at the very least. As for the flouncy satin, lace, and elastic fantasies of high-heeled bedtime femininity concocted by lingerie makers and pornographers, their insult provoked only an inner menaced gyn/ecologist.

Reaching toward the floor Marta secured a pillow and hugged it. Her thoughts ran to Chaz: he'd prefer Bardot in deshabille mode. Or else the cutesy ploy of wearing his too-large T-shirt. Men, in movies at least, found such childishness irresistible; women facing the same strategy from their men, meanwhile, would run for the hills, *Glen or Glenda*'s angora sweater-sharing Barbara the rule's exception.

Scattershot images rose—including an imaginary one: mutual partners in crime conversing at the Husky, friendly waves goodnight, and keys into the locks of separate rooms at the Star-Lite—and Marta fought the urge to organize them into categorical piles that formed a coherent narrative with an obvious thematic thread: here's what happened and here's what it means. The evening's denouement contained comedy of a kind. *Travesty, farce, gallow's humour*, she thought sourly, hands folded on a flannel-clad lap, *better leave it be.*

2.

The botched kiss at the gravel pit had inaugurated an circumspect retracting. Chaz kept a polite distance and resumed professional interaction.

Marta surmised that he saw only a blown chance and that any post-mortem discussion could only worsen discomfort for both parties. Despite the fumble, she'd warmed at the attention and his solid voluble presence; yet in the quest for opportunities to communicate openness, she met only the thick wall of red-faced affability: "I like you, but we're now friends" she understood the demeanor to say.

She hoped an unmistakably cordial engagement with him would encourage efforts, but feared gameness had been misread as collegial, or the teasing good humour between siblings. As for the direct and obvious—"Let's grab a bite after the final scene is shot today"—moxie, not to mention SRLFI's coarse bluntness, evaded her, though the sentiment stayed nestled in her thoughts. Marta paused in wait for the moment to present itself.

Immediately following Jake's abrupt departure from the Husky, no psychic was needed to translate the aura of gloom enveloping Chaz. After minutes of silence and scrutinizing the trickles of gas pump activity, Marta glanced at Chaz—avoiding eye contact, crestfallen, studying the menu's fine print—and wondered about the best strategy to raise the man from the morass-like slump. Between the polar extremes of "Let's talk it over" and "Let's change the subject altogether" stood a handful of choices, one of which, she supposed, must be correct. When, apropos of nothing, Dianne's long-ago telling of "The Three Caskets" floated up, Marta thought, *Three choices, as if anything's ever that simple.* Were the situation reversed, she'd want nothing except to be left alone to sulk and, upon reaching equilibrium, indulge in fantasies of complicated revenge.

Marta tapped the pie crust remnants and said, "I've had better."

"Oh." Chaz looked out the window.

A child could be distracted by a new activity, she'd seen, but a man-child came with a hyphen that muddied any tried and true solution. Marta half-believed men reacted with primordial unease to take-charge and breadwinner women, an atavistic strand of hunt-and-protect DNA transmission that manifested as panicked urgency: "Warning, warning, this is unnatural, the order of things has been capsized." Whether verified or not, that factoid was not an idea she cared to respect. The kid-gloves treatment nonetheless seemed warranted, and that stalled actions completely. "Jake's comment really was uncalled for," ready on her tongue, gradually disappeared.

Marta considered for a moment to dumb down the steely professorial mien, reshape herself, play with hair strands, become acquiescent, and murmur stereotypical lines—"What are you thinking about?" "What do you think we should do now?"—to tilt his world back into balance, but she snuffed out the very notion as hopeless and reactionary. Chaz was a big boy. She'd let him nurse the ego wound until the story he heard about being bested and humiliated by a tyrannical superior in front of an audience faded. Once the heart's beating slowed and the adrenaline metabolized, she predicted, he'd return to his former self.

"Astutely professional," she said finally, confident that she could not stare at the lack of activity under the gas pump canopy for another milli-second.

"Huh?"

"You were talking about branding and self-promotion."

"Oh yeah, right. The idea is to have two, um, adjectives, as in 'astute' and 'professional.' "

"What does it matter?"

"I dunno, those are just the rules we were taught."

"What do you think of mine?"

"They're okay, but not exactly head turners. Any white collar drone is going to say 'professional.' It's a no-brainer, it goes without saying, like a plumber would say 'reliable.' The idea is to differentiate yourself from the horde, you know, to establish your brand as unique and desirable."

"What are yours?

"I dunno. Actually, it kinda depends on what I'm going to market myself as. Back in the lab I'd be one thing, but for this winner career I'd have to be another. 'Whipping boy' and 'Just crap on me' is too many words. I'll keep you posted. Anyway, I suppose I'll go make sure Jake paid up. I have the feeling that tomorrow—that means today, I guess—is going to be a real back breaker."

3.

Marta had listened to what the radio's display identified as the "Olde Tyme Hour" on a country and western station on the return to the Star-Lite, schmaltzy hits about truckers and heartache preferable to the bother of scanning for another station or asking Chaz for help. She breathed thanks at the sighting of the free parking slot directly at #10. Lifting the hand brake lever Marta raised her eyebrows and gave Chaz a quick nodding smile, intending to convey "It's been a weird long day, right?"

Chaz had remained completely quiet—brooding, staring out the side window—during the drive, even in the midst of the plaintive wails of "D.I.V.O.R.C.E." He released the safety belt without comment.

"Thanks for the ride," he said once Marta hip-checked the door and set the alarm.

"My pleasure." Marta wondered at the duration of Chaz's self-pitying silence. Perhaps Jake's chew out recalled an earlier precedent, in Chaz's mind's eye a chilling reverberation from a staggering adolescent humiliation. "Will you need a lift in the morning?"

"I'm good, thanks." Chaz rested his chin on the roof the the car. "The mechanic dude said a cap or a wire or something like that had come loose. No big deal. Still charged me a hundred bucks for the 'diagnosis,' but I guess that's the price you pay for not knowing the basics."

"Welcome to the world of womankind," she said, wishing she'd bitten her tongue: a membership there would be the last honour a pummeled ego needed. "So"—eyes widening with enticement—"do you want to see my room?"

"For real?" Chaz cocked his head expectantly, like a dog hearing "Walkie?"

"Yes."

Rarely drawn to the spontaneous, impulsive act—the sudden purchase of a ticket to Honolulu during the December semester break or a hardcover novel before reading a handful of reviews—and the improvised reactions follow-through typically entailed, Marta decided on the gesture's necessity—of good will? of interest? of blind reach?—if only to breathe life into the funereal dwindling of a memorable evening. "Get the ball rolling," her father would say. Even Jake had commented on their flirtation, she remembered, and the man's observations typically extended as far as his own reflection.

Stepping toward the door, Marta thought of *A bang's better than a whimper*, one of Judy's mirthfully crude encouragements to get Marta—and others: Judy being just as fond of recycling coinages as Wilde—in touch with the teeming banquet outside of blinkered graduate student drudgery.

Unsure about the exact outcome she expected, Marta kept quiet. If asked, she'd have predicted that the distance between soaring erotic ideal—images deep-seated in everyone's minds: the meticulously choreographed and beautiful dance; the profound exploration of kama sutric spirituality; the grand mal seizure of besotted passionate abandonment, as though the ardent, ravenous participants wanted nothing except to tear away cumbersome layers of clothing and even flesh itself in order to gain access to the substantial core, something indisputably real, weighty, and essential in an otherwise shallow material existence of illusions and dispiriting evanescence—and the hobbled eventuality would be mammoth, the breathtaking difference between drunks bellowing off-key Elton John ballads with eyes glued to the cartoon-coloured screen of a pub's karaoke machine and Jessye Norman embodying the soaring tragedy of Jocasta in *Oedipus Rex*.

"Step right into my parlour."

"I say, you're too kind, madam," Chaz threw in a Foghorn Leghorn drawl. Picturing Miss Prissy's virginal bonnet and bottomless appetite for a husband, Marta chose against running with the routine.

In the realm of romantic intimacy—flirting, dating, intercourse, even sleepovers—Marta counted herself as being long out of practice, and never a seasoned vet to begin with. Hardly an impeding handicap, the lengthy "dry spell" (Dianne's recurring phrase, despite Marta's unmissable warnings: "This topic is really not appropriate for family discussion, Mother") was not, in her estimation, the missing ingredient of a contented life. Nor permanent, not necessarily. Celibacy happened naturally in the best of marriages, she'd heard, and romance could be found if and when she set out to accomplish it. The process would be akin to a job search strategy, more or less.

In reply to Dianne's occasional, increasingly sporadic, and uncharacteristically gentle outreach—"Your time will come, don't worry, dear"—and to her own brain's occasional "What's up with that?" Marta murmured, "My career is my primary relationship; I have no time for anything else right now" with a bright attenuated laugh that meant *It's no big deal, whatever, let's move on.* Some circles placed brides of Christ on a pedestal, viewing them as paragons for a bygone commitment to self-denial and good works, so why shouldn't her enterprises be granted identical respect?

When on a rare day a colleague asked about her personal life outside the campus, or if an undernourished albeit out of sight and ordinarily quiescent chamber in her heart whispered lyrically of desire and lack, she would offer a placating line that suggested a short deferral of a low-priority item on an ever-growing to-do list: like repainting the kitchen and the two-week bicycling tour of the Amalfi Coast it would get done, perhaps not next semester but soon.

It wasn't always easy to brush aside cravings and generate neat compelling rationales. On the closed-in winter weeks of constant rain, Marta lamented her vocal sense of incompetence as well as the men who admired her CV but could not apparently perceive any romantic appeal; on cramped humid buses and umbrella-clotted streets, she rolled her inner eye at the notion of solitude being comfortable, fitting, and right. With clouds lifting and a clear day, however, she'd feel grounded and contented, and write off the blue episode as the kind of despondency even Hare Krishna celebrants would feel under the drab regime of Seasonal Affective Disorder.

4.

Out of practice and by no means an Old Testament queen of carnality, Marta focussed on Chaz.

Though she'd known him for less than a week, she saw that her failure as a femme fatale was outclassed by his shortcomings. Chaz possessed little of Casanova's erotic artistry and charisma—and, more dismaying still, he felt self-conscious about the deficit: mentions of packed-on weight, low-totem status, and overall lack of expertise in diverse areas only left room for the belief that Chaz lacked whatever molecules his boss emanated from the fine pores of his flawless skin. Hyper-conscious of the fact that only an hour ago he'd needed woman's protection, Chaz's nerves abounded.

Once Chaz stood inside the room, Marta closed the door. As she secured the chain, he remarked, "You might want to keep that open, just in case." Marta didn't request clarification; plainly, the man planned to orchestrate a face-saving exit strategy for when—not if—things fell apart.

She sat on the bed facing the television and he followed, close but not touching.

Giddy and suppressing laughter, Marta imagined them as a photographic portrait of low rent North Americana: two lumpy, awkward figures in an off-highway motel room staring at a dead TV screen. She stamped down a related urge to pace, converse, and fill the silence with distracting, tension-shattering, and anti-aphrodisiacal scholarly verbiage. Facts, figures, asides: a definite pall.

They proceeded haltingly, insecurely—nervous jocularity followed by a self-deprecating assessment and a period of quiet concentration. There was earnestness and nothing bungled, and yet few moments could be described as artful or graceful: she helped when he fought to peel off the stubborn sweat-damp T-shirt and stood poised for a cue about the removal of her own clothing—shuck them off piece by piece, hips swaying, in halting reference to a burlesque dancer's routine, or would Chaz prefer to unbutton and unzip?

Aware of the need for an adroit intuition nowhere in the room and the avoidance of questions, Marta began by crouching to untie sneaker laces. Stripped to boxers, Chaz waited; feet bare, they embraced tightly.

Face pressing the bristle of his chest, Marta could detect the faint odour of canal water commingled with salty sweat. The kiss—their first successful one—felt comfortable yet reasonably intense; through closed eyes Marta yielded to the warm endearing tenderness and welcomed the urgency of Chaz's desires, for a instant conjuring thoughts of an alternate universe where a bear held a surrendering deer in a fervent, affectionate grasp.

Simultaneously fully-fledged participant and note-taking critic, Marta saw that if replicated on C-print and hung in an austere white gallery as "IAM, Room #10, Star-Lite Motel: *Un Couple Solaire*," their ardency might not inspire a viewer to exclaim "My, what breathtaking eros!" Then again, neither would the majority of real world couplings.

The purity of the moment, not to mention the seamless coinciding of intent and outcome, waned quickly. Concentrating, Chaz soon replaced self-directed chiding evaluations—"Really smooth, man," as though alone—with a different mode of reluctance, posing question after considerate question—"Is that okay?" "Alright?" "Is this comfortable?" "Do you want me to . . . ?"—designed to guarantee comfort and pleasure, but resulting in conversation that approximated a diplomatic negotiation, or a pair of dyslexics puzzling through the elaborate instructions for newly purchased some-assembly-required IKEA cabinets.

While the idealized lyricism of intercourse tethered the act to effortless transport and communion, they both understood they'd missed that ascension to mythic heights and fought against admissions of inadequacy and failure.

It could have been far worse, Marta thought, later watching Chaz's heavy slumber, men being notoriously self-absorbed and unintuitive, quick-to-finish lovers.

"There is such a thing as trying too hard," she said after a bout of queries that succeeded patience-trying minutes of effort during which fatigue pressed down and nothing else, no hormonal kick, thumping in the chest cavity, or weak-at-the-knees flowering of febrile desire. "Don't you think?" Marta had wanted to sound lighthearted, part of a comic scene in which they played actors and audience, co-conspirators in a forgivably minor folly.

When Chaz replied with "Sorry," Marta realized he'd misunderstood her helpful phrase. Once mutual acute sensitivity of recognized shortcomings melded with paralyzing awareness of a looming fiasco—one that would recast the first literal misstep at the crash site as a portent they'd have been wise to heed—their movements slowed until they lay side by side.

Chaz had snuggled then—tentatively, the degree to which he made contact hovering gingerly between lover and companionate bed mate. A compromise gesture, Marta mused, and not a white flag of defeat. He did not sit up with an abrupt or defensively angry movement and mutter, "Well, it's getting late," unreeling further apologies while tracking down an errant sock.

Nor had he persisted in the face of evidence informing him otherwise. He'd fallen asleep soon after, the sapping hours of the work day ultimately too powerful to resist.

5.

Marta had lain awake, uncomfortable in the oddness of the moment; she'd slipped in to the bathroom to change once Chaz began to sleep. The flannel nightgown—a birthday gift from her father that prompted Dianne's dismay: "George, why don't you just buy her a one-way ticket to a goddamned nunnery?"—wasn't sexy, and the fabric too heavy for the desert night. Even so, cream and patterned with pink rosettes, the tent volume comforted her, a billowing latter day security blanket.

When the birds and the farmer's noise guns had roused Marta completely, the only question loomed simple and momentous: "What next?" Moments later, short pulses of mechanical vibration on the floor sounded. Marta unfolded her arms and nudged Chaz awake.

"Your phone, Chaz," she said in a loud whisper, noticing a moist patch where he'd drooled on the pillow. "I think someone's leaving a message." Unsure of the proper degree of intimacy to assume—phrases to choose, tone of voice, or duration and pressure of touch—she jostled an exposed shoulder tentatively with a closed hand as she might a corpse or a drunk whose prone body blocked the path.

"What? Crap, oh crap, it must be Lora. What time is it?" Sliding over the edge of the mattress he reached toward the jeans and withdrew the phone. "I really gotta go, she's on the war path. See you later, okay?"

Comradely, jovial, and himself once again, on the surface Chaz was not knotted up over acts and implications. Marta smiled at that seeming canine ability to launch forward, free of a shackling past; fretful, she tended to move in the opposite direction. *Maybe*, she thought, *he's more experienced than he appears*.

"When you see her, please tell Lora that I'll be in within the hour." She remained upright in bed.

Chaz, already stepping into his jeans, "Sure, no problem. Do you keep Scope or something in the bathroom?"

"Yes. It's there, you can't miss it."

He rushed into the bathroom, emerging short minutes later toweling his hair. "By the way, nice outfit, Grandma Moses," Chaz said, smirking. Seated on the bed to slip on shoes he stretched across to the opposite corner and kissed Marta's cheek. "You gonna rustle up some flapjacks and possum jerky before Jethro heads off to the barn?"

Saluting, he swung open the door and ushering in the day.

6.

With Chaz departed Marta showered and dressed. Keen to avoid picking apart scenes that had passed mere hours before, she allotted time for a quick breakfast before making an appearance at Joan's. She rushed through tooth-brushing and sunblock application. If she had nothing to regret, neither did she feel a great need to speculate about consequences or ultimate meanings. Not before tea and a few bites of toast, at least.

Along the short drive she thought approvingly of the nimble pace and the absence of wobbly, tank-like RVs. In an hour the highway would be bumper to bumper with families who'd pulled up stakes in quest of another water slide five hours up or down the highway; by then Marta would be immersed in conversations with people she'd be grateful to never meet. Word was, the new Lizzie needed to be on a flight well before the sun set. With that acceleration came frayed nerves—and with them j'accusing and buck-passing from all parties.

Marta pictured the cool metal tanks and grapevine trellises of a placid winery tour. That wouldn't be right: Lora's wrath and the sheer unethical irresponsibility would be difficult to swallow.

At the O-K breakfasting farmers had departed for orchards. Luna, nearly completed clearing away the mess of plates and coffee mugs, waved. Marta wound through the tables and watched Luna from the back booth. The ceiling fan turned lazily, the air heavy with savoury smoky drifts from the kitchen.

"G'morning, doc, seems you're running late," Luna said. "You're like clockwork, normally. So, want to break with tradition this morning? The cook has french toast on special, with your choice of fruit fresh off the tree."

Marta asked for toast and ordered the special for Chaz. She'd offered to order a meal for Lora once and had been told, "Thanks, sweetie, but momma always skips breakfast." As for Jake, she hadn't bothered: he struck her as someone who preferred to fend for himself.

"I hope you don't mind my saying so, but there's something different about you today." Luna stomped around glowering and short-fused, the pinched expression a clear warning.

"My hair's back. 'Keep your perm off them plates,' that's from the boss. As if anyone perms their hair anymore." Luna beckoned in a tourist family at the entrance. "And, to be honest, my other half, or my lesser half, as I've been calling him these days, came home stinking drunk last night. Again. I'm still on the warpath about that."

Marta said, "Men," hoping she sounded convincingly seasoned—*Oh yeah, I've been through the wringer too*. Anyone could see that Luna's confiding urged commiseration.

"Can't live without 'em, and can't shoot 'em, right? Tea?"

Marta nodded.

"Be back in two shakes."

Marta, following Luna's heavy-footed approach, took note of the newly chilled demeanor and the fathomless black eyes. A compressed brow arch, also making a trial run this morning, suggested the potential for retribution in the manner of Lorena Bobbitt.

"Do you think you can keep your mood going awhile?" Marta asked as Luna cleared the table with practiced efficiency. "You know, that sounds wrong, so please let me explain. Do you have a minute to spare?"

Luna surveyed the diner and yelled toward the kitchen: "Henry, I'm on break for five. It's dead in here, okay, and my feet are killing me." She said, "It's a done deal. The next order up will be yours."

"Do you remember me saying that there'd been an accident on set?" As Luna sat facing her, Marta mapped out the production's dilemma and the technical requirements of the position.

Intrigued, Luna asked about the character.

As Marta outlined Lizzie's key traits Luna interrupted with concerns about lack of preparation. Marta backpedalled, realizing she'd overstepped; she couldn't say if the idea had merit or whether union regulations would allow for a local. It wasn't as if Luna could show up and audition. "I don't mean to set you up for disappointment," she said. "I'll check at the office and see if there's any possibility. It's not exactly my area of expertise, so it could be that you'd need an agent or some representation or, well, who can tell? It won't take but a minute to find out. If it's good news, I'll let you know. And if not: sorry to get your hopes up. I probably should have asked my superiors before opening my mouth."

"What the hell, eh? Why not. Just give me a call. I'll write the number here. It'll give me something better to do than go home and pace around until His Highness gets done at his shift."

7.

Lora appeared to be alone at Joan's when Marta pushed open the door. She'd set up dueling fans at the command post desk, and her hair fluttered. "Blanche has called half a dozen times already," she said before Marta took two steps. "The woman's a force of nature."

Eyes adjusting to the half-lit interior, Marta could see they were alone save for Jake, who paced in the back office on a call punctuated by frequent resolute hand gestures. "Good morning, that looks refreshing."

"It's not A/C, but it's better than nothing," Lora said. "Anyway, it seems there's actresses lined up around the block. Being a celebrity is the number one career choice of girls these days, thank you very much Paris Hilton and all those child stars that later show up on the news as stories about prescription drug overdoses. I informed Blanche you'd be ready for a massive conference call before eleven, that okay?"

"About that, Lora. Do you have a moment, because I have a proposal." She thought to sound tentative but inspired. "It may be a viable alternative to conference calls and Blanche and digital auditions and jet fuel. Would you like to hear it?"

"You know me, I'm all ears for creative solutions."

Marta studied Lora's eyes for a sign; the woman's incarnation as a stickler for protocol hardly counted as a secret. She emphasized the cost and time benefits as well as the relative puniness of the role. Striving to sound neither dismissive nor cynical, she also outlined *Battle's* product status, and how as a commodity ordered, manufactured, and consumed with no huge premium placed on it attaining Palme d'Or quality—filling time slots its raison d'être—efficiency trumped casting perfection. "Luna would be perfect."

"What?"

"The waitress at the O-K would be a great replacement for Dol'rez." Marta expanded on the declaration. "And I think you mentioned that a Canadian being cast would be likely, right? She even belongs to a union, she's ready to go right now—and the sooner the better, you said."

"That's nice of you, Marta."

"Well, she seems a reasonable choice." Lora mistook her motivations. Another day of telephone exchanges with unpleasant people might turn Marta ballistic.

"Okay, okay, that could work if she has the right paperwork with dotted i's and crossed t's. Where is she right now? What size is she? Do you think she'd be free to take a few days off? We'll set up a pow wow in a jiff when Jake's done. Chaz has to drive him to set, but I figure the whole deal won't take up an hour."

"That sounds great, thank you."

"In the meantime, you'd better grab a coffee." Lora pointed at the kitchen. "Someone looks like they didn't get enough sleep and will get all testy and difficult to work with inside of ten minutes."

"Yes, ma'am."

Trek

I.

"Hello, sleepyhead," Jake called out. "Coffee's on, but it's getting kinda old."

"My oh my, you're here bright and early." Lora clicked on computers before beetling for the rear office. "No rest for the wicked?"

"Well, someone has to be." *You're not the only one who can play martyr,* he thought.

"And did someone not sleep well?"

"I've got to take off for the Hebe farm in twenty. The maestro behind the lens wants to go over the shooting changes mano a mano." Gnawing and sucking, Jake's teeth worked toward a splinter lodged beneath the thumbnail.

"Got it. Be sure to pick up a good mood on your return trip."

"Ha ha." Watching Lora bee-line to the front desk, Jake reached to scour a blooming rash on both ankles. Calamine lotion could be picked up en route; combing the countryside for jewelweed, the natural remedy he'd read about online, hardly seemed practical.

When Jake unlocked Joan's an hour before Lora appeared, he'd already jerked off twice, put on chastity belt tight Calvins, and express-posted operating principles—Another day another dollar; Nose to the grindstone; The sooner it's done, the sooner it's over—to the front of his thoughts. Redtube, Xtube, RetroXXXtube, Wanktube, sniffing around online, and poring over hard drive porn, keeper scenes (real chemistry to savour amidst a glut of robotic, dubbed moaning performances) he stashed away and viewed time and again: also disallowed.

Evidently the situation called for new rules, put in place from now on. He'd even lay off those herbal enhancements for awhile, eyes steady on the prize.

All work and no play: clichés had their uses.

After last night's debacle and waking with an open mouth and hips pushed urgently into the soft mattress, Jake realized the location shoot, and its tanking after-hours especially, would be best viewed from hindsight. In the meantime, the shoot itself needed a fresh approach: as a task to focus on exclusively, an unpleasant laborious term of employment like community service while wearing an orange prisoner's jumpsuit, and a series of hoops and hurdles that, once completed, would be filed away and moved on from—no harm, no foul, and forgotten as a worthless but mercifully short-lived trial.

You have to choose your battles wisely, he conceded, and this bad luck blast furnace of a valley had it in for him like nobody's business. Key strategies: staying busy and being surrounding with upright non-enablers; quitting smoking years ago had taught him that trick.

2.

Minutes into the witching hour drive from the Husky, Jake had replayed scenes—punitive, detailed snippets of conversation, a deluxe, art-directed package complete with multi-angle visuals, scents, temperatures, and rustling winds—and decided that from the moment he'd left the office in search of the promised land in the peach orchard, the evening had not translated well into the kind of anecdote enjoyable for teller and spectator alike. He had complete faith he'd never share the low points, definitely not at the office and—probably—not even with Jeremy during one of their periodic 'fess ups over beers. The live and learn tale deserved a private burial and his solitary respect.

Whereas fashion foibles—the stubborn rat's tail way back when, the Statement Sideburns, the penchant for frat boy ball caps and surfer dude brands that went unchecked for too many seasons—could be joked about, and select revealing miscalculations, preferably with some kind of snappy laugh track moment, might be auctioned off here and there after a few drinks as part of the normal evolution of an intimate friendship, the cuts caused by this OK Valley debacle made him secretive, vaguely shame-faced.

Last night wouldn't convert into a good story, anyway. Jake could tell: besides possessing not much in the way of a build up or punchline, its revelations—such as they were—merited no public consumption. His sense: to mull it over. If he wanted to trot out a revised version later, at a safe distance, once the goading points had been dulled and the lessons gleaned, then he'd do so.

As for Lora—the watchful and curious circling of a seen-it-all mother who can tell that something's up—he'd avoid her attentiveness and the polite lack of interrogation as she set up for the day's impending in-pour of calls, requests, and emergencies. *Sullen*, Jake thought, yearning for his cavernous and restful condo, the city, and all the amenities a real metropolis contained. The phone, desk, and laptop would be an imposing wall for a few hours until busyness consumed Lora full time.

Even though no colossal embarrassment or shameful faux pas dogged him—nothing in that ballpark—Jake felt self-protective, in need of a quiet solitary place to lick wounds. From the outside, the episode looked like no big deal—a brief series of stumbles, a resounding non-event, and nothing he hadn't visited before. In the sobriety of the early morning Jake realized his reaction didn't add up. He faced no momentous road fork, no feet at a precipice; and he possessed complete awareness that he'd had a weird evening—that's all, whatever. Still. The doubt—a gradual, though glacier-steady loss of faith in the prized ability to grab a place in the world and forge any trail of his own making—teased, a resilient vestige. And unwelcome: like a scarlet rash of back acne or an unappetizing set of misaligned teeth, that questioning recalled an earlier, keen-to-belong wannabe self that Jake imagined as so remote its former concreteness had dissipated into spectral nothingness.

He always pictured self-made cock-surety as solid and unmoving, not a fragile, porcelain-thin veneer. Alternate takes on that script, those he could live without.

3.

Accelerating away from the Husky after the orchard no-show and head-butting with Chaz, Jake had ballooned his cheeks and slowly released the air; with turtle-velocity traffic the natural enemy of peaking testiness, he smiled, shoulders relaxing, in gratitude to find the road to Kaleden nearly deserted and shrouded by darkness.

Loser gamblers he'd watched in a casino north of Palm Springs had risen to mind again as he passed by the strip of orchards near the Hebe lot. At mid-morning on the way to Los Angeles during hiatus last spring he'd stopped at Morongo, a roadside high-rise dropped in the middle of nowhere, for a walk through. The gross house-favouritism of gambling rubbed him the wrong way; the stroll was pure voyeurism.

As dealers at the poker and blackjack stations practiced card tricks, watchful for the influx of evening customers, the only activity clustered within one section—row after row of video slots where dumpy men and withered women fed tokens with hypnotic factory regularity. The mirthless expressions struck Jake—they may as well have been punching time clocks at the end of grueling shifts—as did the Pavlovian compulsion to keep the machine plugged with tokens and to smack the lit rectangular button that caused the screen to imitate the whirring reels of a yesteryear machine—cherries, lemons, apples. A blink of an eye separated each round; the loss was registered in that time, then washed over with ridiculous hope that the next game would be the winner recouping all previous damage. *Fat chance*, he'd thought.

Those desert automatons had first sprang up soon after he'd flirted—automatically, habitually, without a syllable of invention—with the matronly cashier at the Husky, saying "Nice night for a drive" and "Must be nice when your shift ends" with snaky insinuation, staring intently into her eyes. In that fraction of a minute he'd become part of the same species at the casino. What a joke, the lines so dead, the ploy so transparent and so *expected* that she hadn't even burned the calories required to lift a smile.

Between making moves on a woman he'd sooner have polishing the kitchen floor than his knob, being a major jerk-off with

Chaz, and getting a deserved wrist slap from the prim professor, Jake's frame of mind turned manic, unbalanced; off his game, he'd decided, would be putting it mildly.

Five minutes past the Oliver town limits sign, Jake couldn't shrug off the hard knot of frustration building from shoulder to shoulder and into his grip of the wheel.

"Sleep it off," he mumbled, "there's nothing that can be done about it now."

When the sleepy lakeside trailer park—reputed habitat of the drunken, Gravol-popping nympho Xtina—rolled into view, Jake grimaced. His right hand, already resting lap-level, inched upward, the obedient servant of an impulsive creature with willed deafness to half-measures, firm denials, and a hypnotist's benign suggestion—"Relax, you're getting very sleepy."

"What's the plan, big boy," Jake asked, judging himself, as an uncharitable outsider might when catching sight of an unhitched man driving alone in a SUV on a two-lane highway late at night and posing a question at a dumb tool of reproduction, a matter any fool knew as better answered by the larger grey organ situated behind the eyes.

Here's the gruesome flip side of adventuring, he'd thought, *and of taking pride in being a wolfish predator.* Ordinarily Jake's perspective felt secure: regarding personal habits and tendencies from one unswerving prospect: no big deal, right, a consequence of appetite, how organic is that? You naturally fed a physical need; and in fact the absence of appetite indicated a red flag, a sign of disorder and ailment in gestation. Ask any doctor.

Everybody agreed. The only difference: technical definitions—to wake up and crave breakfast drew no remarks; that was no more than an integral but pedestrian check mark on the human condition's daily list, like nose blowing and taking a crap. As for the hungering for hole that gnawed at belly level? Only a fraction of the world would equate that pang with basic human qualities. Judgement declared: too base, an animal vestige that right-minded individuals kept under lock and key. And no one won a Nobel Prize for writing about it.

4.

Driving in blackness on a solitary highway, Jake fell into judgment. Here he sat, a figure of fun, the clumsy and witless comic dolt who'd walk into the door frame and then get up and do it again, on and on, a buffoon never clueing in to the obvious lesson. Or worse yet: an illustration from a textbook of pathologies. Or one of those standard figures in mental asylum movies: the crazed compulsive masturbator, flesh raw and aching, going at himself yet again, a kissing cousin to a nearby cellmate psychotic tearing at the imaginary insects crawling over her skin and soon restrained by orderlies and rendered vegetative with numbing doses of Haloperidol.

Checking the mirror for traffic, Jake turned onto a dirt road cutting a line into a wide tract of scrubland still untouched by agriculture.

Killing the engine and lights he elbowed the door open, figuring that a recess of leg stretching and bladder draining would furnish enough time for his disparate parts—a regular UN of competing interests and ulterior motives—to converse, debate, and reach happy consensus. Facing roadside brush, he stayed seated; cool air rushed in alongside soothing cricket chirps and faint star light. No other vehicle moved into sight.

Weighing options took seconds. The real impulse, revisiting the trailer park, he struck out; that door while tempting now presented itself as slammed, a permanent closure. Ditto Orchard Boy and Hotel Visitor, one a prick who'd played him and the other's offer already declined, a terminated connection.

Jake walked to the edge of a ditch and pissed on unnamable weeds. He stared ahead. Low brush stretched back to the silhouette of sharp mountains and uninterrupted night sky. Awesome.

Barring an impromptu stop at a tavern or night club—dicey on a weekday night, even the correct choice a low-return lottery—left only two choices. Resting beneath newly laundered blankets at the air-conditioned B & B had all the merits of a sound decision: smart, logical, adult. Then again, training impulse control had always seemed as interesting as taking courses in accounting. Choice 2A: a campground he'd read about on Spooge.org. Though even a lifelong optimist would clue into the Pluto remoteness of success there, a slim chance looked better than none at all. Worse case scenario: lost minutes and Lora commenting on eye bags in the morning. Haggard was no big deal. He'd bark at everyone within range without good reason, a privilege of seniority.

Jake returned to the seat to grab the phone. Studying a saved map, he saw a partitioned tip of the tiny provincial park reserved for campers jutting into the lake; before it, a skinny peninsula stood officially undefined. Scrolling down the cruising site for relevant details, Jake heeded warnings about poison ivy, wandering families, late night parties near the water, and the necessity for total discretion: a promising location, though too many blemishes for a Shangri-La.

He tapped for another venue listing, gamble 2B, a 24/7 gym—a long-shot mentioned by the site's dedicated pervs. Reading between the lines of the already sketchy details, Jake calculated the beach held greater promise. The gym: too much work, the pursuit of few and unreliable clues that might result in a conversation that could lead to a meeting for a beer likely to end in a frustratingly unproductive hand wave and "Hasta la vista, dude."

Jake wanted results, within the hour, not tomorrow, and minus the desperate ambiguous courtship that produced nothing except crossed wires, wasted breath, and bluer, more engorged balls.

He deleted directions for the gym.

Perusing the first map while attempting to divine secrets from its segmented colour-coded landscape, Jake's mind leapt to ancient seers in rough woven robes who'd ripped open farm animals and based history-making battles on the arrangement of guts. He grinned. At least there was no blood and stench for this roadside oracular moment.

If the area between the beach and the public rest stop consisted of what he predicted—trees, bushes, tall grass, a labyrinth of narrow trails—then, Jake wagered, it would be ground zero for action. In virtually every town he'd passed through pioneer-like necessity concocted out of the way pockets for libido: gravel pits for randy teens, outskirt motels for married types taking on extra commitments, and blanketing forests or pitstop toilets for men who sought out other men. Appetite was a reliable presence even if it might be perpetually frowned upon; it usually dug up a shadowy place to slake itself. Nicos said the crash site pit definitely played that role; the lakefront campground might easily be another. The fact of an address posting on a website likewise implied cause for living hope: if he'd found the place with minimal searching, then others could too.

"Okay, buddy, you win, we'll go take a peek." Immediate problem solved and feelings leavening, Jake's ongoing negotiation caused no further embarrassment. Finger of accusation folded away, mind and body rejoined in a stable relationship once again.

5.

The fits and starts of oncoming traffic had increased to a trickle as Jake shot by the stretch of orchard farms preceding the lake; with no sign of Chaz and the professor approaching from the opposite lane, he huffed thanks. Answering a question from Chaz in the morning would encourage Lora to put two and two together, and being ribbed about bad habits would hurt an already tender bruise; he could live without the professor's stock taking too.

Grimacing at the cock-teasing cornucopia fruit stand, Jake silently blamed its owners for this late night ramble. He rechecked the map and signaled left; and spotting the log cabin facade of the public toilets, he parked in front. The lot stood discouragingly empty.

Jake switched off the headlights. Bathed by yellow light from a bare bulb outside the men's toilet, he pondered the pros and cons, the lack of cars powerful testimony in favour of turning the car key and flipping into reverse. He decided on giving the area a look; a short reconnaissance mission would take no time.

The padlock on the men's toilet shut down one venue, never a quirk of his in any case. Jake caught the glow from distant RVs, but heard no laughter or drunken words and not a note of party tunes. Wardens enforced rules here, apparently, and polite campers obeyed them.

Checking the Ford for a flashlight, he said, "Damn it." Another coin to toss: wandering along moonless trails or bailing on the search? He opted for a compromise: a few minutes only, and if the time passed without making contact he would walk directly back to the vehicle, put the engine in gear, and drive away without a second thought.

The treed landscape ahead looked faint, like X-ray images. The underside of slender willow leaves revealed the faded colour of sage, while chest-height bush masses stood barren, long stripped of the unmarred green of early spring. Jake believed that poison ivy grew vine-like and close to the ground; he'd never seen it before and kept an eye out for leaves that looked like the poinsettias Lora carted in each December. Caution would be needed only if he detoured from the path; well-traveled and free of any triffid-y plant life, the sandy and dry trails offered safe passage.

The trail forked and Jake chose the least trod on the right: the maze appeared to lead away from the lake and into confounding aphrodisiacal darkness. He continued along in a bush-choked morass, where low cloud cover reflecting dim light from the town undercut the disorienting power.

If a pleasant ambling hike in the middle of a fragrant night had been the goal, Jake could have breathed with satisfaction. Instead, his awareness of clock-ticking futility increased with every turn. Skirting the campsite's forlorn branches Jake thought of how unfriendly the landscape would become when winter landed.

Veering left, he crouched when approaching a group of teenagers singing around a fire. With peals of laughter and carefree teasing they rehearsed "Macarena" and stumbled through the elaborate dance. Jake wondered if they were practicing for an upcoming wedding before he noticed the joking in Spanish between flubbed dance steps. Tourists. The hearty innocence struck him as a cosmic accusation, and he retreated away from the water before delving into that corridor of self-loathing. Entertainment, for him, took another form, a different path.

Each trail segment spread open emptily; no litter-strewn secluded alcoves off the edges hinted at past rendezvous, mating dances, and frenzied rutting. If a thriving underground community had once frolicked within these pointless offshoots, its heyday had passed. Jake squinted around for the typical signs—discarded condom wrappers, tissues, butted cigarettes, gum packs—and uncovered none. The locals could be tidy or cautious, there might be a diligent maintenance crew: with those rationales, Jake grew conscious of the foolish grasping at straws.

Seeing the parkland changing into an unnavigable jumble, Jake's feet stalled: in a matter of seconds he'd lose his bearings completely.

In the dark and lost: that fact seemed inevitable. Between the profusion of trails, the miserly and varying levels of light, and a devolved instinct for direction, Jake would feel no surprise if he, to all eyes a bristly drifter with unknown designs, burst into the middle of the RV camp looking dazed and suspect to onlooking families relaxed around a fire. He'd calculated that the best probable location would also be the quietest—a midway between the parking lot and the lakeshore. Stopped to listen for singing, Jake heard silence; catching no flicker of flames he trudged forward, smothering the spiking urge to giggle.

6.

Once cleared of the chemical aura of the public toilets near the parking lot minutes before, Jake had inhaled the weedy lake water air and hay odour of the desert; and in pockets here and there spews of diesel exhaust and inviting drifts of campfire smoke had passed through his nostrils, sweet marshmallows aflame inciting hunger pangs.

Now with each step, though, he rubbed his eyes and felt particles of former lake shore catch inside his nose.

Jake slowed to listen; catching no movement, no cough, no murmured conversation, or, better still, throaty groans, he concluded that precisely one mobile body patrolled the area. *Not much of a consolation prize*, he thought, recalling the porn masturbator-siren plan from the failed orchard rendezvous.

A rustling of branches and murmuring baritone voices grabbed Jake's attention.

"About time." He course-corrected.

He peeked into an off-trail grotto furnished with skinny pine logs and a pair of tree stumps. As Jake stepped inside two wizened men froze in mid-motion, one handing a buddy a bottle. An interloper, Jake wanted to confirm his good intentions: the newbie's sudden arrival was no accident and the men should carry on. Jake understood that all communities liked to preserve traditions.

"Hey," he said.

"Oh boy, you scared the bejesus out of us," the ball cap wearer said. "You came out of nowhere."

"We weren't expecting company." Ball cap's friend drew from a cigarette.

"This here's Jack," ball cap said, pointing.

"And this here's Jesse." Jack's hand, shaped into a pistol, had fired an imaginary bullet.

Jake smiled at the vaudevillians and dropped his voice. "Howdy, old timers. What's going on tonight?"

"We're having ourselves a symposium." Jack tipped his hat.

"We're seeing what the night will drag in," Jesse said. "Find yourself a stump, we ain't going nowhere."

Jake had no intention of staying long and remained unseated. "I'm good. You expect anything, this place see much of a crowd?"

"It's like fishing," Jesse showed off imaginary fly reel skills, "some days are better than others."

"And some nights there's nothing at all. More like hunting deer, seems to me," Jack offered. "Fishing's about waiting, see, hunting deer's about tracking the bastard down."

"Fishing's not waiting, it's tracking. Just need good bait."

"How's your bait?" Jack lifted the bottle. "Want a swig? We got plenty."

"No complaints," Jake intended to stay at the entrance, "I'm good."

"You gonna show us?" Jack persisted.

"Yeah, buddy, give us a little show," Jesse said.

"Nah, c'mon guys." Jake could see this exchange would drag on forever unless he shut it down. "I'm having a dry spell, so I figured I'd take a look out this way, maybe find a tourist or two in the same boat."

"Two, eh? Ha! Once in a blue moon. If you're lucky."

" 'Round here you get it where you can, truckers at rest stops like the one you musta parked by," Jack said.

"Last week, this young kid, a hitchhiker, let me jack him while I drove."

"You tell that BS story to anyone in the bush, it's always last week, like you got the Alzheimer's." Jack grabbed for the bottle. "Summer's better than winter."

"Winters are for the wife," Jesse said. "Sometimes for Indian gals too."

The men traded the wine as they spoke. When Jim raised it, Jake, conscious of appearing stuffy, said, "Nah, I gotta drive." He couldn't stomach shooting the breeze for long, that strategy handy only with a grasp-worthy prize in close range.

Jake listened as the men bantered grandfatherly about fishing and hunting and supposed past triumphs. At home on their tree stumps, they could be hobos killing time before the next boxcar. The only missing elements: the Depression, a few empty tins of beans, and a rabbit roasting on a wooden spit.

"Shh," Jesse said, suddenly still.

"Heads up," Jack lifted the bottle.

"Oh, speak of the devil." Jesse lifted himself from the stump. "We're just talking about what the night'll drag in."

"I figured I'd see the pair of you tramping around here," the newcomer said. "Who's this?"

"A pleasure meeting you, gentlemen." Eager for an exit, Jake capitalized on the opening. "It's getting late for me."

"You sure you're gonna take off? Jesse here can pull out his dentures. Shut your eyes and it's the same as pussy, believe you me."

Jake caught an infantile whine in Jack's voice. Stuffed deep into the pocket, his thumb stroked the head of his rarely shy tool—a lusty keener with a seldom hibernating exhibitionism. The momentary contact prompted an instantaneous affirmative response: Let's put on a show! *C'mon, really?* Jake thought.

He knew the stereotype contained a hefty chunk of truth: men would put their dicks in anything—a carved melon, a knot hole in a fence—as long as it looked receptive enough. The response made sense, like that study on the news where scientists proved babies react positively to a standard facial configuration. It didn't matter if they saw a snowman with a carrot nose and charcoal eyes, they'd still reach out for Mama or Papa. Hardwiring.

So why not the toothless, wine-doused oral cavity of an ancient tramp? Stranger things had happened.

Jake remembered a z-grade clip Jeremy had sent: a farmer wearing a wide straw hat strides toward a donkey in a equatorial field with banana palms in the background; the guy approaches while the animal chomps on grass; it doesn't bolt as the stalker draws closer, nor stop grazing when in one confident motion he steps behind, drops his pants, shoves the beast's tail aside, and begins fucking. Though Jake had peered closely and enlarged the screen size, the grainy resolution and the camera's distance made it impossible to tell whether the horndog actually poked into the animal or faked the act as a stunt to post on the Internet or sell to the makers of *Barnyard Lovers* or *Filthy Farm*. Jake had checked: aficionados could chose from countless titles, horses easily the farmyard's big men on campus.

Jesse belonged to a different league, but compared to what Jake had in mind when he'd turned around near trailer park Xtina's, the offer stood miles below lame. "You never know," he said. "Gentlemen, I'm going to wander a bit more, see what I can bump into."

"Watch out for coyotes," Jesse said.

"Happy trails, buddy." The men spoke as a chorus.

7·

Slogging through prehistoric lake bottom in search of the parking lot—any optimism about roadside fun now DOA—Jake wondered about the men, their friendship, and the routines they followed beyond nighttime hunting. Had they known each other when they were his age and considered themselves adventurers thumbing noses at convention and the humdrum routines of Wonder Bread neighbours across the lane?

He imagined Jeremy and himself twenty-five years in the past: the summer of 1985, a time not so far removed from the present—or, for that matter, from Flower Power, Free Love, Women's Lib, Sexual Liberation, and disco. The men on the stumps didn't seem to belong to that era, forty years old then and humming along to Huey Lewis or Bananarama. Maybe time was different—slower, clinging—outside of the ADD of cities and urban itching for the next season's trends, the latest restaurant, and the flavour of the moment.

If casting these guys, he'd drop them in a buddy movie set in the depths of the Dirty Thirties. Something black and white with Bogart, maybe.

Mulling over parallel lives provoked another thought, a jump into the future the same distance. Was it a done deal that he'd become the spitting image of Jack or Jesse, or one of those men he nodded at politely while being steadfast in avoiding close contact with their knee-jerk badgering, their bottomless cup of need? Would he take drives with feverish dreams—hopeful but in fact bereft of hope—of stopping for agreeable hitchhikers or running into pent-up tourists on the down low? And with diminishing cachet would his choice of nightspots decline steadily? Would a flashy car and open wallet lure bar stars and street trash—or prostitutes, the grade of which relied on retirement savings?

Jeremy had told Jake about a patient, one of his down-and-out Eastside types who budgeted for rock-bottom alleyway servicings exactly twice a month. Jeremy unreeled the story for gossipy pleasure, of course, but really, should they be smiling? Would he eventually sit with Jeremy on stumps or equivalent, living disasters, absolute proof to intimidated passersby that decadence came with an exacting toll and the wages of sin is death, and all that evangelical hellfire and brimstone?

Vulnerability to whatever the world throws at you is one thing, he conceded. But hamstrung and thwarted by your own bad habits? Not on his watch, thank you.

Jake backed out of the lot feeling chastised, rebuked by a fickle cosmos—giving, then taking, at whim—and tonight deciding on a Sunday school talking-to about priorities. And though he'd bet with fair confidence that the future would never include weekly bouts of skulking and drinking cheap wine while squatting in the barren cul de sac of a family campground, he felt shaken by the possibility that his philosophy of private life had encouraged a wild misstep, or that, in the favoured scolding parental phrase, his failure to live up to his full potential grew visibly each day. At least he might make room to remap the usual after-hours vocations.

Fuck that noise, Jake thought.

Scared Straight tactics might work on all-bark, no-bite teenagers. Lesson givers could kiss his ass. Pot-bellied Mr. Zsi-something, that black-eyed physics teacher gleefully assigning an F in Grade 12—"Sooner or later, Yak-ob Neu-gent," the man scolded time and again, voice Eastern Bloc guttural and war-weary despite having fled Hungary right after "dat bald murderer" was sent to the Soviet Union at the start of the Cleaver family's run, "you vill understand dat you can't just coast by on dat smile"—and the cold eye of the universe dead set on schooling him with a wake-up call, had nothing worthwhile to tell him, each no better than a hypocritical circle of hardcore drinking buddies staging an intervention.

Besides, that regret and repent bullshit wasn't part of his vocabulary, never would be. As for raw deals, the universe could hand them to somebody else.

AC blasting, Jake gunned the engine and shot toward the respite of an empty room.

An Artistic Interval

1.

Marta scrambled to greet Luna, who peered through Joan's front window, face strained with apprehension about the could-be star turn awaiting steps away.

"C'mon in, we won't bite," Marta said, wrestling with the off-kilter door and relishing the change in air quality. "Have you kept that mood intact?"

"Oh yeah, I've got fury for days." Despite the proclamation Luna looked cowed. "This here's Lornette. She's my moral support."

"Pleased to meet you, Lornette. I'm Marta."

"It's my pleasure," Lornette said. Flustered and shy, the freckled redhead appeared ready to curtsy. "I can wait out on the sidewalk if I'm in the way here."

"So much for moral support. You stay put." Luna clasped her friend's arm.

"Really, it's fine. People drop by all the time, trust me," Marta said, seeing Lornette's perplexed expression.

"Alright then." Marta herded the women in. "I'd better introduce you to the first half of the powers that be. It's those two, Luna, and not me, that you'll be needing to impress. They're the gatekeepers. Wait right here, alright, the chairs are comfortable. I'll be back in a minute."

Lora shuffled papers in Jake's office and pointed vaguely as Marta approached the desk. "That's her? She looks the part, a bit bigger framed than Dol'rez, I think. Mind you, that was one rack of bones, so who isn't?"

"Luna's friend's closest to the door. You're right, though"—Marta mimed the pretense of a Solomonic evaluation—"but she's in work clothes. Blanketed in the maid's caftan, she'll be a match."

"This is really doing things back-asswards, you know."

"Oh, I thought you were agreeable to a trial run." Marta felt the creep of anxiety about an impending marathon conference call and unbearable voices transmitting hardball attitude from Vancouver and Los Angeles.

"I am, honey. I'm just fretful. Naturally. You should see my family reunions. Mama hands out Prozac with Abilify chasers!" Lora gathered supplies for the meeting. "I'm surprised you haven't picked that up by now, Doctor."

Marta smiled, tongue locked in place.

"Okay, let's take a look. Jake can sell the penny-pinching and the time-saving agendas in his sleep, so no worry there," Lora said. "It all comes down to being a good fit."

The waitresses sat politely—legs crossed, hands folded on laps—as Marta approached to make introductions. "Luna and Lornette, this is Lora," she said. The women stood to shake hands.

"Gee, where's Laverne?" Lora asked with a giggle. "Before we get the show on the road, we need the big cheese. After that we'll shoot a few lines and then upload them to other bigger cheeses. And then after that it's all in the hands of fate."

"Here are a few pages to look over while you're waiting. I've highlighted germane lines."

"Ladies, don't believe that Miss Manners routine for a minute," Lora quipped, expertly putting them at ease. "I swear she's after my job."

2.

Marta watched Luna pace and rehearse variations on lines; comfortable playing the sounding board, Lornette sat, listened, and commented in murmurs. They froze, startled, as Jake strode in with Chaz and Nicos in tow. The boisterous men herded toward the back office, barely nodding to the visitors. "Curly and Moe here need a junk food stop," Jake said.

"Hey." Chaz veered toward Marta. "We gotta grab some snacks for the road."

"I left the O-K's breakfast special on the counter by the microwave. It's a bit past its prime now. I'll show you."

"Who's the tourists hanging around out front?" Nicos said.

"One's a stray Marta here dragged in off the street," Lora said. "And her friend."

"And?" Babysitting locals didn't fit on Jake's agenda.

"Oh, the professor's acting out Hollywood mythology," Lora said. "Just call her Maximillan Carey."

"What?" Nicos checked his phone.

"No idea. Lora loves her golden age melodramas, though," Jake said.

"*A Star is Born*, is that better? *Showgirls*? Um, *Glitter*? You know, a small town nobody becomes bigger than life, tragedy ensues? Marta thinks the local will be a good—convenient, that is—replacement Lizzie," Lora said, "so Luna—she's the one in that lovely nylon waitress slash nurse's uniform—is prepping to read. It's okay, I figure. Nothing ventured, nothing gained, right?"

"Sure, why not. As long as she's paid her union dues, we'll be fine." Jake reached across the desk, jerked open the centre drawer, and switched on a camcorder. "Good, the battery's still charged. Okay, you guys can hit the road any time, give us some room to work."

"C'mon, Jake," Nicos said. "If it's a go, she'll be acting in front of the entire crew, not to mention a camera. We'll be helping her out."

"Good point, but you and the Chazster need to be somewhere, like five minutes ago, right?"

"Okay, boss." Nicos shouted toward the kitchen, "I'm already waiting behind the wheel, Big Boy. Let's get the show on the road."

"Yeah, yeah, Hootie, I'll be two shakes." Paper plate in hand, Chaz rushed for the street.

Jake turned the lock and waited at the front door. "Alright, ladies, let's make this happen."

Luna grasped the photocopied pages Marta had pulled and read the lines in a monotone: " 'My dear Sultan, you are too kind indeed. Verily, I cannot accept so extravagant a gift. That you hold me in such high esteem is surely enough! You insist? Such a wealth of gems could only attract the covetous eyes of my impudent servants.' "

"That'd be great if you we were making *The Jetsons* and you were playing Rosie the robot maid." Lora ignored the persistent ringing of the phones and waved *Don't bother* when Marta moved to answer.

"I just needed to say the lines at full volume, not in my head. Okay, I'm ready now." She spoke the lines at Jake.

"Better, but it's not a race. Third time's the charm?" Lora winked at Marta—*You gotta be tough with the talent.* "And remember: you're an English servant, not a Canuck."

"Okay, here goes," Luna said. Seated but rapt, Lornette offered silent encouragement with raised eyebrows and two thumbs up.

"Not bad at all. We need to try a different scene," Jake said, "to see how she emotes on cue."

"How about the death scene at the crash site." Lora reached for a script.

"Professor, you ready for your close-up?" Jake grinned, swinging the lens in Marta's direction. "Can you stand in for the alien?"

Marta stepped back, her first impulse to scurry off. *The flight response of a marmot,* she thought. "Yes, certainly. What do you need me to do?"

"Nothing much. Just stand there, the wall's green screen basically. You'll give Luna something real to focus on."

Eyes seeming panicked, Luna shuffled through the pages.

Marta explained. "You've just ridden a horse to the crash site because you are planning to negotiate a deal with the alien."

"For real?" Luna asked. "That sounds kinda weird."

"Oh it is, absolutely." Lora handed gestured cosmic resignation. "But we're here to make it happen, my dear, not write a movie review."

"Just run with it, okay?" Jake said.

"Then what happens?" Luna read the page.

"Pretty much what you'd expect: you try, you fail, you get decapitated, you pay the price for fucking with a bad customer, end of story." Jake adjusted the lens. "Let's get a move on, folks."

"No second act for her, I guess. I thought maybe I'd become the alien's queen or something."

"No such luck," Lora said. "Ready?"

"Okay, it says, 'Lizzie walks toward the spacecraft,' " Luna flipped through the sheets, "but she doesn't find anything. Then she sees a cavern and goes toward it. Okay, got it. If the professor stands right there, I'll come in from outside and then begin."

"Go for it," Lora said.

Marta stood with her back to the side wall and watched as Luna struggled with the door and crept in.

" 'Is there anyone about? Good sir? Please, we must speak at once,' " Luna stopped, awaiting direction. When none arrived she read further lines. " 'I am in possession of valuable intelligence.' "

" 'Silent, the alien steps closer to Lizzie,' " Marta read, unsure whether to move.

"Stay put, professor. Basically, after that Lizzie realizes that her time is up and that the alien's not going to play by her rules, so she decides to go out in a blaze of glory," Lora said.

" 'O charcoal fiend, begone. Vile insect, I implore you to retreat,' " Luna tried out the words. " 'Abhorred monster. Treachery!' 'Charcoal fiend'? Man, that's a mouthful."

"The camera is on," Jake said.

Luna read the lines tentatively.

"Will you let me do that one more time? I've got the rhythm figured out now."

"Sure thing, honey." Lora adopted her occasional persona of maternal encouragement.

"Yeah, but we don't have all day. Once more and we'll edit it down, load it up and send it out."

Luna paused to regard Jake scornfully. "I'll come in again, and begin with 'Is there anyone about?' Are you ready, Mar?"

"Yes, certainly. Any time you are."

3.

"Alright, it's a go," Lora shrieked halfway through hanging up. "Marta, go snare your waitress and tell her everyone thinks she's a bona fide soon-to-be-cable-TV-star. That's not the wording, but it'll get her stoked. We need her here, then shuttled over to Costume and Hair."

"That was fast," Marta said. With luck, she'd never again cross paths with graceless Blanche, that surly assistant, or dismissive higher ups in remote production hub offices.

"The threat of money down the drain is very inspirational, don't you think?"

"Very." Marta drew nearer to Jake's desk. She preferred not to yell.

Lora explained that there'd been unanimity from Los Angeles and Vancouver, one happy with a photogenic enough face and budgetary plusses and the other speaking of the time crunch, government incentives, and the virtue of thinking outside the box. Lora passed Marta a yellow sheet of paper. "Okay, here's what needs to get done, in order of importance. Since Chaz is on a run now, I corralled a PA from second unit. They're just out there twiddling their thumbs on establishing shots right now anyway. He ought to be here by the time you're back here with the waitress. Got it?"

"I do, thanks."

Marta beamed as she rushed toward the O-K Café. She'd spared herself duress and in doing so made an actual contribution; her ordinary tasks—answering calls, shuffling papers, purchasing supplies—might be technically useful, but they barely registered on her scale of accomplishment. *So what if Luna's lucky break was inadvertent*, she thought. A good deed still counted even if it came from self-serving motivations.

"Eh, what's up, Doc?" Luna stood at the till counting bills. Marta summoned a smile; she'd heard that line countless times before, although only outside of campus borders.

"We have news," Marta said, looking around. The town couldn't boast of a brunch crowd; the O-K was unoccupied save for the coffee counter regulars.

"Wow, time is money, eh? I'll bet one look at me and they slammed the door shut."

"To the contrary, they're interested."

"For real?"

"For real. And Lora's asked me to tell you in person. To expedite the process."

"Okay." Watchful, Luna waited for further cues.

"In other words, the office needs you for paperwork and then we'll send you to Wardrobe. How soon can you be ready?"

"Um, I gotta call Lornette again. When she offered to cover my shift, I'll bet she thought it'd never happen in a million years. I owe her big time."

"We'll see you soon."

"Thanks a lot, professor."

"My pleasure." Helping had cast a warm light over her stay in the valley. "See you shortly."

4.

Facing away from the sun's glare on the return to Joan's, Marta noticed the efficient miracle of heat evaporating the very perspiration it prompted. The hot brisk current reminded her of lakeshore picnicking and family meals under long tendrils of weeping willow shade. While knowing that the bouncing-step mood resulted directly from the balm of total relief about solving the Lizzie and teleconferencing problems, the facile kitchen conversation during Chaz's stop left her unsettled.

Chaz had thanked Marta for the take-out breakfast and slammed the plate into the microwave. "I hope you aren't too bagged today."

"It's nothing that a full night's worth of sleep won't cure." With the reply she'd strived for nonchalance, as though possessing a venerable history of sleeplessness due to bed guests.

"Cool. They've got me in beast of burden mode today, so I'm not going to be around much." Nicos bellowed from the front. "Shit, looks like I'll have to wolf this down on the road. Catch you later, okay?"

"Alright."

A check-in conversation taking place as microwave beams singed rotating french toast and Jake coordinated an impromptu audition had been by no means ideal, Marta acknowledged as she glowered at a rumbling RV towing a small car and a trailer loaded with an ATV—people would haul entire houses if they'd fit on the road. And even if a deeper exchange had been possible, her inner jury questioned the desirability or necessity: "Um, about last night . . ." would sound neurotic at best, the dullest of womanly clichés at worst. What to say, what policy to effect?

"Let's get the show on the road," the intervening shout from Nicos, had been an instrumental by-product, akin to the career kick for Luna. "A self-correcting mechanism," her smug day trader of a brother might label it to end a discussion. At equal intervals he'd fondly trot out "Everything happens for a reason" too. Marta could never fully grasp what he thought this mass-market article of faith really meant.

Great Irregularity

I.

"Okay, okay, we're closing up shop." Lora unleashed a short round of claps and strutted exultantly through the office. Marta and Lora worked alone; following the seventy-minute stint as a star-maker Marta had returned to wearisome clerical duties—since nothing else exciting rolled down the pike—as Lora hollered into telephones and typed reports in Jake's office. "After that, my dear colleagues, you are simply going to have to wait. The call centre is now closed, please leave a message at the sound of the beep."

Lora peered through the lettering on the front window. "We need a break from this place anyhow, trade in recirculated office air for that invigorating OK Valley oxygen." On a bee-line for Marta, Lora's flattened hands pressed the sides of her face and pulled tight: "Dah-ling, I hear it turns back time."

"What's going on," Marta said, on hold and watching Lora's hummingbird movements. The dreaded conference call had been scrubbed, but Lora had insisted that Marta contact Blanche to give the woman a final update. With a chilly "I see," Blanche transferred the call to the monosyllabic assistant, and she immediately sentenced Marta to on-hold exile. Metronoming a pencil in time to a medley of easy listening classics for five minutes, Marta needed a fresh distraction.

"The final scene is being shot, and we're going to watch it up close and personal. We don't have a lot of traditions in this biz, but that's one of them." Lora's bellowing from the kitchen echoed. "Are you going to be okay with taking the wheel?"

"Yes, of course."

Lora returned to Jake's office, and Marta loaded paper into the photocopier while waiting for the surly voice of Blanche's assistant. Thirty placating seconds into a love ballad from the '70s whose streak-haired singer verged on familiar, Marta hung up. *It's not as though I'm going to get fired,* she thought. Blanche represented nothing but a bridge she could afford to burn. She typed an IM to Lora: "The call is completed."

"Okay, grab your keys and let's get out of here before the phones ring again." Lora slammed down the lid of the laptop on Jake's desk. "There's no bugs out there, right?"

Idling the engine while Lora locked up the office, Marta watched pedestrians, welcoming the speed of the AC as bracing currents wafted across her feet.

"So much for that theory." Lora swung open the passenger door.

"Pardon me?"

"My refreshing outdoors air theory." She placed an index finger on her tongue and then held it in the air. "Not enough wind to rustle a goddamned leaf. You could fry eggs on the hood, though, I'll bet." She fastened her hat with a thick string. "Ha! We're looking like Thelma and Louise of the ozone-hole generation."

Marta laughed. "Do you want to use my lip balm? It's SPF thirty." Barry Manilow, she recalled: the troubadour with whom she'd been trapped on hold, the thick schmaltz the ideal torment for any impatient customer.

2.

Marta had not driven the route, but retraced it easily enough from the to and fro runs between locations with Chaz. She pointed toward the crash site soon after passing by the unmoving radio transmission dish monoliths; on the approach she was struck by how much the habitat had grown since that late night visit, the pattern exponential and jumbled, like a desperate refugee camp. The occupation of turquoise portable toilet rows and pell-mell white trailers flattened wild field grasses; in between, rigid tent canopies provided shade for extras and served as makeshift cafeterias for crew meals. *This time next week,* Marta thought, *passersby will see nothing out of the ordinary except trampled grass*. Such stealth reflected movie magic of a different kind.

Attended cars loitered along the roadside. "Lookie loos and local reporters playing paparazzi," Lora said. "Probably here to catch a glimpse of Michelle Pfeiffer, and good luck with that."

The barbed wire gate lay rolled up by a wooden post. Marta slowed, awaiting directions.

"Everyone that's legit is over there in crew parking, thataway." Lora's thumb jerks directed them to a lot with tape borders rustling in the breeze.

Leaning close to Marta, Lora spoke to the PA guarding the field of vehicles. "Hi, honey," she said tucking her chin and peering over bee-eye sunglasses. "You gonna let us into this blazing mess?"

"ID."

"Um, hello?" Lora pointed to the sticker on the windshield, Chaz's doing.

"Straight ahead, then make a right."

"Christ, what a jerk. There's a rent-a-cop in the making," Lora said as Marta drew into the makeshift lot. She waved to men smoking near the horse trailers. "Animal handlers and extras wrangling, it's a virtual rodeo here today. At least there's a bit of a gust now."

Marta could ignore bladder alerts no longer. "Lora, before we take another step, is there, well, a dedicated trailer for washrooms?"

"No sweetie, it's all for one and one for all here unless you're royalty on the talent totem." With a sly smile, she jerked her head at the turquoise row. "I'll wait over there under the extras tent."

"Do you mind?" She handed Lora the tote bag.

Abuzz with flies, the cubicle's semiopaque, off-gassing plastic walls also oozed an aura of blistering heat while the liquid chemicals and body excretion stew below suggested toxic waste and recent mass graves. Marta pulled a sanitary seat cover from the dispenser and sat reluctantly. Once finished reading the maintenance schedule with its commonsense warning—"Excessive use will result in unsatisfactory conditions before the next regular servicing"—she focussed on the company's humble motto: "We're #2 in Number Two." She imagined a cutthroat rivalry with the frontrunner in the portable toilet sector—industrial espionage, kickbacks, headhunted sales staff: who could say?

"Pretty ripe, eh?" Lora sat under the shade of a tent. "I always go back at the office." The plastic rental tables remained unoccupied except for a group of swarthy men throwing down pennies and cards.

"That's a good call; I'll remember for next time."

"Shall we take a stroll down the hill, my dear?"

"Yes, let's."

Another PA stood guard at the rim of the pit, the young man's hand gestures as standardized as sign language: halt, the camera is rolling, there's radio silence, all non-essential personnel need to hold their tongues and keep still, thanks for being patient.

When the walkie-talkie squawked two minutes later, he muttered into the receiver. "Alright, ladies. It's a go. Watch your step, we've had a few twisted ankles on that hill already."

"No snakes?" Lora raised her sunglasses to peer down the slope.

"Not a one, ma'am."

"Let's go. We'll find Jake and station ourselves by him." Lora took the lead.

Congested and to all appearances volatile—well-behaved movie house patrons the instant someone shrieks "Fire!"—the scene below struck Marta as textbook Hollywood film set. Radiating from the bull's eye plot of gravel, now void of the actors who'd finished speaking their lines a minute earlier: a thriving settlement's worth of tasks and sweat-drenched personalities—handlers corralling excitable horses, extras in desert garb smoking by a butt receptacle, tradesmen inspecting generators, electrical cables, and the camera track, PAs receiving instructions and hustling from A to B, urgent conversationalists on walkie-talkies, capped men adjusting equipment under a miscellany of spindle-legged white canopies that Marta ordinarily associated with outdoor weddings, underling slackers in twos and threes chatting as they awaited instructions, and complete strangers standing docile with hands deep in front pockets. At the far periphery a young woman in a peasant skirt and print head kerchief held a green hose and misted the powdery ground.

"Craft service has a coffee slash snack bar set up over yonder," Lora said. "Most of the talent is usually huddled there, or smoking out of sight if there's a big break between takes. I figure we have a couple of minutes before they're ready to go again. I'm going to grab a cup."

Marta followed. She wanted to stand at a central but safely tucked away spot from which to watch the proceedings and considered Lora—winding through the crowd while tapping a message—an invaluable guide.

"Can't figure out where Jake and the boys could have disappeared to. No answers from them, either." Lora reached into her satchel. "Cappuccino?"

"Do you think they have soy milk?"

"Oh, I'd say so. Craft Service is used to special needs diets, so they'll have all those kinds of products. Agave syrup too if you're vegan. Or watching your glycemic load."

3:

Marta had re-read the pages of the crash site scene in anticipation of Luna's morning audition. Outwardly fearless, Lady Swinburne—Delacroix's heroic Liberty, but possessing heavily-draped Victorian propriety—led the ragtag entourage toward a destination of unclear significance. Though the script skipped details, Marta supposed that the farmhands and servants would look shifty-eyed and reluctant, instinct in the form of raised arm hairs having whispered "Pawn! Cannon fodder!" and summoned gory scenarios to show how better off they'd be fleeing in the opposite direction.

As Lora and Marta approached the crew cluster, the AD relayed word from the director. "Okay, okay, listen up, folks," he said, pausing until the group fell silent. "We need more of a gap between Swinburne and the rest. It's like she's the warrior and then the other riders are a bit chicken shit and the villagers have been ready to crap their pants since they left, got it?"

Murmurs of assent sounded.

The AD clapped. "Alright. Everyone ready in place in two."

4.

"The powers that be now want a practice run for the rear guard," Lora said. "It's easy to see how going over budget is par for the course."

Horses cocked their ears as Dr. Potter, Lizzie, and a pair of nameless male villagers drew closer to the crashed spacecraft; a mute handful of scared villagers—raised scythes, machetes, and sticks in hand—filed in behind. *It might as well be outside of Frankenstein's laboratory*, Marta thought, *the only items missing are fiery torches.*

Watching Luna, Marta felt impressed by the apparent veteran confidence; she rode naturally, unfazed by the swirl of cameras, mikes, and crew. "Won't the wind interfere with sound quality?"

"Oh it will, but that's no big deal. They'll re-record chunks of it later, under studio conditions. Always do."

5.

On the ninth take, Tracy Scoggins achieved the desired balance of dignity, sensible trepidation, and steely martial ferocity.

A tantrum eruption—"Will you please . . . and by that I mean are you truly capable of letting me speak without stepping all over my lines? Is that too much to ask? Is it?"—following an unbidden burst of laughter, two wardrobe malfunctions, flubbed lines, a stumbling extra, horse dung clean up, and technical glitches turned the preceding takes into editing screen trash.

Watching with mounting boredom, Marta wanted to applaud when the scene finally hit its stride: with so many handicaps failure seemed fated, an ironclad guarantee. Besides heat, extras, crew, equipment, horses, and other actors, the star rode swaddled by a heavy linen caftan; further encumbrance by a red wool tunic and equestrian boots with brass spurs restricted her movements. And in keeping with historical portraits of Lady Hester Stanhope, a woman notorious for donning the attire of manor-born Levantine males (here interpreted as a fur-trimmed cloak and epauletted ceremonial finery that could have inspired Michael Jackson's latter years), Lady Swinburne wore an embroidered turban. Errant strands of the actress's signature chestnut hair slipped out behind her left ear. The costumer's inspiration also included a decorated steel scimitar, positioned to face the camera.

Seeing the wardrobe here in the Middle East's body double convinced Marta that madness underlaid Lady Stanhope's legendary eccentricity: besides unwieldy, the layered ensemble would have been oven hot after ten minutes of riding. Small wonder elaborate visions of grandeur assailed the woman: she'd been slow-roasting herself into a delirium.

And for these takes Marta exhaled slowly, relieved that not a word deviated from the pages. Double-checking the script, she heard no note of improv or free association with the characters' personalities—

EXT. CRASH SITE - DAY

LADY SWINBURNE

It is my sense, Dr. Potter, that the facts of the matter cannot be ascertained until we discover what tumbled from the heavens. Otherwise, we shall continue only to blunder like a company of dunces.

Potter rides closer to Swinburne to catch all her words.

DR. POTTER

We share one thought, Lady.

SWINBURNE

Lizzie, fall to the rear with haste.
Misplacing villagers in this dusty maze is a fate we must avoid.

LIZZIE

Yes, milady.

They halt their horses as they approach the crash site.

SWINBURNE

Merciful heavens!
It appears to be a mechanical device, but as nothing I have before witnessed.

POTTER

I concur, Lady.

(nods)

Not even within the great mills of Lancashire have I seen such a leviathan mechanism.

LIZZIE

The villagers have fallen back, whispering of protection from demons. Perhaps it is a craft, milady?

POTTER

(impatient, dismissing the idea with his hand)

Nonsense, chavette.

LIZZIE

(shades her eyes)

What is your supposition, then, good Doctor?

POTTER

I cannot hazard a guess.

SWINBURNE

It is a scientific marvel, sprung from minds greater than those of the Royal Society. We must investigate!

LIZZIE

Take care, Milady. There is darkness to it, an evil.

Marta grasped the fact of a direct relationship between what she observed under bright lighting on the scraped floor of a gravel pit carved from a field miles from the nearest town and what would eventually broadcast in the near future on the Psy/Fi Network and its international affiliates. Lack of experience forced her to speculate about the relationship's exact nature—what would be edited out, how well would Luna come across, what impressions would Lady Swinburne, weighted down by a museum's display of costumery, make, how much difference did the visual field outside the lens frame cause, and how would computer wizardry affect the tone or look of the finished product? Answers, she knew, existed short months into the future.

Lora had pitched Lady Swinburne as larger than life—as Amazonian, as Lara Croft and Eleanor Ripley combined, as fearsome warrior material—but here, despite intermittent seconds of heroic chin and fiery eyes, the thrift store layering recalled a character Carol Burnett might have played in one of the affectionate movie travesties of her variety show. To a casual viewer Swinburne passed as an eccentric traveling merchant, literally carrying wares on her back.

Marta pictured her excitement to see the finished product as a house sitting on wobbly stilts; the whole edifice swayed precariously, poised to collapse at the next slightest tremor.

A Giddy Thing

I.

"That's a wrap, folks," the AD announced, sliding off bulky grey headphones. He wound the long coiled cable around puffy ear cups and heaved the set toward the sun. "Woo fucking hoo!"

The loud round of cheering abruptly ceased. Expecting a roaring, rowdy atmosphere of TGIF celebration, Marta mouthed "What?" when the crew began swapping instructions, dialing calls, and busying themselves with equipment. Others dispersed, wiping dusty faces streaked with sweat as they strode toward the pit's narrow road. *Of course*, Marta thought. They'd been under the sun and breathing dust for days; icy beer and showers or lake water would easily best another minute milling about and talking shop inside a rocky heat trap of a hole.

As Lora made a call, Marta watched the animal handlers assist with dismounts, waving when Luna approached.

"Hey. They need me 'right away' at some trailer up above." She kept the index finger quotation marks raised high. "So can I talk with you later?"

"Yes, of course."

"Except for this godawful blanket and getting orders and 'advice' from every direction, that was fun, way better than the used car commercial, so thanks again." Luna patted her forehead with a linen sleeve and joined the cast exodus. "We have to do interior shots next week, so they're flying me down to the studio."

"Great. I was glad to help." Luna turned as Marta spoke, waved, and trailed the others. She mimed "two minutes," and Marta tracked the practiced efficiency of the crew who, she supposed, could strike a set in their sleep like carnies.

"Well, here's to another fine quality MOW almost ready to be launched at chubby faces across couch potato land," Lora said, offering a toast with a styrofoam coffee cup. "It's a living anyway," she added, studying Marta. "Keeps the repo guys at bay too."

"What's next?" Marta felt eager to change the topic. Judgmental muscle tugs reflecting half-baked thoughts about Marx and worker alienation during Lora's speech had apparently registered across her face.

"They'll shoot the rest back in the city and ship it over to the CGI guys. Oh, you mean for us? Back to the office, tie up loose ends, et cetera, et cetera, get ready to say goodbye to Joan's and this burg. Shall we?" Motioning toward the incline road, Lora secured the indigo bucket hat and began to walk. "You know, 'Shooting on location' has a nice ring to it, like 'Going to Hawaii,' but in truth after the first twenty-four hours or so everyone's just itching to get back home again. Keyword is, be careful what you wish for. We shot a snowboarder comedy a couple of years back, *Shreddin' Too* or *Boardin' II* or something memorably sequel-y like that, at two ski hills hours apart. It shoulda been called *Cabin Fever Revisited*. Christ, I thought the whole crew was going to go all Jack Nicholson. We could not get out of there fast enough."

"Hey, ladies," Nicos yelled. "Puh-leeze wait the hell up, it's not a forced march, you know. Chill for a sec."

"Well speak of the devil." Lora said. Although the black sunglasses seemed impervious to light, she shielded her eyes as the men caught up. "Question: Where did you three disappear to?"

"Out of sight, but actually in the vicinity," Chaz said.

"Yeah, Jake wanted to hang back by the video hut." Nicos stood back and lit a cigarette.

"I didn't want to," Jake said. "*El cineasta* wanted an information session, so I was obliged. I texted that, right?"

"No, that's not a courtesy you extended to me."

"Ah, well. Me bad. Anyway, you're up to speed now."

"Thanks a heap." Everyone watched their usual rowdy sibling badinage go off the rails; petty squabbling appeared to be the next destination.

"Would anyone like coffee before Craft Service slams shut?" Marta said as Nicos asked, "Okay boss, where to, what next?"

"Sure," Chaz said.

Marta stepped back from the informal circle, pleased with Chaz's acknowledgement.

"The Hebe farm, anywhere but this drought zone," Jake said. "I need to check out how much is left to clean up. Then the office." He addressed Chaz while checking for messages: "As for you, you can get coffee later."

"That's where we're heading, so let's meet in an hour." Lora tapped her watch. "Do you want me to write that down?" Phones in hand, Jake and Nicos turned their backs to the overhead glare.

"We are going to the office now. We will see you in one hour," Lora, speaking in a slow robot voice, directed the words at Chaz. "Six zero minutes."

"See you later, ladies," Nicos said as he and Chaz scrambled to catch up with Jake.

2.

Speeding along White Lake Road, Marta listened politely. The receding location in the side view mirror provoked a twinge of wistfulness; second by second the crash site solidified as a pin-point in history, an episode now relegated to memory.

Lora went over a raft of immediate goals and furiously tapped reminder notes. She apologized for thinking out loud and caving in to OCD. "Pulling up stakes is just a matter of checking off items from an accurate list."

"Then we disappear, like thieves in the night?"

"Exactly, as if we were never here, ninja-style."

"I'm already half-packed." As for why, Marta saw no legitimate reason to share.

"Don't forget to pick up your per diem," Lora said as Marta approached Joan's.

"Thanks, I won't. I have a few last-minute items to attend to as well, so I'll grab it then."

3.

Lora scurried to the front desk and unlocked a metal box in a lower drawer. The envelope she retrieved featured Marta's name and a peel-on sticker of a roulette wheel.

"Just a token," Lora said.

Marta checked inside: a printout of a map, casino tokens, and bills banded by a piece of folded paper that exclaimed, "What Happens in Penticton, Stays in Penticton!" The other side listed the specifics of the wrap party: time, place, dress code. "Come as you are!" she read.

Marta caught up with work email within an hour; while deleting junk, departmental administrative updates, and the usual miscellany of queries and requests from incoming and outgoing students, textbook peddlers, and conference promoters, she scanned the tidings of sin dispensed by Exconfessio—the standard assemblage of guilt, misanthropy, and sexual misdeeds, with one poignant exception: "I have an overwhelming sense of not living up to my capacity, but can't seem to generate the missing ingredient"—and weighed each word of an unexpected note from her Floridian publisher, its subject line characteristically direct: "*Holiday Archetype Personality*: 2.0???" She committed to holding off on that reply until resettling in the city.

4.

When Nicos drove by the trailer park at Vaseaux Lake, Jake snorted at seeing a lawn chair near a parked car. *That figures*, he thought. Xtina must be holed up there right now bored, alone, available at a computer screen, and trying her damnedest to lure visitors while he was stuck in the SUV's passenger seat. He'd kill to be straddled across that warm body, building up to spray long strands of pearl necklace. It wouldn't take a minute. Jake pulled the seat belt forward and turned to Chaz in the back seat.

"So, what's going on with you and the egghead?"

"What do you mean?"

"Don't play dumb. You know what I mean."

"What's this," Nicos said. "A showmance?"

"Showmance? Christ, do real people say that? I thought that was reserved for reality TV dregs."

"What's your problem, man? You've been crapping on everybody all day."

"My problem, man—" Jake's mouth gaped, an answer caught between brain and larynx. The truth—"I'm tired and pent up and frustrated because I have not gotten laid despite the fact that I have literally walked for miles in fricking desert sand looking for it like some deranged bible prophet and the closest I got was in that trailer park we just passed by and a campground back a few kliks, where I could have gotten a sloppy blow job at midnight from a troll cupping a set of dentures in his palm"—belonged in a locked vault. Nothing else clever and foe-demolishing came to mind, and he couldn't smile away Nicos's charge. "How many years have you been in this business, Nicos? I mean, c'mon. A short-tempered boss can't be news to you, so enough with the ragging and cut me some slack. It's the last day of the shoot, do I really need to say more? So sorry, okay? Just give it a rest. How about I buy you guys a beer"—Jake remembered Nicos's stream of declarations about sobriety—"or whatever. There's a beer parlour just down the street from the office."

"A tavern." Nicos said. "Really? I didn't see one."

"Yeah, really. It's there. And technically it's a beer parlour because we're in Canada, not the U S of A, eh."

"Jeez, okay, professor."

"A beer sounds great, Jake," Chaz said.

"Head there now?" Nicos said.

"No, slack ass. We'll do the Hebe place first. I can be in and out in ten minutes."

"Okay, boss, whatever you say." Nicos accelerated.

"We're good?" Jake studied trees, guessing at what fruit they would bear.

Nicos focussed on the highway. "It's history."

Jake nodded. The past behind them, order restored.

5.

Marta pruned the contents of the inbox listlessly and overheard Lora making arrangements with her boyfriend for airport pickup—detailed and repeated, as though instructions for a child: "Okay, okay, good, now just tell me exactly what you've written down on the pad." Marta realized the email make-work project disguised unconscious dawdling. After all, hours stretched until the second—and, this round, surely successful—wrap party of her life began, and since both cruising up and down the valley in search of purpose and perspiring while staring at daytime TV in #10 ranked as equally unappealing, killing time claimed the lead.

Being candid, though, she recognized the excuse beneath the empty hours rationale. Chaz's return and the inevitable conversation pressed on her mind; she'd noticed her eyes flitting toward the front of Joan's each time a shadowy form passed by. *Nesting already*, she thought with disdain. Really, no different than a caterpillar entering chrysalis? Just like that, hapless in the face of ancient, fundamental biological imperatives, the cocoon-spinning begins? As she sat at a desk making plans, had microcellular processes begun—neurons activating and chemical instructions racing through arteries and creeping into organs, all aiming to direct actions and assure species continuance? Was she no different than a marionette?

Men kiss in order obtain sex, while women do so to evaluate potential mates; this factoid her brother had touted last Christmas, taking a digression from justifying the breakup of a twenty three-month second marriage to unsympathetic familial ears. "Is that a fact, Mr. Science." Marta's doubtful tongue poised readily with counter-arguments.

"Yup, it's a fact, proven in controlled lab conditions."

"And I suppose infidelity with your secretary can also be explained away in a lab," Marta said, always the able cross-examiner to Les' fumbling testifying witness.

"Ka-pow! She's got you on the ropes," Dianne said.

"Now, now, you two." Their father's placating caught no one off guard; he'd long played the impartial referee to Dianne's knee-jerk instigator. *The George and Dianne Speck Show*: a long-running family joke.

No, Marta decided. She desired a clarifying exchange and, as Lora would say, needed to tie up loose ends. Biochemical ulterior motives didn't come into the picture. Really, who wouldn't want illumination?

"Lora," Marta shouted, "when are we expecting Jake and Chaz?"

"Just a sec, honey," Lora barked from Jake's desk. "Believe it or not, I'm on hold. Really, I do not ever want an answer to the question, 'Dear God, how much of my adult life has been spent on hold?' " She stood before Marta's desk a minute later. "You were saying?"

"Oh, Jake and Chaz, when do you expect them to return?" Marta had clicked off the computer and tidied papers. With the desk's surface in order, she'd have no reason to linger.

"To be honest, I expected them by now. Jake said an hour, right?" Lora sipped from the lidded coffee cup. "Christ, that's hot. I dunno, could be they're off drinking somewhere dark and dirty. Men like their brass poles and exotic entertainment. Wouldn't be the first time. You can always text if there's something important. Is there?"

"It's nothing. Actually, I guess I'll see everyone at the party."

"I'll let Chaz know where you are, if you'd like that." Lora winked.

"That's not necessary, but thank you." She surveyed the dingy room. "Okay, I've done all I can do here, so I'm going to, well, I'm not quite sure what yet. Float where the winds take me?"

"Sounds like a plan. We'll see you in a few hours, okay?" Lora's cellphone trilled from the back of the room. "And there's my cue."

"See you later." Marta walked to the computer at Lora's desk and typed an email to Chaz: "Need a lift to the wrap party? I'll be at the Star-Lite until then."

6.

Before returning to #10, Marta dropped by the front desk to remind Mrs. Simms about the morning check-out, the visit a formality since the production company footed the bill. Still, it couldn't hurt to double-check; perhaps the contract excluded calls.

"We'll miss you," Mrs Simms said. "I wish all my guests were as quiet as you movie people."

Counting the red doors en route to the room, Marta thought about souvenir options for her family. She struck fruit off the list—too perishable, and delivery would push her into an unscheduled early summer visit. Ordinarily wine made for a reasonable generic choice—but her parents, practically teetotalers, would say obligatory thank yous and stow the bottle away indefinitely; and Les already drank too avidly. *A jpeg*, she thought: easy, inexpensive, novel, efficient. No one had mentioned setting aside time for a group crew photo at the crash site or at Djoun. She'd find out later. Lora, the queen of details, must have arranged documentation of the shoot. When Luna arrived at the party Marta would ask for a memento, and email the shot with the tie-in story once comfortably ensconced in Vancouver.

With luck, a new photograph would inspire Dianne to remove one of four variation on a theme cap-and-gown snapshots of Marta in the living room's digital photo frame. Their sameness might lead a casual viewer to conclude, based on available evidence, that the only daughter of the Specks had disappeared mysteriously—along with a promising career—on the afternoon of her final graduation ceremony.

Marta shut the door after the breeze had swept out the room's stale air. The cavernous stillness encouraged her to stretch out with closed eyes. Marta didn't expect to nap. Instead, she'd use the time to organize and prioritize—summer's writing and research schedule needed to be pieced together, as did preparative reading for autumn's graduate seminar. She decided those details couldn't be mapped without a notepad and a calendar, and turned to the *Holiday Archetype Personality* sequel. The publisher's proposal had gnawed since the email at Joan's.

"A companion volume does not serve my interests at this time, thank you": she knew the intelligent and unequivocal response to compose. Still, Marta's mind circled the offer. Her own ethical core demanded to be swayed, a compelling justification outlined and proposed. If the first effort had been more or less successfully rationalized as an experiment—a series of experiments, to be accurate—the next one required stronger logic and allowed for fewer permissions; she'd slump, feeling miserable, if pursuing a follow-up volume, an exercise in advanced cynicism featuring a sad grab for petty cash and pitiful and anonymous demi-celebrity that would also look like a finger of self-accusation.

And if improving creative reach or pursuing fame or dabbling with alter-egos truly named her fundamental goal, then she ought to evolve and try for something else. Larger too: a serious work of realist fiction, perhaps, or complex allusive verse sent to small-circulation literary journals. Or, admitting multiplex-or-bust motives, then why not a genre exercise, *Angel V: The Return of the Killer*? Chaz would say, "Go for it!"

For the grand experiment that included Sadie Lighbody's *HAP* to have further value, only full committal made sense—"Go big or go home," as she'd heard Jake declare?

Marta opened her eyes. The hour for that decision could be postponed indefinitely. Sadie, a junior member of Apate+Global's stable of financial gurus, psychics, dietitians, and self-help royalty, lacked status; and in light of total sales figures, Marta guessed, she stood a hair's breadth from never being contacted again. Not one of A+G's cadre of publicists stored either Marta or Sadie on speed dial.

Unable to resist dwelling on worrisome details, Marta recalled that the crew—and their girlfriends in particular—had appeared decked out for the wrap party she'd attended in the city years ago. A suitcase inventory revealed no suitable cocktail party items in reach; still, she felt sure that the location shoot's party would be wall-to-wall T-shirts and jeans: "Come as you are" did imply informal attire. No alternatives sprang to mind; the valley towns were no fashion meccas, and purchasing anything she'd wear exactly once meant wasted money. Another party, glitzy and cosmopolitan, might be in the works for the city once all the studio work ceased. She'd ask Lora.

Marta sat up, any hint of relaxation or refreshment scattered; she'd practically fallen into a chagrined dream as soon as her lids joined. The radio alarm clock informed her of slow-running time and that remaining penned up in the room served only as an invitation to fret. Picturing herself behind the wheel of the rental, Marta reached for the keys. For Chaz she'd leave a note under his door—the corner unit a refuge for which he'd offered no walk-through—before sliding into the driver's seat.

She signaled right at the highway for no other reason than she'd be turning left later for the casino party. *This is the last of my workation*, she thought, *whither shall I wander?* Sentimentality, a personality aspect that usually lay dormant, whispered about the windmill ice cream shop that she'd visited before the hairpin turns to Anarchist's lookout.

Lactose intolerance be damned, Marta ordered two scoops—one chocolate, one vanilla: the unwavering choice for childhood visits—and scrutinized the vineyards, tenacious grasses, and sage on the tawny hills above while seated atop a shaded picnic table. Lines of vacationing vehicles and squabbling families, the other immediate views today as with yesteryear, would have ruined the moment.

Wrap

I.

Marta stood a few paces from a round curtained table set with plates and cutlery. After striding though the hotel's lobby—a boxy affair countrified with a deer antler chandelier and rustic-effect lampshades with visible stitching—at twenty minutes past the time printed on the invitation, she'd been chagrined to enter a hall populated with meagre pockets of crew. The majority arrived a half hour later, and she now watched the rhythmic convergence and dispersal of these small groups near the banquet room's centre.

The multipurpose space adjacent to the casino that Lora had booked presented its occupants with architectural clip art—a standard rectangle featuring painted metal fire doors and perpetually lit Exits on two opposing walls, the room was papered pinky-beige and carpeted with an unobtrusive pattern. It could be anywhere, as though such rooms, like the pie Marta had ordered at the Husky, came pre-fabricated from one warehouse in a flat manufacturing hub. At conferences in Boise, Orlando, Toronto, Vancouver, and Dallas, Marta had stood in near-xeroxes of the venue; and while attending Les' two wedding receptions, she'd scooped up lasagna from identical steel trays set on buffets skirted with spill-resistant nylon fabrics in soft tints that blended with the domesticated pastel of the walls.

"Ghastly, isn't it," Lora said. She'd slipped on a fresh camouflage T-shirt; the v-neck offered viewers clearly displayed Points of Interest. "It's like a crime scene: the mother of the bride exploded. We should alert the local CSI."

2.

Nicos arrived with Jake and toasted the clique with a bottle of Perrier. "All hope abandon, ye who enter in. And, folks, remember the motto of this place: 'Know Your Limit, Play Within It.' "

Marta tracked the Location Manager's weaving. He marched up to another departmental klatch, and raised the green vessel for an identically foreboding toast. "My, what is that about? The rancorous witch in *Sleeping Beauty* could be his ancestor."

"All I'll say is somebody, no names, had a little problem with online gambling a few years back," Lora said, leaning close, hand cupped close to Marta's ear.

"And booze too." Jake opted against Lora's low decibels. "Now's he's got the born-again bug, big time." He held up a highball glass and rattled the ice.

"Oh, I see."

"And here's to getting the hell out of Dodge." The others touched their glasses to his.

Marta, familiar with the easy smile—wide, baring dentist-straightened polar drift teeth—saw little humour in eyes that swept the half-circle of crew before terminating at an Exit's red glow.

3.

Marta spotted Luna, who cut through the crowd with Lornette trailing a step behind. She waved them over. "You made it." In flip flops, a short denim skirt, and a black T-shirt, Luna hadn't bothered to dress up, but Marta noticed that her sidekick, in tendrils and tiers, could pass for Loretta Lynn attending a prom.

"Yeah. I'm not keen on parties, but 'bite the hand that feeds you' and all that," Luna said, fingers quoting. "Besides, Miss *National Enquirer* here wanted to snap some celebrities."

"Oh, shut up, you." Lornette turned to Marta, "This is a fancy spread."

"Yes, it's not bad. There's a good chance that most actors will opt out of the party."

"Oh. I guess they're itching to get away from country living."

"That may well be. Luna, I asked Lora to take a picture when she saw us." Marta spied the room for a suitable location. "I'm guessing that you're not at all shy in front of a camera."

"A picture would be great. Something to pin up at the O-K and show off to the regulars after the hubbub dies down."

"As if, Luna," Lornette said. "You wait and see, they'll be fighting each other to get you into their movies."

"I dunno, the O-K's not so bad."

"Hmm, let's see," Lornette displayed her open palms as a mock-scale, "a limousine and driver or twenty-five cent tips during the breakfast rush? Like there's any comparison!"

"What limousine?"

"Say 'Djoun' everybody," Lora said. The camera's screen provoked a frown. "Okay, once more, but this time keep your eyes open, my dears."

4.

"Well," Lora said, "was all this movie stuff what you expected?"

"It was and it wasn't," Marta said. "Sorry for the politician's answer."

"No problem. I take it you're not ready for a change in career?"

"A change in scenery was what I needed. I guess."

Lora reached for her phone. "His Nibs demands an audience. Pick this up after my tour of duty?"

"Sure, that'll be fine."

"Hey guys." Chaz held a plate and a highball glass; he bent forward in a flourish and achieved the semblance of a bow-curtsy. "What's going on?"

"I'm about to track down Jake, then I'm going to gamble away the futures of my unborn children," Lora said. "You're here sooner than expected."

"No problemo, not a hitch, everything just fell into place, and we're set to go."

"Impressive, miracles never cease! I'm off, ladies, wish me luck."

"I'll see you in there," Marta said. "I need to finish this lasagna first." She'd have to turn over the remaining waterlogged noodles to one of the servers or, failing that, maroon the plate on a nearby table. Catering staff witnessed all species of slovenly manners at these events, Marta had noted, and opted to wait for a server instead of contributing an anecdote to an after-shift bitch session.

"*Hasta pronto*," Chaz said. "That's it for you? I'm thinking second helpings for me."

"I had a late lunch." Marta's habitual white lie came out easier than exposing a judicious diet others might categorize as finicky and high maintenance; and by now Chaz was partially up to speed and ready with Princess Pea quips.

"That was quite a long day, eh?"

"Yes, it was that. I've begun to get used to them. In another week I'd be a veteran."

"Can you hold on here a sec? I wasn't joking about the second helping. I'm starved. Jake kept us at his beck and call all bloody day and then thought a pint would smooth over the slave driving and assholery."

"Sure, I'll wait here. The gambling next door doesn't have much appeal."

"I figured as much. It's hard to picture you chucking dice and yelling 'Mama needs a brand new mink.'" While Chaz's observation was essentially astute, Marta heard a backhanded compliment.

Chaz set the plate on the floor. "Man, this place could really hire a few more waiters."

Marta smiled. "You'd better head over to the buffet table before the food's gone. You know, now that you mention it, I think I'll take a brisk tour through the casino. I won't be but five minutes."

"No rush. See you." Chaz turned for the buffet.

5.

The deserted triangular foyer between banquet room crew talk and the neon enticements of the afterthought-sized casino contained a monitor bolted to the ceiling that advertised husband and wife country and western acts appearing next month in the hotel's lounge—Doc and the Missus, The Petermanns, Jonny & July. Tan papered walls remained bare except for pioneer-style sconces and a poster announcing PPV fights; from it, a trio of surly tattooed bald white men glared thug challenges to onlookers. In one corner a pair of two-foot yuccas in pebble-effect plastic urns stood at opposing edges of a trickling fountain on whose cultured stone rim sat an empty wine glass containing a balled napkin.

Feeling a barely tepid curiosity cooling with each breath, Marta charged into the adjoining room. She viewed the loud decor as culturally threadbare, the climate profane, forced gaiety needful of an alcohol crutch. A chasm stood between the garish carpet beneath her feet and the affluent Monte Carlo sophistication of Bond film set casinos.

Further scrutiny revealed the enthralled faces and boisterous laughter looked authentic. Marta admitted that perhaps her personality lacked an essential something that prevented her from humming with the hopeful, nail-biting tremor of tossed dice, selected cards, and pressed buttons.

Whereas recklessness barely registered in the ranking of her daily traits, Marta predicted Chaz would take to gambling like the proverbial duck to water—the Brat Pack tie-in served as reason enough.

The meander was expedient—a circuit by noisy machines flashing lights of candy brightness and tight groups leaning into games. At one table, a groom hooted encouragement as his new wife breathed good luck on dice cupped in his hands.

As though secured within a spacesuit, Marta couldn't breathe in the ebullient atmosphere. She studied the windowless room. From the piped-in muzak to the flashy neon- and brass-accented decor, gambling struck her as a spectacular void—bread and circuses—not to mention a costly waste of time.

Still, she mused, the history of letting loose made for a respectable volume. And an authority as reliable as Nietzsche had claimed there'd be no real art without chaotic irrationality. *Perhaps my Dionysian rite should begin with the purchase of a lottery ticket one of these days*, she thought, lips curving into a grin. Or not. Hope against hope, the whole enterprise—to live deep and suck out all the marrow of life—seemed so unreasonable, so wishful, and so ridiculous, but perhaps that was the point. *Another time, another place*, Marta thought. Steadfast—a nun at an orgy—she knew she could wait in vain here all night for the moment of her unfastening.

Pushing against an inbuilt aversion Marta veered toward an unused video slot machine at the end of a short aisle. She stood by two grey-haired women, sisters evidently, if not twins, and watched them insert tokens; as one pulled the lever the sibling gestured like an orchestral maestro—conjuring a charm for good luck.

When bounty failed to pour from the machine's mouth, the duo switched roles. As the newly-appointed luck hunter, the other sister dispensed with hand movements altogether: "C'mon, you dang one-armed bandit, we've been at it all night."

The women sat entranced, but they didn't smile; huddled, both held straws in their fingers, replacing outlawed cigarettes with the nearest passable substitute. Marta wondered if their stance signaled territoriality: the machine's luck belonged to them and no one else.

Marta slid a token into the slot. Pulling the lever she noticed a large raised lit lozenge near the place where other players had rested drinks: a start button. The lever had no real physical purpose—with guts entirely computerized, the machine's arm offered comfort as decoration, a nostalgic emblem.

The device became animated with carnival lighting and the nerve-jangling clang of recorded bell noise during the ten-second interval that coloured images on virtual reels appeared to whir. When the unit returned to relative calm, Marta stared at twin cherries, a grimacing clam, and a can of spinach through square viewing ports. She'd lost, and grew aghast calculating how many dollars a player could lose in a single hour.

"Better luck next time," the sisters chimed automatically.

Next time? Marta smiled politely, but received the encouragement critically, certain she'd never be part of this dire community and its textbook enabling. Preparing to insert another token, the canned spinach reel caught her eye. *I 'yams whats I ams, and dats all that I 'yams*, she thought, and nodded with approval at Popeye's self-acceptance, the figure's fundamental at-homeness.

"You know what, I think my luck has finally run out." Marta wished to appear weary, as though gambling since breakfast. "Here are my tokens, ladies. Maybe you'll strike it rich with them."

"Why, aren't you an absolute dear!" Twins definitely, Marta concluded, fondly calling up a Diane Arbus retrospective poster hanging back in the Dark Tower's office.

Marta couldn't help but hear surges of excited voices around the adjacent tables—unsure about the full range of games that the government allowed, she pictured blackjack and roulette. Freed of the gift tokens she felt no inclination to mill about and watch additional women and men—*on a losing streak* or *on a roll*—throw down cards and bless dice: she understood the gist of it.

Turning for the exit, she walked directly into Jake. His body was solid, as expected.

"Oh, I'm sorry." She stepped back and looked up.

"No worries. I was watching over your shoulder, so I was asking for it. That sucks, eh?"

"Pardon?"

"Gambling. I get the idea and the charge and all that shit, but c'mon everyone knows the cards are stacked against them. Me, if I'm going risk my ass for something, I gotta at least think there's a good chance I'll get what I want. Why bother otherwise?"

Marta, wondering about the man's sudden volubility, noticed the tall drink in his grasp.

"We're on the same page there."

"I'm heading to the bar for a refill. Can I get you anything?"

"Thanks, but no. I think I'm going to make my way back to the banquet room."

"Alright. Cheers."

6.

Tipping his glass, Jake caught Marta's eyes as she mimed a raised glass in reply. *Self-righteous goody two-shoes*, he thought.

One last vodka and tonic; he figured handling that would be no problem. He'd toss a double back and beg off, tell Lora that he'd done his part and that a headache demanded a quiet room.

Trailer park Xtina and the bush codgers tumbled into Jake's consciousness as he strode toward the bar, insistent, like those *Night of the Living Dead* zombies once they've caught sight of living flesh. He swept the images aside, focussing on the drive ahead and the details of the morning's flight.

7.

Chaz gnawed on a rib as Marta approached. "Hi Fido, how's the grub?"

"Woof. You weren't lying about five minutes, wow. It's good, actually. I'm surprised. Buffets are wall-to-wall crapfests usually. So, was mini-Vegas really mini-Reno?"

"I'm not a great judge of character. You might like it, but it's not my cup of tea."

"I'll check it out in a bit."

"Okay." Marta recognized the contribution of words intended to pad a conversation thinning out.

"Are you planning on staying at this shindig for long?"

"I don't think so. Do they usually last long?"

"Depends. I figure with the casino and bar within spitting distance of each other, some hardcore crew will be letting off steam for quite a while yet. A couple of teamsters dropped by the office earlier, though. They're already loaded up and ready to hit the road."

Marta stepped back from Chaz and looked around the room. "I'm not far behind them."

"I could go back with you. If you'd like."

"I'm fine, really. The quiet will do me good." She wanted to say little else; she'd sound neurotic or silly growing serious and questioning as Chaz blithely chewed. "Enjoy yourself here. I'm planning to get up early anyway."

"Okay, that's cool." Chaz reached out the plate as a waiter passed by. "Thanks, man. Hey, if I get back early enough I'll drop by to say Hi. Maybe I'll be loaded down with booty if Lady Luck's good to me in the casino. You like mink?" Marta imagined the smiling ghost of Frank Sinatra watching over the scene.

"Gold bullion has some appeal, actually. Good luck then." In lieu of an embrace she waved; slumbering, intuition hastened her in no direction.

8.

"Time for me to cut out," Jake said. Antsy from shop talk and logistics with Lora and tired of Nicos crowding in, bleating about "inebriates" like a Prohibition-days do-gooder, or pointing out the endless faults of "this puny dime store Reno," he craved a radical break. Also, the remaining advertised sources of entertainment looked verboten—*Dallas*-wannabe locals in tight Wranglers, their mates in satin blouses over push-up bras—exhausted, or never promising to begin with. "Should get back to my room and pack. The flight is at some godawful time in the morning."

"Want me to track down Nicos?" Lora surveyed the crew clusters. "He's sober as a judge and you've been putting back a few, I think."

"I'm fine, mother."

"Okay, you're the boss. Just don't expect me to haul your ass out of jail or identify remains later tonight. I need my beauty sleep. The phone will be shut off."

"You're all heart." He swallowed the vodka and tonic—definitely the final one of the evening—in a gulp, and made for the casino exit.

"Give me a call from the airport, alright?"

"Of course, dear. Don't stay out too late."

9.

Marta smoothed the floral quilt until it stretched perfectly across the bed. Standing back, she judged the effect to be wrong—too neat—and produced the asymmetry of use with a swift tug. She'd like to be regarded as a respectful guest and, unaccountably, wanted Mrs. Simms to have evidence that she'd slept in the room. With the bed's appearance for the morning departure set, Marta opened the front door and watched ungraceful moths fluttering near a fluorescent tube above.

In no rush to arrive home, she charted tomorrow's drive as leisurely, even whimsical. She'd pull over whenever a roadside attraction proved alluring: the lake with the unearthly mineral crust, the Depression-era covered bridge painted an eye-searing orange, the riverside picnicking area opposite a gigantic rock from which risk-takers dove in summer months.

The nervous anticipation she'd carried in her midriff while driving into the Interior would have long since dispersed. Embarking on the inevitable katabasis, she'd signal right just past the Husky and see the fledgling orchards, once home to the Silver Sage Drive-In; perhaps she'd stop at the first look-out at the crest of the inaugural climb. Not expecting to return soon, she'd want to have the valley's geography gel, to reset images held so long by imperfect memory that the edges had become blurred, the details scant or absent. Surveying the vista she'd breathe in an incense current of dust and withering vegetation; she might step over the guardrail and crouch to snap off sprigs from nearby sagebrush that would later perfume the car.

Leaning against the warm red surface of #10's door, Marta envisioned the gradual change in landscape—from low-density single story outposts, valley-wide orchard swathes, and steep needle-thatched hills of pine to voracious, pulsating, multitudinous city: expanding grids of glass towers and invasive growth of rooftops from numberless residences, freeways of single-occupant vehicles barreling toward clogged overpasses and arterial roadways, pooling autumnal, then wintery rains preceded by urgent multimedia alerts—beware, beware—about incoming low-pressure systems and diluvian rainfall, competing herded black umbrellas with metal ribs delivering sharp pokes and bracing trickles of water, and crammed superheated buses of Bangkokian humidity to and from classrooms filled with slouched, keen, and indifferent students—their cell phones never out of reach—who would sit mutely, check Facebook statuses, or ask questions that could intrigue, challenge, exasperate, or infuriate.

The inordinate volume, strength, and velocity of the visual torrent was dizzying, overwhelming. In centuries past it might be called a sign from God, but despite the attractiveness of the idea Marta had no real faith in visions—if pressed for an explanation, she'd propose that Jean d'Arc had suffered from schizophrenia—and decided she preferred *montage* instead.

She paused, pensive, moths still on erratic orbits above.

Watching *Koyaanisqatsi* decades ago she'd been enraptured, convinced that the bombastic score and manic procession of slow-motion and time-lapse imagery declared something profound, ideas that could be keenly sensed but never adequately translated into mere words. Ineffable.

As another RV came into Marta's field of vision, she marveled at the strange workings of the mind. How simple. Apparently she'd developed a smidgen of anxiousness about returning home. Eager to bring that to attention, one brain compartment had colluded with another, seizing on a vintage memory and casting it with relevant local details. *Repurposing*, she thought, *that's the word.*

III

Gastown to Chanakyapuri

With these facts bearing upon the behavior during the establishment of orientation before us, we may now well ask the question: how does the rat attain orientation?

—Harvey Carr and John B. Watson,
Orientation in the White Rat (1907)

Post-Production

I.

Earth, the first projected image, floated colloidally in the infinite substance of space. Its frozen poles nudged the frame of the screen.

"Credits and other shit will be added later," Chaz whispered to Marta. "This workprint isn't the rough cut technically, but it's not much past that stage."

Jagged scars and scorch marks blemished the planet's life-breeding hues. The camera zoomed in, passing through dingy clouds and ominous drifts of smoke before quickly cataloguing tourism brochure vistas from India, France, China, Russia, and the United States. A generic image procession—burned and crumpled architectural icons, miserable lines of refugees trudging blindly toward the mirage of safety, CGI blast craters, exploded military vehicles—hinted at battles fought and lost. Vignettes of hopelessness, the gloomy scenes announced a foolish wager in favour of humanity's continued existence.

Marta chewed inside her lower lip. These dystopian vistas came from a lazy hand—not homage, not derivative, but virtual plagiarism, a compendium of notions shoplifted from a warehouse of historical film reels.

The title, in *Star Wars* yellow, replaced the camera's dolorous globetrotting: *Alien Advance*. A second later, the final half materialized: *Desert Assault*.

A scrolling legend replaced the fading title—

Cambridge, England 2091 AD

THE GLOBAL WAR BETWEEN HUMANITY AND THE KREPLON IMPERIUM HAS BEEN RAGING FOR DECADES, THE COST

DEVASTATING. RIVERS AND SEAS POISONED, ENTIRE CITIES DEMOLISHED, AND HUMAN POPULATIONS DECIMATED, CIVILIZATION NOW STANDS ON THE BRINK OF A NEW DARK AGE.

DESPITE HEROIC EFFORTS, THE BEST MILITARY AND SCIENTIFIC MINDS HAVE PROVEN NO MATCH FOR THE TECHNOLOGICAL SUPERIORITY OF THE KREPLON FORCE. FOR THE REMAINING HUMANS A SINGLE HOPE REMAINS: TO LOCATE AND DESTROY THE KREPLON PRIME NEST, THE PLACE WHERE THE KREPLON QUEEN ONCE DEPOSITED HER EGGS.

HAVING RISKED THEIR LIVES TO STUDY KREPLON REPRODUCTION SCIENTISTS BELIEVE THAT THE ENTIRE ALIEN ARMY WAS LAID BY A SINGLE QUEEN, WHO HAD ARRIVED SOMEWHERE ON EARTH CENTURIES BEFORE.

IF THE PRIME NEST CAN BE ELIMINATED, THE KREPLONS WILL HAVE NO MEANS TO REPLENISH THEIR NUMBERS, AND THE TIDE OF WAR WILL AT LAST TURN TO SAVE HUMANITY.

"What is this," Marta whispered. " 'Kreplon Imperium?' "

"They've made some changes."

"Oh, really, I hadn't noticed."

"I'll explain later."

The next scene depicted a litter-strewn pebbled walkway. As wind blew, the camera panned to a sign in front of a formerly august building, now smoke-streaked and fortified by razor wire, spiked metal barricades, and boarded-over windows: Cambridge University Main Library.

Marta recognized the facade. Belonging to a venerable library on campus and a two-minute walk from her office, the strangely hyperreal building had proven a versatile godsend to generations of production companies with specific exterior shot requirements, not to mention the university division responsible for come-study-here promotional materials. During Marta's tenure, the library had played a posh Ivy League faculty club, the backdrop for athletic cheerleading practices at a state university in Memphis, laboratories specializing in misguided research (of the usual kinds: genetics, cybernetics, robotics, exobiology, virtual reality), and head offices of nefarious high-tech American corporations operating above the law. Marta felt confident that it had also served in dozens of feature films and television broadcasts she'd missed.

Marta puzzled over the dire scrolling legend. With the exception of battle strategy and weaponry design classes, choosing a major and fulfilling degree requirements while hostile extraterrestrials marauded—never mind running an entire university with the human race shuffling toward extinction—seemed counterintuitive. Where would the operating budget come from? What would anybody study and why? Surely seminar discussions of Jane Austen's juvenilia and Plato's cave allegory at a time of mass extinction would be decadently pointless activities, not to mention suicidal.

Inside the library, a young woman seated at a long wooden table read in an otherwise empty room, low stacks of leather-bound books the objects of her scrutiny. Marta noticed that even though the woman wore an improbable white lab coat, she handled the antique volumes with bare hands, turning the pages without care as though slouched in a salon and impatiently flipping through a ratty copy of *People* as the technician dabbed at unsightly roots with viscous dye. For the graduate student—a beautiful, flat-ironed blonde—production had hired a strikingly athletic actress recently spotted on campus and watched by a steadily dwindling audience on a short-lived TV series targeting the teen demographic. There, as Cyd—a sexy but curly blonde—she'd played a reluctant Tennessee cheerleader from the wrong side of the tracks.

Running an index finger along a page, the student reacted with mounting excitement and jotted down notes. She slammed one volume shut, and grabbed it, a pair of stuffed accordian folders, and a spiral notebook, and began a purposeful arc toward the study hall's exit.

A nondescript librarian wearing a cardigan the exact shade of porridge raised a hand, glaring over low-slung reading glasses to explain that rare books must never leave the building. "Rules are rules, young lady." *Suspension of disbelief required,*

Marta thought. Perhaps a century of warfare had retarded the digitization of books and snuffed out the cycling of fashion. The man's professional dedication at an hour of global extinction, however, baffled her.

"It's a matter of life and death, for all of humanity." The student's whisper grew hoarse. "Please," she said, leaning toward the clerk while removing her glasses, the unencumbered eye contact promissory. "Just this once, alright?" Marta smiled as the nameless functionary's posture stiffened. What bureaucrat could resist a meal of life-and-death urgency served on a platter of raw carnality?

With an editing cut, the student ran down a lengthy dark-paneled hallway, high heeled boots echoing. She approached and knocked on a heavy door decorated with a carved wooden frieze. The opening door revealed a professor's office furnished with shelves bowed by innumerable volumes. A lean elderly man with sunken cheeks sat behind a colossal oak desk.

All that's missing is the Droeshout portrait of Shakespeare, Marta thought, *our holiest relic.* Her eyes settled on the scholar's herringbone jacket and club tie, the delicate floral pattern tea cup and saucer amongst the clutter of books, and the terminal antiquarian air of the office.

"Professor Highsmith, I need you to contact the military command centre," the student said.

"Sit, my dear child," the man said with a magisterial English accent that evoked afternoon Darjeeling, crustless cucumber sandwiches, and triumphant canal rowers. "Please take a deep breath and then explain yourself. This is certainly no time for hysterics. May I pour you tea?" He polished his glasses, as though wearied by student self-importance and impatient to return to studying *Samson Agonistes*, a daft tweedy Nero fiddling as Rome burns.

"It's all here, plain as day."

"Yes?"

"It's one of the journals of Lady Harriet Swinburne." The Californian vowels of the accent were pronounced, Marta noticed, evidently a foreshadowing: New World ingenuity would soon make a hash of the professor's British backwards-glancing unworldliness, the impotent fuddy-duddy snobbery. *Hitler woulda kicked your asses if we hadn't stepped in* the implication of her every word.

"Just listen to this, okay?"

"Of course. Please do go on."

The student began to read:

" 'May 22, 1825. Within the last fortnight, a dark and dreadful cloud has settled over the land. There are whispers of livestock torn asunder. Lizzie, unrepentant gossiping maid that she has become, reports that two entire families in a nearby settlement have vanished overnight. From dawn 'til dusk mothers arrive with infants, both suffering from a malady I do not recognize and for which I can offer no curative. . . .'

" 'May 24, 1825. The troubles grow worse. . . .' " At the professor's throat clearing, she stopped.

"It is base conjecture, no more. The evidence is circumstantial at best. Someone with my reputation would become a laughingstock if presenting this fantasy of yours as fact."

"There's more."

"Of that I am certain, my dear. Your imagination rivals that of Louis Carroll and C.S. Lewis combined." The professor's eyes twinkled.

"Perhaps you're right, Professor. I've been working so hard on my thesis, it must be getting to me."

"Don't give the matter a second thought, young lady. Indeed, I've already forgotten the whole unseemly episode. Good day."

That's got to be a set, Marta thought, *no one has an office that palatial.*

Standing at the steps in front of the library, the student said, "Asshole," and withdrew a clamshell phone from a purse fold. "Military Command, please. It's urgent." The creation of future telecom technology was another item not included in *Desert Assault*'s budget, Marta surmised.

"That'll get dubbed with 'ass' or something when the network broadcasts it," Chaz whispered. "Psy/Fi's family entertainment and doesn't use bleeps."

"She wasn't carrying a purse when she left the library," Marta whispered in reply.

"Yeah, continuity's a bitch. But no biggie, it's not like any guy will notice that kind of thing."

2.

Yellow words appeared, explaining the change of scene to stock footage of a submarine descending into dark choppy water: NATO MILITARY COMMAND VESSEL ANACONDA, NORTH ATLANTIC OCEAN. 1130 HOURS.

A second later *Desert Assault* dissolved to an oval table—cluttered with papers, maps, and coffee mugs—bolted to the metal floor of a cramped room. Not a touch screen could be seen. Marta guessed that the rust-specked walls and World War Two equipment of the vintage submarine's cabin had been chosen as reminders about the losing side of the war.

At the head of the table, Cambridge's intrepid graduate student, dressed in a snug black nylon paratrooper's jumpsuit, paced as she lectured; she'd gathered the abundant locks into a no-nonsense ponytail.

"No, gentlemen, the evidence is not, as General McBride says, 'a pipe dream.'" The aggrieved student swept off her glasses. "An exceptional gift has fallen onto our laps. In fact, it's the only real opportunity we've been given in nearly a century of warfare to exterminate the Kreplon force." The camera zoomed back. Arms crossed, she stood in front of a whiteboard filled with the symbols and numbers of an ersatz mathematical equation.

Four men in military uniforms sat opposite, their collective mien adversarial. They began talking at once; the General, gesturing angrily, muttered "wild goose chase" and "preposterous."

"Gentlemen, please. Let me walk you through this one more time from the start. It's a matter of life and death." The student slammed a book on the table.

"Simmer down, missy," the General said. "Don't get your panties in a bunch." The other men laughed.

"I'll outline it simply. 'May 22, 1825. A scouting expedition is planned for before the sun sets. Perhaps then we shall uncover the origin of the maladies.'

"Next. 'May 23, 1825. Words fail me. Following many minutes of vexatious conversation, the Doctor and I have come to share a momentous conclusion. A great machine, a leviathan of its kind and blacker than the pits of Hell, has plummeted from the stars. Cold to the touch and as impenetrable as Mongol fortresses, we cannot fathom its utility. It has caused grave misgivings. . . .' Okay, you can see where this is heading."

"Yeah, yeah, we get it," a younger man seated next to General McBride said. "Some old broad thinks she found something in the desert back in the day."

"The next entry, a few days later—"

"Right," the young man continued, "so some whack job blue blood that probably breathed in too much lead paint in her nursery loses it after years of solitary confinement in the desert eating goat stew. And you expect us to deploy troops?"

"Our resources are already stretched to the limit, young woman." With a sweeping motion the General surveyed a map. "We can't go off on a wild goose chase without better evidence."

"And how are your other strategies working out, gentlemen? So, let's take this from the top. . . ."

As the student began to read, the scene blurred; a sepia-toned image came into focus, a close up of a hand dipping a quill into a glass inkwell.

"That'll be smoother too," Chaz whispered.

Marta watched as Lady Swinburne, dressed in a simple white robe, wrote "May 22, 1825" in a journal with the quill. Oil lamps cast delicate light over her bed chamber. Without the turban, ceremonial sword, and horse, Lady Swinburne possessed surprising gravitas. At the knock on the door she ceased writing.

"Enter."

"Will you require any further service before I retire, Lady Swinburne?" Lizzie asked.

"Your service has been adequate."

"It is beautiful, milady." Lizzie stood at the desk and stroked the cover of a silver jewelry box.

"Your fascination with trifles is cause for concern, Lizzie." Evidently weary, Lady Swinburne did not look up from the journal. "Leave me. My writing . . ."

Lizzie cast a hateful stare at the inattentive mistress and left without a word. *Impressive*, Marta thought, *Luna's bad boyfriend turned out to be good news*. For a minor character uttering largely rote lines, Lizzie's black mood and clipped sentences commanded positive attention.

3.

Reaching into the pocket of her zipper-front sweater Marta pressed the button beneath the cellphone's impassive glass surface. She'd been resisting the temptation for what seemed like days. 9:02. Eighty nine minutes had passed by, during which she'd fidgeted through logic holes, flat-lining exposition, and risible dialogue jumping between 1825, 2009, and 2091; and all the while she'd strived to project shiny finishings on roughly edited scenes and half-complete imagery courtesy of keyboard technicians. Granted, the crudity of the rough draft instructed her about post-production; and the un-special effects of this early version of *Desert Assault* provided a fresh appreciation for the art of computer rendering.

Even factoring in the unrefined facets, Marta's silent review of the scenes had arrived at the inevitable conclusion that *Alien Advance: Desert Assault* achieved workmanlike heights at best; and when the director reached for epic—so far, she had noticed flagrant thefts from *The Lord of the Rings* and *Saving Private Ryan*—he attained merely passable. *Dregs*, she thought, *ridiculous, immune to parody*. The characters fared slightly better. The era-spanning scribbling women cum action heroes kept her attentive, although befitting the trope the graduate student's role slowly degraded to cliché: moments of weepy sideline farewells began soon after she met a handsome Air Force pilot, a square-jawed lone wolf with a Clint Eastwood squint and black, side-parted hair who said,

"Lady, I play by my own rules" to the student's heartfelt entreaties, and, "General, I play by my own rules" when a blinkered, regulations-quoting superior expected his subordinate to "do this by the book."

Desert Assault sputtered out with ostensible human victories in 1825 and 2091. Marta knew that a half century ago a drive-in feature of this sort would have left viewers with winking tantalization: "The End" and a question mark slowly rotating. For the Psy/Fi network, though, the ambiguity presaged slots for a sequel. Marta guessed that if the ratings, advertisers, or critics reacted warmly enough, the writers could find a way to insert the Kreplon matriarch laying a separate cache of eggs in a Middle Eastern cave never discovered by Lady Swinburne; naturally, those reptilian hatchlings would lead to another terrorizing Kreplon force: and voila, *Alien Advance 2: Another Desert Assault*, pouring from television screens in 2014.

Detritus, then. Still, when placing *HAP* and *Alien Advance* set on the Scale of Cultural Worth, Marta foresaw them achieving a perfect balance, consumed and forgotten shortly thereafter, and—perhaps—exhumed as a future footnote in a survey article by a Cultural Studies graduate student seeking access to the ivory tower.

Disappointed by the absence of credits, Marta half-listened as Chaz explained the changes.

"And it'll be smoother when they finish it, way better in the CGI department at least." The light came on in the room. "They're doing a *Lost* kinda set up in different time periods."

"Pardon me?"

"At some point someone—at the network maybe, but I don't know for sure—thought there was enough material for a 'television event' "—the rolled-eyes tone unmistakeable—"you know, what used to be called a mini-series. As opposed to a television non-event, I guess." Chaz followed the film school custodian's progress in stacking chairs. "Wow, they're efficient here. Anyway, then some genius—in marketing maybe, again I don't know how that works, maybe it started with a focus group or something—decided that since they couldn't really stretch out the OK Valley scenes, they could have parallel stories in different time periods instead and shoot them in studio and near the city. Kinda like *Lost* or the *Terminator* movies."

The audience milled around, watchful of the staff's group dispersal agenda and awaiting directions from higher ups.

Moving whispering distance from Marta's ear, Chaz said, "Hey, by the way, um, Miss Sadie—"

Faintly audible, Marta's sudden breath intake disguised the complexity of its components: resignation, intimacy, regret, vulnerability, affection. For better or worse, the price one pays for honesty is standing at the confidant's mercy, she'd learned. There it materialized, a truism worthy of her mother.

"There's no way I'm going to drive back to Bellevue tonight," eyebrows raising and lowering suggestively, "so can I stay at the Pits?"—Undre Arms generated nicknames easily—"I'll be out of there at the crack of dawn."

After swallowing the urge to point out the difference between can and may—Chaz having stated during their only real quarrel that in his estimation pedants deserved their destiny of the ninth circle of hell, right next to pederasts—Marta said, "I don't see why not." She'd welcome the distraction. *Gestation*'s unfolding had grown obstinate, sincere creative writing a greater task than she'd imagined. A screenplay about abject femininity came freighted with a peculiar set of challenges; and despite attentive viewings of Bong Joon-ho, splicing that theme into horror genre tropes had so far proven a Herculean obstacle.

Seeing Lora break away from Jake and some other crew she didn't recognize, Marta waved.

"So, what did you think?"

"I'm not sure what I was expecting, but that wasn't it."

"I told you'd there'd been some changes when I emailed you, honey."

"Yes, and about that you didn't exaggerate."

"See, the network liked the basics, but then some ambitious executive type thought they'd pull a mini-series out of the hat. It'll stand alone as a movie, but can morph into a series if there's interest. Aliens are a hot topic again these days since TV's exhausting vampires and everyone's getting sick to death of hobbits and pubescent wizards."

"I see."

"It'll be in the vein of that '80s alien show, you know the one they made in TO."

"*V*?" Chaz said, "No, that was here. Oh I know, *War of the Worlds*."

"That's it. With the creepy alien tentacle grabbing onto Earth in the opening credits."

"Bingo," Chaz said. "Guess what? Somnia and Hibertrin X."

"Okay, I'll bite," Lora said. "What's that?"

"They're the names Marketing came up with for the DIDIs, launch date pending but the rumour mill says late next year. Somnia is for cats and Hibertin X for dogs, but both are getting 'Deep Sleep, Within Reach' for their ad campaigns. Turns out the species have big enough genetic differences that they're required to market them as completely different products even though they're almost the same. Well, basically. It's like how a dog will die if it chows down on coffee or grapes or something but we can eat it, or cats can't have aspirin but dogs can or maybe the other way 'round. Weird, eh?"

"How about a pill for birds?" Lora said. "I could use a few of those."

"Nothing doing. There's not enough money in it for Vedmedica to have a 'whole family of products,' as they say. Yet, anyway, right? I guess birds and gerbils and so on just aren't that popular, and God knows it's not like Big Pharmacy is in it for the wellbeing of pets."

"We'll be expecting caviar and champagne when the big bonus comes through," Lora said, and waved Jake over. "Hello, boys. Marta, you remember Jake of course. This fine specimen next to him is Antony."

"Pleased to meet you." Marta held out a hand to Antony.

"How goes it, guys," Chaz said.

"Sequel anyone?" Jake said. "I'm taking bets."

"I'll vote for no."

"That makes two of us," Lora added.

"It wasn't so bad," Antony said. "I liked the scenes in the desert."

"Would they shoot the sequel in BC?" Marta asked.

"Probably, but Bulgaria is grabbing some of our action these days, bigger tax breaks, so it—or we, I guess—could end up there."

"Jake, do you want to say it?" Lora surveyed the room.

"Oh right, sure. Alright folks, that's the latest cut. I hope you enjoyed the show. We'll send out info once the world broadcast date is set."

"And . . ."

"And thank you all for work well done." Jake's mechanical tone undermined the sentiment, a sentence read from a cue card.

A round of claps closed the evening.

4.

"Catch you on set for the sequel, Professor?" Jake asked. Marta was buttoning her coat.

"Yes, certainly."

"We'll be in touch if the deal goes down."

"Thanks again. It was a valuable opportunity." She sensed the ridiculousness of the words and their stiff, empty formality, but even at this late date Jake's reserve made her tense.

5.

"You ready to head out?" Jake had MC'd countless screenings, attendance a cemented line in the job description. "I need to check with the guy locking this place up, so five minutes."

"Sure," Antony said. "Where's the men's? My bladder's about ready to burst."

"Out the door, down the hall, and hang a left." He watched Antony wind through the talkative stragglers of the audience; at the sure tug of lust, he felt glad about reading body language correctly that first night. The moment had been wrong, that's all.

Timing's everything, he'd learned.

At the location shoot in the valley, Jake had tumbled off the chastity express wagon less than twenty-four hours after he'd climbed aboard—a sequestered failing and remaining so. Sharing had grown into a plague of the times, anyhow; silence helped stamp it out.

Jake frowned with puzzlement when he later burped up pieces of the scene at unpredictable intervals as though expelling a build-up of guilt, like the murderer in that Edgar Allan Poe story he'd worked on for *Masters of Horror*. He'd question the eruption each time a chunk surfaced. Eventually, he dismissed the possibility of guilt, and decided the process reflected his brain's processing of disgust, as though he'd been forced—or, far worse, chosen of free will—to eat a bowl of vomit, or swim in a sewer.

Like those woeful self-loathing drunks confessing the exhaustive details of their latest disaster to empathetic peers at the rebound AA meeting, Jake suffered as much disdain for the failure of resolve as machine gun pangs of humiliation about the seedy choice of venue. After all, the failure wasn't just a sleeve of lager that he'd ordered with lunch, but a trashy bender in which any liquid containing alcohol served his needs.

The episode right after the casino wrap party represented a serious misstep, the sexual version of a Lysol and hairspray cocktail chugged while sprawled under an overpass. And while the bush geezers no doubt congratulated themselves afterwards for talking him into lowering his pants and letting them go to town, Jake alone comprehended the reality: he'd gone there with resigned conviction about the eventual outcome. Slumming had never been part of his repertoire; and after trying it on for size, he wanted only to have the memory dead and buried. With that, he suspected, the remorse would scatter too.

Still blue and repelled a week later, Jake walked into the trendy place decked out in the style of an old Chinatown apothecary. Nursing a scotch in the dim light while waiting for face time with Jeremy—running late, as always—he became conscious of a figure approaching.

"Hey," the man said. Jake recognized him easily.

Jake nodded.

"It's Antony. We, er, met at The Recovery Room."

"Oh right, how could I forget? Where's the other half?"

"Krysta. Not really sure where she's at. Long story."

"Gotcha." Antony wanted to unload, but Jake wasn't interested in a sob story.

"Anyway, I just wanted to say Hey."

"Cool." Jake checked the door for his delayed buddy. "See you around maybe." Jeremy would snap him out of his sulk with tales of midnight exploits, dedicated internet trolling, and crazy medical histories, casually bending the rules of doctor-patient confidentiality—names withheld, of course.

"Sure thing, man. Here's my card. If you're ever, I dunno, in the area or something."

Jake read it as Antony disappeared into the fashionable murk: ANTONY THAQI - CONSULTANT, FINANCIAL INSTRUMENTS. He pocketed the card.

6.

Feet crunching on the diamantine litter of smash-and-grabs, Marta surveyed the few remaining cars in the parking lot—intact but slick from an early winter downpour that had passed through during the screening. A sense of misconduct assailed Marta when she caught sight of the shiny, newly leased black German coupe. Hearing of it, her father had shaken his head and muttered "money down the drain," hurt that his only daughter hadn't called for advice.

Chaz huffed. "Snow soon?"

"I doubt it. None tonight, definitely."

"I thought with La Niña or El Niño or whatever we're in for. . . ." Chaz kicked a beer bottle cap. "Never mind. So, what did you think of the ambiguously gay duo?"

"Sorry?"

"Jake and Antony."

"Really? I thought Antony was a colleague."

"An ass colleague maybe. He's a stock trader or something financial like that." Chaz stopped. Running late, he'd wound up parked at an adjacent lot. "They're 'friends,'" the quote from an unnamed source. "But Lora says they're really tight, like a couple doing the nasty, not a couple of dudes bromancing over beer while watching the Canucks lose."

"I wouldn't have guessed."

"Yeah, Jake's a total skank; he'll get with nearly anybody. And a Kinsey three."

"He didn't pursue me." Marta enjoyed the novelty of an incidental conversation at night in a darkened parking lot in an iffy part of town. "You?"

"Nope. He doesn't do industry, that's what Lora told me."

"That Lora's a fount of information. I'm loath to think what she'd say about me."

"Nothing but good things." He smiled. "Scout's honour."

"I see."

"I could handle a bite before we turn in. Light on the fat, though, I'm cutting back."

"I've noticed." Subtle hints about fitness, she'd discovered, a poorly received tactic. "There's fruit and yogurt at my house."

"I said cutting back, not in complete self-denial. I'm not the Gandhi type."

"You choose then."

"Pie somewhere."

"Okay." Intuition and experience told her to stamp down the ready lecture about pie as a diet item. "This is not the greatest city for pie, but how about that place we tried before, The Refinery?"

"Deal. I'll get there way before you, Professor Ten and Two. Want me to text Lora and company to say where we're heading?"

"Sure. Why not?"

Regional Markets

I.

IMDB.com
User Reviews
★★★★★☆☆☆☆☆
Low expectations exceeded!!
5 Sept. 2012 | by Amit-Chanakyapuri (India) – See all my reviews

The plot=weird, the acting=so-so, the science=huh?!? You could drive a bus thru the plot holes!

The special effects are convincing here, not convincing there. Same with dramatic scenes.

The end is disappointing (a sequel set up, totally) and there is zero suspense.

The only reason not to give this a lower vote is because it is a TV movie and I believe the budget was pennies to start off with.

If you can overlook the badness, overall it's fun to sit down with and watch if you can deal with mid grade B films. Has some gore here and there, some nice scenery, some decent sets, and some interesting characters. But you have to be into these kind of stories, time period, etc, to begin with. It's worth watching to see Tracy Scoggins, who is better here than she ever was in *Dante's Cove*. Good effort overall for what it is.

Probably there could have been more gore and blood in the movie to keep horror fans happy.

It wasn't a tenth as scary as *Aliens* but it was still reasonably good, absolutely not a time waster.

Definitely worth a watch.

I have to give it a 5.

2.

Exxtreme Outer Limitz: The Online Fanzine of Science Fiction, Horror and Fantasy Film Reviews
February 2012

The Wrap-Up: "Alien Assault": Entertaining cheese, worth a look if it's snowing and you have nothing better to do. And *AA* might inspire you to rent the way better movies it rips off.

Alien Assault is a typical package the Psy/Fi Channel churns out these days: the cookie-cutter monster movie. (Maybe Psy/Fi ordered an expensive computerized script-writing robot and needs to get its money's worth?) Okay, a bit different than usual was the story shifting between centuries.

AA has been made without much effort beyond disguising the wooden formula's unmissable thefts. The movie's purpose is to set up scenes of makeup effects (meh) while members of the supporting cast—unknowns, with one exception—are dispatched by the CGI alien every few minutes. We did like the maid with 'tude, true, and the sight of her severed head landing in the sand was cable-level genius.

Three Words or Less: Hackwork, Occasionally Inspired.

2.5 stars.

ACKNOWLEDGEMENTS

Unbeknownst to me over a decade ago, ideas for this novel began to coalesce during a late-night visit to Stanley Park. I'd been invited there to catch the shooting of a scene from *First Target*, a TV movie starring Daryl Hannah. Readying 'Washington State Park' for camera took an eternity, so I eventually left without having seen Ms. Hannah's Secret Service Agent Alex McGregor or heard the director's "Action!" From that point, a brief exchange about Alice Munro's reputed personality at a dinner with my ex and three of his American film industry colleagues and encounters with Lytton Strachey's *Books and Characters* and Virginia Childs' *Lady Stanhope: Queen of the Desert* (plus: non-encounters in the form of overheard bus and classroom conversations, postings on Craigslist, and so on) provided me with an abundance of source material. While invention is no doubt foundational to storytelling, *This Location of Unknown Possibilities* could be reasonably called an instance of repurposed found objects.

Emily Morse Symonds, Walter Pater, Mary Shelley, Joseph Conrad, William Shakespeare, Emily Dickinson, and Edna St. Vincent Millay may be rolling in their graves at my borrowings throughout the novel. To them I apologize: no disrespect was intended. As for Lady Stanhope and Doctor Meryon's alien stalking, that spectral twosome can blame Hollywood.

Pen in hand, redoubtable Carellin Brooks laboured over two cruder versions of the manuscript and handed me tart but invaluable reactions and suggestions over pleasantly combative lunches. Further gratitude: a small grant from the Canada Council arrived with perfect timing.

Chris Needham expressed immediate interest in my project and for that I'm all kinds of grateful. A few other publishing industry professionals set aside time to read the entire manuscript before rejecting it, and I'd like to thank them for pushing on after the first chapter and offering feedback.

Listed last but foremost in my heart, there's Alex, whose initial enthusiasm for (and later tolerance of) my self-assigned, intrusive, and financially counter-intuitive part-time occupation of writing fiction ought to earn him the heights of prosperity and happiness in his next incarnation.

Brett Josef Grubisic's first novel, *The Age of Cities*, was a finalist for the City of Vancouver Book Prize. He's the author of *Understanding Beryl Bainbridge* and co-editor of *National Plots: Historical Fiction and Changing Ideas of Canada*. He lives in Vancouver and teaches at the University of British Columbia.

Author photo: Alexander Crouse
Cover design: HonkHonk Graphic Arts
Tomorrowland film set photo: Brett Josef Grubisic